The Three of Us

SAREETA DOMINGO

Previously published as *The Nearness of You*

PIATKUS

PIATKUS

First published in Great Britain in 2016 by Piatkus as *The Nearness of You*
This paperback edition published in 2022 by Piatkus

1 3 5 7 9 10 8 6 4 2

A CIP catalogue record for this book
is available from the British Library.

ISBN 978-0-349-43215-1

Typeset in Bembo by M Rules
Printed and bound in Great Britain by
Clays Ltd, Elcograf S.p.A.

Papers used by Piatkus are from well-managed forests
and other responsible sources.

MIX
Paper from
responsible sources
FSC® C104740

Piatkus
An imprint of
Little, Brown Book Group
Carmelite House
50 Victoria Embankment
London EC4Y 0DZ

An Hachette UK Company
www.hachette.co.uk

www.littlebrown.co.uk

For those seeking serenity
and sweet inspiration

This novel was previously published under the title
The Nearness of You

Prologue

It was about a year ago, on my mother's 'anniversary'. Much as I tried to ignore it, Anita was all I could think about. I was already off sick from work with a flu thing, and then remembering my mother and everything that surrounded her, me, us ... It all just made it worse. Marcy had an important dance rehearsal, but she'd wanted to stay home with me. I made her go, but then I couldn't stand to be in the flat on my own, so I decided to go to the cinema – early, the first show. The film was a black-and-white reissue. I didn't really even know what it was, I just wanted to stare at something for a while, not think. There was not another soul in the red velvet theatre, and as the lights went down I suddenly felt so lonely, so frightened, and I missed my mum so much. The tears burned in my eyes until the screen was just a fuzz of light, and once I let them spill, they wouldn't stop. But it felt good, crying in the darkness – a huge release.

And then he walked in.

He was a stranger to me then, of course. Still is, really. But somehow, maybe even then, he felt known to me in a way I don't understand. In a way I know I can't explore.

He stood in the aisle and looked around, running a hand through his hair as he waited for his eyes to adjust to the gloom. Then he heard me sniff and turned, and his amber eyes met mine in the flickering light from the screen. Every seat was free, of course. But he sat on the end of my row, not saying anything. I should have felt awkward – normally I might even have moved. But something in his gaze made me feel unjudged, unthreatened. Safe.

We both stared forward, with occasional muffled sobs emanating from my throat, until I saw something move in my peripheral vision, and I heard the thud of a folding chair springing back up. He shuffled closer, until he was one seat away from me, and then he held something out towards me. A packet of tissues. I stared at them, and let out a small, short laugh. Here's this guy just trying to enjoy a quiet film and I'm slobbering and sniffling. His brow furrowed for just a moment, and then his expression broke into light. He smiled at me, right at me, for the very first time. I drank it in. It was like air.

I reached out and took the packet, our fingers brushing. Neither of us spoke, but I pulled out a tissue and wiped my cheeks and nose, then took a deep breath, and noticed him take one too. We looked at each other, took another breath, smiled, then turned back to the film. And then I don't know what made me do it – loneliness, attraction – but I stood up and moved one seat over so that we were sitting next to each other. He glanced at me, but did nothing else. I looked down at his arm on the armrest, and then leaned my own up against his. Our little fingers were so close they were almost touching, and he seemed to freeze for a moment before relaxing, his muscles softening and his arm pushing ever so lightly against mine. Through our clothes, I could feel his warmth. I could smell him, his scent like cut grass, fresh with possibility.

And then slowly, incrementally, his hand moved – his fingers gently, then firmly, found their way between mine, and suddenly our palms connected.

He held my hand.

His gentle heat seemed to slowly envelop my whole body, until my tears stopped falling, until my breaths stopped shuddering.

We stayed like that for the rest of the film, my hand in his, not looking at each other. Neither of us had said a word. But the minute the credits began to roll, I pulled away, stood up and grabbed my coat. I looked down at him, studying his angular face, his dark brows against the contrast of his pale skin. His wide, expressive mouth ... Then my gaze fell on the packet of tissues still in my hand. I laid them on the armrest where my arm had been, and looked back at him once more. His eyes held mine for a moment, and he took a breath as though he was finally about to speak.

But I turned, and walked away.

Chapter One

It's only twelve days into the new year, and already my resolution is being broken.

The morning air hangs gauzily over the river – it's not one of those crisp, clear mornings where the air whips into your lungs and you feel glad to be alive. It's just cold. A heavy kind of cold. I stare over the water towards Tower Bridge in the distance, but today it looks out of place. Gaudy, even. Sighing, I feel the wind take up my coat, opening it like wings, swaying me back and forth. I let it. Usually I notice the cold – I'm definitely one of those people who'd rather be hot – but maybe what I'm feeling right now is more like numbness.

I blink hard as ash blows into my eyes from the end of the cigarette, and I know I should probably feel bad about already smoking again, but I don't. It actually feels really fucking comforting having a cigarette clamped in between my lips. And anyway, I'd say twenty-two is exactly the age when I should be getting these sorts of vices out of my system, right? I let the acid cloud of smoke swirl around inside me and then float out between my lips, mingling with the droplets of my breath on the air. I mean, promising to quit on the stroke of midnight on one random day is such a cliché, isn't it? I only did it to please Marcy, and now I realise what I *actually* should have resolved is to never, ever go against my better judgement and walk her bloody dog.

The tips of my fingers sting vaguely with the chill where Charlie's licked them. He's dropped the leash out of his mouth at my feet, and now his big liquid-black eyes are gazing up at me imploringly. As I stare back down at him, his nose twitches, and he turns and trots back towards the water's edge. Back towards—

'Sorry, miss? Are you OK?'

I turn towards the direction of the voice, which belongs to the tall, thin woman in a fleecy electric-blue sweatshirt and black leggings standing next to me. She puts her hand on my shoulder, but then withdraws it quickly. Yeah, it didn't feel quite right to me either.

'Look, they're here. The police,' she continues. 'I think I might just . . . I mean, do you think I need to wait? It's just, I'm late for work, and seeing as it was your dog who found, um . . .'

She trails off, and I glance at the headphones hanging around her neck, wondering what she listens to when she runs, and if I'd be into it. And there's the packet of cigarettes; the outline protrudes from the pocket of her sweatshirt. That's where mine came from. If she's going to leave me here, at least she's been helpful for something. Going for a run carrying a packet of fags? Nice. I kind of think this woman and I could have been friends, if she wasn't passing the proverbial buck right now. I don't blame her, though – I'd call finders-keepers on this little discovery too if I could get away with it.

I try to say something, but my voice is grainy. I cough and try again.

'Could you possibly spare another one of these?' I pick the fag out from between my teeth and gesture with it. She looks at

6

me for a moment before taking the Marlboro Lights out of her pocket and pulling a lighter out of the packet. She pushes both into my hands.

'Here you go. Take the lot.' She puts her hands on her hips and sighs. 'Look, will you be all right?'

I shrug and nod, pressing my lips down hard on the spongy filter of my dwindling cigarette and sucking emphatically. Looking over the thin woman's shoulder, I see Charlie standing over the man lying on the pebbles. The dog nuzzles at his pale, lifeless arm again, to no avail. I close my eyes and listen to the paper crackle as I finish my fag. I can hear Charlie coming back towards me, kicking up the tiny loose stones with his paws, and open my eyes just in time to see the woman scrabbling away from us, back up the riverbank to the concrete steps, her arms held akimbo in search of invisible support. I drop the butt on to the ground with a sigh.

It's just the dog, the man and me now.

The river whispers conspiratorially against the shoreline and the wind picks up again, and for some reason I get that panicky feeling rising in my chest, the kind you get when you suddenly realise you might be sick. I exhale hard and Charlie turns to look at me quickly, startled by the noise. I'm really starting to feel cold now. I pull my coat around me, folding my arms tightly over it and tucking my hands into my armpits, turning deliberately away from our companion on the bankside. Charlie scuttles around to me, huffing and trying to catch my eye, like it's playtime. I know it's not rational, but the happy-go-lucky look on his little canine face sends a prickle of anger up the back of my neck.

'Are you fucking joking?' I hiss at him.

Charlie whines a little and I look away, feeling bad immediately. Jesus, it's not his fault – he's a dog, for crying out loud.

7

But his yelping this morning was worse than Marcy's was with Ryan last night. How does she sleep so soundly anyway, that she couldn't hear her own dog? I'm not sure I want to think about the answer to that, given that it's probably something to do with the cause of her nocturnal yelping.

My heart sinks even further as I think about her with *him* ... like that.

I distract myself by looking out towards the car park. The electric-blue-sweatshirt lady didn't manage to make the quick getaway she was hoping for. She's standing next to a stocky policeman now, and he nods a couple of times, jotting down what she's saying. I suppose it will be my turn next. I reach into my coat pocket and pull out another one of her cigarettes. Waste not, want not, as Anita used to say. Of course, I *would* think of my mother right now. But if this man has done what I think he's done, then Anita coming to mind is only natural, I guess. My heart starts racing a little, but I tell myself it's because of the nicotine.

Another policeman's arrived now, this one taller and older-looking. I watch all three sets of eyes follow the path the skinny lady's arm points down towards us – the awkward triumvirate down by the water. Finally free to leave, the woman jogs away, and I stoop down to retrieve the soggy leash that is now back between Charlie's jaws. I clip it to his collar, take a shaky, shallow breath and wait. God, why am I so nervous? It's just a ... a *thing* that happened, and then I happened upon it. Upon him. Or Charlie did. I'll just answer some questions and get on with my day, forget any of this even happened. I bite my lip and wait.

The stocky policeman's partner holds a radio up to his mouth as they make their way down the concrete steps, and the two men squint against the pallid sun as they trudge towards me with matched strides.

'Thank you for waiting here, miss,' the taller one calls out as they near me. 'We understand this must have been a bit of a shock. We just want to ask you a couple of questions, and then you can be on your way.'

I clench my jaw, straighten my back and tuck a wayward curl behind my ear. They're right in front of me now, and the stocky one starts patting Charlie on the head absently. The dog pants amiably, his tail drawing a V on the ground. He's clearly feeling no remorse whatsoever for discovering the mother of all day-ruiners. I flick fag ash on the ground next to him pointedly.

'Uh, yeah, bit of a shock,' I repeat dully.

'I'm Constable Martin,' the stocky officer says. 'And that's my colleague, Sergeant Lyndhurst.' The older policeman has already begun to stroll off in the direction of the man.

Constable Martin pulls out his small, battered notepad again. 'OK, first things first, love – could I take your name please?' He smiles at me encouragingly. I've pretty much taken an instant disliking to him.

'Uh, yes. It's Taylor Jenkins.'

'Taylor.' Constable Martin nods as he scribbles it down in his notebook. 'That's unusual.'

'I was named after my dad,' I reply, then add, 'My mum chose it.' Why did I say that? My heart's beating fast again, and I drag quickly on my cigarette.

'So, how did you come across this unfortunate chap, then?'

'Well, I was walking my flatmate's dog and he ... we came across him.'

'I see. Border collie, right? He's a sweet pup, isn't he?'

That's one way of looking at it.

Constable Martin glances down at Charlie, who stands up eagerly, panting. I'm gripped by a burning desire to get home. Or anywhere away from here. 'Was there anything else, or ...?'

The officer smiles, and even chuckles a little.

'Yes, just a few more things, I'm afraid, Miss Jenkins. So I take it the gentleman was, uh, deceased when you came upon him?'

I nod, peering quickly over at the bloated figure then back to Constable Martin. 'Yes.'

Sergeant Lyndhurst strides back over to us. 'Weights around the ankles,' he murmurs to his partner. 'No immediate signs of anything untoward. Think he waded in, and the tide must have pulled him back up again in the end, poor bastard. Anyway, I'll get on to the coroner's office.' He nods at me once with a tight smile, and heads off back towards their car.

'What time was it, when you found him?' PC Martin asks.

'Sorry?' My throat feels drier than sandpaper. I try and swallow. 'Oh. Uh, around eight, I think. Maybe quarter-past. And then that lady, the jogger, she came over a couple of minutes later. I did try to ... Sorry, I don't know if it's a problem but I did try to roll him over, but he was too heavy. And I kind of felt for a pulse too but—' I stop, remembering the cold, solid feel of his flesh under my fingertips. I take a deep breath. 'I mean, it was obvious, really.'

PC Martin looks at me for a second, then writes down what I said in a spidery scrawl on the dog-eared notepad. When he finishes, he nods and sort of cocks his head to one side, like it's what he is supposed to do.

'Right. OK, love, well I don't want to pre-empt the coroner, but it looks to me as though he might well have, er ... taken his own life.' He purses his lips together, looking in the direction of the body. I make a faint noise in my throat, and he seems to take it as some sign of agreement with his assessment.

'OK, Miss Jenkins,' he says, turning back to me. 'Could I just take your address and phone number, then we can let you get on.'

'Thirty-four Dockley Road. Flat nine,' I say, gesturing need-lessly away from the river in the vague direction of our flat. Charlie pulls suddenly at the leash as I do, thinking I've thrown something, and my arm yanks away from my body. It hardly feels like it belongs to me. 'Um, I don't know my number off-hand yet, I'm afraid: I dropped my phone the other day and I had to get a new one.' I fumble in my coat pocket for my mobile, my numb fingers jabbing at the screen. Finally I find my number and give it to him, then turn to leave.

'Just a mo, love, let me give you my card,' Constable Martin calls, a brightness already back in his voice. 'We may need to have just a quick follow-up with you. Nothing serious.'

I nod swiftly and take it from him. I'm really not sure I can handle being here a minute longer.

'All right then, Miss Jenkins. Give us a call if you need any-thing.' His radio crackles loudly, and he holds up his hand in a wave before reaching down to answer it.

My hands are burning from the cold by the time I reach the door of our flat, and they tremble as I try to put the key in the lock. I keep missing. To my surprise, I hear Marcy stumble towards the door and peer through the peephole.

'Babe? What are you doing?' she says, swinging the door open. My hand is still hovering by the space where the keyhole was. Charlie bounds eagerly inside, and I follow. A plastic bag slips from my wrist and I realise I'm still carrying the dog shit. Damn it.

'What time is it?' Marcy says, in a sleepy voice that extends all her vowels.

I sigh. 'Nine-ish? A.K.A. time you sorted your own bloody dog, M. Didn't you hear him? I couldn't sleep.'

Marcy scoops up the shit-bag and takes a few long-legged

strides into the kitchen, her bare feet slapping on the linoleum. She's dressed only in one of Ryan's T-shirts, and I can tell she's naked underneath. She swings the bag deftly into the open bin, and I start to protest, but I don't really have the energy right now. I'll take it down later. Following her into the kitchen, I go over to the sink and begin washing my hands under a stream of hot water. The cold-burn flares, then starts to dissipate at last.

'Sorry, T,' Marcy says, leaning against the counter next to me. 'I'm really sorry. Seriously. Thanks, yeah?' She leans over and tickles my neck playfully. I flick water at her and smile a little. I really want to just forget this morning ever happened.

'It's fine,' I say, drying my hands. I walk through the flat to empty my pockets amongst the unopened bills on our little round dining table in the living room, because I know it annoys her when I do that. Marcy follows, eyeing me but saying nothing. She does cough exaggeratedly when she spots the cigarette packet, but I ignore her. Then I notice the police officer's card among the change and lip balm. I pick it up again quickly and stuff it back in my pocket.

'I'd better jump in the shower,' I mumble. 'I'll be late for work.'

Marcy's looking more closely now, scrutinising me. She knows something's up, but I really can't go into it now. *Please don't ask me what's wrong.*

'Yeah. OK then, hon,' she says. I can tell she's still suspicious, but for once she might be letting it go. 'Listen, honestly, sorry about Charlie . . . ' She pauses for a second as if she's about to say more on the subject, but to my relief she just shakes her head. 'Anyway . . . Can I use the loo quickly before you go in?'

I nod, and linger in the hallway as she dashes into the bathroom. Through her open bedroom doorway, I catch a glimpse of Ryan's naked, toned torso, his lower half only just covered by the rumpled duvet where Marcy's climbed out of the bed. Before I can look away, he stirs and raises himself up on his elbows, contracting the taut muscles in his stomach. His eyes meet mine; clear amber, even in the gloom of the morning light.

'Everything OK?' he asks me quietly.

I swallow, my gaze skimming down his body and back again. Nothing feels OK this morning. I'm irritated that he's even asking me, *now*, with things the way they are. Angry, almost.

Or I want to be.

'Um ... Yeah. Well ...' I hesitate, clear my throat and nod. 'Yeah. Thanks.'

The skin between his eyebrows wrinkles a little, like he doesn't believe me. He presses his mouth into a sympathetic line, and we both glance away as the toilet flushes.

'OK,' he says.

Marcy opens the bathroom door and dashes past me on tip-toes, obviously starting to feel cold.

'Have a good day, T. Speak to you later.'

'Yeah. You too.'

Charlie trots along to follow her, his claws scrabbling on the floor as he leaps up to join them on the bed, leaving wet pawprints as he goes.

I head into the bathroom, and hear Marcy apologising. Then giggling. Then there's softer whispering. Then the sound of kissing ...

I listen for a second too long, then nudge the bathroom door with my heel until it clicks shut.

Steadying myself with one hand on the sink, I push my jeans down my legs until they fall in a heap on the floor. After a moment, I step out of them, and pull the loose sweatshirt over my head. Yeah, this look is really some competition next to Marcy's T-shirt-and-a-smile. I shake my head and stare at my reflection. Even now, with what happened this morning, this is what I'm thinking about? I bite the inside of my lip guiltily. Still, I guess it's better than thinking about finding a dead body.

A suicide.

I look at myself in the mirror a moment longer, studying my smooth, sandy-brown skin, my big, bouncy, tightly curled dark hair. No matter how many years pass, edging me closer to the age she was when she died, I know I'll never fully resemble my mother, with her straight auburn hair and luminous pale skin. But that had never been an issue for me – I had so many other things to worry about when it came to her. The only thing that bothered me about my appearance was the occasional idiot seeing us together and questioning if she was really my mother. The truth is, for good or bad, it was always just the two of us. Sometimes I still can't believe I've carried on without her.

From time to time, I do wonder if maybe I look like Taylor Senior. But African blood is the only thing I ever got from him. I sigh loudly, and it echoes around the tiles.

I reach out and turn on the shower, but again I pause, looking down at the bath. It's been a while since I really hesitated over getting into a tub. It's been a while since I thought about how hard it was to do little things, to do almost anything, right after Anita ... Thank God Aunty Sylvia had a separate shower, or I would have been one stinky sixteen-year-old. I try to smile, but it falls away. Some days, especially today, trying to control where my thoughts wander is hard. I shake my head again. Can I shake the memories away? If only.

Taking a deep breath, I step in under the spray of water and let it run down my face.

Chapter Two

Twenty-three minutes later, my handbag bumps heavily against my side as I pound along the pavement, breaking one of my rules and running for the bus. Luckily my driver hasn't had his Weetabix this morning, because I just make it. I head upstairs, panting hard, and flop into a seat. I really need to work out more.

Usually I like being in transit – that period of time *in between*, when your only purpose is to be transported from A to B. On the bus to work, I can indulge my own mind for a while, with nobody I know around me to make me embarrassed at my thoughts. Well, except myself. And that's mainly because the majority of my daydreams end up involving my best friend's boyfriend. I close my eyes for a moment and try not to think about Ryan this morning, asking me if I'm OK. I try not to think about his naked body. I try not to imagine stealing his warmth by climbing underneath those covers into the bed with him, letting him comfort me against the gloom growing inside me . . .

I try, but I fail.

Gritting my teeth against painful impossibility, I open my

eyes. I'm still surrounded by commuting strangers concerned only with their own little lives. We're alone in this together. The thing is, this morning I'd really rather not think. Complete and utter blankness in my mind would be fantastic – something like the 'snow' you used to get on old TV screens. I push in my ear-buds, turn up the volume on my phone and stare out of the window at the grey morning and the tops of people's heads at bus stops. I already feel like I've been up for hours.

The bulky guy in the seat in front of me by the window is fighting sleep; I see him reflected out beyond the surface of the glass, nodding off. The strip lights inside the bus make it brighter in here than outside, and it's sort of mesmerising that I can watch him and he's oblivious. His chest rises and falls, and his chin slowly leans against his chest, his eyes close, his mouth opens and slackens. Pale face, puffy cheeks. He looks sort of like—

I try not to remember, I try to keep my mind afloat, but it's useless – heavy thoughts begin to sink and settle, down to the bottom of a river next to a man whose name I don't even know.

Stop it, Taylor. I mean, that man this morning was a stranger. This is nothing like it was with Anita; it's just an unfortunate coincidence. Yes, there's a vague sense of the universe singling me out for this particular type of shit, but I'll try not to be offended. I can't help wondering, *What if I had got there earlier? What if I could have talked to him, stopped him?* I know he must have waded in hours before Charlie and I even got to the river; it's stupid. But I have that churning, angry *what if, why, what if,* why stirring in the pit of my stomach. How the hell am I going to get through today? Friday mornings at the shop are quiet at the best of times.

The sleeping man jerks awake as we pull in to a stop, his face reanimates and I feel a little better – but then the music in my ears abruptly ends mid-song. I fumble in my bag for my phone and grit my teeth at the blank screen. I obviously forgot to charge it last night. At least I have my charger in my bag for when I get to work, but I suppose, for now, ambient noise it is. I pull the earphones out and twist their wires around my fingers absently as a uniformed teenager plonks down in the seat next to me, his legs wide and inconsiderate. I edge closer to the window pointedly, but he doesn't seem to notice. *He's* got music – large headphones balance on his slim head, emanating a jumble of tinny sounds just loud enough to irritate but not loud enough for me to make out any melody. His nylon Puffa jacket rustles as he bops to the insistent beat, and out of the corner of my eye I watch his jaw move up and down silently as he mouths the words to the song.

I used to do the same thing, in another lifetime. I'd heard the words to some of the songs so many times that, when my mother couldn't find a babysitter and took me along to a club in Soho or wherever, I'd mime along from the wings. Every time was like watching another person altogether. A kind of alchemy occurred when Anita stepped out on that tiny stage; her face painted, her dress tight, her shoulders back, her red lips ready to manipulate the notes. I'd stare out at the handful of expectant faces in the audience, catching the reflected spotlight, like small beacons of happiness out in the shadows. When my mother drew that first breath, my own throat would almost close, and I'd feel a prickling heat rising up from the soft skin underneath my eyes until liquid threatened my vision. Air would move in and out of my lungs too fast, and my mouth would hang open in genuine awe of her. Then my lips would begin to mirror my mother's silently as I watched her sway to the drums and the piano and the bass ... *that voice*. She'd tease, bending right up to the final note, never just hitting it dead

17

on. In moments like that, I loved her so much my heart would nearly burst.

But backstage, after the ripple of clapping hands and the occasional bunch of flowers, I would never let slip how I felt – how the beauty of Anita's voice had almost made me want to take bites out of the air. Instead, I'd kiss my mum on the cheek that she proffered, and then sulk as one or two devoted admirers whirled around the dilapidated dressing room. It was childish, but it was one of the rare occasions I could afford to be.

That adulation was so temporary; thinking about it now, the effect it had on my mother was probably more negative than anything else. As soon as the praise died away, she was back to being just plain old Annie, unhappy mum to a bastard daughter, and I'd be left to pick up the pieces.

The bus jolts to a halt, and I hear the hiss of the doors opening. Bollocks, I've almost missed my stop. This is exactly why I shouldn't be left alone with my thoughts. Springing up and pushing past the boy with the headphones, I run down the stairs and out on to the street.

Obviously, there was no need to rush. There's no customer waiting impatiently outside the shop, and the street, lined with chair designers and conceptual ad agencies, is quiet as always. Who buys those weird chairs made of contorted plastic anyway? Pulling the set of keys from my bag, I unlock the shutters and the heavy glass door and push my way inside. I head towards the counter, past the expensive tomes artfully displayed on the rows of shelves by yours truly. The OCD in me, I guess. Plus, boredom.

There's always that new-book smell in here, but its familiarity isn't giving me much comfort right now. And the pending tedium, which I was hoping might give me some kind of anchor to normality, only seems to be increasing the feeling that something inside me is close to coming loose.

I flick on the lights, watching the whole room illuminate in subtle hues, with back-lit cabinets designed to emphasise tasteful luxury. Expensive books on art and architecture, the type that people buy and never read. Cultural accessories. By contrast, the storeroom-cum-staff-area behind the counter is in its usual state of disarray. Huge coffee-table books are stacked up against the walls, and a pile of rejects is casually strewn in a corner, waiting to be boxed up, the books' spines broken or their glossy pages torn. Value's all in the perception, I guess.

Sometimes, during the days when seven hours go by with hardly a customer coming into the shop, I think, *Why did I bother with that History of Art degree again?* But I know why. I was just following Marcy and her Performing Arts scholarship. I wanted to forget about being responsible for a while. I'd been preparing for the inevitable moment when Anita would be gone and I'd be left on my own, needing to fend for myself. But when the time came, I realised I was actually free, free to be a 'normal' young woman without a ... burden. A dark part of me felt relieved. Everyone else my age seemed to be able to shirk responsibility, to be reckless, and I was finally allowed to do that too. Guilt prickles over my skin even thinking that now, but it's true. I wanted to move away, hang out with my best friend somewhere nobody else knew me, get fucked up and make mistakes. And not have to think about whether Anita would be light or dark the next day. Not to be the kid in sixth form whose mum had just topped herself.

But after three years of 'study', here I am sitting in a customer-free bookshop in east London. I feel like I have NOW WHAT? stamped permanently across my forehead. If I close my eyes and imagine where I would like to be in five years' time, what I would love to be doing, the faintest of ideas nudges at my mind, but I push it away. I don't have time for dreams. Not when I've seen them played out in front of me, to end in disaster.

At least I sort of get to be my own boss here – the owners only check on me once in a while. I could be getting up to all sorts: running an under-the-counter drug cartel, writing a magnum opus. But I pretty much just count time, and think entirely wrong, lonely thoughts about someone I can't have. Oh, and occasionally I rearrange books on shelves, of course.

Still, it's a job with a pay cheque, and if living with Anita for sixteen years taught me anything, it was to appreciate a regular income. I dealt with enough threatening electricity companies, phone companies and landlords to learn that. And at least this job is vaguely connected to art, right? I half chuckle at the thought, and the sound dulls appropriately in the carpeted shop.

I make sure to plug in my phone to charge before going to boot up the till. But just as I do, to my surprise I hear the electronic beep of the door. Someone's come in already? That's a turn-up for the books, so to speak. I look up. The woman has shoulder-length, fluffy ginger hair, competing angrily with the vivid cashmere wrap draped around her shoulders. In her heavily wrinkled hand is a plastic bag with the shop's intricate logo. A return, I'm guessing. The woman glances around, slightly confused; this is probably going to take a while.

'Good-morning, madam,' I call. 'How can I help?'

She turns to me. 'Oh. Oh, hello, dear. Do you ... do you work here?'

What else would I be doing behind the till? She takes in my face and glances up to my hair. Oh, right. It's like that.

'Yes I do, madam. Can I help?'

The woman flicks her hair over her shoulder ineffectually. 'I wanted to find out if I could return this. I had bought it as a gift for my nephew, but I think it might be rather graphic for a thirteen-year-old. The young man who recommended it should have known better. You ought to be more careful, you know.'

She purses her lips and raises her thin eyebrows. I look down at the expensive David LaChappelle coffee-table book that the woman pulls out of the bag and try to stifle a smile. Arty photographic smut practically drips from it. Lucas, who covers my lunch hour, must have been responsible for this one.

'Certainly, madam,' I say breezily. I set about running the refund through the till, and hand the receipt over for the woman to sign with her shaky, veined hand. 'Sorry about that.' I'm not sorry.

As I watch her cape swoop back out of the door, I look down at the book. I run my hand over its smooth cover, appreciating the vivid colours and kitsch, escapist imagery. LaChappelle is one of my favourite photographers, and I spend a few minutes idly turning the pages. I glance up at the door, and back down at the book. My hand lingers at the top of one page, and I look around one more time to make doubly sure nobody's there. I turn my body away from the CCTV they installed after that time a weird guy came in and started stripping down to his undies.

Then I rip.

I exhale hard, scoop up the book and head to the back room, adding it to the pile to be returned to suppliers – or claimed by staff – at the end of the month. I mean, it's fine. They account for the damages. It's no big deal. My heart's beating hard, and I head back out to the counter, staring blankly at the shop floor for a moment. I've never done anything like that before. Jesus, I need this job. If they found out . . . ? But they won't.

And anyway, today I feel like a little recklessness is justified.

Two hours later, the electronic beep sounds once again, but to my relief it's just Lucas arriving to do my lunch-hour cover. He looks as though he may have slept in the clothes he's wearing, and he still smells faintly of alcohol.

'All right?' he says, slinging his bag into the back room without looking where it might land. 'Brew?' He stumbles towards the sink in the corner and fills the kettle.

'Nah, I think I'm going to head straight out. Can I grab you anything?'

'Maybe an anvil to crush my head, might stop the pounding . . .' He grins lopsidedly at me and tucks back a lock of lank, slightly greasy hair. I raise an eyebrow but can't help grinning back. He has that effect on people. Women especially, it seems, though he's thankfully not my type. Plus I know where he's been.

'I'll see what they've got in Boots.' I start to head out, then turn around, remembering the return this morning. 'I've got a bone to pick with you, by the way—' I begin, but I then remember the ripping of the page and stop. He looks at me expectantly. 'Uh, that girl in the coffee shop that you never rang back? Every time I go in there she's all, "Oh, can you tell that guy you work with to call me?" in this super-needy, hopeful voice. It's hard enough to get a decent espresso around here—'

'See you in a bit,' Luc interrupts brightly, ignoring me.

I grab my coat and bag and unplug my phone, heading out of the shop smiling, though it feels sort of strange, like something in the back of my mind is telling me not to. I take a lungful of the fresh, cold air and head towards the shops.

As I speed up my steps to pass the cake shop that makes me want to buy a bag of madeleines every day and be seventeen stone, I notice an elaborately decorated birthday cake in the window and suddenly I remember today's date. Fuck. Aunty Sylvia's birthday. I pull my phone out of my bag. I should call, but . . . I wonder if a text would look too . . .

An anxious feeling starts to build up in my chest.

22

I'll send a card. Even though it will get there late, I can always blame the post. I duck into the newsagent's and sigh at the shit selection of cards. They look like they've been there since 1985, but I pick the least embarrassing of the bunch and pay, heading back out to a bench to write it.

My hand starts to get cold as I hold the pen poised, my mind blank. I never know what to write when these occasions come around. Birthdays, Christmas. Mother's Day. After Sylvia took me in, little orphan Taylor, I spent so much time thinking that I had to dislike her – that liking her would be a betrayal of Anita – it started to feel real. Even though she was supportive, protective and loving, sometimes to the point of stifling.

Sylvia had known just as well as I did, of course, that it was only a matter of time with Mum. The way she'd watch me with concerned eyes if she was round visiting Mum when I got home from school, the way she'd ask cautiously if everything was all right. I knew what she meant: *Are you coping? Has she tried it again? You'd tell me if she did?* But even as a kid, I was no snitch. I felt like it was private – what my mother went through, how it affected me. It was for the two of us to navigate together. Until she decided it was time to break that pact and leave me alone, I guess.

Mum knew that Sylvia was concerned about us. She probably resented being monitored as to how she looked after her own child – well, when she was stable enough to care. Still, even though she resented her sister seeming like the perfect mother even after getting divorced, deep down Anita needed Sylvia to be there. I know my mum actually wished she were more like my aunt: doting on her daughter, getting her life back on track after a crisis. The two of them were so different – but not in the way my mother thought. Not in the way that really mattered.

Either way, Mum still trusted her sister enough, when that

day came, to protect me as much as possible from what had happened. It was Sylvia she called, right before she did it.

It must have been such a burden for my aunt. And how do I thank her? By being distant and pathetic and forgetting her birthday. Thing is, I never know how to put into words everything I need to say to her. So now I just shake my head, scribble

Dear Aunty Sylvia
Hope you have a great day
Love, Taylor x

and stuff the card into the envelope. I wince at the bitter taste of the adhesive as I lick it and seal it shut, and then I jump as my phone rings, thinking, ridiculously, that it might be her.

But no. It's just Marcy.

'Babe? Hi!' She sounds loud and out of breath. 'Sorry, I thought it would go to voicemail. I'm just running into rehearsal.'

'Yeah, I'm on lunch,' I reply, a little tautly, as I cradle the phone against my shoulder so I can stick a stamp on the envelope. I'm still a bit irritated about this morning, even though it wasn't really her fault. 'What's up?'

'Listen, Ryan got guest list for Manna tonight, but he can't make it. He's got an audition tomorrow.'

'Oh, right . . .'

'So he said I should take you and have some fun. He insisted, in fact. Come on, T, girls' night out, make up for this morning?'

She knows I'm still pissed off about it, which is why we're friends. God, and she doesn't even know the half of what happened today.

And, wait, *Ryan* said she should take me out? Why would he—?

'Taylor? What you reckon? I mean René and a couple of those lot are going, but it would be a thousand times better if you were

24

coming too.' Marcy's chatter interrupts my thoughts, her voice dropping lower as the traffic noise on her end of the phone dies down. 'You'll come, yeah?' I can hear the expectant expression on her face.

'Um ... Can I give you a call later and let you know?' Part of me just wants to get a bottle of wine and watch dumb shit on TV tonight, but I don't actually say that or she'll never let me get away with it.

'Course, babe, course ...' Marcy pauses, and I know I'm not off the hook. 'You fucking *should* come though. It'll be wicked!'

I sort of grunt a non-committal reply, but she's barely stopped for breath. 'Cool, cool, OK, I'll see you later on anyway, yeah? Gotta go.'

'Yep, see you later,' I reply, but the line's gone dead before I finish. I drop my aunt's card into a postbox before ducking into Boots to pick up a sandwich and a box of cheap ibuprofen for Luc. As I walk back to the bookshop, I pop two of the pills into my mouth and clench my jaw, swallowing hard. I'm starting to get a headache myself.

When I walk back into the shop, Luc's extolling the virtues of a weighty architectural tome to a short, balding man who winces as Luc's alcohol-tinged breath wafts over him. The man seems to take my arrival as a window for escape, and hastily shuffles out past me as I enter.

'Think he thought I was a crazy person who just crawled off the street while you were in the loo and started babbling about Albert Kahn,' Luc says, chuckling to himself.

'Here you go.' I toss the box of painkillers towards him. 'Sorry, I cracked into them.'

'Tough day already?'

'Could say that.'

Luc hangs about chatting while I finish my lunch. Somehow

we always manage to talk for ages without getting too personal, which I like. But today I feel as though something might accidentally bubble up out of me – bobbing uninvited to the surface. It's a relief when he heads off for the afternoon. Well, it is until the eerie silence settles amongst the bookshelves and plush carpeting again, and I'm alone.

I sit for a while, yawning. I'm so tired, I don't know if I'd have enough energy to go out with Marcy tonight. And going out with her usually means getting hit on, because she's like a magnet that has to deflect on to Single Little Me. I end up feeling like I *should* be looking, because maybe she'll be suspicious that I'm not – and then I feel hot bursts of guilt and envy, because what's the point?

Nobody else is *him*.

I gaze around the shop vacantly, as though it might give me some kind of answer. Then I think of something, and slide off the stool I've been perched on, walk over to the door and turn the lock. I flip the BACK IN FIVE MINUTES sign over, then stride swiftly down the aisle between the shelves and into the back room. I rummage in my bag, a sense of urgency building in me, until my fingers close around the packet of cigarettes. Opening the back door a crack, I light one and inhale deeply, puffing the smoke through the gap and watching it billow out into the alleyway. I'll have to buy some American Spirits; these things taste like shit. I look down at the packet and lighter, remembering the woman who gave them to me, and why. For a split second, I think about throwing them away, tossing them out into the alley, but I think better of it. Instead, I pull my phone out of my pocket, looking to distract myself with some guilty Facebook stalking of Ry—

There's a text from Marcy.

We are going out tonight, yes? It'll be fuuuun xxxx

I bite my lip. Maybe a night out would do me some good – I could do with killing off a few brain cells, perhaps some of these heavy memories will fade away with them. I know Marcy would just go with her dancer mates anyway now she's got her mind set on it, and if Ryan's going to be staying in then chances are I'd be there alone with him. So far, with Herculean effort, I've been able to avoid that.

Marcy and Ryan have only been together four months, which you would have thought would be too soon for cohabitation. But he had some issue with his landlord, and of course, being the masochist that I am, when Marcy asked if he could stay with us for a few days – five weeks ago – I said yes. Even though I remembered him. Even though I hadn't told her about when he and I met. Even though I'd thought about him every single day since *that day*, wondering ... And then there he was. With her. And I said nothing.

Living with him has made my totally inappropriate attraction to him much more manageable, of course. At least he pays a bit of the rent.

So, hours of awkwardness in the flat, just me and Ryan? No, bad idea. Very bad. Although ...

No.

I hit the dial button, and at the other end the phone rings twice.

'T?' Marcy's voice whispers.

'Go on then. Let's do it. I'll come.' I hold the phone away from my ear as Marcy squeals, then return it to hear angry shushing in the background before she speaks again.

'Shit. Not meant to be on the phone. In a bit, babe.'

I hang up, stub out my cigarette and go back into the shop. I have a feeling it's going to be a long afternoon.

Chapter Three

The door to the flat clumps shut behind me, and I wait, listening. No one's home yet – or Marcy's taken Charlie out for his evening walk. No sign of Ryan.

I dump my stuff in my room and take the Sainsbury's bag into the kitchen, where my face falls. It looks as though every pot and pan in the flat has been used to make some sort of pancake breakfast, then left to form a no-doubt-immovable crust. Flatmates, who'd have them? I'm just glad I'm only chucking something in the microwave so I don't need to cook – Marcy can deal with her own washing-up. The obsessive in me does, though, feel compelled to put everything in hot soapy water to soak, and I wipe down all the surfaces while my micro-meal whirrs in a circle, heating up. It's still going after I've finished clearing up, so I lean against the counter, resting my eyes for a moment. Better not fall asleep ...

The microwave beeps loudly and my eyes spring open. Now that I can smell the curry, I'm not even sure I'll be able to eat it, but I peel back the film and half-heartedly stuff in a few mouthfuls before pushing it away with a grimace. I glance at the sinkful of dishes. It's taunting me. Maybe I'll just do a few.

I can't help it, it's an impulse. Probably from being in the same situation as a kid, coming home from school to find Anita holed up in bed after having tried to make me dinner. Half the time it was just lucky she hadn't burned the house down.

I turn to the sink, pull on the gloves, set the water running hard and start to scrub. I feel better already.

'Helloooo?'

Marcy's voice over the sound of the running water makes me jump.

'In here,' I call. Charlie barks at the sound of my voice and comes scurrying towards me eagerly. I turn and squirm defencelessly, trying to pull off the rubber gloves as he jumps up at me with wet paws. What is it with this mutt?

'Hey.'

I look up – instead of Marcy, it's Ryan's frame that fills the kitchen doorway.

'Oh. Hey.' I finally pull the gloves off with a loud snap, flicking water into my face.

'She's just jumping in the shower quickly,' Ryan says, crouching down and patting his knees to attract the dog away from me. 'Come here, Chuck. Leave her alone, come on.'

His sandy-brown hair is freshly cut, shorter than usual. It makes his eyebrows seem stronger, darker; his eyes and cheekbones stand out more too— I'm staring.

'I think he wants feeding,' I say, and then glance at my halfeaten dinner on the counter. I pick it up and scrape it into the dog bowl, then throw the plastic tray away. Ryan raises an eyebrow at me.

'Not hungry?'

'It wasn't great,' I reply. 'I was just feeling lazy.'

'Fair enough.' He's still in the doorway, with his hands in the pockets of his pea-coat. 'You know, if he gets the shits it's me who's going to have to take him out tonight,' he says with a half-smile. 'Though I guess fair's fair. Thanks for taking him out this morning. Marcy said—'

'No, no. It's cool. Anyway, it's her pooch, so . . .'

He chuckles at 'pooch', and his eyes linger on mine for a moment, like they do. God, why *did* I say pooch? Who says pooch?

I want to get out of the kitchen, but I'd have to brush past him, and just the thought makes me feel on edge in a totally ridiculous way. So I turn to the sink and wash my hands needlessly.

'You had your hair cut,' I say with my back turned to him. I roll my eyes as the words come out of my mouth, but then glance over my shoulder to check he's still there – I could be talking to myself.

'Yeah,' he says, nodding and reaching up to touch his head. 'I have an audition tomorrow. Guy who goes AWOL from the army. Thought I should look the part. What do you reckon?' He turns his head to show his profile, frowning to look militaristic, then breaking into a wry expression as he turns back to me.

'It looks good,' I murmur, smiling but looking away, down at the dishcloth I'm using to over-dry my hands. 'Uh, yeah, Marcy mentioned you had an audition. Thanks for the guest-list spot for tonight.'

'No problem. I'm not much of a dancer anyway, I'm sure she'll tell you.' I sense his smile, feel its warmth aimed towards me. He takes a breath. 'I thought maybe . . .' I look up at him, curious about what he's going to say, and he seems a bit nervous all of a sudden. When he speaks again it's more of a mumble. 'I don't know, sometimes a night out just feels full of potential.'

I look at him for a moment, my jaw tensing. I get that sensation again – the one where I want to be angry or defensive at these weird little suggestions that my feelings are somehow his concern. But I think it's his way of trying to do what he did that day at the cinema. A hand reaching out – one that I want more than anything to take.

If only.

'Forget my troubles, come on, get happy?' I say sarcastically, but through another smile.

He shrugs. 'Forget . . . Or don't. There's nothing wrong with that either.' He studies me for a moment longer, and I'm not sure what to say to that. 'Anyway, if forgetting was that easy we'd all be doing it, eh?' he mutters. I swallow. 'Well, hopefully it should be a good time,' he says, louder now. 'Just don't let Marcy get you into too much trouble. Don't want to add to that pile you need to forget, right?' The corner of his mouth turns up a little, and he exhales a semi-laugh, which I echo. Ryan shakes his head, seemingly at himself, and finally turns away into the hall to hang up his coat.

I take the opportunity to slip out of the kitchen, but then decide I'm going to need something to perk me up for tonight, and it's probably best if it's not Class A stimulants. I turn back, pausing in the doorway.

'Actually, I'm going to make some coffee before I get ready,' I say. 'Want some?'

'I can make it if you like?' Ryan replies. Before I can move out of the way, he's in the doorway again too. The length of his body brushes slowly against mine in exactly the manner I'd been hoping to avoid. I catch his cut-grass smell, feel delicate, electric threads of myself pull towards him, like fine hair caught on the breeze. He looks down at me and breathes in. The feeling bubbles up inside me again – the desperate questions I want to ask about that morning at the cinema, the questions we both avoid. If things had turned out differently, if—

Just then, I hear the shower switch off in the bathroom, and he moves away. A moment later Marcy strides into the hallway with a towel barely wrapped around her, dripping water on to the floor. She grins at me.

'It's *showtime!*'

Yeah, it certainly is. She points at me and raises admonishing eyebrows.

'Are you ready? Come on, get a move on, I said we'd maybe meet some of the guys for drinks early doors.'

By 'the guys', she means her dancer friends. I kind of like them, and they certainly have good energy, but nothing makes you feel more insecure than going clubbing with professional dancers.

'Do you want coffee, Marce?' Ryan asks. Just the smell of it starting to percolate is making me feel better.

'*Coffee?*' she scoffs, but scuttles into the kitchen to tease him, still wearing just the towel. I head towards my bedroom to avoid the display, and stare into my wardrobe, hoping some new and exciting outfit has made its way in there without my knowledge. I could borrow something from Marcy, I suppose. I cringe, thinking of what I'd *actually* like to borrow of hers.

Pushing the door shut, I dump my work clothes and pull on my dressing gown.

'Just jumping in the shower,' I call, heading back out.

'Your *coffee* is ready,' Marcy replies disapprovingly. I shuffle over to the kitchen, where she's proffering a mug.

'Thank you,' I say, trying to encompass them both, glad that Ryan's back is turned now, even though he's seen me in this ratty robe dozens of times.

'Want me to make it Irish?' Marcy says as I grab the mug and turn back to the bathroom. I give a short laugh over my shoulder.

I shower quickly, gulping down the coffee before brushing my teeth, then swipe some of Marcy's pricey body oil over my skin before heading back to my bedroom to get dressed. As I pull on a black vest top and black jeans, I glance at the photo of Anita in all her finery that I've tucked into the corner of my mirror. How did she always look so good (when she made an effort)? Red lippy. I feel like she's willing me to wear some, and she's right: it makes all the difference. I brush my fingers over the picture, missing her.

Finally I drag the hairband out of my curls and let them tumble free, trying to shape them into some sort of sensible do with my fingers, then pull on high-heeled ankle boots that I know I'll regret an hour after we get to the club. But fuck it. I stand back, scrutinise my reflection from every angle, and sigh. 'It'll do.'

I emerge into the hallway, but now there's no sign of Marcy, after all the talk of hurrying to get ready. I grab my coat and bag.

'Marcy?'

'Yeah? Uh ... five minutes,' comes her muffled voice, followed by giggling. Ryan's in there with her. I sigh.

'Hurry up,' I say through gritted teeth. 'I'm having shots.'

'Mmm ...'

I go to the kitchen, pull open the booze-cupboard door and pour myself a large shot of rum. I down it and pour another, opening the fridge to prise an ancient ice cube out of the tray and plop it into the glass. Heading to the living room, I switch on the TV, but to my surprise I hear Marcy's bedroom door open, and I spring up eagerly.

'That *was* quick—' I begin, reaching down to pick up my bag and coat.

'False alarm,' says Ryan, coming into the room and sitting on the sofa.

'Ah.' I slump back down into the armchair. 'Course.'

'You know,' he begins slowly, 'I'm kind of starting to feel sorry that I'm not coming with you guys.' I glance over at him and he eventually flicks his gaze away from me towards the television screen.

'Oh, well, if you want to take that guest list, I can always—'

'No, no. I just meant you look . . .' He tails off and shakes his head a little, looking embarrassed. Jesus, I need to learn to take a compliment. Maybe I didn't imagine that moment in the kitchen earlier? 'What are we watching?' he says, changing the subject.

'Oh, I think it's this thing called "the news",' I say with a smile, which he returns wryly. I take a sip of rum, and the ice hurts my teeth. I put the glass down on the table. Better pace myself. 'Um, so what are your big plans for the evening then? You've got the flat all to yourself.'

He turns towards me. 'Yeah, look, thanks for this, Taylor. I really hadn't meant to stay this long. Maybe if I get this gig tomorrow I can start looking to—'

'Oh, no, it's fine, I didn't mean . . . You're welcome to stay. Of course.' I feel myself getting hot, and reach for my rum again.

'No really, I appreciate it though. Having me lumping around the place all the time can't be your dream scenario.' He looks at me and bites the inside of his cheek, hesitating. I stare at the TV, trying not to think of his role in my dreams. 'I mean, I know this is . . . weird. If I'd had any other choice, I'd have taken it.' I still don't look at him. He's silent for a while. 'Taylor,' he says, his tone lower now. I return my gaze to him, drawn by all the things in his voice when he says my name like that. We stare at each other for a moment, and he puffs out an ironic sigh. 'Do you ever feel like you've dropped into some alternative universe, and you just have to go along with it, until things right themselves?'

I raise my eyebrows. 'Like some 1960s sci-fi show or something?'

'Yeah.'

I look down at my glass. 'Yeah.'

Why are we such cowards? Why can't we just talk about it?

I hear heels clattering along the hallway. The 'why'.

'Yes! Gorgeous!' Marcy exclaims as she poses in the doorway. I'm not sure if she's referring to herself, but then she teeters over and reaches down to pull me off the sofa, looking me up and down appreciatively. 'You look amazing. Simple yet sexy. Oof, those boys aren't going to know what hit them.'

'I just want to have a bit of a dance,' I murmur, but I can't help grinning as Marcy mocks me with a 'Little old me?' face. She reaches for my glass, sniffs it approvingly, and downs the rest before slamming it back on the table. Then she grabs my hand and turns to Ryan.

'Don't wait up, babe,' she says with a wink.

'Would I be so foolish?' He slips his hand around Marcy's waist and pecks her lips. I pull my hand away and busy myself taking the glass to the kitchen. I put on my coat and wait by the front door until Marcy emerges.

'OK, let's roll,' she says.

'Have a good time,' Ryan says. Marcy strides out and I follow, glancing back to see him give me a little wave before the door closes.

'So, are you two sisters?'

'Sorry?'

'You and that girl I saw you with. Are you sisters?'

I recoil a little as this guy shouts into my ear. The music pounds around me, pressing in on me. I shake my head, and it swims dizzily with the movement. As he leans over me to speak again, I concentrate on sucking hard on the thin cocktail straw in my glass. The smell of his aftershave is making me want to gag.

'Funny,' he continues, 'I could have sworn . . . '

The line's not working, mate. Drop it. I steel myself to draw in another aftershave-laden breath and make an excuse so I can head to the ladies' and find Marcy, but then I feel her arms snake around my middle and she rests her chin on my shoulder.

'Who's this?' she says with a raised eyebrow, looking at me expectantly then smiling slowly at the tall, dark-blond guy. Yeah, OK, he is pretty good-looking, but he has zero game, and I'm really not in the mood.

'I didn't catch his name,' I say pointedly, hoping she'll get the hint.

'Well, maybe he'll buy us a drink and we can find out.' She grins at the guy, who turns obligingly to the bar.

'God, this place is rammed tonight,' Marcy shouts, smoothing over her pulled-back hair and sweeping her hands down the long ponytail that hangs down her back. It's not even a weave – her mum's Mauritian. I mean, whose mother is *Mauritian*? And her dad apparently has Russian Jewish heritage, though I've never met him; he'd moved out by the time I met Marcy in Year 9, and her bumbling stepdad Kevin was on the scene soon after. I'm certain my own hair is a cloud of frizz by now, with all these sweating bodies around, but there's not much I can do about it. It baffles me that Marcy and I are sometimes mistaken for sisters. I mean, we're both mixed-race, but other than that I couldn't feel more different from her most of the time. I'm a tightly wound ball of wire wool, and she's like free-flowing silk. Or something. Bloody hell, I've had too much to drink already.

'So, any talent yet?' Marcy asks. She eyes the guy at the bar

36

to make sure he's not doing anything strange with the drinks he's ordered us.

I shake my head. 'Not happening.'

Marcy laughs. 'Fair enough, babe. Well, I just thought I'd lend a helping hand if anything *was*. Or at the very least watch our wallets, eh? Drinks in here are bloody expen—'. She breaks off as the aftershave guy turns back to us with two bright-pink cocktails in his hands.

'Thanks!' she shouts.

'Michael,' he finishes, grinning from Marcy to me and back again. 'My name's Michael. You know, I was just saying to your friend here, I thought you two were sisters. Practically look like *twins* ...' We really don't. He pauses, laughing needlessly, and more than a bit sketchily. 'I've never met twins before.'

I roll my eyes and see Marcy purse her lips. She gets it now.

'Hmmm. Well, she's my sister from another mister,' she says breezily, and clinks her glass with mine. We look at each other, taking healthy gulps of our drinks. The concoction tastes like syrup mixed with nail-polish remover.

'Maybe it's my lucky night then?' He licks his lips, his eyes more focused on Marcy now, seeing as he was getting more out of her. 'You two, me, a cab ... ?' I think I'm going to puke. We both drain our glasses, and I step towards him before Marcy decides to slap him.

'Dream on, *Michael*,' I say, looking up at him sweetly. Not exactly the pithiest retort, but he gets the message. Marcy laughs loudly and grabs my hand, pulling me off towards the dance floor as a familiar, pounding rhythm starts up.

We push through the heaving crowd – Marcy always has to be right in the centre of the action. We start to dance, and I close my eyes and raise my hands above my head, getting into it. As I open them, I see Marcy start to *really* move. It's a sight to behold.

Even sandwiched into a mass of writhing bodies, she manages to stand out. Her dancing isn't showy like it would be on stage, but it's still mesmerising – like a singer slipping effortlessly into a complicated harmony. She moves closer, pulling me in to her movements, and with the copious amount of alcohol coursing through my veins mingling with a sudden rush of adrenalin, it doesn't take much persuasion. Soon we're rocking from side to side, my feet are shuffling, I'm singing at the top of my lungs . . . For a moment, I feel free.

Then the music changes. I stop moving, and Marcy spins away seamlessly, shimmying towards a group of her friends. My stomach's churning hard. I stumble towards the edge of the dance floor and glance back to signal to Marce that I'm heading to the ladies', but I can't spot her. I stand in the line for the loos, clutching my middle, and finally get in. Inside the cubicle, I lean over, breathing heavily. My stomach lurches but thank God I manage to keep things down. I hover over the seat to pee, flush, then make my way towards the sinks, jostling for room amongst the sweating women trying to fix their make-up. I run the tap hard and splash some water on my face, then half-heartedly dry it on a scratchy paper towel as another drunk girl asks me if I'm all right. I nod, but I need to get outside. I push my way out of the bathroom and start to look around for the smoking-area sign. I head up the stairs towards the exit.

'No re-entry, yeah?' The bouncer glances at me impassively as I hover in the doorway.

'I've got a stamp,' I say, proffering the back of my hand.

'No re-entry after one a.m., love,' he replies, ushering me out of the way before I can say anything else.

'Fuck's sake.' I need a cigarette badly, and I can't see the smoking area anywhere. There's no queue for the cloakroom though, so I swiftly collect my coat and push my way outside past the bouncer. I pull out a fag and my lighter, lean on a nearby wall and take a deep inhale, trying to calm my stomach and get my bearings. I feel better already. The music pulses faintly from inside, and I watch a small cluster of girls trying to hail a taxi, their bare legs blue and blotchy from the cold. I should text Marcy, tell her where I am, but when I pull out my phone, the battery's died again.

'Fucking great.'

I push my hands into my coat pockets, leaving the cigarette burning between my lips, and try to gather my strength to face the night bus. It's freezing out here – my cheeks feel numb already – and the bus stop is a ten-minute walk.

I feel every step. My boots have my toes in a vice grip, and my head still feels a bit fuzzy, though the wind whipping into my face does help sober me up. When I finally get there, there's only one other person at the stop. I glance at him – tall black guy, hair trimmed low, expensive trainers. Quite fit. Very, actually. But looks can be deceiving this late at night. I clench my fists in my pockets, only partly against the cold, and tense up a bit as he looks over at me. I turn my gaze to look studiously out at the passing traffic.

'I've been waiting for like forty-five minutes now. Must be an accident or something,' he says after a moment. His voice is deep, well spoken. I again remind myself about making assumptions either way, clear my throat and look down the road. The girls from outside the club are making their way towards the stop as well, and I relax a little.

'Oh, right,' I reply, looking up at him and smiling a little. 'Bloody cold, isn't it?'

I nod, not sure whether I should get into a conversation with him or not.

'Not that this lot mind,' he chuckles as the girls arrive at the stop, their heels clattering loudly against the pavement. Their breath bursts in clouds around them as they speak over one another in high-pitched voices.

'Is this the right side of the road for the New Cross bus?' one of them slurs brashly, looking at me with barely focused, mascara-smudged eyes. I hope I don't look as battered as that – I definitely don't feel it any more.

'Uh, yeah, it is,' I reply, folding my arms around myself. It really is freezing; I don't know how these women don't have hypothermia already.

'Oi, do you lot wanna share a taxi? You two?' Another of the girls is flagging a black cab with her handbag, but then she crumples to the ground giggling as its contents go flying. I sigh, but it would be cheaper than getting one on my own – there doesn't seem to be a bus coming, and it's sub-zero out here.

'Yeah, all right,' I say grudgingly, and I hear the guy behind me say the same. He glances at me and shrugs, and we both smile a little again.

All of us bundle into the cab, and there's lots of toing and froing with the driver about where to drop everyone off. Thankfully my flat's on the way to their end-point of New Cross Gate, where Bus Stop Guy says he'll get out too. I'm squeezed in between him and Mascara Girl, and I feel myself bumping from side to side, his leg rubbing against mine every now and then. The girls laugh and joke, asking us if we're together. I say I don't even know his name, and he turns to me and says, 'Leon. Good to meet you.' He holds out his hand and I shake it, wondering how it's already so warm.

I fight the urge to give a fake name – and frown at the fact that I want to tell him it's Marcy.

'Taylor,' I say, and he smiles.

'Nice name.' He doesn't break eye contact.

'Thanks.'

'I think I saw you earlier, with that tall girl?'

Even when I'm not with Marcy, I'm defined in contrast to her. Shit, I hope she doesn't worry about where I am. I'll text her when I get in.

'I— Not that I was . . .' he stammers, realising how that sounded. 'I mean I haven't been stalking you or anything, I just . . . couldn't help but notice you.'

One of the girls makes the standard 'Oo-oo-ooh' noise, and the others giggle.

'Well, she stands out, doesn't she, ladies?' he says, grinning at them. He has dimples that make him look younger when he smiles.

'Charmer you've got here,' Mascara says, elbowing me. I should feel uncomfortable – I usually would – but for some reason tonight I don't. I laugh along with the others.

'Hmm, I didn't notice *you* though, Leon,' I say, raising an eyebrow at him with a slow smile. 'I hope you weren't just hanging around in a corner letching at women?'

He laughs and looks affronted. 'No. I was with a mate and his girlfriend tagged along, they got in a fight, then went off to hers to "make up", I guess.' He pulls a face but then glances out of the window for a moment like he was genuinely annoyed by my suggestion. I pat his arm and he turns back to me.

'All right, Dockley Road,' the cab driver calls good-naturedly, pulling up to the kerb. 'Who's getting out?'

I peer at the meter and rummage in my purse for the cash I owe, but then the other girls start to think about the fare too.

'Shit, I think I dropped my purse . . .'

'Well I've only got a fiver . . .'

'How far is it to walk to New Cross from here?'

I look at Leon, then at Mascara. 'Uh, maybe forty minutes?'

'Fuck it, girls, I think we should get out here. There's probably a bus from here anyway . . .'

They start debating amongst themselves while the cabbie gets increasingly impatient. I hand over my portion of the fare to Mascara and start to get out, leaving them to it, but they pay and pile out of the cab close behind me – Leon included. He lingers for a moment, catching my eye.

'Figured I might as well get out here too,' he says, still looking at me.

I nod slowly. The cab driver doesn't hang around. Exhaust plumes in the night as he speeds away, probably glad to be rid of us. The girls call goodbye to us and link arms, walking off in a teetering line, heading in the wrong direction. I laugh a little self-consciously.

'Are you far?' Leon asks, and I shake my head. I should start walking, but I haven't yet, and neither has he.

'Just up there on the left.'

He sighs and looks at his phone. 'My brother lives round here actually. Franklin Road, 'bout five minutes away?' He looks at the time again. 'Dunno if he'd appreciate me turning up right now though.' He smiles. The girls are still up ahead, giggling and walking slowly in the same direction as the flat. I wouldn't be alone with him for more than a minute or two. Ryan's at home.

I swallow.

Leon speaks again. 'Well, nice to meet—'

He breaks off as I step closer to him. Another step. I look up at him.

The space between his brow creases a little: surprised, confused maybe. I move my mouth closer to his, and he leans in too. He presses his lips against mine, soft but firm. I tilt my head, probing with my tongue. He responds, gripping my waist. I have

42

a vague worry about the taste of my cigarette but I put it aside. He's a good kisser, but he doesn't push his luck either. I pull away, breathing harder. He looks at me, still a little quizzically, but then breaks into a slow smile. I glance around. The girls disappear around the corner.

'This way,' I say, but leave him standing there as I start to walk. My feet still hurt, but I quicken my pace, and listen. A moment later his footsteps are behind me, then beside me. I head to my building and let us in, and he looks at me again, trying to get a read on me, checking silently if I'm sure. I start up the stairs, and feel him press in behind me. We reach the top, and I try to push my key quietly into our front door. Leon pulls my hair aside and starts kissing my neck. I close my eyes for a moment, then unlock the door, turning and pressing a finger to my lips like a teenager. He nods.

But maybe we shouldn't be quiet. Maybe I *want* Ryan to know.

'Which one's your room?' Leon whispers, but his voice sounds loud in the quiet of the corridor. I point, and slip off my boots to pad towards it, my heart beating fast. Without my heels for elevation, Leon feels even bigger now. I take a deep breath, but he follows respectfully, and I close my bedroom door and turn to him. He smiles, and his dimples deepen.

'Hi.'

'Hi.'

I press my lips to his again, up on tiptoes, squeezing my eyes shut. He pushes my coat off my shoulders and I do the same with his. His hands edge up under my top, my hands reach around the back of his neck. I turn him around and he stumbles until his back is against the door. I keep kissing. He pulls his head back for a second, panting. Maybe I was coming on a little too strong. I step away, trying to remember if I have condoms.

He looks at me, wondering why I'm hesitating now.

'Are you OK? We could always—'

'No, I'm fine. I . . . Just a sec.' I rummage in my bag, pick out my phone, find my charger and plug it in by my bedside, bending down to connect them. The phone buzzes to life with missed calls and texts from Marcy. I fire a quick one back, saying I'm fine and home; that my phone died. All the while, Leon watches me, still standing by the door. I flick my eyes back up to his, and then put the phone down.

Straightening up, I walk towards Leon again, slowly now. Taking his hand, I lead him over to the bed and sit down on it, facing him. He stares down at me, edging in between my knees, and I start to undo his belt buckle, but he pushes my hands away, leans down and kisses me again, and we slide back on to the bed, easing each other's clothes off. He knows what he's doing, and I'm surprised how much I like it. *Keep your mind blank, just focus on the physical sensation and don't think about anything – anyone – else, just—*

'Do you have something?' Leon whispers breathlessly.

'Uh, yeah . . . ' I stretch my arm out to my bedside drawer, feeling around blindly until my fingers close on the packet. We pull apart for a moment for that awkward, unsexy fumble, but then he pulls me back close, rolls me on to my back, eases himself into me and moans softly. I close my eyes, concentrate. He feels good. It's been too long. Usually, alone, I'd imagine— *God, don't think about Ryan now. Concentrate. Concentrate. Concentrate . . .*

I turn and look at my clock: 3.57 a.m. I blink, panicking for a moment when I see the figure lying beside me, but then I remember. We must have been asleep for a couple of hours. He's breathing steadily. Quietly I get up, avoiding the piles of our clothes flung from the bed on to the floor, pull on my dressing gown and move quietly towards the door.

As I make my way to the bathroom in the darkness of the corridor, I trip over something and stub my toe hard on the skirting board. I swear loudly then clamp my hand over my mouth, eyes watering from the pain. I look down and see Marcy's chunky platform heels strewn on the floor. Guess she made it home all right then.

I close the bathroom door, leaving the light off, and pee. My mouth feels fuzzy, but I can't be bothered to brush my teeth right now, so I take a long drink straight from the tap and a swig of mouthwash that just reminds me of the alcohol still valiantly trying to party in my system. I look at my reflection in the mirror, a vague blue outline from the moonlight coming through the window. Eyes hooded, hair wild, but less of a mess than I'd expected, considering. I wipe the last of my make-up off with my damp fingertips, and feel for the hairband on my wrist, pulling the nest up into a bun. I hesitate, feeling strange about going back to sleep with a stranger.

'Fucking weird day,' I whisper to myself. Then I jump as there's a soft knock on the door. 'Uh ... just a minute ... ' Shit, is that Leon? Maybe he's going to leave. I kind of hope he is. I wait for a moment, listening.

'Taylor?'

Ryan. I hold my breath for a moment, then slowly unlock the door and turn the handle. He peers into the bathroom, his eyes tired, reaching up to push back his now non-existent hair.

'Hey.' My voice seems to echo around us. 'Sorry, did I wake you up?'

'Well *you* did, then later *Marce* did,' he says with a half-smile, but his gaze is shrouded in darkness. My stomach lurches. That was what I wanted, wasn't it? For him to know that I— 'She was worried. I texted her saying you'd come back, though.' He looks at me, then looks away.

'Yeah, my battery died. Fuck, I'm sorry Ryan – about waking you up, I mean. I know you've got that thing tomorrow, the, um ...'

'No, no, don't worry about it. I just wanted to see if you were OK.'

I narrow my eyes a little, grit my teeth. 'You seem very concerned about that lately.' I immediately regret it. I must still be drunk. 'Why wouldn't I be OK?' My words are still confrontational, but my voice is much quieter now, softer. Like I want him to have an answer. I look up at his face, and I'm vaguely aware of his chest rising and falling under his white T-shirt. His eyes break away from mine and move slowly down my body. The cheap cotton of my dressing gown suddenly feels thin, like it's barely touching my naked skin.

'Your toe's bleeding,' he whispers, pointing downwards. I look down too, just making out little beads of blood in the gloomy light.

'Oh. Ugh. Yeah, I tripped on Marcy's stupid shoe. I'll—'

'Taylor, did you ... did you bring someone home?' he interrupts. His voice is quiet, hesitant.

I stare at him, and his eyes stay steadily on me.

'Yes,' I whisper.

He blinks, but doesn't say anything. I swallow, and he takes a step closer and reaches around me. I can hear my pulse pounding in my ears.

'What are you—?'

'Plasters.' His face is close to mine. I can feel his breath on my cheek. 'They're in here.' He's pulled open the cabinet under the sink.

'Oh.'

He takes out a box, his body still close to mine. 'Sit down,' he says, his voice low.

Taking a step into the bathroom, he gestures for me to sit on the toilet lid. I shuffle backwards and he pushes the door. It's not quite closed, but the proximity of us, together, in this small space ... My breathing sounds loud and urgent, and I can barely make out his face. He doesn't put the overhead light on, but he pulls the little cord that makes the dim light above the mirror blink into life.

I sit down heavily on the toilet seat and look up at him, wondering if either of us knows what we're doing. He kneels down in front of me. I stare at him, not sure if I should say something. He's so near me that I can barely think. I ball my hands into fists to avoid reaching out and touching him. His features are shadowed in the faded light, until he tilts his face towards me and takes a long, slow breath. Then he blinks and looks towards my bare feet. Gently, he lifts the injured one on to one of his thighs. His hands are warm, his fingertips stroking the sole of my foot, the instep, ever so lightly. I feel my lips part, and his eyes travel up my leg as my robe slips off it, just a little. I don't pull it back. I hear him breathe in again. Then his hand moves away, and he opens the box of plasters and tears one open. He leans down towards my foot, concentrating as he presses the plaster around my big toe. He looks up at me again when he's finished, smiling slightly. His fingers rest lightly on top of my foot, which is still on his thigh. The skin where he touches me is suddenly so sensitive, the delicate bones seem to ripple under his touch. Heat begins to build inside me, between my legs.

'Thank you,' I say, my voice barely a whisper.

'Taylor ... I know it's none of my business if you bring someone home,' he says quietly. He sounds like he's berating himself. 'I know that.'

'No. It's not,' I retort firmly.

He nods several times, like he's convincing himself my words are true. I don't know if I'm sure myself.

After what feels like an age, he releases my foot and stands up. He takes a step back, away from me, opens the door and heads to Marcy's room without looking back or saying anything more. I feel like something in the very centre of me is pulling towards him as he goes.

Saturday morning, I wake up alone. I look at my alarm clock – it's well after midday. My head swims a little, and I drop it back down on to the pillow, feeling around on the bedside table for my phone. I see the texts from Marcy, and vague memories begin to filter into my mind from last night. I sit up a little, and glance at the condom wrapper on the floor next to the bed. I turn the other way and see that Bus Stop Guy left a note.

I swallow, staring at the neatly folded square of paper resting on the pillow. My heart beats a little faster for a moment as I remember another neatly folded note with my name written on it like that. But I push the memory aside, pull myself up to sit cross-legged in the dishevelled bedclothes, and unfold the note quickly, squinting to read his small, scribbly boy-writing.

Taylor. Thanks a lot for last night. Sorry I had to go. Leon.

I look at the note for a while. He was nice, a good guy, I think. A gentleman, but not too much of one when it counted. Handsome, intelligent ... Being with someone like him might make my life less complicated. Or at least one aspect of it. I wriggle my toe and feel the plaster on it. A sharp memory of my encounter with Ryan last night jabs me; alone with him in the darkness. His fingertips brushing against my skin ...

I start to think about the first time, all those months ago, before he was who he is now. When I had a chance. I quickly push the thought away. This can't happen.

But still. Why did he ask me about bringing someone home? *Forget it, forget it, forget it.*

I sigh in irritation at myself, crumple Leon's note instinctively, and aim it towards the bin. I look at my phone again, and notice that there's another message on there I haven't listened to. I dial into my voicemail, and hear an unfamiliar man's voice.

'This is a message for . . . uh, Taylor Jennings. Jenkins, sorry. Taylor, this is Constable Martin, we met the other day. We were wondering if you might be free to come in and answer a few more questions about the body you found. Just routine stuff, nothing serious, it's just for finishing up the inquiry. Um, if you could give me a call back—'

I hang up before the message finishes, and lean back against the headboard, staring down at the phone.

Nothing serious?

I take a deep breath, but it brings on a wave of nausea. I stumble towards the bin, with the discarded note at the bottom of it, and heave.

Chapter Four

An hour and a half later, I'm still lying on my bed as the world whirrs around me. The flat is silent except for the dull thud of the blood pulsing in my head, and I jump when I hear a sudden, rapid scrabbling on the bedroom door, and then a low, rumbling 'woof'. I attempt to ignore him, but my mouth is suddenly drier than the Sahara. I need to go to the kitchen to get some water.

Levering myself up slowly, I make my way out to the kitchen, blinking hard at the bright afternoon sun streaming in through the window. Charlie dances around my heels, panting excitedly. Through the slight gap in Marcy's door I can see her, face-down at an angle across her bed, snoring quietly. There's no sign of Ryan. He must have gone out to his audition.

I down three glasses of water from the tap while fighting the memory of him kneeling in front of me, looking up at me ... Eventually I pour a mound of dog biscuits into Charlie's bowl. He crunches gratefully, and I'm searching around for the coffee when I hear my phone's ringtone start up loudly in my room. Marcy stirs.

'Mmmnf ... turn it off!' Her voice grows from a mumble to

a shout as she calls from her bed. I walk quickly back into my room and, without thinking about it, I answer.

'Hello?'

'Hello, is that Miss Jenkins?' It's that police constable. I remain silent for a moment.

'Miss Jenkins?'

'... Yes.'

'It's Constable Martin here, we met yesterday morning? I don't know if you got my message earlier, but we were hoping you might be able to stop by the station to just wrap up a few things?'

I pause. Shit. 'When?'

'Well, we were hoping you might be free to pop by this afternoon? Just to quickly answer a few more questions. It shouldn't take long.'

He speaks as if we bumped into each other in the supermarket, not over a corpse.

'Right ...'

'It won't take long,' he says again. If I say no, or suggest another time, it's just putting it off. I don't think I really have a choice.

'Um, yeah, OK.'

'Great. Could you come in, say, four o'clock? It's just the station in Rotherhithe, by the school?'

'OK ...' I glance at the clock on the oven. It says 14.46, and I know it's five minutes slow. How is it already so late in the day?

'Splendid. I'll see you at four then, Miss Jennings.'

'Jenkins,' I murmur half-heartedly, but he's already hung up.

I touch the End Call button, staring at my phone's screen. I don't know why I thought I could just forget about finding the man by the river. Or *any* of my so-called troubles. I have a vague memory of Ryan telling me that not-forgetting might not be so bad . . .

Still, a stupid, perhaps deluded, part of me thinks that if someone chooses to take themselves out of the world, shouldn't we just respect that? Maybe. But where would we be – *who* would we be – without someone left behind to remember us?

My head starts swimming again, and I realise I must be hungry. Starving, in fact – Charlie ate my dinner last night, and I haven't had anything since.

I pour myself a large bowl of bran flakes and get a pot of coffee going. I only have an hour until I need to be at the station. My stomach lurches again at the thought, and I take a large bite of cereal.

'Mate, I feel *rough*,' I hear Marcy say hoarsely. She stumbles out of her room and into the kitchen, shielding her eyes dramatically. I pour her a coffee and she holds her hands out for it like a three-year-old reaching for a sippy-cup. I can't help smiling a little. Her sleek hair is sticking up at angles, but she still looks annoyingly modelesque in her child-size T-shirt and underpants.

'How the fuck did you even get home?' she croaks. 'I was worried.'

'Cab. I shared with some, um, some girls and stuff who were at the bus stop. Sorry, I couldn't text till I got in.'

A faint glimmer of life flickers into her eyes. 'And stuff? And a *stuffing*, more like.'

'Marcy!'

'I'm just saying, I heard you had company.' She grins. 'Correct?'

'Uh . . . yeah . . .' I start to push past her out of the kitchen. Ryan told Marcy? Or maybe she *literally* heard. I feel my face get hot. I could think of it as payback, I guess. 'Look, I've got to get going.'

'Going? Going where? I want details!'

'Later. I promise. But it was ... yeah, it was nice.'

'Nice?'

'Good.'

'Jesus Christ, T,' she says, laughing exasperatedly. 'We're gonna talk about this properly— Shit, is that the time? I was meant to meet that girl from rehearsal.'

Distracted, she wanders back into her room, and I head to the bathroom to get ready. I shower, brush my teeth twice to get the fuzzy feeling off my tongue, then go to get dressed. But my increasing reluctance means I can't seem to make my limbs move fast enough, like I'm underwater. I force myself to pull on jeans and a jumper, redo my bun. I'm going to be late.

'See you in a bit,' I call to Marcy, then slam the door. I don't want her to ask again where I'm going. I force myself down the stairs and out, sucking in the cold air through my nostrils and exhaling loudly. I can do this. It's just a couple of questions. I can handle it. And then it will be over and done with.

I thrust my hands into my coat pockets, balling them into fists. I'm walking deliberately slower than I usually would, but I soon see the police station coming up on the other side of the road. The traffic is moving past fast and loud, and my cheeks burn with the cold. I finally come to a stop opposite my destination and glance at my watch. Five-past four.

A police car is parked outside the station, quiet and empty. I stare at it for a moment, my jaw tight, unable to move. Obviously, a police car outside a police station is normal – gosh, I don't know, expected, even? *Get it together, Taylor.* I draw a shaky breath.

It's strange; seeing a police car go past with sirens wailing, lights flashing, clearly on the way to some catastrophe – *that* never bothers me. But sometimes seeing one like this, parked up, with nobody inside? It reminds me of that day. After Aunty Sylvia rang my mobile with The News. Or at least started to tell me. 'It's your mum . . . ' I didn't need to hear the rest. I insisted on walking home from school, even though Sylvia tried to come and get me. It was the end of the day, on a Friday, after our last exams. Anita had obviously judged it that way deliberately, so I wouldn't get called out of classes, so it would go straight into a weekend. She thought carefully about that sort of thing.

I didn't tell Marcy anything, but she knew something was wrong. I couldn't make myself speak as we walked back from school, but as we got to my road, I could see that parked police car outside our tiny terrace house. Its blue plastic shell not illuminated, its engine silent. No one inside it. I turned to Marcy and managed to tell her I'd speak to her later. I could see the anguish in her eyes. She knew. She hugged me tightly without saying anything before she walked away, but I couldn't return the embrace. I knew if I did I'd fall apart. I turned and just kept walking towards that quiet police car, feeling a split second of relief. It was done now. It was over. No more worrying about whether it was going to happen, when. Then panic. Then guilt, then sorrow, then utter terror. All before Sylvia opened our front door and I walked inside to face the two police liaison officers and their sympathetic faces.

Putting one foot steadily in front of the other, I force myself to cross the road, stumbling back a little as a black cab almost swipes me. But as I finally reach the other side, something else makes me stop short.

'Oh. Hi,' the woman says. Her blonde hair isn't pulled back now, and falls long and wavy around her shoulders. She's wearing jeans and an expensive-looking camel coat, not jogging gear, but as she pulls out a pack of Marlboro Lights and wordlessly offers me one, she's instantly recognisable. I take it gratefully, even though I must be at least ten minutes late by now. She lights us both up.

'They asked you to come in too?' I ask, realising I don't know her name, though I guess it doesn't really matter.

'Yeah,' she replies, exhaling off to the side. 'It's nothing too serious though, just a lot of repeating yourself.'

'Right.' I glance towards the station's entrance.

'Are you OK? I mean, have you been all right? I think about all this and I just . . . ' She tails off with an exaggerated shudder. I take several puffs on the cigarette, nodding vaguely and trying to make an expression that says 'Yeah, it's bummer' rather than 'I'm a traumatised idiot.' She seems so well-adjusted and chic, even though we had the same experience. I feel like a steaming mess next to her.

I reach out to a nearby bin and stub my fag out on top.

'I better be getting in there. I'm late. Thanks for the cigarette, again.'

She smiles. 'Yeah. No problem.'

She stays on the kerb for a moment as I climb the steps to the entrance and wait for the sliding doors to open.

Inside, the station is a dull taupe colour almost everywhere I look, with posters on pin-boards seemingly having been placed one over the other with no resolution for the ones that have come before.

'Hello there. Can I help?' The uniformed man behind the desk is clearly pushing retirement age, with a considerable waist-line. He peers at me over half-moon glasses, not looking like much of a crime-fighter.

'Er, yes,' I say, my voice coming out small and hoarse. I clear my throat. 'I'm here to see PC Martin?'

'Oh right, yes. About the chap by the river. Come through.'

I nod and follow as he comes out from behind the glass partition towards some double doors. *The chap by the river?* The way they talk, it's like the guy I found had just been down by the river for a spot of fishing. I wonder if this is the glib way those officers talked about Anita when our backs were turned. I clench my teeth.

Following the portly officer through the set of doors into a smaller office, I spot PC Martin leaning against a filing cabinet, sipping gingerly from a Manchester United mug and chatting to a secretary in an ill-fitting blouse. He straightens up when he sees me, but looks unhurried.

'Ah, Miss Jenkins,' he says loudly, smiling. I return it thinly. 'Thanks for coming in, love. Take a seat just here.' He gestures to a padded, armless office chair in front of another desk, and then goes to sit on the other side of it. The chair swivels a little as I sit down, and I reach out a hand to steady myself.

'Tea? Coffee? Water?'

I glance up, realising he's talking to me.

'Um, just water please. Thanks.'

He stands up again and goes over to a water cooler, still talking loudly. 'It's just a few routine questions . . . ' How many times has he said that? He pauses, filling the plastic cup, then brings it back over to me and sets it on the desk. I reach out, feeling its sides give, the cold condensation on its surface. I gulp some water, shivering a little. PC Martin sits back down at the desk and leans forward. I notice a tape recorder, and some official-looking paperwork laid out in front of him. He follows my eyes, then looks up at me with what he clearly thinks is a reassuring smile.

'Don't worry – just a formality.' He reaches over and switches on the machine, then begins reading out a case number and my name and address off a sheet of paper. I take another swallow of water.

'Now, Miss Jenkins,' he says. 'We just need to go over a few things from the day in question . . .' *It was certainly questionable, I* think wryly. 'As you were the first to find the body—'

'Well, sort of,' I interrupt. 'I mean, it was bloody Ch— Sorry, it was Charlie, my flatmate's dog, that found him.' Something in me really doesn't want to have been the one who officially found him. I'd been spared that responsibility as a child. I didn't want it now.

PC Martin smiles at me and nods.

'If only dogs could talk, Miss Jenkins.'

'A-and there was that woman who came along almost at the same time really—'

He holds up his hand and nods again. 'I understand.'

I half expect him to say something like 'Just the facts, ma'am' but instead he begins to ask me a series of questions, making me go over the details again of what time I found the man, what I did when I got to him, all the things I've already told them. When he seems satisfied that I've confirmed everything, I feel like I've passed a test. He leans back in his chair, reaches over to a brown envelope and begins to pull out some pictures.

'OK then, love,' he says, spreading the photographs on to the desk in front of me. I can't look at them. I stare straight ahead, almost forgetting to blink. 'So, just to confirm. As in the pictures here, Mr Barnett was lying face-down when you found him, that's right, isn't it?

'Mr Barnett?' My heart begins to race. I don't want to know his name. I don't want to know anything more about him. But then something else, something deep inside me wants to know every possible detail. The whos, whens. Whys.

'Oh, yes, of course,' PC Martin says. 'My apologies. David Barnett – we've established that was the gentleman's name. His mother came forward and identified him, which is why we're trying to move this case through quickly – a new initiative, you know.' I don't. He pauses. 'She . . . She says he'd tried twice before, and he'd left a note. We think the coroner will rule suicide, as, to be honest, there was nothing suspicious about the death.'

Yeah. It's not suspicious to drown yourself in the Thames. Or to overdose on sleeping tablets and slit your wrists in the bath for good measure.

Not if you leave a note.

My pulse quickens again, and I swallow down bile.

'Oh, right,' I say, a little too loudly. 'Uh, yes. That's how I found him.' My eyes involuntarily drift down to the pictures of the man lying face-down on the tiny rocks that cover the bank-side. I bite the inside of my cheek and try to slow my breathing. One of the photos was obviously taken after the coroner's visit, and the man had been turned over. I look quickly away from his puffed face, the small bits of rock still clinging to his cheek and forehead.

'Is there anything else? I . . . I'm not feeling that great.' I look up at the constable, and he starts to clear the photos away.

'That'll be all,' he says quietly. 'Oh – but if . . . if you'd like to come to the coroner's hearing—'

'Why? Do I need to do that?'

'You don't have to, love. It's just if you'd like to. Sometimes it helps, you know? Put a book-end on it. We're pushing it through quickly, as I say – it'll be at one-thirty, this coming Wednesday at the Southwark Coroner's Court.'

I nod mutely. A book-end?

I have that need-to-get-out-of-here feeling. Standing up, I

send my chair wheeling back, and it clatters into the desk behind me.

'Sorry,' I mutter. 'Er, thanks.'

I don't know why I'm thanking him, but he smiles at me, and for once I believe the sympathy in his eyes is real. I turn away and walk out of the police station as quickly as I can.

Chapter Five

I'm barely five steps from the front of the station before I light another cigarette. Guess it really is starting to become a habit again. I exhale smoke slowly, feeling the panicked tightness in my chest begin to loosen, and without really thinking I start walking towards a café I used to go to all the time a year ago, just after I finished uni. I'd surf the internet there all day, pretending to send out CVs. I stopped going when new owners took over and it got overrun with buggies. And, of course, I landed my illustrious job at the bookshop.

It's a Saturday afternoon, so the place is packed with people – couples reading the paper and not talking to each other, groups of friends, mums with their kids in high-chairs. I grab the only paper left on the rack, and wince as I see it's a rag I'd never usually touch, but it's something to stare at. I order a large black coffee and squeeze into a seat by the window, sipping too soon but almost welcoming the burning feeling on my tongue.

I think about David Barnett. David. Barnett. Did his friends call him Dave? Did he *have* friends? I wonder if he lived around here? He must have done. Maybe he even came into this coffee shop once or twice. Maybe I'd even seen him before. What if I'd somehow struck up a conversation with him, what if we'd become friends, and then somehow none of this would ever have happened? 'What if's . . . '

I sigh. I should know by now that it's ridiculous to think like that, but I suppose it is possible David Barnett and I could have been in the same place before the river. Convergence – that's what Anita used to call it. How your life can intersect with someone else's in ways you'd never expect. I didn't really understand it as a kid, and I'm still not sure it's real. I think things *seem* like they're connected because you make coincidences seem significant in your mind. I purse my lips wryly at that . . . and find my thoughts drifting to Ryan again. I don't know what it is, why we never really say anything to each other. We never get far enough, because neither of us seems to have the courage to really talk about it. But that feeling of connection to him, it won't go away. It's as though he sees me, *really* sees me somehow. Does he want to help me? Take care of me? To be honest, who says he wants anything from me? And what *would* he want with me, anyway? He has Marcy. He. Has. Marcy.

God.

But I remember. Him leaning towards me last night, his breath against my cheek. Delicately wrapping the plaster around my stupid toe. And before, months ago – the two of us alone in darkness, enveloped by a faint glow of light . . .

Maybe what I *want* those moments to mean and what they really *did* mean are two very different things. I mean, last night Ryan could just have been worried I'd get beaten up, or that the guy would rob us. I wouldn't be thrilled about a stranger in the flat either.

I sip my coffee again. Have I imagined everything? Am I just hiding inside the idea of wanting Ryan, so I don't have to want something I can actually have? Look at what happened with that guy from the bus stop. He's an attractive, seemingly nice guy, but

I knew from the start I wasn't going to let it get any further. I wouldn't even let myself entertain the idea. He was there to serve a purpose – fill a hole. Hah. I sigh, swallowing more coffee. I can't remember the last time I just slept with someone, with no intention of knowing them. It makes that desperate feeling come back into my stomach, like I'm on the edge of something, waiting. Or like I'm hungover and a little embarrassed at what happened last night. I shake my head at my inner drama queen, and turn my attention to grimacing incredulously at the newspaper laid out in front of me.

'Tay?'

I freeze, recognising the voice straight away. I swivel around slowly on the stool and force a smile on to my face.

'Joe . . .'

'Hey! It *is* you. I thought so. How's it going?'

'Yeah. Uh, it's going,' I reply with what I hope is a wry yet open expression. I glance down, trying to remember what I threw on this morning. Joe looks good – too good. He's lost weight, or gained muscle, something. And his hair's longer now, pulled back neatly off his face in one of those man-bun things. It really suits him. I had heard he'd moved to the area – well actually I'd seen it on Facebook, reading his updates about buying a house with intrigue and a slight hint of jealousy. If he hadn't dumped me before we all left for uni, who knows – it could have been me reaping the accommodation benefits of his book deal and the inheritance he got from his grandma.

'I forgot you lived round here,' he says, shoving one hand in his jeans pocket. Clearly he's forced himself to say something to me in case I'd seen him and thought he was avoiding me. He always was self-conscious about what people thought of him.

'Not too far from here, yeah.'

I nod. He nods.

'Uh, I heard about your book,' I say. 'That's ... that's really cool. Congratulations.'

'It's mad, isn't it?' He shakes his head. 'It's still sort of sinking in. Yeah, I actually just moved here as well.'

'Cool.' *Stop saying cool.*

'Are you and Marcy still together?'

I roll my eyes. 'You make us sound like a couple.'

'Well there were times I was kind of hoping ... ' His eyes glint, and he grins, and it's so familiar. I feel like I'm seventeen again for a split second.

'We're still flatmates, yeah,' I say with a smile.

'That's good.'

'Some things never change.' I raise an eyebrow at him, and he glances down at the floor. I remember how guilty he looked the night he broke up with me. The whole year we were together was a weird one – it was only six months after Anita died that we started going out, and I was still 'that girl whose mum ... ' He'd been the only one with the guts to ask me out, and it was a welcome distraction. He was a 'good boy', as Aunty Sylvia used to tell me. She was almost more upset than me when he broke it off, like she thought he'd been some kind of anchor, and that I'd go off the rails if he left me. He wasn't, and I didn't. I was only a kid, I wasn't in love then.

'True, some things don't,' Joe's saying. 'But then again ... It feels like we're really grown-up now, you know?' Translation: The past is the past.

Until it makes its way back to the present.

'Speak for yourself,' I mumble, but he ignores me.

'God, it's so funny to think ... I mean, I've got a fucking *mortgage* at twenty-three. Jesus,' he says, like it's just sunk in. We share a look, then a laugh.

'Was it a double shot, babe?' A willowy brunette strides over

63

and touches Joe's shoulder, her eyes flicking to me then back at him. 'Oh, who's this?'

'Oh, Yaz – this is my friend Taylor. We went to college together,' he says euphemistically, with a smile at me. 'Taylor, this is Yasmin.'

She holds out her hand, which I notice she's removed from a perfectly protruding middle. 'Oh,' I say as I shake it. 'Wow, er ... congratulations!' No wonder he's feeling like a grown-up.

'Yeah,' Joe says bashfully, but looks at Yasmin proudly. I study her and realise she's a good few years older than us.

'Nice to meet you, Taylor,' Yasmin says through a tight smile. I don't blame her: you can always tell an ex, can't you? 'I'll go and grab those coffees,' she says, and heads back to the queue.

'So what are you up to these days?' Joe asks. 'Seeing anyone, or ... ?' He trails off. I know he doesn't mean it competitively at all, but I feel a crushing sense of the inertia of my life.

'Oh, ah. No ... And I just work at an art bookshop, you know, waiting for something more ... I don't know, deciding what I really want, I guess.' God, that sounds a bit too real once it's out of my mouth.

'Yeah?' He glances over at Yasmin at the counter. I can tell I'm losing his interest.

'Yeah. I'm actually not usually round this way much, but I had to go to the police station.' *No. What are you doing?*

His eyes flash back over to me.

'Shit, really? Everything all right?'

I nod quickly. 'Yeah, yeah, fine. I just ... It's kind of crazy but ...' Am I really going to say it? No, I can't. 'I just had to go in and answer some questions. I was a ... a witness to something, sort of.' Fuck. Have I made it sound worse than it is? I know he'd get the significance if I told him exactly what happened. Why did I say anything at all? I guess because it's the most interesting thing that's happened to me in a long time. I feel a prickle of sweat form across my forehead at the notion of suicides being the interesting pinpoints of my life.

'Bloody hell,' he says, and clearly my ploy to seem intriguing has worked.

'Yeah.' I swallow the last of my coffee. It's lukewarm. 'It's been pretty mad.'

'Are you sure you're OK?' He leans towards me with a worried face, and my heart sinks. 'What exactly did you—?'

I breathe a sigh of relief as Yasmin comes back over with their coffees and he breaks off.

'That queue was insane,' she says with a benign smile. 'Baby, we'd better get going.'

Joe is still glancing at me with that look in his eyes like I'm a broken toy. Dismay, concern. Feels familiar. If only he really knew. 'OK ...' he says vaguely, like he's unsure if he should leave me.

'Yeah, I'm going to get going in a minute too,' I say, trying to sound bright. 'Really good to see you, Joe. Nice to meet you, Yasmin. And oh, good luck with the, uh ...' I point vaguely at Yasmin's midriff, then turn back to my mug as though I have a little left to finish.

'Sure you're ...?'

'Yeah, I'm fine. Thanks.'

'Give me a call if you want a chat or anything, yeah?'

I'd never do that, and I think he knows it, but it's sort of nice that he said it. Yasmin glances between us, but takes Joe's arm.

'Mm-hm. Thanks,' I say quickly. 'See you.'

I wave, even though they're only a metre away from me, and finally they're out of the door. I pull on my coat, wait for a minute or two, and then head out of the café myself.

*

The wind's picked up, and I walk along feeling as though the Earth is rotating under my feet like a treadmill, like I'm just walking in the same spot, getting nowhere no matter how hard I push. That coffee's made me jittery – and the police station, and seeing Joe. Maybe I should have had something to eat at the café. I feel like there's a hollow space inside me that I need to fill. I stop at a pedestrian crossing and squeeze my eyes shut for a moment, but open them suddenly as a car honks. I push my hands into my armpits, fighting the urge for another cigarette.

David. David Barnett. Now I can't stop thinking about it – his name. A normal name. Probably a normal guy. He had a mother, a woman who'd been worried; for a time she won't have known where he was, what had happened to him. Then the realisation: he was gone, and in his place was a note. Or, more likely, she would have known what had happened, but she won't have wanted to believe that it really had, finally. I feel that conflict all over again, on her behalf.

I wonder when he'd gone down there, to the riverbank? Very late at night, looking up at the cold, dark sky? Had he gone down there many times before, thinking about doing what he eventually did? Planning it, getting up the courage? Had anyone seen him drive up that night, park his car? Had they asked him what was wrong? Maybe he felt nothing *was* wrong. Maybe he was calm, relieved. He'd made a choice, made a decision. Perhaps a selfish one.

But we're all selfish, aren't we? Do we know any other way to be?

'T?'

I turn and see Marcy jogging up beside me in a hoodie, leggings and gloves, with Charlie galloping beside her on a long lead. Only she would think of going for a run after the night we've just had.

'Hey, you OK? You were in your own little world.' She smiles, but her eyes look concerned.

'Yeah, yeah, I'm cool. Cold, actually. And hungover.'

'Yeeeah,' she says, nodding, though her peppy step as she slows to my pace says otherwise. 'So, where did you go off to in such a hurry earlier?' she asks, panting lightly. Charlie doubles back and circles around us, tangling his lead. I glance up as a streetlight flickers on, and link my arm in Marcy's as she offers it.

'Um, I just wanted to clear my head, get a coffee and stuff,' I mumble towards my chest, pretending there's fluff there I simply have to get off. I feel bad that I told Joe about the police station but haven't told Marcy any of this. One more thing I haven't told her.

Though at least I know she'll understand and appreciate the excruciation of having bumped into my ex. 'Guess who I saw in Woodson's?'

She chuckles as I relay most of my encounter, and raises her eyebrows when I tell her about Yaz's baby bump.

'Christ, that could have been you! Barefoot and pregnant . . .'

'And free from financial woes,' I counter, though we both know we'd be horrified at the idea. She laughs.

'Speaking of preggo; you used a rubber with last night's mystery man, right?'

'Yes, thanks Mum.' I regret it as soon as I say it, but she just squeezes my arm in the crook of hers without saying anything more.

'So who was he? *Tell* me it wasn't that sleazy arsehole we were talking to before? Although, on second thoughts, he would have been beating down my bedroom door as well, right, *sis*?' We both grimace.

'Give me some credit, babe. He was, uh, this guy called Leon. We met at the bus stop.'

'Oh, that is classy,' she says sarcastically, but grins and arches a brow. 'Any good?'

I know I can't brush her off this time. 'Yeah. Respectful . . . Good with his mouth – and everything else. Yeah. Definitely . . . good.' I feel heat rise under my coat.

'Niiice,' she drawls, her grin widening. 'Good for you, T! Sounds like a good un. Are you going to see him again?'

'I don't know.' I don't even have his number, obviously, but if she thinks Leon's a possibility, maybe I won't feel so guilty every time I look at Ryan. Or think about him . . . Though keeping things from my best mate doesn't seem to be helping in the guilt department, funnily enough. I look up and notice it's getting properly dark, but at least we're nearly home.

'Coming up?' I ask.

'Nah.' She bends down and fusses over the dog. 'Little Chucky hasn't had a poo poo yet, have you, baby?' She straightens up. 'And anyway, I want to go around the block a couple more times. You should join me, you know. I swear, a run will sort you right out!'

I look at her dubiously. If only.

'I'll see you upstairs.'

Chapter Six

'Crikey, didn't there used to be, like, decent shit on TV on a Sunday?'

Marcy screws her face up and reaches for the remote, leaning over Ryan and pausing to brush his cheek with her lips as she does so. I look down at my lap, pushing the last pizza crust around in the box.

'Leave it on this?' I suggest. A low-key, low-budget American indie film seems about right as far as I'm concerned. Sitting around vegetatively while watching other people in their twenties sit around vegetatively – perfect. Something sort of contemplative, something—

'Ah, brilliant. Cop thing!'

Marcy sinks back down into the battered sofa that she and Ryan are sitting on, and I shift a little in the armchair, irritated. Ryan looks sort of annoyed too; he was rhapsodising about the director of that film only ten minutes ago.

He had tried to get me to keep my spot on the sofa when he first moved in, but it seemed churlish not to let them sit together. And snuggle up ... and kiss ...

'I think I'll clear up, then,' I hear myself say.

'Oh, we can do that later,' Marcy murmurs as I stand up and start to gather the detritus of our takeaway. She cranes her neck around me, trying to see the TV. I ignore her and gather pizza boxes under one arm. Ryan stands up and starts to help me with the glasses and screwed-up napkins.

'Guys, chill . . . ' she mutters.

'Well, we've done it now.' I glance at Ryan and he gives me a faint smile. I head to the kitchen, and feel him following me. Dropping the boxes on to the floor, I take a little too much pleasure in stamping on them so I can fold them into the bin. Ryan pauses and looks at me.

'I know it wasn't the *best* pizza, but . . . '

I give a sort of sighing laugh, trying to avoid looking at the dimple that forms in his cheek as he smiles back at me. He turns and puts the glasses in the sink, then moves next to me by the bin, throwing the rest of the stuff away. His shoulder brushes against mine a little before he steps back. Jesus, only I could find standing next to an open bin sexy. I clear my throat.

'Um, so how was the audition yesterday? Sorry about – sorry I woke you up.' I look at him, trying to get a read on his reaction to my mentioning Friday night. He doesn't *seem* like anything about it was weird. *Let it go, Taylor.*

Sometimes I feel like the very definition of wishful thinking.

'Well, I want to say it was good. It felt good, you know what I mean?' He leans against the counter and folds his arms, like he's in no hurry to go back to the living room. 'But sometimes they feel good, then no call-back.' He presses his lips together.

'Go with your gut, I reckon.'

He looks at me for a moment, then gives a half-smile. 'Yeah.' I look away.

'Well, I should know next week, anyway.'

'Cool. Fingers crossed.' I actually do it, and hold them up, cringing internally as soon as I do, and laughing a little in spite of myself. Ryan's smile widens as he looks at me, and I feel a warmth spread across my chest. But then his expression changes, and he lowers his voice.

'How's your toe?'

Again, that should not sound even remotely erotic, but the way he leans towards me, the memories it sparks . . .

'Better,' I say, my voice hoarse.

He shuffles, unfolding his arms, scratching the back of his neck. 'I . . . sorry if that was overstepping the mark.' He looks at me, and my heart sinks. He regrets it. Maybe he just wants to forget it. Maybe— 'I mean, asking about that guy,' he says, and his eyes fix mine again. We're silent.

'You lot, come on, you're missing it!' Marcy calls from the sofa. Ryan sighs briefly before calling out that he'll be there in a sec. He looks back at me, but I cut him off before he can say anything else.

'It's cool. Honestly. Don't worry about it.' But I will worry about it.

He's been thinking about it too?

Even though I'd rather go to my room now and bury my head in a pillow until the world, and all my messed-up thoughts, go away, I don't want to seem weird. So I head back to the living room with Ryan and watch as Marcy leans forward automatically so he can slip his arm in behind her neck. I try not to notice his fingers snake nonchalantly into the opening of her T-shirt. For goodness' sake, I just had a shag, I shouldn't be this . . . aware.

Marcy is clearly well and truly engrossed in the police procedural, so there's definitely no changing the channel now. I try and make sense of what's happening on screen. Two fat detectives are ringing the doorbell of a run-down apartment, then a woman lets them inside and they start showing her black-and-white mug-shots, then crime-scene photos of a dead man partially covered in a white sheet. My stomach lurches, and a little noise escapes my throat as I close my eyes quickly. To cover, I bring my fingertips up to my face as though I was rubbing them sleepily, but as I open my eyes I notice Ryan looking at me with a slight furrow between his brows. After a moment, he pulls his gaze back to the screen.

Yeah, great job seeming not-weird.

I need to forget about all these memories and images and thoughts jostling for position. *Focus on the here and now,* I think. Not for the first time, I wonder if I should talk to somebody. I never did after Anita died, and sometimes I think that was a mistake. Sixteen years old, that's formative shit. My wiring's probably all messed up. That would explain the David Barnett issue. The Ryan Harding issue is something else altogether ...

I decide to take my own advice and focus.

'Who was that guy again?' I ask, pointing at the screen and turning to Marcy.

'Shh! Hang on.'

'The bank teller from earlier,' Ryan replies, jabbing Marcy lightly in the ribs and smiling apologetically at me. She giggles, and as the show cuts to an ad break, she begins a garbled explanation of what has been happening, but my mobile vibrating on the coffee table interrupts her. She glances down at the screen.

'It's Sylvia,' she says with a note of caution in her voice, and passes the phone over to me, watching my face.

'Oh, right. Um, it was her birthday the other day ...' I say vaguely, then look down hesitantly at the Answer button, hoping it will ring off. But eventually I press it:

'Hello?'

'Hi, Taylor?'

'Yeah. Yes. Hi, Aunty Sylvia. How are you?' I stand up and move into the hallway as I see the ad break end, but I can feel Marcy watching me. It kind of bothers me that she knows me so well. She knows that a call from my 'erstwhile guardian', as she used to call my aunt, can make me feel on edge, in spite of everything Sylvia did for me.

Because of it.

'Oh, I'm fine, sweetheart,' Sylvia's saying. 'How are you? Thank you so much for the card, that was very thoughtful of you.'

I cough. 'Sorry, it probably arrived a bit late—'

'Not at all,' she lies smoothly. I smile a little. 'Listen, darling . . .' I'd forgotten how many terms of affection she has. I used to think it was over-compensatory, but more likely I was just a brat. 'I know you haven't been down here for a while, but I was wondering . . . Linda's turning sixteen next weekend, and we're having a little party. Just in the daytime, you know, before she does her evening thing with her friends. I told your cousin to send through the invite but you know how she can be, so I just thought I'd check.'

Linda's an *angel* compared to how I was in the sullen-teen stakes. 'Oh, no, I hadn't got anything, but uh . . . next weekend?'

'Yes. Saturday, around three? You can bring someone if you like,' she adds, and I can hear the note of hope in her voice – not only that I'll come, but that I might be with someone.

'OK, yeah. I . . . I should be able to come. I, uh, it'll probably just be me . . .'

'Oh.' Disappointment, but she recovers quickly. 'Of course. That's fine. I mean, that's great. It would be so good to see you, love.'

I cringe at how grateful she sounds. Why haven't I been in touch more? If the idea was to help me forget that period of time, clearly it's not working. 'Yeah, it'll be good to see you too, Aunty. Thanks for the invitation,' I say.

'OK, sweetheart. We'll see you then,' she says, her voice bright with happiness.

As I hang up, a cloud of anxiety at the idea of going down there and seeing my family – *Mum*'s family – settles over my head. I walk back into the living room, and Marcy looks straight up.

'Everything OK? What did she want?' she asks, eyeing me closely, protectiveness radiating from her. I reach over and squeeze her hand briefly as I flop back into the armchair, thankful for her concern, if a little irritated.

'It's cool. It was nice to hear from her, actually.' I feel Ryan look between us curiously. I suddenly wonder if Marcy's ever told him anything about back then, or if he's ever connected it with That Day, when we first met. Probably not.

'It's just Linda's sixteenth. They're having a little afternoon thing next weekend.'

'Are you going to go?'

I nod, and I know she wants to offer to go with me. I try to head her off. 'It'll be nice to see them. It's been ages. I mean, I haven't seen Linda for, like, two years or something.'

'OK. Cool.' Her eyes communicate 'I'm here if you need to talk,' and I nod again. Sometimes I wonder what I did to deserve a friend like her. Not a lot, lately.

'Yeah,' I reply.

Marcy sits back again and turns towards the TV. 'What's happening, babe?'

'Fucked if I know,' Ryan says, and we all laugh. I try not to hear Marcy murmur, 'Mmm, you will be,' as she leans in to kiss him. I hold a vague smile on my face, but decide it's time to draw a line under the day and go to bed. I can't believe it's already Monday again tomorrow. I stretch and yawn, a little too emphatically, and they both turn to look at me.

'Might head to bed, guys,' I say, as if it needs explaining.

'Really? It's only ten o'clock,' Marcy says, disentangling herself from Ryan.

'Yeah, well, we can't all live a life of artistic leisure, you know,' I say sarcastically. Ryan chuckles, and I feel stupidly rewarded.

'Har har,' Marcy says. 'I'll have you know I have a tap class at *eleven a.m.*' She folds her arms, a glimmer of humour in her eyes.

'Blimey, butt-crack of dawn,' I retort, glad she's not giving me that concerned look any more.

I realise what I'm really going to do is stay up too late reading because I can't sleep, and then feel like hell when my alarm goes off in the morning. Unless Charlie gets there again first, of course. Jesus, we definitely don't need to repeat that.

'Night, you two.'

'Night, hon,' Marcy says, swinging her legs into Ryan's lap.

I start to make my way out of the door, and then I hear Ryan, softly:

'Sleep well, Taylor.'

Chapter Seven

My eyes drift open, and I see the glowing green lights of the clock: 7.52 a.m. Eight minutes before the alarm is due to go off. Of course. I close my eyes again, my mind in that liminal state between waking and consciousness, and I'm thinking about Ryan, *again*. For the first time in a while, I really let myself turn to that memory – that one moment when it all could have been different.

I think about the two of us, alone, that day. I think about the chiselled planes and angles of his face in the intermittent light from the cinema screen, the warmth of his eyes like dark honey as his gaze settled over me. His breaths slowing mine until tears dried on my cheeks. I think about his fingers easing between my own, about the feel of our pulses pushing against each other as our palms connected. The quiet between us. The calm I felt, with a stranger – a person who later fell back into my life, but not quite in the right place.

Of all the unfair things, sometimes Ryan feels like the most unfair. I know that's stupid, but when I think about my mother's belief in fated encounters, I have to wonder if she was right. If I were the type to believe in that sort of thing, perhaps I would think she sent him to me, from somewhere beyond. But I messed up, missed my chance. What if I'd told him my name that day? What if he'd asked me? We might have gone for coffee, tentative but knowing that it was *right* somehow, that we were destined to be—

No. I swallow hard, unwilling to let myself what-if now. It never gets me anywhere, it just causes an ache. The two of us are not fated, apparently. And I don't believe in Anita's ridiculous convergence theory anyway, right? I smile sadly to myself. But God, I wish I'd kept that stupid packet of tissues. It could have been like an artefact, like evidence – proof it actually happened. Sometimes I think I dreamed it. Here, now, lying in bed, I open my eyes and see if it still feels real.

But I know it was.

I don't think 'I met him first' would really work now though; it's far too late. When Marcy introduced Ryan several months after that day at the cinema as the guy she'd been telling me all about, the gorgeous actor she'd met on a video shoot, my throat almost closed with the shock, like I'd dived into ice-cold water. It was *him*. I could see in his face that he remembered me too, and apparently he could see in mine that I didn't want to talk about it at that moment. I'd never told Marcy about That Day, and then I *couldn't*. Even though Ryan's with her now, I wanted *that* encounter to be just mine. Just ours. A silent secret between us.

He tried once to bring it up, a week or two after they started going out, when we were briefly alone in the pub while Marcy took Charlie outside. But he wasn't sure where to begin, and I cut him off, shook my head. Since then we've never spoken about it again. Not in the four months they've been together, or in the five weeks Ryan's lived in our flat. He let it go, I guess. Obviously. Although sometimes, even now, when he looks at me, when we talk … The other night? God, I don't know. Maybe that whole thing at the cinema was nothing – just one person comforting another when they clearly needed it. And the rest is just coincidence and conjecture.

The only thing I do know is that both of us have kept it safe, secret – that day. That memory.

I sigh, and then jump as my alarm finally screeches on, scrambling an arm out of the duvet to switch it off with a frown. The warm feeling of remembering is already gone, and I pull my arm back under the bedclothes.

Monday bloody morning.

My motivation is completely shot at the moment, and it's not good. Lying in bed in darkness, lacking the will to move? Sounds familiar. But I can't let myself be like Anita. More than once I've wondered if I might inherit it, if it could be something passed down to me, that slow sapping of will. I lie back staring at the ceiling as the minutes tick by, but eventually turn back to my clock: 8.11 a.m. I can't stay here.

I'm going to be late.

With huge effort I bring both arms out of the warm cocoon of my duvet and peel it down my body. Cool air hits me like a bucket of water, and I swing my legs out of the bed and pull on my robe. Just as my hand is on the knob of my door, ready to head to the bathroom, I hear Marcy's door open and rapid footsteps crossing the hall. Shit. I stride over to the bathroom, knocking hard on the door.

'M, hurry the fuck up! I need to get in there!' Last thing I need is her taking one of her random half-hour showers. I bite my lip as I suddenly realise that of course it might be Ryan. Silence for a moment, then a flush.

'Sorry!' comes a throaty baritone voice. I freeze outside the door, hearing the tap run. Then the bathroom door opens, and he's right in front of me, wearing only boxer shorts and a surprised expression – I don't think he expected me to be still standing here. My eyes drift down his torso: slim, toned, with dark hair clinging to places I'd love to—

I clench my jaw to make sure it's shut, and step aside.

'No problem,' I murmur, then blush, realising it might sound as lascivious as I feel.

He smiles a little, but his eyes say something else. I take a breath and shuffle round him into the bathroom. I let the shower run cold.

By the time I'm rounding the corner towards the shop, I'm close to half an hour late. And as I pull out my keys, I also realise I'd forgotten about something.

'Shiiit,' I hiss under my breath, quickly checking my reflection in the glass door before I push it open. The electronic beep sounds like a death knell.

'Taylor. How good of you to turn up.' Rosamund's soft voice has an edge of bored expectation. How would she know what the norm is anyway? She barely ever leaves head office.

'Uh, hi. Sorry I had . . . public-transport issues.'

'Well, lucky I was here early, then,' she says with a thin smile.

'Oh, did someone come in already?' I can't resist.

She looks at me for a moment and then shakes her head, clutching an iPad to her barely-there chest. Her hair is freshly highlighted, and she's wearing a well-tailored burgundy dress. I pull at my slightly misshapen green cable-knit jumper, and hustle through to dump my bag and coat in the back room. As I return to the shop floor, I notice Rosamund hasn't booted up the till yet. I switch it on, thinking she probably has no idea how to do it, and suppress a smug smile – until I remember that it's not exactly a vital life skill. She begins to stroll amongst the shelves, nodding to herself. At least I've been keeping things in relatively good order. Oh yeah, that's job satisfaction right there.

'How have things been this fortnight?'

'Fine. Uh, a bit quiet.'

'Yes, it is a bit,' she says with a note of worry, studying the figures on her tablet. This better not be the part where she tells me they're closing down. A thin seam of panic rises in my chest, but she looks up and gives me her tight little smile again. 'Online's been good, though. Retail dips are to be expected.'

I try my best to seem interested, though I choke a little when she moves into the back room and stops by the pile of reject books. Here comes the ambush – she'll calmly show me CCTV footage of me ripping that page on her little screen and then tell me to get my things—

'Quite a few damages and returns here,' she says. 'We need to be careful about those.'

'Uh, yeah ...'

She turns to me. 'Help yourself before you box them up.'

I swallow. 'Oh. Thanks.' Maybe she's not so bad after all. Must be the pallid look around my gills from hardly any daily human interaction; she feels sorry for me, trapped in here every day. I smile at her, and then we both turn around to the door as we hear the sound of fingernails tapping against glass. I see a tall, slim silhouette, waving wildly. *Marcy?* I groan inwardly – it was all going so well.

She flings the door open and strides into the shop with a grin so wide it almost leaps off her face.

'Babe! You will never. Fucking. Believe this!'

I'm actually pretty surprised she's up and out this early. She can't have been too far behind me. Her grin is infectious, but as I stand behind Rosamund, I shake my head, trying to indicate to her with my face, eyebrows, head-tilt, cough, that I shouldn't be messing about – but of course Marcy barely registers.

'Marce—'

'Seriously! Guess what?' I open my mouth again, but she barely leaves a gap before blurting out in a garbled rush, 'World tour. They've booked me for a whole leg of a world fucking *tour* – a last-minute sub. Remember I told you about Ruthie breaking her ankle? She was meant to be on it, and at one point it was looking OK, but now it's not, poor thing, but they were like ,"We saw your head-shot and we need three girls with your look and you're the best fit," and I did the audition a week ago, smacked it, or at least I thought so, but I didn't hear anything and I'd totally forgotten all about it, well almost, but then they called me this morning and said can you be ready and I was like *fuck* yeah!'

She finally finishes, panting, and stares at me with her hands spread wide as if she's ready to catch a big ball of my enthusiasm. After a moment her hands retreat to her hips, though her smile can't be tamed. I clear my throat, and pause for a moment.

' . . . Can I help you, miss?'

Marcy stares at me, then at Rosamund, then back to me. Then she bursts out laughing, and I do too, and we both turn to Rosamund, whose face breaks into a genuine smile.

'Congratulations,' she says to Marcy. 'Now, I'm afraid Taylor has a little work to do here – perhaps you two could catch up on her lunch hour?'

'Oh, shit. Yeah, of course,' Marcy says, still grinning.

I wink at her. 'That's amazing news, babe. Listen, I'll meet you at the place round the corner, twelve-thirty, yeah?'

'Yeah. OK. Sorry, er . . . Sorry about that! Nice to meet you,' she nods at Rosamund, then blows me a kiss before striding back out of the door. 'In a bit!'

81

As the door swings shut, it feels like a hurricane's just passed. Rosamund and I stare at each other, feeling the energy levels drop. She glances down at her tablet, then back up at me.

'Very exciting for your friend,' she says.

'Yeah,' I say, nodding and rearranging the notebooks by the till.

'She's a . . . ?'

'A dancer. You know, like a backing dancer for music acts, music videos, that sort of thing.'

'Gosh,' Rosamund says. Yes, I think, it's a million miles from what I'm currently doing. I can feel her struggling with the connection between the two of us. 'That's unusual. And you two are good friends?'

'Yes,' I say resignedly.

'Great.' Rosamund pauses. 'She seems very . . .'

'I know,' I say with a smile.

I turn back to the notebooks.

Lunchtime, and by some miracle Lucas seems to have remembered that we're due to have company – he's bang on time and even seems to have run a comb through his hair. He looks almost . . . fresh. I have to admit, it kind of suits him.

'Good-afternoon,' he says in his politest voice. Rosamund smiles at him, and I think I see something glimmer in her eyes as he grins back at her. How does he do it?

'Hi, Luc,' I say, raising an eyebrow at him when I know Rosamund can't see my face. 'Well, I'll be off on my lunch then.' I grab my coat and bag, and pull another face at him on my way out. He gives the tiniest of smirks.

I check my phone as I head out, surprised it hasn't exploded under the barrage of texts and voicemails Marcy's left. She's been hanging around the area, clearly having far too much caffeine.

She's in the coffee shop with three mugs lined up in front of her and newspapers spread all over the table. She springs up, grinning, as I walk in.

'Still got a job?' she asks with a laugh.

'Yeah, just about. Bloody hell, Marce.' I grin at her.

'I know, sorry – I didn't think you had, like, a supervisor or whatever?'

'I don't, usually. Rosamund comes over from head office every two weeks – I'd totally forgotten about it myself. Anyway, let's *both* forget about that.' I grip her shoulders. 'A world fucking tour?' I pull her into a hug, and she squeezes back tightly.

'Mental, right? It's just a leg of it, Australasia and Europe, but if I'm lucky they might book me for North America too. I had to come and tell someone! Ry's in some locked rehearsal thing all day, so I just hopped on the bus over. Let's get out of here – we need to celebrate, get some champagne or something—'

I grimace. 'I don't know if that's a good idea right now. Rosamund will probably give me a breathalyser when I walk back through the door.'

'Well, you don't have to have any. You can just watch me,' Marcy says, her lips curling devilishly.

Ten minutes later, we're sitting in the pub with a bottle of prosecco and two full champagne flutes.

'Cheers! To booty-shaking!' I say, planning on just a few sips as we clink the rims together. But the minute the bubbles hit my tongue, I know that's not going to happen. We stare at each other beyond the stems of the glasses, down our drinks in one, then laugh as Marcy refills us.

'That's the spirit!' she chuckles, then goes to give our food order to the barman. I sit sipping on my second glass, already feeling my face start to tingle. No breakfast. Great. But I feel warm and light for the first time in days, like I'm floating inside one of the bubbles in my drink. I watch them drift to the surface and burst, but the light feeling doesn't last. Just like that, it's gone. Marcy strides back over to me.

'All right?' There's an edge to her voice like she can tell I'm *not* quite all right, and in that moment I want to tell her everything, most especially about finding David Barnett and what it's done to the even kilter I'd previously thought I had finally achieved after all these years. Right now the slightest thing seems to throw me off balance. And I want to tell her about—

'So anyway, listen, T. About Ryan.'

She levers herself lightly back up on to her stool, and I take a gulp of prosecco.

'Yeah?'

She presses her lips together and looks up at me from under her considerable eyelashes. I take a shallow breath of relief; she's about to ask a favour.

'I was kind of hoping . . . if it was cool with you, of course . . . if Ryan could stay at the flat while I'm gone. I mean, it's five-six weeks, but we'll be in Europe for loads of dates, so maybe I'll be able to get back home in between?'

Ryan staying in the flat. With me.

I stare at her, and she starts to look unsure. Oh, God. *Say something, Taylor.*

'It's just, well, he won't really have anywhere to go,' Marcy continues, seeming to think she needs to plead her case. 'He's getting work now, but he's still a bit short – I'll cover his bit of the rent if I need to. I just wanted to see what you thought?'

I try to keep my face neutral. Why hadn't I thought about it? Where else would he go? Why would he—?

'Of course!' I hear myself blurt quickly. 'I mean, yeah, of course he can, don't be silly. No worries.' So many worries.

'Brilliant,' she says, reaching over to squeeze my hand. 'He'll be good, I promise!'

Finally the food arrives, and I busy myself with cutting into my sausages and piling mash on my fork while Marcy chatters happily. I nod and smile, fighting to concentrate on feeling happy for my friend, not sorry for myself. How am I going to do this? Six weeks alone in a flat with him?

'I'd better get back, I can't be late,' I say as the floor guy clears our plates and glasses. 'Rosamund'll have a shit-fit as it is – bet I reek of bubbly.'

We both stand up, and Marcy sniffs me exaggeratedly. 'Nope, just pork and gravy. Oh, and fags, of course.'

I punch her in the arm, but we link them and head out of the door. I feel unsteady on my feet, and not just from the prosecco. Out on the pavement we hug again, and I feel like a traitor. I blink away sudden tears as she smiles into my face.

'I'm proud of you, Marcy.'

Now it's her turn. I see a thin film of tears, but she coughs and they're gone.

'Thanks, babe.'

As I turn and walk away, she shouts, 'Dinner!'

I swivel back, chuckling as she winks at an old man who stares at her disapprovingly.

'We should have dinner tomorrow night, the three of us, to celebrate. Queen of the Nile?'

I give her a thumbs-up. *The three of us.*

'Wicked,' she shouts. 'It's a date!'

Walking down the street back to work, I lean into the wind as it whips past me. Before I know it, I'm standing outside the bookshop, trying to make my head stop spinning.

Chapter Eight

I stare out of the glass doors of the shop at the quiet street out-side, the grey pavement glowing orange in the light from the streetlamps. I'm closing up late because I had to do a stock-check, but it's been dark for hours. I cannot wait for spring – it's starting to feel like we're living in Alaska or something. I purse my lips at my reflection as I turn over the CLOSED sign and turn the lock.

After the 'excitement' of Rosamund's half-unexpected visit and Marcy's news yesterday, today has felt even less eventful than usual, although that could all change as I have my date with Marcy and Ryan this evening. Part of me is looking for-ward to it – especially the food at the Queen of the Nile. When Marcy and I first moved into the flat after university, we used to go there all the time. She'd just landed a job teaching music video dance moves to twentysomething 'creatives' after a hard day's work at their ad agency internship or whatever (yes, I was and am jealous). I'd just started the job here at the bookshop, thinking of it as a stop-gap on my way to something much more exciting. We felt like the world was at our feet. And sometimes on a Friday night, instead of heading to a club or a gig, we'd go to the Queen and order too much food and spread it all out on the big spongy disc of shared injera bread, and talk about what we were going to do, where we were going to be, and who with – aside from each other, of course. Thinking about that time envelops me in a warm feeling of nostalgia, but my stomach tightens at the thought of how many of those dreams have come true for Marcy, and how few for me.

What *did* I want back then? It wasn't long ago really. What do I want now? Deep down, I do know, but I'm scared to answer those questions honestly, even in my own head. Who am I? I spent so long thinking about who I'm *not* – who I didn't want to be – that I think I lost sight of the truth. So what if my path collides with my mother's? We're different people. Aren't we?

But since I'm too frightened to admit I want a little of what she wanted, even if it's risky, my life just seems to be happening around me without my being able to control any of it. And if nothing else, Anita never let her dreams float out of reach. She chased them, fiercely. Until . . .

I swallow hard, let it go. I slip on my coat and grab my bag and keys. Switching off the lights in the shop, I resist the urge to be a complete weirdo and tell the books good-night, but then say it in my head anyway; at least it raises a smile to my lips. There is something quite peaceful about looking at them all in rows on the shelves in the dark. I set the alarm, messing it up first time, as always, and then finally head out into the chilly evening, and miraculously, for once a bus arrives immediately.

I put my earphones in, check my phone for messages and see Marcy confirming dinner at eight with an array of emoticons conveying her excitement, and I have to chuckle. But when I get back to the flat, all is quiet. It's seven thirty – maybe Marcy and Ryan have already left for the restaurant? I freshen up and brush my teeth quickly, then hear my phone beep. I read the group message: Marcy, saying she's still at a fitting for the tour and will have to go straight to the Queen. She thanks Ryan for walking Charlie, and suggests we all meet there – the reservation's in her name. I text back **Roger that xx**, then grab my coat and bag. For some reason I really don't want to bump into Ryan and Charlie coming back from the walk; then we'd have to head over together and I just … I should get used to it, I suppose, it's going to be weeks of this sort of thing, but for now I'm taking my traditional coward's route of avoiding the situation.

I stop in the corner shop to buy more cigarettes, and I don't even need to finish my sentence before the man behind the counter hands over a packet of Spirits. Probably a little challenge he sets himself to stave off the boredom of working there. *I can relate, my friend.* I test out my smile on him, but having to consciously think about it doesn't bode well for this evening. It's supposed to be a celebration, after all. And it really is – Marcy's getting this amazing opportunity to do something she's wanted to do ever since she started dancing as a kid. She can do something so expressive, creative, *free*, and she can actually make a good living at it. I think that was all Anita wanted, but of course it never worked out. Dreams unfulfilled. Maybe that really is reason enough to give up. How long do you keep trying? Is that what happens when you run out of goals – you force the finish line to come to you? I wonder if that's what happened to David Barnett. I feel an odd wave of empathy, but then remind myself that this is bad headspace.

I pull on my cigarette, pausing just around the corner from the restaurant to finish it so Marcy doesn't tell me off. It's silly that I care, but I do – even though I'm sure she'll smell it on me anyway.

'Taylor.'

I spin around, dropping the cigarette guiltily and stepping on it. But it's not Marcy.

'Oh, hi.' I exhale the last of the smoke with an embarrassed laugh, and Ryan smiles down at me. He's turned the collar of his coat up against the cold, and the honey colour of his eyes is darkened as he's silhouetted against the streetlight. He's all cheekbones in shadow.

'I won't grass you up,' he tells me with a slow smile, still not looking away.

I shake my head. 'It's ridiculous, I know.'

'Trust me, she does it to me too . . .'

'I didn't know you smoked?'

'Exactly.'

We both laugh, and then he and pulls one hand free of his coat pocket, aims it towards me and sweeps it in an awkward gesture towards the restaurant.

'Shall we?'

We start to walk, side by side, and I try to glance at my watch in the dark. Marcy should be here soon. I hope she is. I hope she isn't.

'Oh, Marcy said she's still running late, I just spoke to her,' Ryan says, seeing me check the time.

'Ah. Cool. I mean, right.'

As he reaches out to hold the restaurant door open for me, the smell of spices hits my nostrils and I inhale deeply. I duck under his outstretched arm, and then for a moment I'm enveloped by him. His arm brushes down my back and guides me inside, and I move slowly, savouring the feeling of him touching me.

'There should be a booking for three under Marcy McGregor,' I tell the expectant waitress, who smiles and nods then leads us over to a table by the large glass window, and sets down some water in a jug with stout little glasses.

'I'll be back to take your order in a minute,' she says.

It's dark in here, with the brown carved-wood furnishings and trinkets all around, and the gentle flicker of the tea-lights on the tables. It feels far too intimate. Ryan settles down in the chair opposite me, pouring a glass of water. He slides it over towards me before pouring his own, which is totally normal, obviously. But for some reason the slow, bubbling sound of it seems impossibly sensual. I take a deep breath. Gentle chatter from the tables around us feels distant, like we're inside a cocoon. I shrug out of my coat, realising I should have taken it off before we sat down. He watches me wriggle, a half-smile on his lips, his eyes still dark.

'Did you take Charlie out?' I say inanely, trying to keep things to small-talk.

He nods. 'Yeah. I don't think he likes it when I do, though, to be honest. He's so tense. It's like he has poop anxiety around me.'

I laugh. 'Poop.'

'Pooch,' he retorts. I feel ridiculously happy he remembered me saying that, days ago. Jesus. We both grin. I flick my eyes down to the candle, because it's hard to look at him in this light without—

'You look tired.'

I glance up again, feeling defensive, but his eyebrows are drawn together as he studies me, his face more concerned than judgemental.

'So do you.'

His eyes stay on mine, and then he sighs. 'Yeah. I guess rehearsals have been kicking my arse, and I didn't get much sleep last night ...' He tails off and looks away from me. I think Marcy's celebration tactics had something to do with that. I swallow.

'Wish I had some excuse,' I reply, trying for a light smile.

'Preoccupied mind,' he says, almost a question, but somehow not. His eyes are back on me.

'Maybe,' I murmur.

He takes a slow sip of water. 'What are you preoccupied—?' he begins, but then stops and puts his glass down, wiping his mouth. I watch his fingertips as they touch his lips. 'Taylor, I know we don't really talk about . . . that day.'

My pulse surges in my throat, and I can't reply.

'But I think about it. I just didn't want you to think I don't. And . . .' He looks around the room, like he's thinking carefully about what to say next. 'If I ask you things . . .' he looks at me, 'questions. It's not because . . .' He puffs out a breath, his brow furrowed. 'I don't want you to think the only memory I have about you, about that day, it is that you were crying.' He says the last word softly. 'I suppose what I mean is that I'm not judging you.' He rolls his eyes, and I continue to stare at him. It seems to be making him flustered, and I wish I could think of something to say. 'Far from it. I mean, if you hadn't been there, in that screen, that day, who knows? It could have been me with tears on my face,' he murmurs, looking down at his glass.

I'm stunned, not expecting that. Every cell in my body wants me to reach over and touch his hand, but I don't.

'Ryan . . .'

He looks up at me, but while I'm searching around for more words, he speaks again. 'My point is,' he says, taking a deep breath and smiling a gorgeous, embarrassed smile, '*feeling at sea.*' He spreads both his hands like he's finally alighted on something close to the words he was searching for. I can't help smiling a little too, and his eyes soften in relief. 'A lot of times, feeling at sea is, like, my default position. And I suppose I recognise it in other people sometimes. And it helps. Me, I mean. To know it's not just me. So I thought maybe . . . ' He lets out a growl of frustration. 'Fuck, sorry, I'm not making any sense.'

'No,' I say quickly. 'You are.' It's weirdly true. It actually frightens me how much I want to grab him, right now, take his hand and run.

Ryan leans forward a little, like he's about to say something else, but I glance through the window and see Marcy waving from outside, blowing kisses at us and darting nimbly across the road.

'Oh. There she is,' I say quickly, a tremble in my voice.

We both lean back again and, what feels like seconds later, Marcy's weaving in between the tables to reach ours, shrugging elegantly out of her coat and sliding in next to Ryan. The tables next to us suddenly seem louder. Marcy reaches over to squeeze my hand, and I rub her cold fingers, returning her infectious grin with a touch less wattage, genuine though it is.

'Hi, babe! Hi, baby!' she exhales to us both in turn, leaning over to kiss Ryan. I look down at the table.

'How was the fitting?' Ryan asks.

'Well, for a lot of it they may as well have just given us a couple of plasters. The look is *minimal*, to say the least. But, hey! We'll work with it.' She waggles her eyebrows and grins, then swivels around in her chair towards the restaurant floor. 'Shall we get some drinks? I'm bloody starving too, have you guys ordered?'

'No, we waited,' Ryan says, glancing at me. Marcy raises a hand, and the waitress comes over. We all order food without looking at the menu, even Ryan, which surprises me a bit. In spite of everything, I feel kind of irritated. I guess he and Marcy have come here too, without me. For some reason I thought of it as *our* place, just her and me. Pathetically, I feel a twinge of jealousy. I guess that's the problem with nostalgia – a hit of reality can ruin it forever.

'. . . And a bottle of champagne,' I add as the waitress finishes taking our order. 'My treat,' I say, smiling at Marcy. The waitress nods and heads off.

'What would I do without you two?' Marcy looks between me and Ryan, and I can see a film of tears start to form in her eyes.

'Hey, don't, M, come on.' *Please don't.* 'You deserve this.' She really does. You get what you deserve, right?

'Hey, yourself,' she says in a low voice, and I know my face must have fallen. Self-pity, never a good look. I force the smile back on to my lips, glad I practised.

'No, I'll just . . . We'll miss you, that's all,' I say, glancing at Ryan, who quickly looks away from me, back to Marcy. The waitress arrives with the champagne just then, and I flinch as the cork pops. We all clink our glasses together, Marcy insistent that we look into each other's eyes or we'll have bad sex for seven years or whatever her superstition is. I swallow down the sharp bubbles.

'Hey, how was your audition?' she asks Ryan. She turns to me. 'They called him back for some new BBC thing, the one about fifties TV journalists. It's a long shot, but still – right?' she says, turning back to Ryan.

'It's actually about newspaper journalists,' he corrects her.

I nod, the smile still a little stiff. 'Cool.'

He glances at me, then back to Marcy. 'But yeah, it was good . . . I, uh, I got it.'

'You got it?' she says. 'Seriously?'

He shrugs, seeming slightly irritated that Marcy sounds so surprised. 'Yeah. I mean it's only two days, a small part but yeah, it'll be pretty good exposure.'

'Oh wow. OK. That's fucking brilliant!' Marcy says, her voice high, and she tops off our glasses with more champagne. My stomach feels a little queasy suddenly, and I can't wait for the food to turn up.

'Congratulations,' I say quietly. 'Seems like everyone's got something to celebrate. Well, almost.' God, that defeatism just comes tumbling out of me. I take a (hopefully) cleansing breath, and get a faint hit of Ryan. It helps.

'It'll be your time soon,' Marcy says, reaching over to squeeze my hand again. 'I know it.' I'm glad *she* does – but time for what exactly? I can't see any path to my own ... creative destiny, or whatever, so I'm not sure how she can. She studies me again closely, a little frown forming between her eyebrows. I know she's going to corner me about this shitty mood later, and I know I'll deserve it. I wish, for the umpteenth time, that I could just be happy.

Thankfully the waitress arrives with our injera and delicious pots of different foods that she spreads lavishly in front of us. That's one way to perk me up. My stomach rumbles loudly, and I clutch it, embarrassed.

'Hear, hear!' Marcy says with a laugh, and I can't help smiling too. After cleaning our hands with the warm towelettes the waitress hands out, we get stuck in, tearing off bread and scooping up delicious meat and vegetables with our fingers. Marcy of course has to feed some to Ryan, who blushes a little as she makes him suck remnants off her fingertips, but then it's my turn. She leans over and I open wide, both of us giggling so much that food almost flies out of our mouths in a *very* attractive fashion. The champagne's creating a nice buzz inside my head now, and I actually start to feel sort of good about tonight. I watch the large, flat, spongy bread disappear in front of us as we eat until we start to feel sick, and finally we're done. We all lean back, satisfied.

'So, listen, hon, I got an invite to this show for Fashion Week on Saturday,' Marcy says as the waitress clears away the debris and brings us dessert menus. 'Fancy being fabulous for the afternoon? I'll be gone already.' She nudges Ryan with her elbow teasingly. 'I don't think it would be his vibe, but you could see who fancies going with you, using the other invitation?'

'I'd love to, but I can't,' I say. 'It's Linda's sixteenth so I'll be going to Aunty Sylvia's.'

'Oh, of course, right.' She raises her eyebrows, wrinkling her forehead. 'Shit, I won't be here for that.'

'I'll be fine, M. I'm a big girl. I told you, I can handle it.' I intend it to come out jokingly, but I realise my voice is a little tight with irritation. It's bad enough how much I build things up in my head; I don't need people around me helping.

'I know, but I just . . . '

'Marcy—' I begin but, glancing down at the table, I see Ryan cover Marcy's hand with his. He turns to me.

'Where does your aunt live?' he says, trying to steer the conversation away from an argument. I swallow and look at him gratefully.

'Uh, Sevenoaks. When I moved out to go to uni they decided to head out of London, I suppose.'

His fingers loosen a little on Marcy's hand, like he's forgotten they were there. 'Oh right, you lived with her? How long for?'

'Ryan . . . ' Marcy begins.

'Um, just a couple of years, from sixteen to eighteen. I went to live with her after my mum died,' I reply, keeping my voice steady. I wonder how much Marcy's told him, if anything. I look up into his eyes, scared I'll see pity, scared I'll see puzzle pieces clicking into place. And in a way I do, but not in an I've-figured-you-out way. It's something I can't quite read,

95

and I can't look away from him. I *should* look away. I swallow. He blinks.

'Well, getting out of town for a day could be good,' he says softly.

'Yeah, Sevenoaks is quite nice,' I say, glancing at Marcy and trying for a smile. 'Thanks, hon. For worrying, I mean. But I'll be fine. You have lots to be thinking about – sorting out stuff for your trip and, like, all the amazing things that are going to happen. You should focus on all that, you know? Don't worry about me.'

Marcy nods. 'Yeah, fair enough. Sorry.'

Shit. I feel bad for making her feel bad.

'Anyone going for dessert?' I say, taking a deep breath. Both Marcy and Ryan groan and clutch their stomachs. I smile a little, and then excuse myself to go to the loo.

'I'll come with you,' Marcy says, standing up quickly.

We make our way through the restaurant, push aside the beaded curtain and step into the tiny ladies' toilets. There's only one cubicle, so Marcy just leans against the main door while I pee. She checks her make-up in the mirror, then turns to me when I flush and come over to wash my hands.

'T . . . ' she begins tentatively.

'I'm OK, Marcy—'

'I know. I just don't want you to feel like you can't talk to me if you're . . . I don't know, feeling down or whatever. You just seem a bit . . . ' She looks up, searching for words. 'You're smoking again.'

'Marcy, they're just cigarettes.'

'Yeah, tell that to Kevin,' she says, folding her arms. As well as being a health nut, she's been down on smoking ever since her stepdad got emphysema. I sigh.

'Listen,' she continues, touching my arm. 'I just think maybe going to Sylvia's, and with your mum's anniversary coming up, maybe you're just feeling a bit blue, right? It's understandable. I just don't want you to feel like you can't talk to me about it.'

I feel like a boulder's lodged in my oesophagus. *Tell her about David Barnett. Tell her about the police station. Tell her . . .* For some crazy reason I feel like if I tell her one secret I have to tell them all. I look down at a trail of wet loo roll on the floor to avoid Marcy's eyes. Why does everything pile up inside me? Why am I so afraid to let it out? I open my mouth to speak, but someone bangs on the door, and we jump.

'Come on, we should go. Ryan's out there all by himself,' I say. I pull Marcy in for a quick hug. 'I'm OK. Really,' I whisper into her ear, glancing at my lying reflection in the mirror before we step outside.

As we return to the table, I notice Ryan's ordered another bottle of champagne. Marcy grins as she sits down, and pecks him lightly on the lips. He looks up at me as I hover by my seat.

'Liquid dessert?' he says with a hopeful smile, which drifts a little as he registers my face.

'Uh, yeah. I might just pop out,' I say, making an apologetic face at Marcy. I need some air.

I slip on my coat and grab my packet and lighter. From outside, I can see Ryan pouring Marcy another glass. They're facing away from me, and I can see the muscles of his back through his light sweatshirt. I hold the flame against the end of my cigarette, watching them for a moment before looking away. They don't seem to be talking much, but they're *together*. She has someone – she has *him* – and I don't. I feel sick at my own jealousy, knowing how lucky I am. Knowing that, if I wanted to, if I wasn't a coward, I could get rid of *some* of this burden on my brain at least. I have a friend, a good one, who would be willing to listen. Maybe even two. I glance back over at them, and blush as I see Ryan looking at me over his shoulder while Marcy chatters away, looking down at her phone screen in front of her. As his eyes catch mine, I see him mouth something.

You all right?

I stare at him, and a wave of honesty comes over me as I think about what he told me earlier. I shake my head a little, then shrug and half smile. The corner of his mouth quirks a little, sympathetically, then Marcy says something and he turns back to her. I blow out the last of my smoke and go back inside.

Chapter Nine

My alarm pierces down through dark layers of sleep, and I stare at the clock, disbelieving. Time for work again. I feel like my life's on an endless loop, desperately in need of some variety. I should probably get a hobby of some sort. Well, besides general obsessing. And finding dead bodies by the river isn't the sort of variety I'm thinking about.

I sit up in bed and pull off the covers. The thermostat must have been cranked up; it's stiflingly hot. My jaw hurts, and running my tongue over my teeth I realise I must have been grinding again. Marcy used to tell me I did that when I would sleep over at hers, needing a break from Sylvia's.

I hear a faint grunt outside my door from Charlie, but he's obviously learned not to push his luck with me now. Small victories. But thinking about the dog makes my head hurt even more. Something's trying to jog itself loose in my memory . . .

Wednesday. The book-end. David Barnett's inquest.

I need a cigarette, and go over to the window, staring out at the dull morning and letting the chill wind swoop over me through the crack while the grey fog of cigarette smoke runs over the morning fuzz of my tongue. It's too late, isn't it? I should have arranged longer lunchtime cover if I was going to ... No. It's fine. I don't need to go. I don't want to.

Dropping the butt into a half-empty mug of tea on my bedside table, I head to the bathroom to get ready. After my shower, I wipe away the condensation from the mirror and look at myself closely, staring into my own eyes until they seem like they belong to someone else. As if thinking about myself at a slight remove might help me decipher something, get some distance from my 'problems'. It sort of works. I pull at the skin under my eyes, wishing I had a reason to feel beautiful. Really beautiful, like someone who loves you can make you feel. I think of my mother, squeezing my face when I was a little girl, kissing it.

I think of Ryan, watching me.

I stop myself.

What feels like minutes later, I wait as the bus pulls up and then climb aboard and up the stairs, earphones in, moving automatically. Suddenly, Billie Holliday is in my ears and I fumble for my phone and skip away from her. Too Anita. The air outside is dark and thick, threatening rain, reflecting my mood. Reflections. I feel like I left myself back in the mirror in the bathroom, and someone else is now going through the motions for me. If only: someone else can live this life for a while, and I'll just watch.

I get to work and do the usual. God, I wish I'd never remembered what day it is. I can't shake it, the idea of going to the hearing. I try and concentrate on rearranging the books on contemporary sculpture, to little avail. I think about my mother's hearing. It was really just a formality – like David Barnett's will be, I suppose. A foregone conclusion. I didn't go to hers – Sylvia said it was probably better if I didn't. I guess my aunt was in the position I'm in now though, having been the one who found her. I suddenly feel a wave of empathy and sorrow at the idea Sylvia had to find her own sister like that. For all her planning, for all her wanting to protect me, Anita hadn't really thought about how traumatic it would be for Sylvia. My stomach lurches as I think about it. I head over to the cooler out the back and gulp down a couple of little paper cones full of icy water. A creeping sense of obligation begins to build inside me.

An hour later, I stare at the clock in the corner of the computer screen by the till, edging closer to one o'clock. Lucas will be here in less than a quarter of an hour. If he's on time. But it will be too late if I wait – it starts at one-thirty, I remember PC Martin saying. I blow out a breath of frustration and stare harder at the clock, wondering if it's likely Lucas will have his set of keys. I could text him, but he'll probably already have left his flat. I need to set off now if I'm going to make it. I need to lock up and go. If I'm going. Shit. Blood pounds in my ears and I scribble a BACK SOON note, my hands shaking as I tape it to the door. Jesus, I'm really doing this. I grab my coat and bag, and as I head out of the door, the alert beeps accusatorily. I glance at the note and clench my teeth, locking the door quickly.

A cab. I'm going to have to get a cab. Thankfully one is passing and I flag it down desperately, barking the address I looked up online through the half-open window. As I slide along the black leather seat I ring Lucas, and at least it goes straight to voicemail so he must be on the tube.

'Luc, please tell me you've got your keys. I . . . I had to go. I'll be back by two-thirty . . . two-forty-five at the latest. Please get there soon, yeah? I . . . Just, please.' I hang up, instantly regretting how wobbly and dramatic I sounded. He's going to think it's some major emergency. I fire off a quick text message to back it up, saying it's nothing serious and that I'll be eternally grateful if he can stay a little longer than usual today. I even add a smiley face, then realise he'll definitely think something's up because of that. Smiley face?

I look at the time on my phone as the taxi pulls up to the coroner's court, and fumble for change to go with the ten-pound note I press through the sliding partition into the driver's hand. One-twenty-eight. God bless London cab drivers.

I take a few deep breaths and then go up the steps and pull open the door: a drab lobby with a few rooms leading off it, and a set of lifts at the end of it. I'm not sure where I'm meant to go. Shit. But then I see PC Martin, standing in the doorway to one of the rooms. He turns and catches my eye, smiling at me like he knew I would be here, gesturing silently for me to come over. I head to the doorway, then stand beside him and stare into the room, with its sad rows of chairs. They're plastic, with cushions moulded on to them like an afterthought, spongy stuffing showing out of some of the more worn seats. The coroner sits at the front of the room facing the chairs, his stack of cases piled next to him on a run-of-the-mill desk. A smattering of people in the seats. I think I expected something more like a court that you'd see on TV: marble, wooden rows of benches, a raised judicial podium. Even if the coroner only determines how someone died, in a way this is a place for passing judgement on people's lives – lives they've had taken from them, lives they threw away themselves. How is it even possible this could look so ordinary?

'Glad you could make it, Miss Jenkins,' PC Martin says, reaching out and touching my arm a little hesitantly. I wonder just how strained my facial expression looks after the frantic escape from the shop. My phone beeps.

No worries T. Your love affair with Homeless Bob from two doors down is safe with me. See you in a bit. L

My shoulders sag in relief.

'You'd better switch that off for now,' PC Martin says quietly, nodding towards the front of the room. The court is back in session. I walk into the room and sit down in the back row automatically. My mouth is suddenly so dry it hurts to swallow. I hear the coroner read out the case number, 'DB15'. DB – dead body. I remember that from reading Mum's report a few years ago, and looking up some of the procedures. Fifteen initially unknown dead bodies found this year already? Then they assign his name. David Barnett. No middle name. Same initials, DB. The coroner reads out his date of birth – 14 July 1989. He was five years older than me. I can feel the room pressing in on me, seemingly unremarkable but shot through with dread, with things being absolutely wrong. We're here for an inquest, to question, to ask 'why' about something that probably can't ever be explained. The resounding agency of the fact that as human beings, we can take our own lives. I've always hated that phrase, but it's oddly appropriate.

'We have some testimony,' the coroner says in a matter-of-fact voice. 'The first from . . .' he checks his notes, 'Cynthia March. Ms March?'

I watch as a tall woman steps forward, her face worn with seemingly premature wrinkles, her hair dull, auburn, frizzy.

'What was your relationship to Mr Barnett, Ms March?' the coroner asks, a more gentler tone to his voice now.

'I'm – I was – his mother. Barnett was my married name,' she adds quickly, then shakes her head like she knows the information isn't relevant. The coroner continues asking questions in a quiet, sympathetic voice, and I lean forward, watching David Barnett's mother, my stomach tight. Cynthia March's voice stays steady, like she doesn't want to give away that private part of herself, the part that's feeling everything about this moment, every emotion, with every fibre of her being. The part that's barely holding it together. The part where her cells might collapse at any moment and she'd simply cease to be, just like her son has done.

I understand it completely. It's a state I've almost never left. But she keeps her voice steady.

'And what did Mr Barnett do for work?' the coroner's asking.

'He didn't really have a job. He tried, but it was hard for him ... Sometimes he helped a friend who was a plumber, that was his most regular work. He'd begun to train as a social worker, but he wasn't able to finish.'

The coroner nods and jots a few notes, like he's deciphering something. I stare at his pen as it flickers across the page.

'Did your son suffer from depression? Or any other illnesses?'

'Well, he was asthmatic. And yes, he suffered from depression. Since he was thirteen years old. Maybe ... maybe even longer.'

I watch her jaw tighten slightly, the muscles clenching and unclenching. She wants this to be over. I silently beg for it to end, for the questions to stop. Finally, after a few more, the coroner tells Cynthia quietly that she can step down, and then calls the next witness. I watch her walk steadily over to sit in one of the chairs in the front row, and a young man takes the seat beside the coroner's desk.

'Can you state your name for the record please, sir?'

'Jonathan de Witt.'

'Thank you, Mr de Witt. And may I ask, what was your relationship with Mr Barnett?'

The man clears his throat. 'I was his flatmate. His friend.' He glances over at David Barnett's mother with a look in his eyes that I also recognise – guilt. He thinks he's let her down. Or maybe he knows, deep down, that he hasn't, but it's still there; he can't get rid of the worry. Cynthia March nods her head almost imperceptibly.

'When did you last see Mr Barnett?'

'On the evening of the eleventh. He brought us back a take-away. Burgers and chips, which was his favourite, even though I told him the chips always got soggy and cold.' He smiles a little. 'Dave said he'd been at the library. He loved the quiet. And then, I don't know, we chatted about this girl I was seeing, we watched TV. I went to bed, and when I woke up the next morning he wasn't in his room. There was just the ... ' He glances over at Cynthia again, takes a deep breath. 'The note. He was gone.'

The coroner nods. 'And did you have any indications about Mr Barnett's state of mind?'

Jonathan frowns for a moment. 'Do you mean did I think he was going to do this?' He sighs. 'He sort of used to talk about it. He wasn't always happy, but he had this exaggerated world-view on everything. Love, his friends, his family. I don't know, just the state of the world in general. He'd talk about that a lot. He *felt* everything so much ... ' He trails off for a moment and then clears his throat a few times. I swallow hard. 'But when someone tells you they're OK, even someone like Dave, and if they *seem* it ... you want to believe them, don't you?' He looks at Cynthia again, his eyes shining a little, and she looks down at her lap. Eventually he is dismissed too, and goes to sit next to her. Cynthia reaches over and takes his hand, and they're both resigned in their grief. Did David know he was so loved?

Did Anita?

Suddenly I wish it was *my* hand his mother was holding, and the feeling makes me shift in my seat with awkwardness. No matter how old you get, you're still someone's child, I suppose. Except my own mother would never know me as an adult, despite how much I used to try and act like one when she was alive. A desperate need for comfort overwhelms me, and I take a deep breath. A flash of memory again, the cinema That Day; needing *someone*, and Ryan being there. My heartbeat steadies a little.

Constable Martin is on the stand now, going through the full details of David Barnett's discovery. Of the discovery I made – I glance up as my name is mentioned, worried that I'm going to be some sort of surprise witness, but thankfully they move on to talk about time, place. I think about those moments before that time 'around 8.30 a.m.' when I found him. The quiet moments when he lay still, peaceful and undisturbed. And the moments before that, when he waded into the freezing-cold water to greet death.

As PC Martin continues, he says that there were no witnesses to the moment when David Barnett entered the river, but that CCTV from the car park showed him pulling up in his car, and fixing what they now known to have been weights to his ankles before heading down to the riverside. There was nobody there to ask what he was doing. He must have just waded slowly in, and waited. Finally the constable steps down, and the coroner surveys the room, asking if there's anything further, shuffling some papers on his desk a little distractedly. Then he settles, looks over at Cynthia and asks if there is anything more she would like to say before they conclude.

'No. Except he was … David was my only son. He was a good boy.'

The room is quiet for a moment, and I watch her take a small sip from a bottle of water. At last the coroner concludes the hearing, officially ruling the death a suicide. I feel the air rush out of my lungs as he finally says it. Others begin to file out of the room, but I'm rooted to my seat.

'Miss Jenkins?' Constable Martin is beside me, saying my name like he's been repeating it. I look up at him and he smiles a little. 'Glad you were able to come.' I'm not sure if it's a question or a statement, but I nod. He lowers his voice. 'I know these things are difficult, a bit bleak perhaps, but like I say it can some-times be good closure. The burden of discovery—'

He breaks off as I stand up suddenly and push past him, mut-tering a faint apology, trying to reach her before she gets to the door.

'Mrs Bar – I mean, Ms March? Sorry, I ...' Looking down at my outstretched hand, I realise it's trembling. Cynthia pauses a moment, then takes it, not quite shaking hands, just sort of grasping it. She looks down, then back up into my eyes.

'You're the one who found him?' She glances at the constable, then back to me.

'Yes.' I don't know what else to say.

'Thank you. I ... I'm sorry,' she replies. 'I'm sorry about that.'

Her eyes stay on mine a moment longer, then she lets go of my hand, and she's gone.

Chapter Ten

As I walk into the pub, the icy air that had surrounded me seems to turn into a warm vapour. Luckily the place is only a short walk from work, and the fresh air was actually pretty welcome – I'd told Luc I'd work through lunch to make up for my extra time yesterday, for which I was grateful he didn't ask any questions beyond some deliberately far-fetched teasing, but nine hours straight in that shop damn near defined the word 'stifling'.

I scan the brown, carpeted interior of the pub and see Marcy already here, flicking through a copy of *Vogue* next to the roaring fire, and I'm a little surprised at her punctuality. She has her back to me and Charlie's nestled at her feet, dozing. I start to sneak up on her, but the dog raises his head and starts wagging his tail, giving the game away. Killjoy.

'Hey!' Marcy springs up and gives me a hug. I soak in her warmth, and the heat from the fire.

'Hey indeed,' I reply. 'I thought I was going to be late. Bev's not in the loo, is she?'

Marcy shakes her head. 'Nah, she texted saying she was running a couple of minutes behind. Are you going to the bar?' She drains her wineglass for emphasis.

I smile and roll my eyes, then head over and order a bottle of red and three glasses, bringing them back to the table in two trips.

'Oh no, don't get up,' I say sarcastically.

'I have to keep the table, don't I?' Marcy retorts with a grin.

'You know, for someone who uses their body for a living, you're kind of lazy.'

'Gah, you sound just like my pimp.' She laughs, pouring out the wine.

'I don't know why you decided this is how you want to spend your last night before the tour anyway,' I say, shaking my head. 'You know she won't let us get out of here before closing.'

We both glance up towards the pub door guiltily as it opens, but it's not Bev.

'It's all good,' Marcy says with a sigh. 'We never all get to catch up, and besides, Bev was pretty insistent about tonight. It's really hard to say no to her, T.' She feigns a haunted look, but immediately recomposes her face as we see Beverly breeze in through the doors. She stands for a moment, looking around for us, and Marcy mutters something under her breath. 'Oh shit. Ring. Brace yourself.'

'What?'

Beverly strides over to our table and throws off her black wool wrap, beaming.

'Hey, girls!'

'Hi!' we both chorus. Marcy springs up and kisses Beverly on both cheeks, then I do the same. As I do, I clock what Marcy was on about. On Beverly's left hand is a diamond the size of a cherry, glinting against her smooth mahogany skin. Crikey.

'How are you both?' she asks, grinning as I pour her a glass of wine and top ours off, and we clink them together.

'Good. Really good,' Marcy says, glancing over at me with a

glint in her eye. 'What's this though?' she exclaims, reaching for Bev's hand. 'Bloody hell, you could take someone's eye out with that! Congratulations are in order, I presume?'

It was sort of cruel, but I could see Marcy couldn't help herself. If there's one thing she loves, it's taking the wind out of people's sails. I suddenly remember a furtive evening around Marcy's laptop a few months ago, when Beverly changed her status to 'in a relationship', and with whom. This could be interesting.

Beverly holds up her hand, the rock winking brightly even under the dull pub lights.

'Well, yeah. That's sort of why I wanted to see you guys – you know, hear it from the horse's mouth and all.' She clears her throat, smiles a little nervously now, and states the obvious. 'I'm getting married!'

I look over at Marcy's rigid grin, and almost have to bite back a laugh. Her mouth may be smiling but her eyes are looking daggers at the bling.

'Fantastic,' she says flatly. 'Who's the lucky bloke then? Not that guy who had the photocopying business?'

Marcy knows exactly who the 'lucky bloke' must be. Tom. He was Marcy's boyfriend when we first went to university, and she was completely doolally over him for the first few months we were there, but then she learned there were bigger, sexier fish in the sea. They broke up, and she was over him within a few weeks, but clearly she's stuck on principle now. She just wants to make Bev squirm, and it's pretty much mission accomplished. I wonder, if she and Ryan broke up, would she get over it quickly? Would she make me feel guilty if he and I then got together? God, why am I even *thinking* this?

'Uh, it was a printer's, and no, not him. That was ages ago,' Bev replies, pressing her lips together and taking a breath. 'You know I've been seeing Tom? We, uh, reconnected – I mean, not reconnected, but uh, bumped into each other a while ago. I know it's been ages since we've all met up so maybe you didn't . . . ' She shifts in her seat. 'Anyway, we've been seeing each other for a while now and it's been wonderful, and then last week he just . . . He popped the question!'

Marcy gives her nothing. She sips her wine carefully, and Beverly glances at me for rescue.

'Wow. Tom,' I say, kicking Marcy under the table. 'Who'd have thought, eh? Good for you guys! Congratulations, Bev!'

'Thanks! I know it's a bit awkward, Marce, but you know, you guys were together years ago . . . '

Marcy looks at her a moment longer, fake-frowns, then breaks into a genuine smile. 'I'm just playing, hon. I'm really glad you guys got it together.' She reaches over and touches Bev's arm. 'Honestly, I'm happy for you.'

'Are you sure?' Bev says, somewhat ridiculously. I feel a bit irritated at Marcy for having made her feel bad about it.

'What, if I say no, are you going to call the whole thing off? Just ignore me, B, seriously, I'm only teasing,' Marcy says and laughs fluidly. The nervous tension eventually disperses, and we all reach for our wine simultaneously. Bev regales us with the somewhat clichéd story of Tom's proposal, and shows us photos of the two of them beaming from her phone screen, and I can't help smiling. Even if it's a bit swift, at least they've found each other, and they're looking forward to a future, whatever it might bring. I try to ignore the hollow in the pit of my stomach as I think about that, but then talk turns to Marcy's tour, which doesn't really help matters.

'Fucking hell, Marce, that's amazing!' Bev enthuses, and I can just feel what's coming next.

'So what's new with you, then, Taylor?'

111

I draw in a breath. Why does something always have to be new anyway? What if I like old, what if I want things to stay exactly the same and never change? I think I'm scared of what 'new' could mean. Unknown, out of my control ... I know things staying the same is really not what I want, but I've got nothing to tell them in answer to that question besides the one major unforeseen incident I've been trying in vain to push to the back of my mind. My face must show that I'm thinking of *something* though, as both Bev's and Marcy's eyes light up.

'That's quite the pause,' Bev says. 'Go on! You've got some mystery man, haven't you? Spill!'

Marcy leans forward too, smiling but with a hint of wariness.

'Honestly, I don't. I was actually just thinking I wish I *did* have something to report, but there's really nothing. No tours, no weddings ... ' I smile at them, trying not to sound pitiful.

'Well, everything to play for then,' Beverly says kindly. She raises her glass. 'Here's to infinite possibilities.'

'Hear, hear,' Marcy says, like she always does, and I feel grateful to them both for their hopefulness. I hope I can drink it in with the wine.

We order another bottle, and get into some reminiscing about our days at university: Bev's different weaves, Marcy's most embarrassing auditions, my weird tutor with the too-big gums who tried to crack on to me. Then talk begins to turn back to wedding planning, and Marcy emphatically checks her watch.

'D'you know what, guys, I think Charlie and I are going to have to get going. It's my last night, and Ry should be getting home soon ... ' I see Bev eyeing the third-full bottle of wine still on the table. She wants me to stay, I can tell, and my heart sinks at the thought of discussing different types of organza. 'Speaking of early starts, babe, you look exhausted.' Marcy reaches over and taps my knee sympathetically. God, I love this girl sometimes.

'Yeah, you know what, I am pretty knackered. But it was great to see you, Bev; congrats on everything. We'll have to sort out getting together again soon.'

'Yeah, definitely. I'll call you. You'll need a pal while Marcy's away,' she says with a wink. I smile warmly. 'And you, darling, with your fancy tour, who knows when I'll see you? There'll obviously be the hen night if I don't see you before . . .'

Marcy's eyes widen imperceptibly, and I bite the inside of my cheek to keep from chuckling. Marcy's worst nightmare. We pull on our coats and hug and kiss goodbye.

We head off, Charlie trotting ahead of us, eager to hit each lamppost with the requisite amount of piss.

'Are you really cool with that? Her engagement?' I ask.

'Course. Jesus, Tom was bloody years ago. I have so moved on,' she says with a grin.

I look down at the ground in front of us. 'Do you . . .' I begin hesitantly. Why am I even bringing this up? She turns her head to look at me. 'Do you think that's where you and Ryan are headed?'

She blows out a sort of laugh, her breath clouding up in the dark sky. 'God, I don't know about *that*. I mean, we're good at the moment, but babe, if I'm honest, sometimes . . . I just wonder how much we have in common. Do I picture us going for the long haul?' She leaves the question unanswered. I meet her gaze, and she looks at me contemplatively for a moment before her grin returns. 'For right now though?' She waggles her eyebrows suggestively. 'It's pretty damn good.'

I exhale a breath I didn't know I was holding.

'And I will miss him,' she says. 'I'll miss both of you. You more, though, by a long shot.' She links her arm with mine, but immediately has to unlink it to scoop up Charlie's shit. It suddenly occurs to me that will probably be at least partly my job while she's away. Great.

Marcy drops the plastic bag into the bin outside our building, then turns back to me. Charlie trots towards the downstairs doors, but I don't move for a minute.

'Marcy.'

'Yeah.'

'I'm going to miss you, too.'

She steps towards me quietly and we hug. I feel Charlie tugging her hand away with the leash, and I break towards the door, swiping my entry fob. I feel her watching me again as we head up the stairs and I open the door to the flat.

'Cool?' she says.

'Yep.'

'Hungry?'

'Yep.'

I head into my room to change into my sweatpants, feeling sad and nervous and ridiculous at the tears prickling my eyes. I hear Marcy phone for Japanese takeaway. It's getting late for eating, but I didn't have any dinner. It's Friday tomorrow anyway; I can handle being tired at work for one last day.

'What do you fancy, babe?' she shouts.

I open my bedroom door. 'Usual,' I call.

'Cool.'

I pull my hair into a bun and head to the bathroom to wash my face. I was hoping putting on some comfy clothes and washing the day off would help me feel more relaxed, but my back is tense and as I watch the water drip down my face, my lips are drawn in a tight line. I feel like I'm counting down to something, and I don't know what to expect when the clock hits zero.

I head to the living room and slump into the chair, staring at the sitcom Marcy's put on the TV.

'Food'll be here in fifteen or so, they said it's quiet.'

'Nice one.'

We both watch for a while, laughing occasionally. It sort of helps.

'Where the hell is Ry? I know he said they had to rehearse late, but I was hoping for an earlyish night,' Marcy says, an anticipatory look in her eyes. Just then we both turn towards the door as we hear a key in the lock. She grins and springs up to go and greet him. I try not to listen to them kissing in the hallway, but after a few minutes the buzzer goes, and I realise I need to get cash from my room to pay for my part of the takeaway. As I head into the hallway Ryan quickly pulls his lips away from Marcy's, and they finally answer the door. Marcy goes into the kitchen to arrange plates while Ryan pays the delivery guy. I try to give him some cash, but he pushes my hand away and smiles down at me.

'It's cool, I'll get it,' he says.

I reach out for the steaming food, sweating in its plastic bag and foil containers while Ryan gets his change, and as he closes the door, he glances at me again and for a moment, just a moment, I think I see a look of worry in his eyes.

After eating in front of the TV, I thank Ryan for getting the takeaway and then decide I should probably make myself scarce. I clear the plates away, then walk slowly back to the living room.

'So ...'

'So ...' Marcy replies, standing up from where she's been snuggled against Ryan on the sofa. He watches us both, his expression unreadable. He looks down as our eyes meet.

'This is it, eh?' I say quietly. I'll have left for work by the time she sets off tomorrow. When I get home, it will just be me and

Ryan. I clench my jaw, hardly able to keep up with the thoughts and emotions battling in my mind. I see tears in Marcy's eyes, and we both take a deep breath. She squeezes me into another hug.

'I'm on the end of the phone, OK?' She pulls back and looks at me meaningfully. I nod. 'I love you, T. Be good, yeah?'

I hug her again. 'I love you too,' I murmur. 'You're going to smash it. Have a great time.' I push the corners of my lips out into a smile as we pull apart, and blow out a breath. 'Right. Good-night.' I glance down again. 'Night, Ryan.'

'Sleep well, Taylor.' He runs a hand over his growing-out hair.

I brush my teeth, then silently walk back to my bedroom, shut the door and sit down slowly on the bed, feeling chaotic. I turn, looking down at the messy bedclothes. I stand up again, and begin meticulously straightening, smoothing, pulling tight, fluffing. I turn one corner of the duvet down and then look at the bed again.

I pull off my clothes, get in, close my eyes and hope to fall asleep.

Chapter Eleven

The electronic bus lady announces my stop, muffled under the sound of my earphones, and I stand and walk slowly down the aisle between the upstairs seats, trying to get a look at the woman up ahead. I'd had this odd feeling before, looking out of the corner of my eye – something about the way her hair was ...? But no, it's not Cynthia March. As I walk down the stairs, I glance back up at the middle-aged woman sitting near the front, just to make sure.

I don't know what I would have said if it was her, anyway. Since the inquest, I find myself seeing her – or thinking I do – everywhere I go. The corner shop, walking past the storefront at work, outside our building. Even if I don't know exactly what I'd say, I feel like I didn't say everything I needed to that day, and now I'm looking for that opportunity. Or perhaps I'm just looking for a distraction from the issue immediately ahead of me tonight. Though I'm not sure if, as distractions go, having an awkward chat with the mother of the man whose body I found would be the best one.

The bus doors hiss shut behind me and I walk slowly along the icy pavement, trying not to slip, and in no rush to find out what awaits me at home. Will he be there? It's Friday night, but it's early, and now Marcy's gone ... It occurs to me that in the few weeks he's lived with us, I've never really thought about what Ryan does when he isn't with her, who he hangs out with. My heart beats faster as I walk slowly up to the flat, the echo of my footsteps following me up the staircase. Maybe he's still out at rehearsal? I should have phoned Bev or someone to go for a drink, then maybe I could have just come in late and gone straight to bed. I reach the flat before I'm really ready, but just as I'm about to put my key in the lock, the door opens.

Ryan jumps. 'Shit!'

I put my hand to my chest, as though it will slow my heart, but no such luck. Especially now he's in front of me. We both laugh nervously, in that way people do when they're scared.

'Sorry,' I say, still chuckling a little. He shakes his head and smiles broadly enough that I see the little chip in his canine, which somehow emphasises the beauty of his face. He steps aside to let me in. Although he has his coat on, and layers ready for the cold, I can tell he's freshly showered. I inhale slowly. Soap and ... him.

Charlie slopes into the hallway, wagging his tail and snuffling at me, but calm. He's obviously been walked for the evening already, I think gratefully.

'Good day?' Ryan asks, watching me absently pat Charlie's head.

I shrug. 'Same old.'

'At least it's Friday, eh?'

'Definitely,' I say, and then notice he's carrying a guitar case. He lowers it off his shoulder and rests it on the floor for a moment. I've never seen him with one before. I nod towards it. 'I didn't know you played?'

'Yeah, I ... ' He looks down at the guitar. 'I haven't for a while.'

I want to ask why not. I want to ask him to play, now, just for me, from the look in his eyes as he says that. Although the front door is still slightly ajar, he makes no move to leave, and I stand in the hallway, coat still on, bag on my shoulder. Neither of us seems to want to go anywhere.

'Oh,' I say. 'Well, I guess it's like riding a bike . . .' Ugh. I roll my eyes as I finish speaking, and the corner of his mouth turns up a bit.

'Yeah. Sort of.' His dark eyes gleam with repressed amusement.

'I wish I'd learned to play an instrument.' I smile as a memory suddenly pops into my head, spreading warmth from my heart. 'There was this guy who used to play piano with my mum, and for some reason he was convinced I would be a natural. Like, he thought my fingers *were* somehow perfect for piano-playing. I suppose maybe they were freakishly long for a kid of seven or eight.' I look down at my hands, turn them this way and that, and glance up to see Ryan staring at them, then back into my eyes. 'But anyway,' I continue, because I've started now, 'I remember she was rehearsing once, and he sat me next to him on the stool so he could nod to me when he wanted the last note played at the end of one song. But my mum . . .' I start to chuckle, but tears prickle my eyes suddenly. 'My mum just held her note for ages, throwing me off. It made me laugh so much. Like, you know when as a kid things are just much funnier?'

Ryan nods and smiles along with me, his eyes warm.

'And she was laughing too, like *really* laughing, and it was just . . .' I tail off and shake my head. I can almost hear her. It was like magic, a rare and beautiful thing, her laughter.

Ryan's quiet for a moment. I realise it's probably the most I've ever said to him, and that it was a bit out of the blue.

'Your mum was a singer?' he says eventually.

'Uh, yeah. Jazz, mainly.'

He nods and raises his eyebrows a little, like it makes sense to him. 'Nice.'

We look at each other for a moment.

'Anyway ... I'd like to hear you play sometime,' I say, feeling heat creep up my neck a little.

'Maybe after my training-wheels come off again,' he says, then smiles slowly.

He's teasing me. 'All right.'

He looks at me a little longer, then, 'Got any plans tonight?'

I shake my head. 'Nah. You?' Clearly yes.

'Uh, I've got a bit of bar work, then ... Yeah, I don't know yet. I might be back a bit late.' He holds up the instrument a bit, as if it explains what he means. Sinking disappointment mingles in my head with pure relief that he'll be out for the rest of the evening. He looks at me and opens his mouth as if he wants to say something else, but then thinks better of it.

'I guess Marcy gave you a call?' I say quickly. 'She texted to say they've arrived at Hong Kong for the stopover.' I smile at the memory of her excited message, but my expression slackens a little as he looks at me. Like I meant it as a reminder, for both of us? Maybe I did.

'Yeah, she did,' he says. He hoists the guitar-case strap on to his shoulder again. 'Well, better get going.'

I look down at a loose floorboard. 'OK, yeah. Have a good evening.'

One side of his mouth turns up again, and I see the dimple in his cheek. 'You have a good one too, Taylor.'

I exhale hard as the door slams shut. Charlie raises his head from where he's settled in his basket in the kitchen, and I shake my head at him, at myself. The dog's looking sort of depressed, probably because of Marcy leaving. For once I know how he feels.

*

Actually, it's quite nice being totally alone in the flat for once – well, alone except for the dog. I change into a hoodie and sweatpants, make some lazy scrambled eggs and toast for dinner, then settle down on the sofa with a cup of tea, ready to be decadently numbed by the big dumb action movie just starting up as I switch on the telly.

I watch the film to the end, and then decide I might as well go to bed. I've been trying not to think about tomorrow. Linda's birthday party. I try to tell myself that there's no point getting nervous at least until I get there, but it doesn't really work. The queasy feeling builds in my stomach each time I think about what I'm going to wear, about getting on the train, about getting in a taxi, about ringing their doorbell. If I'm going to struggle to get to sleep thinking about it, I might as well start trying now. Charlie lopes towards me as I head to the bathroom to brush my teeth, staring at me dolefully.

'Cheer up, mate,' I say through toothpaste. He looks at me as if to say, 'You're one to talk.' I shrug, spit, rinse and head to my room.

'Come on, then,' I say, holding open my bedroom door for him to follow me in. He does, and sits reluctantly by the door for a moment before heading back to his basket in the kitchen. Apparently I'm no replacement for the real thing.

I awake from half-sleep with a start as my stomach growls. My body's protesting against the meagre dinner, and I didn't really eat much at lunchtime either. I sigh, looking at the clock: 1.32 a.m. Has Ryan come in yet? I didn't hear anything, and suddenly I have a nervous feeling in the pit of my stomach, familiar but unwelcome – needing to check that everything is OK, that nothing bad has happened while I was asleep.

I push back my duvet cover and pad over to the door,

startled when I hear Charlie's low snuffle – he clearly changed his mind and nosed his way in to sleep on my floor. He follows me as I edge out into the corridor. It's nice that he has my back, even if he wouldn't be much of an attack dog. I glance along the dark hallway and see Marcy's bedroom door is still open. Ryan's not back. I frown, wondering just for a moment if there's someone else he might be seeing. A pang of embarrassing jealousy rises in me, and I tamp it down swiftly and head to the bathroom.

As I flush, I hear a scraping, scrabbling noise, and wash my hands quickly, peering out into the corridor again. Charlie is staring at the front door, but then he trots towards it calmly. Before I can dive back into my room, it opens, and light from the stairwell seeps into the darkness of the flat.

'No, Charlie, come on, boy,' I hear Ryan whisper as the dog ruffs and pants at his entrance. He reaches down for Charlie's collar and edges him back into the flat, but as his eyes clock me, standing awkwardly in the middle of the corridor, he does an almost comical jump.

'Jesus Christ!'

I can't help laughing. 'Nope. Just me.'

Ryan starts laughing too, and turns around to close the front door. It's dark again; just slivers of bright moonlight coming in from the kitchen window and into the corridor.

'Twice in one day?' he says, exhaling the last of his laughter.

'Sorry. I was just going to the loo, and—'

'No, no, it's OK ... I didn't mean to wake you up.'

'No, you didn't.'

We look at each other, eyes adjusting to the lack of light, recalling a similar exchange a few days before.

'Uh, I was actually going to grab some cereal or something. I didn't really eat much today.' I realise I'm whispering unnecessarily mid-way through my sentence, and clear my throat to speak in a normal voice. 'How was your night?'

I head into the kitchen and switch on the light, blinking at the glare. Ryan props his guitar against the wall, hangs up his coat and follows me, leaning against the kitchen counter.

'Yeah, it was good, thanks.' He folds his arms, and I see his eyes travel up my body from my bare feet. I'm suddenly very aware of the fact that I'm wearing old short-shorts, a T-shirt and no bra. It's simultaneously getting a little cold, and uncomfortably hot. He looks away as I catch him staring. My breathing quickens and I turn to the cupboards to quickly begin fixing a bowl of cornflakes. *Think about the cornflakes.* Deeply unsexy.

'What . . . uh . . . Did you go somewhere to play?' I say, shaking cereal into a bowl, eyes down.

'Yeah, well, just a late-night open-mic thing, just trying a couple of things out. Like I say, it's been a while.'

I turn to him, intrigued. '"Trying things out" like you write your own stuff?'

'Yeah.' He shrugs, then opens the fridge to pass me the milk. He steps towards me to hand it over, and though his eyes look at my face, nowhere else, his expression makes me even more self-conscious.

'That's cool,' I murmur. I'm not sure whether to excuse myself and eat in my room, or whether that would be really weird. Though maybe having milk dribbling down my chin would help lessen the tension.

'So,' he says, drawing a breath. 'How about you?'

I frown, unclear what he means.

'How was your night?'

'Oh, ah, nothing special. Sofa action. Early night.'

He smiles a little. 'Sounds pretty good actually.'

It's my turn to shrug, and I spoon more cereal into my mouth, chewing as delicately as I can. The crunching still sounds ten times louder than normal in the quiet flat. He watches me eat, and I feel strangely less and less embarrassed. He laughs a little, quietly, and I grin, though I don't quite know why. I finally finish, and put my bowl in the sink.

'Better try and get some sleep,' I say. 'Got to get up early to get the train.' I feel the tension back in my jaw as I speak.

'Right. I remember. Your cousin's birthday.'

I nod, and though he doesn't say anything else, I see a reassurance in his expression that really does help. I look down, fighting the urge to do something, to take his hand in mine. Glancing up, I see his eyes still on me, his broad chest rising and falling noticeably, like he's making a deliberate effort to breathe. I feel like I'm doing the same.

'Good-night,' I say finally.

Ryan lifts one hand out towards me, hovers it above my shoulder like he's scared to touch me. I'm scared too. He sighs a little, and brushes his fingertips gently, almost imperceptibly down my arm, in a gesture that could be merely one of support or reassurance. But it feels like slow-motion feathers, like electricity, like blades of soft summer grass on my skin. His fingers trail away as they reach my wrist, before I can grab them, weave them in between mine.

'Good-night, Taylor.'

I blink hard for a moment, and he's out of the door, heading into his room.

Their room. *Their room, Taylor.*

After a while, I move. I climb into bed, listening to my duvet crackle as the cold bedclothes surround me. Sighing, I turn on my side, trying not to think about any of it. I wait for sleep, but it feels like it never comes.

Chapter Twelve

I can already imagine the smell of the hallway, and I'm not even inside yet. Menthol cigarettes and air freshener. I desperately want a smoke now, in fact, but as the taxi pulls away behind me, there are only a few steps up the drive to the door, so it seems unlikely I can fit one in. I strongly consider heading around the corner and having one quickly, but I'm self-conscious enough as it is without stinking of cigarettes for all the greetings.

Making my way slowly up the path, I check my reflection in the wobbly surface of the frosted glass, hoping none of my curls have sprung free from their tight bun. I feel a little stab of disappointment in myself that I decided to put my hair up at all – as if it could somehow disguise the ways I'm different from Sylvia's family. Mum's family ... The brown sheep. I press a wry smile away from my lips, then take a few long, deep breaths. If I did go round the corner, call the cab company, how long might it take for them to turn up again? I could hide in the neighbour's bushes until I see the taxi pull up, then make a run for it ...

I press my finger to the doorbell, looking at it like the digit belongs to someone else. If only. I can hear faint music coming from inside, and then Sylvia's voice getting louder as she nears the door.

'I told you there was somebody at the— Taylor!'

She throws the door open wide and stares at me for a moment.

'Hi, Aunty,' I say, trying for a broad smile.

'Oh, darling! I hope you haven't been standing there long?' She makes no move to let me inside, just looks me up and down, an overwhelmed expression of surprise, warmth and worry on her face. Every time I see her now, she's smaller than I remember, less statuesque than Mum. But Sylvia's frame always did belie her strength.

'No, no, I just got here.'

She shakes her head, like she's remembering herself, and steps aside. 'Come in, come in. Oh, sweetheart, it's so lovely to see you.'

I step inside and inhale the familiar scent. It's somehow reassuring, even though this isn't the home I moved into after Mum died. I think if it had been the same place, today would have been even more difficult. This is familiar, but different enough not to flood me, drown me, with memories. As it is, I'm fighting the hollow, sick sensation in my stomach at the recollection of us all piling back to Sylvia's living room after the funeral, staring at one another and having to listen to the music my mother loved without her there to enjoy it.

Sylvia's a little different too. She's lost weight, dyed her hair – I guess finding a new man has given her a new lease of life. The phrase sounds oddly unfortunate in my head.

'Taylor,' she says, then pulls me into a tight hug. I wrap my arms around her shoulders awkwardly, fighting the sudden urge to push her off – a teenage instinct that has flared up in me again. She releases me, but holds on to my shoulders, looking up into my face searchingly.

'How are you, love? You're looking so beautiful.' She touches

126

my cheek, and her eyes glaze over a little. Maybe I look more like Anita than I thought. 'Come in, let me get you something to drink.' She leads me into a large, brown kitchen.

'Where's the birthday girl?' I ask, feeling like some kind of spinster aunt as the term leaves my lips.

'Oh, she's out there with her friends,' Sylvia says, gesturing through the living room where I can see people milling about, to some sliding glass doors leading to the garden. 'God knows how they aren't freezing to death.'

I recognise the instinct to separate. I bet Linda can't wait for this portion of the proceedings to end so she can go and have some actual fun. On the day of the funeral, I wanted to get out of there just so I could pretend something wasn't terribly wrong, that I hadn't just thrown a handful of dirt on the grave of my own mother, that she was just away on a trip for the night, and she'd be back any moment . . . I swallow hard, and try to focus as Sylvia holds a bottle of red and a bottle of white up towards me. I point, then watch the dark liquid splash into the glass.

'This must be Taylor!' a deep, jovial voice says, and Sylvia and I both turn towards the kitchen door. I take a large glug of wine.

'Oh darling, yes – this is Malcolm. My, uh . . .' she chuckles, 'my fiancé!'

'Of course! Nice to meet you,' I say, extending my hand, but knowing I won't get away with it. Malcolm steps forward and pulls me into a quick hug, his soft, pale jumper stretching over his generous middle, which bounces into my side. Although he has a walrus moustache and not a big white beard, I can't help thinking he'd make a great shopping-centre Santa. My smile is genuine as I pull away. Sylvia grins between us.

'I've heard so much about you,' Malcolm says, his eyes shining with sympathy. I nod, imagining the main thing he heard; the defining element of my relationship with my aunt, the loss that unifies us. I smile towards Sylvia, and she presses her lips into a line. She understands. My gut twists with love and guilt.

'I have a present for Linda ...' I begin, and Sylvia wipes her hands on a nearby dishcloth with a sense of finality.

'Yes, of course, darling. Let's go and find our little sweet sixteen.'

The three of us head into the living room, and I begin to chew the inside of my cheek as several pairs of eyes turn towards me. I don't recognise many people – must be mainly family friends and neighbours, and it's not a big gathering, but somehow I feel hugely self-conscious, like all the details of my who and why are written in a big neon sign above my head. Sylvia grips my hand and introduces me to one or two people, proudly telling them I'm her niece. I scan their faces, trying to decide if they know about my mother, why she's not here, how Sylvia took me in. I try not to think of the words 'burden' or '*de facto* orphan' or 'abandoned', in case they might be telepathically transferred into these strangers' minds.

Finally, Sylvia slides open the patio doors, and we're greeted by a wall of chilly air. Linda and a boy her age are sitting on an old swing set at the bottom of the garden, their breath dispersing as they glide through the air into the clouds in front of them. Next to the swings, a red-headed girl seems to be telling an animated story that the other two are mostly ignoring.

'Linda!' Sylvia calls. 'Why don't you lot come in now? It's bloody freezing! And your cousin's here, look!'

Linda steps gracefully off the swing in mid-air, her long dark hair dancing behind her. Her friends follow somewhat sullenly. She walks quickly towards me with an eager smile, and as she reaches the top of the garden, I'm amazed to find her eye to eye with me. She's suddenly almost a woman. I really do feel like that spinster aunt; the next words out of my mouth better not be 'Oh, haven't you grown!' Linda was only ten when I moved in, and we never got close. She wasn't looking to make me her surrogate big sister, and maybe it was just as well – I was pretty self-involved back then. Now, of course, I'm the very *picture* of selflessness . . . I smile at her.

'Hi, Taylor,' she says shyly, and we hug clumsily. I catch the faint musk of cigarette smoke on her coat and inhale deeply, smiling wider as we separate. Another familial connection.

'Happy birthday!'

'Thanks.'

'Come inside,' Sylvia frets, waiting by the glass doors. We head into the living room and she slides them shut and clicks the lock, her shoulders relaxing like she's finally herded the last sheep into its pen.

I remember Linda's present and reach into my bag, pulling it out and trying to smooth out the crumpled ribbon before I hand it over.

'Thanks,' she says again. Teenage monosyllabism has definitely kicked in. She unwraps it and hands the paper and ribbon to the boy hovering behind her like a butler. He crumples them into a ball and holds it, looking around fruitlessly for a bin. Must be her boyfriend, though Sylvia's probably in denial about it. Either way, Linda clearly has him trained well. I try not to feel jealous of a sixteen-year-old's relationship.

'Nina Simone,' I say. 'She was one of my favourites when I was around your age.' There's that spinster aunt again. 'I mean, I think that's when I first got into her. Um, yeah. Let me know what you think.'

Linda turns the box set over in her hands, looking a bit unsure. Jesus, she probably doesn't even use a CD player. I bite my lip and glance at Sylvia, both of us remembering Nina's imperial voice booming off the walls of my little box room, years ago.

'Cool. Thanks, Taylor,' Linda says, reaching over to hug me again. I exhale in relief – four syllables: can't be that bad.

She heads off to join her friends, sitting in a row on the long sofa along the far wall, and they lounge together, counting time and gossiping unsubtly about the adults. I wish I could slump on to the sofa and join them, but I'm one of the grown-ups now, supposedly. I chat stiltedly with some of Sylvia's friends, and then I'm accosted by a tall, blowsy woman with grey-brown hair, who says she's Mum and Sylvia's cousin. She looks at me with inquisitive-sympathy eyes.

'So nice to see you doing so well after all these years,' she says. I'm not sure how she's assessed that I'm doing well, but I can practically hear the 'in spite of' in her tone.

'Thanks,' I say, glancing around the room for any form of escape.

'Your mother was . . . She was quite a character. Lovely singer.'

I nod and smile, draining my glass.

She lowers her voice, looking at me like I'm a walking misery memoir whose covers she can't wait to crack open. 'Must have been difficult, you know, with you so young when she—'

'I'm just going to grab some more wine,' I interrupt quickly. 'Can I get you anything?'

She shakes her head, holding up her orange juice piously. Bet it has a slug of vodka in it. I head back to the kitchen.

This hasn't been so bad, though, overall. At least that's what I try to tell myself – and it hasn't really, but somehow I still feel like I'm untethered, like I have no real ties to this place, these people even. Would it have felt different if Anita was here? I've not wanted her to be with me quite so badly in a long time. We were a unit, Mum and me. And now I'm on my own. It really hits me again, all of a sudden, and tears threaten from the back of my throat.

Bypassing the kitchen, where a small gathering has inevitably converged, I open the door to what thankfully turns out to be the downstairs loo. I vaguely hear Sylvia call to me from the group in the kitchen, but I close the door and sit down on the toilet seat, wineglass still in my hand. I place it next to the sink, taking slow, deep breaths to try and calm myself.

'Taylor, sweetheart?' I hear Sylvia's tentative voice coming through the door. Déjà vu – that same tone, muffled by a wooden door, would be the response to my latest 'You're not my mum'-based teenage tantrum. I quickly wash my hands and open the door.

'We're going to do the cake,' Sylvia says, studying my face as I emerge and force a smile.

'Ah, OK. Listen, Aunty Sylvia, I think after that I'll need to be heading off. I'll just ring for a cab and then after the cake—'

'Nonsense, love. I'll drop you.'

'Oh, no, it's fine—'

'Of course not, Taylor darling. I can run you down there straight after.'

'OK. Sure, yeah, if you don't mind.' I smile gratefully. I realise there's actually not enough gratitude in the world for how patient Sylvia's been with me, and guilt coils tighter within me for not being able to show her that. I wasn't the only one abandoned by Anita; I wasn't the only one hurt. I'm not the only one that must constantly think, *What if I had*, not the only one that feels her absence every day. But Sylvia never did like a fuss – in so many ways the opposite of her sister.

She gives me a quick wink, and heads back to the kitchen, rummaging in the pocket of her cardigan for a lighter for the candles on the cake.

*

Sylvia's Micra rumbles along loudly as I stare down at the slice of cake, wrapped in foil and nestled in my hands rather than my bag, so as not to get crushed. The icing will probably be mashed into the aluminium anyway, but Sylvia insisted, and frankly, who can say no to cake?

'The trains are on the half-hour, so you should be fine,' she says, and I nod. 'You know which platform it is, don't you, sweetheart?'

I nod again, grinning at her.

'Sorry, darling. I forget you're not a teenager any more.'

'No, I . . . It's nice,' I say, and she smiles over at me as she flicks the indicator. She pulls in to the station's car park, both of us silent as she reverses into a spot.

'OK, love,' she says, blinking hard as she glances at me. I suddenly notice she has tears in her eyes. 'I'm . . . so glad we got to see you, especially now. When it's this time of year, coming up to the anniversary, I just get a bit . . . I miss her.'

I swallow. 'I know. So do I.'

She switches off the engine and reaches over to squeeze my hand, taking another deep breath. 'But you're all right.' She says it as a statement, not a question.

I nod, unable to reply. Am I?

'Thanks for the lift,' I say, clearing my throat of the thick wad of my own tears that has nestled there. 'It's been really nice to see you all.' I mean it, I realise. I reach over to hug her, and she rubs my back, angling awkwardly over the gear stick, then pulls back and nods out towards the station.

'Go on, you'll miss your train.'

I open the car door and step out. 'Speak soon.'

'Yeah. Keep in touch, sweetheart. Thank you so much for coming.'

I shut the car door and she waves jauntily. *Back to business.* I smile back at her, and then head into the station just as a train pulls up to the platform.

As the carriage doors hiss shut behind me and I fall into a seat, a knot in my stomach that I hadn't really noticed was still there begins to unravel. It's kind of sad that I feel tense around the only family I have. I try to imagine a future when that's not the case – when Sylvia and Malcolm are long and happily married, and Linda's left home to do some impossibly cool thing, and I'm ... well, I don't know. That part's tough. But we might all go round for Sunday lunch and laugh and joke and be a family of sorts.

I notice I'm staring at a little girl sitting opposite me in a green coat, her short legs jutting over the edge of the seat as she sits next to a young man, barely past the stage of acne, who has one hand draped protectively around her tiny shoulders while the other holds a mobile phone, texting rapidly with his thumb. She grins at me and I grin back, glancing at her father – brother? No. Father. Of course, Sylvia and Linda aren't the only family I have – just the only family I know. There could be half-siblings, cousins, grandparents out there on my dad's side – there more than likely are.

I turn and stare out of the window at the green fields rushing past, wondering why I'm so incurious about him. Anita was always my mother and my father. And my child, in a way. Taylor Senior probably knows nothing about me – and worse, if he did or does, he clearly hasn't felt the need to find me in twenty-two years. He was itinerant even in the way he chose to pursue music – a session musician, not a permanent fixture. Just passing through on his way somewhere else.

Maybe that's what I should do. Follow in his invisible footsteps, move on, keep moving, never stop. Perhaps I've got a restless spirit? When I do think about the one thing, the one

person who really makes me feel grounded, centred, still ...
The feeling scares me, and I shake away the image of Ryan's face.

I can't hold on to him. I'm not allowed.

The girl and young man stand up, ready to get off at the next stop, and she turns and smiles at me again.

'Bye,' she says.

'Bye,' I say, smiling at her and glancing up at the young man, but he ignores the interaction. He takes her hand and gently but firmly guides her off the train. I watch them walk off, hand in hand, as the doors slide shut.

Glancing at the empty seat next to me, I notice a tabloid newspaper. I scan the showbiz section, killing time, but when I turn the page, my finger grazes the serrated edge and I manage to give myself a paper cut. As I raise my hand to my mouth to suck away the pain, something on the page makes me freeze. It's only a tiny article, a little square in the column headed IN BRIEF.

Body by Riverbank Ruled Suicide.

It's about David Barnett. No more than a handful of words, probably picked up by a solitary reporter trying to fill space. There's a short quote from Cynthia March, and I stare at the words.

'My son will finally be at peace now. It was very difficult for him ... very difficult.'

I reach down and touch the corner of the page, and a pinprick of blood from my finger seeps into the paper. Slowly, carefully, I begin to tear around the small square of writing, folding it into an even tinier square. I pull my purse out of my bag and tuck the square inside, deep into one corner. I feel like I need to take it with me.

'Are you finished with that?' a voice across the aisle asks.

134

I glance up and see a middle-aged guy in a suit, looking at me with a smile that says he doesn't necessarily just want the paper. I refold the pages back to the start and hand it to him.

'Go ahead,' I murmur, then turn away from him back to the window.

It's beginning to get dark outside, and I push my gaze out through my reflection to the gathering lights of the city.

Chapter Thirteen

Five cheerful musical notes wake me early – far too early for a Sunday. They repeat themselves, over and over again, until I push through the fug of sleep and realise they're messages coming in on my phone. I blink at the screen, then smile. They're from Marcy, typically unaware of time zones. She sounds happy, she says she misses me, and I tell her the same. I'm pleased that I can genuinely tell her the visit to Sylvia's wasn't the cluster-fuck it could so easily have been, but I do feel like I'm being a little dishonest when I type that I'm feeling better.

I'm definitely feeling hungry. I pull on my tracksuit bottoms and dressing gown, and head to the kitchen to pour myself some cereal. As I crunch, staring out of the window at the white sky, I bite my lip a little, remembering Ryan's smile at this same sound the night before last. Charlie trots out of their room to come and investigate, letting out an experimental yip that makes me jump guiltily. He stands, looking up at me in judgement, then yawns. I shake some biscuits into his bowl before returning to my own. Seeing as I'm up, I suppose I could take him out, get some fresh air. He looks up from his kibbles, as though he can read my mind. I wish I could say it's because I want to spend more quality time with the mutt, but I have an ulterior motive. One that makes me feel guilty for another reason.

I don't know if it's morbid curiosity, or if I think it might set me on the path to some magical answer, but I've realised, since they read out his address at the hearing, that David Barnett's flat can't be more than a ten-minute walk from here. I just want to see what it's like, where he lived. What he saw as he came out of his building and walked to his car, those last moments.

I look up as I hear Marcy's bedroom door opening, hangers rattling on the back of it like a warning system. I glance down at my attire, disappointed at its tattiness, but glad that at least I have more on than last time. But when Ryan emerges, I can't say the same for him. Charlie scampers over to him and Ryan pats his head, giving his own forehead a sleepy rub. He's wearing his long cotton pyjama bottoms and nothing else. I hope the dog will keep him distracted a while longer so I can ogle, but Ryan looks up at me a moment later, and I sweep my gaze down to his bare feet and then away, my face warming.

'Morning,' he says through a yawn. He rolls his shoulders, causing the tight muscles in his chest and stomach to ripple, and squeezes his eyes shut for a moment.

'Morning,' I just about manage to murmur. 'You're up early. Coffee?' I turn quickly to start a pot before he can answer, using it as a distraction from the heat spreading rapidly over my body.

'Mmm,' he says, his voice fading, and I turn to see he's gone back into the bedroom. He emerges again, pulling on a T-shirt, and I sigh a little in disappointment and relief.

But then he smiles and walks closer to me, and the look in his eyes makes my own begin to widen in strange hope and confusion. He reaches around behind my head and opens the cupboard to grab two mugs, setting them on the counter as I look up at him, frozen to the spot. He stays next to me for a moment, and when he steps away I feel the ache of an unfinished gesture, like I need to find a reason to touch him. I take a deep breath and listen to the coffee machine begin to percolate.

Ryan folds his arms tightly, as if he's trying to restrain them, then leans against the fridge. 'So how was yesterday?'

I open my mouth, about to answer, but then I think again. I wonder if Marcy told him to keep an eye on me, with all the Aunt Sylvia stuff. Maybe he does feel sorry for me, in spite of what he said at the restaurant. The thought makes my shoulders slump. I glance down at the tiled floor, noticing a stray cornflake has fallen there, and bend down and pick it up, put it in the bin. I realise I haven't answered his question. He looks at me, his eyebrows drawn together in concern.

'Uh, sorry,' I say. 'Yeah, it was actually a lot better than I thought it would be. It was . . . it was nice to see them all.' I try to make my face look open and together and worry-free. I probably look like a maniac. The machine croaks out the last of its coffee into the glass jug and I turn to it gratefully. I take a couple of steps over to hand Ryan his.

'Good,' he says. 'That's great.'

'Yeah.'

I press my lips together, feeling like he has something over me, whilst I know nothing really about him. A bead of irritation settles in my chest, and I take a hot gulp of coffee.

'Do you see much of *your* family?' I ask, looking at him challengingly.

He gazes into his mug for a moment, considering. 'Not as much as I'd like to, no.' He looks like he wants to say more, but doesn't quite know where to start. I regret having asked; it's too early in the morning to be getting into this. Charlie trots between us, and I look down at him.

'I was thinking I might take Charlie out for a walk. I could use some fresh air,' I say, clumsily changing the subject.

'Oh. Are you sure?'

'Yeah, yeah, it's cool. I don't mind doing the early run, maybe you could take him out later?'

'Course.'

He sips again at his coffee and we fall silent. Eventually I put my mug in the sink, still half full, and start to leave the kitchen.

'They live in Warwickshire. My mum and dad.'

I stop and turn to him, and his eyes hold me steady.

'Oh, right,' I say. 'Not too far.'

'No. Couple of hours on the train.' He takes another sip of coffee. 'My ... birth mum lives closer. Lewisham.'

I look at him for a moment. 'Oh. That ... that is close.'

'I only ... I didn't know – didn't want to know – where she lived. But last year, I suppose curiosity got the better of me and I looked her up. Talk about your awkward visits,' he says, his mouth curling in a wry smile.

I take a step towards him, wanting to reach up, to touch his face, say thank you, like they do in those therapy groups. *Thanks for sharing.* He didn't say a lot, but it feels like he's told me something very important. I push my hands deep into the pockets of my dressing gown to keep them safe.

'Yeah, I bet,' I say, returning his smile, hoping I'm conveying some degree of gratitude. And not too much burning hot desire. I draw in a deep breath. 'I should probably take the pooch out.'

His smile broadens into a grin, and he laughs. God, what a beautiful sound.

'Yeah, you'd better.'

I turn away, my fists clenched tensely inside my pockets, and head into my room. I take off my dressing gown and throw it on to the bed, then pull on my trainers and a hoodie. Charlie trots eagerly over to me as I come out of my room again. Ryan's still standing in the doorway to the kitchen, and I realise he's staring at me as I unhook the leash from its place by the front door. The dog pants in anticipation.

'Uh, I've been looking for that,' Ryan says, still staring, half smiling, half frowning.

'Huh?'

'My sweatshirt.'

I look down at the faded yellow hoodie. *Oh my God. It's his?*

'Shit, I – I thought it was Marcy's. I've had it for a while, I just thought—' Jesus, does he think I stole it, so that I could . . . who knows what? I blush and start to take it off, and he holds up his hands.

'Please no, no, I didn't mean . . . It's . . . It looks good on you.' He looks at me and bites his lip. His words hang between us, and my breathing speeds up. I blink a few times, but he doesn't look away.

'I suppose it did seem a bit big,' I say in a quiet voice, almost involuntarily. I can't help chuckling at how ridiculous it sounds, and soon he laughs softly too, but then shakes his head.

'No. You're . . . It's . . . fine.' He swallows visibly.

I chuckle again, nervously now. 'Thanks.'

I turn and open the door, grabbing my coat and patting my thigh. Charlie rushes eagerly out, and I give Ryan one last glance before I pull the door shut. Standing at the top of the stairs, I watch the dog jog down, oblivious. My heartbeat feels like it's being played by Jack DeJohnette. I close my eyes for a second, then open them and race down and out on to the street.

Outside, I clip the leash to Charlie's collar, cursing the fact that the sweatshirt thing made me forget my purse and cigarettes. My face feels tight with the cold and with the effort of trying not to replay the look on Ryan's face. Why should it seem so intimate, wearing his clothes? Why does any of this feel the way it does? Am I imagining things? I don't think I am. And it's starting to scare me, because it makes me feel hopeful – something I haven't felt in a long time. For something I know I can't have. It's like a kiss and a slap at the same time. Jesus, I really need a smoke.

There's some loose change in my coat pocket, and the jingle of it between my fingers makes me think of Anita sending me down to the shops for her Marlboro Reds, during the times when she stopped caring about whether they would ruin her voice. A handful of coins from her, heading to the corner shop eagerly, feeling so grown-up. The guy in there knew my mum, and I think he felt sorry for me so he let me buy them, as long as nobody else was in the shop to see him sell fags to a minor. But tasks like that also brought a rolling, acid worry in the pit of my stomach – the start of a slide. The lack of care. A burst of laziness, no warning me to be quick, not to talk to anyone. I'd come back and hand her the cigarettes, and she'd thank me absently, staring out of the window, her limbs seeming a burden.

I look down at Charlie, pissing merrily against a lamppost, and when he finishes I remember my intention to walk a particular path today.

I've got about halfway to David Barnett's street when an almost-familiar figure rounds the corner and almost collides with me.

'Whoa—'

'Sorry, I—'

We both speak simultaneously, and then stop. He looks from me to the dog and back again, and I blink up at him, his breath coming in rapid, panting plumes in the air, the front of his grey T-shirt soaked with sweat. The edges of his hair cling in thin tendrils to his forehead. Realisation begins to dawn on him.

141

'You were there, the other day,' he says.

I nod. 'Yeah.'

'You were . . . You found David, didn't you?' His eyes search my face as though I might still have some of the experience imprinted on me. He'd be right, I guess. 'The police officer said you—'

'Yeah,' I say again. 'That's right.' I'm not sure if I should apologise, or if he was going to thank me.

'Sorry, I'm Jonathan. I was his flatmate.'

'Yeah, I remember. I'm Taylor.'

He wipes his hand on his T-shirt and then extends it towards me. It's still a bit clammy, and he pulls it back and rests it on one hip, his breathing starting to slow. 'Do you live close by?'

'Yeah, not far.'

'Actually, yeah, makes sense,' he says, almost to himself, but then meets my eyes. 'Is this your dog, then?'

'My flatmate's, actually. I just seem to end up walking him a lot.'

Jonathan nods and smiles a little. Charlie sniffs busily around his trainers and his taut, hairy legs. I wonder if he's not getting cold now he's stopped jogging. He reaches down and pats the dog's head dismissively – I can tell he's not a big animal person. I pull on the lead, and Charlie scuttles off to sniff some fascinating area of pavement. I start to feel a bit uncomfortable, like I've been busted trying to stalk David Barnett's life after death. Jonathan draws in a breath and I look up expectantly.

'Listen, Taylor. I know this is going to seem a bit weird—'

My eyes widen in spite of myself, and he stops at my expression and smiles a little.

'It's nothing bad. Well, not really, it's just . . . There were some words in the note Dave left, for whoever found him.' His jaw clenches and he glances down at the ground for a second.

My throat has gone dry. 'What do you mean?'

'He ... Dave left a suicide note. He'd not done that before, the other times. That's why I knew this one was serious. When I saw it, I just knew: he was really gone this time.'

I don't know what to say, so I just nod again, and Jonathan shuffles his feet.

'Look, I know this wasn't you were expecting when you just popped out to take the dog for a walk. I meant to say something when you were at the hearing, but Cynthia said we should just leave it,' he says, looking off at Charlie distractedly for a moment, before returning his gaze to me. 'She has it now anyway,' he says quietly. 'The note.' He stops, and shakes his head. 'Do you know what, actually I think she was right. It was the funeral yesterday, so it's all just a bit raw.' He frowns, like he's angry now, and I can understand. Helplessness, anger, sorrow. The feelings all fighting for position.

'Oh. OK,' I say, sad for him, but almost relieved. I'm not sure I want to know what David Barnett said.

'Basically, he was sorry. To us, to you for discovering ... ' He shakes his head again, and when he looks up at me again, his eyes are slick and reflective. 'Dave always was quick to apologise.' His voice is quieter now, remembering.

'Thank you,' I murmur. 'For telling me.' I feel bad because I'm not sure if I mean it. David Barnett was sorry. But sometimes a 'Sorry' can sound more like a 'Fuck you.' I try to tamp down memories, of wanting to believe that word, but wondering why, if she knew it would hurt us so much, she would do it in the first place.

Jonathan clears his throat and swallows, and I can't help echoing him. Then he begins to flex his feet, bend his knees and shake out his legs, as though they're starting to cramp up.

'I'd better get going. Sorry, that was ... ' He tails off, shaking his head, and laughs a little incredulously.

'Yeah,' I say, and smile back sympathetically.

He pauses, lowers his voice. 'Or ... Look, actually, the flat's not that far, if you wanted to have, like ... a cup of tea or something?'

A look passes over his face, and I understand what he means by 'or something'. He's hopeful, lonely, throwing caution to the wind. I have to admit, I find the offer tempting – and not because I want to sleep with him. The only reason I'd entertain the idea is because I'd really like to see where David Barnett lived. But I know that would be a step too far. I do understand why Jonathan asked, though. Another body, some comfort.

'Oh ...' I begin, and he blanches, fearing his gamble was poorly judged.

'Sorry—'

'No, thanks for the offer. Tea would have been nice. I just ... I need to be getting back myself. Thanks, though.'

'OK. Yes, of course. Sure,' he stutters quickly.

'Uh, take care.'

'You too.'

I pat my thigh and Charlie comes trotting closer to me. Jonathan begins to jog away at a fast pace, and I feel a bit bad. Maybe he really just wanted someone to talk to. Was that selfish, to deny him?

I turn round and start to walk back to the flat, thinking about David Barnett's apology. It seems so English – *terribly sorry for the inconvenience*. I shake my head and smile a little. It's kind of crazy, leaving a note at all. The idea that you could even attempt to explain an act so inexplicable, so seemingly *impossible*.

Anita's note had an odd clarity to it; the writing and the words were so meticulously clear, like she didn't want to be misunderstood this time. I wonder if that's how David Barnett's was too.

Charlie pulls up suddenly, jerking me out of my thoughts, and I pause with him. He looks up at me, then squats and begins to take a shit on the pavement. I nod.

'Yup. That's about right.'

Chapter Fourteen

'How long now?'

I roll my eyes. It's been sort of nice having Luc here for the whole afternoon, but he really has no clue quite how slowly time passes when it's heading towards closing up.

'Ten minutes.'

'Still?'

I laugh. 'It was fifteen five minutes ago. That's how time works, isn't it?'

'Ugh.' He leans against the counter with exaggerated fatigue.

'It's not my fault you were too lazy to go home.'

'Well, you clearly need company or you're at risk of going crazy in this shithole. I mean, bloody hell, it's like some sort of time-sucking vortex. I can't believe you do this every day.' He straightens up a bit. 'Anyway, like I said, I'm meeting my mates at six so I figured I might as well hang out.'

'And I appreciate it deeply, Lucas.' I finish cashing up and push the till drawer shut emphatically. He's right, though; this place really is starting get me down. I mean, it's only Monday and it feels like the week is stretching out ahead of me without end. I wonder, not for the first time today, what Marcy's doing right now. Why didn't *I* force myself to do something more exciting to earn money? But then again, Marcy has the uncertainty of auditions, the competitive back-biting, the up-and-down pay. Not that I'm exactly swimming in riches.

I turn to Luc, curious. 'So when you're not here, having your time sucked and all,' I begin, and he grins at me suggestively.

'Yes?'

'You manage to, like, make your rent and pay your bills just by doing the photography?'

'Just about. I mean, selling to papers or magazines, licensing . . . it's a bit tooth-and-nail, but yeah. Why, are you thinking about jacking this in?'

'If only,' I say. 'What would I do?'

'You can do anything, Taylor Jenkins.' He looks at me earnestly, and I shake my head.

'In the real world? Not so much.'

'I'm serious.'

I raise an eyebrow at that, and then puff out a breath in frustration. 'I see all these people around me doing things that are just . . . what they love. Creative things. And you're all managing to get on with life just fine. You, Marcy, Ry – her boyfriend. I mean, it's like, did I miss a memo or something? Or did I just miss my chance?' My voice rises at that and I shake my head, realising I'm getting a bit too het up about it. I'm thinking of Anita and how hard she found it pursuing her dream. When you hit middle age and the dream of success is still floating out of reach, when you haven't yet soared on its wings into the realms of reality, then what? 'Sorry,' I say, turning to Luc, who's studying me with his head cocked.

'You'll find the thing. That *thing*,' he says.

I don't tell him I think I already know what 'that thing' is, but I'm too scared to pursue it. I can't even remember the last time I tried to sing – *really* sing – even by myself.

Luc takes a step towards me, unsatisfied with the expression on my face. 'You will.'

I nod. 'Thanks, mate. I hope so.'

'Would a snog help?'

I laugh. 'Come on. Let's close up.'

Luc holds his hand up for a high-five and I slap it emphatically, then head over to the door to turn the CLOSED sign over. Only he can pull off ironic hand gestures. I'm actually pretty glad he hung about.

'So you're gonna come, yeah?' he says, grabbing our stuff. I'm not sure I can face a table full of strangers at the pub, but maybe I should try and force myself to have some fun. Jeez, I almost bit Luc's head off for just enjoying life a minute ago. 'Come on. Just for one,' he says, handing me my bag and coat. He can't get out of here quickly enough, it seems. I consider things for a minute. I'm still not entirely sure of Ryan's routine, and it might actually be better if we didn't spend long evenings in the flat alone . . .

'Yeah, go on then. Just for one.'

A triumphant grin spreads across Luc's face. We take the short walk to the pub mostly in silence, and while that's usually not a problem with me and Luc, now I'm starting to worry he's a bit concerned by my everyone's-having-fun-without-me speech. But he's never been a judgemental sort, and definitely not one to dwell. I suddenly think, *We're friends.* Not like me and Marcy, but it's nice to have someone uncomplicated in my life. I smile over at him as we stride down the pavement, hands in pockets, and he winks back with a look that makes me wonder if he thinks of our relationship as purely platonic. But I'm fairly sure he's more of an opportunist than a pining brooder; that's my department.

'So, Ben's a bit of a cock, just as a heads-up,' he says in a low voice as we arrive, holding the pub door open for me to pass through. 'Sara always insists on inviting him. The others are cool.'

I chuckle, but feel a bit nervous as he guides me over to a table for two that has four of his friends huddled around it.

'Guys, this is my mate Taylor, from the bookshop. Taylor, that's Sara, Ben, Nico, Dom.'

I wave a bit self-consciously and wonder how we're all going to fit around the table. I glance around, but the guy who was meant to be a cock has already stood up to retrieve some chairs. I raise an eyebrow at Luc and he mouths, 'Trust me.' I smile, and Sara looks at us in a slightly curious, slightly territorial manner. I hope I haven't horribly misjudged this and it really was some surreptitious way for Luc to ask me out? But my ego is clearly getting away from me; he leans over to Nico and asks eagerly about a girl with a name that already screams muse or model or impossibly beautiful something, particularly by the way Luc practically drools on the table when his friend tells him she'll be arriving soon. Ben gestures for me to sit down, but I decide I need a minute to acclimatise.

'Actually, I might go to the bar ...'

'No, don't worry, I can—' Luc begins, but I wave him off.

'Honestly, it's cool. Are you guys all right for drinks?' I look at their full glasses with some relief, and they all nod and decline. 'What'll you have, Lucas?'

'Pint of Guinness?'

'Cool.'

I head over to the bar, sort of glad that it's so busy that I'll have a bit of a wait, but as I fish in my too-big handbag for my purse, someone leans over to me.

'Come here often?'

I roll my eyes, almost amused that a guy would actually

use that line, but then my pulse quickens as recognition floods through me. I turn to him, my stomach leaping nervously. Our eyes meet, and for a moment it's almost like we could start again, now, as if we'd never met before.

'Hey,' I murmur.

'Hey.'

'What are you doing here?'

Ryan laughs a little, a warm rumble from his chest, and reaches up to scratch the stubble on his chin. I badly want to touch it. 'Oof. You really know how to make a guy feel welcome,' he says.

I feel prickling heat rise up the back of my neck. 'No I didn't mean . . . Sorry.' But I feel a smile on the edges of my lips. 'To be fair, it wasn't much of a pick-up line.' God, why did I say that?

'True. I think I can do better,' he says, smiling too, but his eyes burning with something more than mirth.

We regard each other for a while, like we're deciding whether to continue flirting or fall back to our agreed parameters.

'Yeah. Well, these things are important, you know,' I say. 'You have to consider what sort of answer you're hoping to get. I mean, "Come here often?" gives the impression that your follow-up question is going to involve, like, asking for tips on what to order from the bar-snack menu.'

He laughs gorgeously, and I feel like all I ever want is to make him do that.

'So what would you advise is best to say?' he asks, his voice low and warm. Someone pushes in front of us to reach the bar, but I hardly notice.

'Uh . . . ' I swallow. 'Start simple. Introduce yourself. Ask a woman her name.'

He looks at me for a moment. 'OK.' He reaches out his hand. 'I'm Ryan. May I ask your name?'

I look down at his outstretched palm and slowly put my hand in his. He's still wearing his coat, and my fingertips brush the navy wool of the edge of his sleeve, then my hand nestles into place. He doesn't try to shake it or pull away, just holds it there as silence settles between us. I pray my palm doesn't start to sweat – I'm sure he can feel my pulse quickening; I can feel his . . .

'My name's Taylor,' I whisper.

His eyes bore into mine. 'A beautiful name, for a beautiful woman.'

Just then, a teenage girl carrying two large white wines stumbles, knocking into my shoulder, and our hands spring apart. She squeaks an apology before tottering away, and I turn back to Ryan.

'Too much?' he asks, his jaw tense now.

'M-maybe, yeah.'

'Yeah. I'll have to work on that,' he murmurs.

He takes a step towards the bar, but it's still busy. He leans his guitar case up against it, not looking at me, and I wonder foolishly if I've done something wrong, if he's angry or irritated. I want to reach out and touch his arm, but I don't. I rest my arm on the bar and put my elbow straight into a puddle of beer.

'Shit,' I say, swiping at it ineffectually, and finally he turns and looks at me again. 'Uh, so are you meeting a mate, or . . . ?' My heart sinks at the small-talk being emitted by my mouth. I want to rewind time a few minutes.

'No, I'm just on my way somewhere, killing a bit of time.' He gestures to a paperback sticking out of his pocket. I wonder if he was trying to avoid being at home with me?

'Are you playing somewhere tonight?'

I try not to sound hopeful or inquisitive. Though I'd love to hear him play, I don't want him to think I'm angling for an invite. I glance up just in time to see the barman give up on us and move along to the next people at the bar. Ryan sighs a little at that and cranes his neck to try and catch another server's eye. Remembering my question, he shrugs a little without looking back at me.

'I might do later,' he says.

I look up at his profile, at its perfect angles and contours, as he flags down another barman and then turns to me suddenly, catching me staring.

'What would you like?' he asks quickly.

'Oh, don't worry, I'll get it. I'm with a workmate, so ...' I glance at Luc's friends, who are chattering away happily, not seeming to notice how long I've been gone, and then turn to the barman, blushing, though I don't know why I'm finding this all so awkward now. 'Could I have a pint of Guinness, a gin and tonic – single – and ...' I look expectantly at Ryan.

'I'll have a Beck's, please.' He looks at me. 'Thanks.'

His gaze drifts over to Luc's table as I pay for the drinks.

'Do you want to come over and ...?' I begin.

'No, no, it's cool,' he says. 'I'm not going to be here long. I should leave you guys to it. Have a good evening, though.'

'Oh, I'm not going to be late, I just got sort of dragged into a drink after work. Luc's going off with his mates after ... I mean, I'm not going with them.' Ugh. I think he gets the point. Ryan reaches over to pick up his drink, and his shoulders seem to relax a little. He nods, and that beautiful smile finally returns.

'Cheers,' he says, and I clink my glass to his. It reminds me of Marcy, and that familiar stab of guilt is back in the pit of my stomach. His face falls a little too.

'Well, I'd better be getting back over there,' I say. 'I'll see you later, I guess.'

'Yeah.'

We look at each other a moment longer, then I pick up Luc's

Guinness, feeling the inevitable cold slosh of it dribbling down the glass over my fingers. I walk back towards the table, feeling Ryan's gaze on my back.

Luc grins up at me as I put his drink down in front of him and wipe my hand on my jeans. He raises his eyebrows at me and glances towards the bar, but doesn't say anything – he must have seen Ryan and thought I was getting hit on while I was buying the drinks. If only this was some *Sliding Doors*/bizarro universe where it could be that simple, and not the complicated, unhealthy, torturous thing that it really is.

'Who can be arsed to go all the way west? It's a Monday fucking night, Nico!' Sara is saying.

'But he's really good and he's not doing another show for, like, three months after this,' Dom protests.

'We probably won't even get in,' says Ben, nodding at Sara supportively.

'Well, I don't give a shit, but the carpets in here are giving me S.A.D.,' Luc says, nudging me gently with his shoulder. 'What do you reckon, T? Should we stay east or jump on the tube to this gig?'

'Oh . . . If it was me I'd probably just stick around here.'

'What, aren't you coming with?' Dom says, pulling one hand over his full-on hipster beard. 'You should! Blow off some steam – you probably need it, hanging with this reprobate at work all day.'

Luc throws a pretzel at him, but it hits Ben, who picks it up and eats it.

'Oh, thanks, really,' I say. 'Maybe another time. I'm pretty knackered, to be honest.'

Dom nods in understanding, and Sara holds up her hand. 'Let's have one more here then head off to wherever.' She stands up, smoothing down her Van Halen T-shirt. Pretty much every one of Luc's friends seems to have an ironic fashion sense. 'Taylor, another G and T?'

'Erm . . .' I look down at my almost-full glass, then turn and crane my neck to try and spot Ryan at the bar – I'd offer to help her with the drinks if he was still there – but there's no sign of him, and I have a feeling he just had a couple of swigs of his beer and then left pretty much as soon as I came back to the table. He didn't say goodbye. I curse my sinking disappointment.

'Yeah, go on Taylor, one more,' Ben says, getting up.

I shake my head. 'Honestly, I'm good.'

He shrugs, then turns to Sara. 'I'll help you get them in, little lady.' They head over to the bar and Luc rolls his eyes, but then Nico's phone beeps and he looks at it and grins.

'She'll be here in fifteen minutes, she says.' He and Luc bump fists, and it's my turn to roll my eyes.

'Who's this mystery lady, then, Luc?' I ask.

He sighs dreamily and says Xiomara (yes, with a freaking X) is Nico's Colombian cousin who's just moved to London as she's landed a big modelling contract, and who sounds like she's a few catwalks away from strapping Victoria's Secret wings to her back from the way he's practically turning into a puddle at the mention of her name. I decide it's best I get out of here before she turns up – I feel inadequate enough as it is. I turn to Luc while his friends continue to chatter.

'I think I'm gonna head off.'

He faux-pouts. 'Sure?'

I nod, touched that he really does seem to want me to come out with them, but I know if I have any more to drink my thoughts are going to edge too far into the morose. Already memories of bumping into David Barnett's flatmate yesterday, and that apologetic missive from beyond the grave, are starting to edge into my mind. Luc stands up and gives me a hug, making

154

sure I'm fine to get home. I do feel a bit unsteady, but I realise it's because I haven't had dinner. I decide to stop for some chips on my way home. Go nuts, I tell myself wryly.

'See you tomorrow, yeah? Have a good one.' I say goodbye to his mates and head out.

It's dark and cold and raining. I pull out my umbrella, open it and balance it on my shoulder while I light a cigarette, watching the smoke dance between the raindrops. I then quickly pace the few streets over to the fish-and-chip shop. I order, over-salt my chips and drench them in vinegar, grateful the rain's stopped by the time I leave so I can eat on the way home. By the time I get in there's only a soggy piece of cod left, which I scrunch into the newspaper and chuck away. Just a shade too late, I notice Charlie's hopeful gaze as he patters towards me.

'Sorry, mate,' I say, and my voice echoes against the kitchen lino.

It's quiet. Ryan's not home yet, and I don't expect he'll be back for a while – it can't be much past nine, but it feels more like midnight. The fish and chips have made my stomach feel better, but I think it's too late to rescue my mind from the morose thoughts. I wash the grease and vinegar off my fingers, and stand for a moment, listening to the silence. The slow, regular drip of the tap that won't tighten no matter how much we turn it. Charlie beginning to snore; he's gone back to Marcy's room and I can see him settled on the bed, head on his paws. Everything else still, quiet, waiting. If I weren't standing here, this would all still be happening, unobserved, in the darkness. If I weren't here, it would still all exist.

Is that how they feel, when they decide? That removing themselves from existence wouldn't make a difference to the world? After all, people say it like it's a comfort: 'Life goes on.'

But it's not true. I know nature supposedly abhors a vacuum or whatever, but that's all that seems to be left behind when someone dies. Not a neatly filled space where they used to be, but a gaping hole of emptiness. I feel like I walk around with a big jigsaw piece of my heart missing where my mother should be.

I sigh shakily, pressing a tear away from my eye. Why am I so lonely? It's ironic, considering the people always crowding my mind. Anita. Marcy. David Barnett. Ryan. Ryan. Ryan . . .

Switching on some lights might help, I think, and laugh at myself mirthlessly. Allegedly it's the best medicine, but Anita used to say singing was better, and I think I agree. When she could bring herself to, if she hadn't sunk too low, she'd sing and sing until her spirits lifted, and mine too.

If I shut my eyes, I can almost hear her, still.

I clear my throat and try a line from one of her favourites, 'The Nearness of You'. It's not quite the same. It's nowhere near. But those words – they're romantic, but they're also about comfort. I miss hers. I miss when she was my everything, when I didn't know that any harm could come to her.

I take a deep breath and sing another line, louder now. It bounces back to me from the hard kitchen surfaces. Through Marcy's half-open bedroom door I see Charlie's head move, his ears prick up. I smile a bit, dedicating it to him. Closing my eyes again, I let the song flow out of me, hearing each word as it escapes my throat, playing with scales, imagining harmonies, unthinkingly letting my body become music—

I stop as I feel a gaze on me. Not the dog's.

My heart judders and I clamp my mouth shut, opening my eyes. Anger wells up unexpectedly.

'Sorry—' Ryan begins.

'You scared me,' I say through a clenched jaw.

'I didn't mean to, I just . . . You didn't hear me come in, and I didn't want you to stop. You have a great voice. A *really*—'

'You should have said something.' I feel tears threatening, along with hot, skin-melting embarrassment. 'You shouldn't have been listening.' Yeah, that was a stupid thing to say.

'I couldn't really help it.'

'Still, it's . . . it's private. I don't—'

'I'm sorry,' he says again, holding his hands up apologetically. 'I should have made it obvious I was here. It's just I've never heard you . . . I didn't really expect it, that's all.'

'What do you mean?' I blush, having a feeling that I know. That's why I try and avoid singing in front of people – they might start paying attention, and that's sort of my fear and my out-of-reach hope, all rolled into one. Anita used to try and encourage me, telling me how good I was, but when she was there, with that voice of *hers* . . . Why even try to compete? Sometimes I have a nightmare where I'm forced to wear one of her old dresses and stand on the stage of one of the tiny dark clubs where she used to perform, and I'm made to sing one of her songs, but only a high-pitched scream comes out, and I wake up with that scream still in my throat—

'I mean . . .' Ryan is beginning to reply, but trails off and looks at me. 'Are you all right?'

I nod and then turn around to run a glass of water from the tap. I take three sips, swallowing hard, before I face him. He's taking off his coat, and he hangs it up in the hallway before walking over to me, his frame silhouetted in the light from the corridor.

'Are you sure?'

I want to say no. I want him to put his arms around me.

'Yes. I'm sorry, Ryan . . .' I have to pause, feeling his name on my lips. 'I don't really sing in front of other people, it's a weird thing of mine. I didn't mean to bite your head off.'

'You should,' he says quietly, then realises what it sounds like, and I see his teeth gleam white in the gloom as he chuckles. 'I mean, other people should hear you sing.'

It reminds me of his own secretive musicianship. 'What about you? I thought you were playing tonight?'

'Oh. I didn't go in the end. I decided I'd rather . . . just chill, I guess. Pretty tired.' He glances away.

Maybe he wasn't avoiding me after all. I bite my lip.

'Yeah.' I take a deep breath, smelling the damp as the rain evaporates off him, leaving a heady scent in the air around us. My lips part. His eyes roam down towards them, then flick back up to meet mine. We stare at one another for what feels like eternity. I have to move away or—

He sighs loudly. 'I better . . . I think I'm just gonna hang out in the room. Read a bit. I'll say good-night.'

'OK.'

I might as well get ready for bed. I head to the bathroom and squeeze toothpaste on to my brush, cleaning my teeth for longer than usual as I try to sort through all the feelings jumbling in my mind. I spit hard into the sink, rinse and straighten up. Wash and dry my face. Pee, wipe, stand, flush. Wash my hands. Then I pause with my hand on the bathroom doorknob, listening closely to make sure the coast is clear, hating how ridiculous it is to sneak around avoiding him, like I can't control myself. Like I don't trust myself.

I walk across the hall quickly and into my room, slumping down on to the bed. Leaning against the pillows, I flip open my laptop, plug in my headphones and decide to try and watch a film. I start one up, but after a few minutes my gaze drifts from the screen over to my wooden chest of drawers.

I stare at the bottom drawer.

I keep the note my mother left me in there. Folded tight, right at the back, as though that might keep the words from flying out at me unexpectedly. I take off my headphones and swing my feet off the bed, then lean over and open the drawer – a crack at first, then a little wider. I take a deep breath, waiting. Looking at the dark space I've created there. There's no need to hesitate, I know that. It's only a piece of paper. But it was one of the last things she touched. That paper, a pen, and then ... something altogether more violent.

I grit my teeth and pull the drawer completely open. It's full of old socks, underwear I never use any more. Some of my mother's old stuff too. I stare at the jumble of material, hovering my hand over it for a minute before plunging into the cool acrylics and fuzzy cotton. I rummage around, even though I know exactly which corner it's nestled in. My hand closes around the small folded paper, and I hold it there for a moment, cocooned, before pulling it out, keeping my fingers clenched tight around it like a butterfly that might escape. I feel its corners digging into my palm and then open my hand, seeing how worn the edges are. They hold the memory of countless foldings and unfoldings. Sometimes when I read it it gives me a sense of peace, makes me feel that I've actually forgiven her for what she did. That I can just love her, not feel love *and*. But other times, like now, I can't even bring myself to open it up. In spite of that, I can picture the words, Anita's handwriting, and of course I know everything it says off by heart. I hold it in my palm a moment longer, and then put it back in its corner, shutting the drawer with a thud. No. Not tonight.

I lie back on the bed, trying to focus on just breathing. Next door, I hear something – a guitar, being strummed quietly. For a moment, it stops my mind rushing. Music; like a memory of time past, before I knew anything was wrong with the world. I get up and quietly walk to my door.

His bedroom door's open a crack. I pad towards it, my bare

feet soundless on the floorboards, and lean closer, listening. Ryan's playing with his eyes closed. His back is to me, but I see him reflected in the mirror facing the door. His long fingers move over the frets and strings expertly, playing a slow, melancholy melody. I lean my head against the doorframe and close my eyes too. When I open them, he's looking right at me in the reflection. He doesn't stop playing, and I know it's his way of apologising for what happened earlier. I close my eyes again and listen for what feels like an hour, but eventually I turn and slowly go back to my room.

His chords float through the air after me.

Chapter Fifteen

The flat's quiet now, and I should be sleeping, but I've remembered something. Pushing the covers away, I clamber out of bed and find my way to my bag as it hangs on a chair. I reach into it, groping around until I find my purse. I feel into the corner, and there it is.

Heading back to the bed, I turn on my bedside light, looking at the torn piece of newspaper as it rustles between my fingers, then pull my laptop on top of the duvet cover and tuck my legs back beneath its warm down. I smooth open the small, wrinkled piece of newsprint and stare at the words for a moment. Slowly, I type in the Google box and hit Enter. I have to scroll through quite a few Cynthia Marches before I find the right one. A café and cake shop in Kentish Town, with her picture, smiling in an apron, on the home page. It's odd, seeing her smile. I scroll up and down the site, and see their closing time – 5.30 p.m. That's too early; I wouldn't be able to get there after work. I could wait until the weekend, but ...

Fuck it. It's only one day, and I can't remember the last time I called in sick. This is a completely shit reason to, I realise that, and there is of course the weird fear I have that any indiscretion work-wise will leave me penniless and out on the street. But it should be fine. To be fair, I don't even know what I'll say or what to expect when I get there, but I know I just have to go and see Cynthia March. I should probably leave it alone, but that book-end PC Martin said I'd get from going to the hearing seems to have fallen off the end of the shelf. Things are still unfinished and I need to stop feeling like this is surrounding me constantly. Before I can talk myself out of it, I shut my computer and set it aside, pulling the covers back over me. That's settled. I'm going. Tomorrow.

I let the cool of the pillow settle against my cheeks, and a while later, I fall asleep.

'Rosamund?'

'Yes?'

'Uh, hi. It's Taylor.' I swallow, trying to sound hoarse. 'I'm really sorry, I don't think I'm going to be able to make it in to the shop today.'

'Oh, right, OK. Have you spoken to . . . '

'Luc, yes, he's fine to go in and cover.' At least I think that's what I can glean from the barely comprehensible text I got back this morning when I sent a begging message. I'm sure he'd be proud of me for bunking off. I'll call later and make sure he's there. 'I've just . . . been coming down with something for a few days, I think it should be fine if I can just have a day in bed to get rid of it, you know?'

'Yes, yes, of course, Taylor. I'll just make a note. Hope you feel better.' I think I hear a hint of suspicion in her voice, but for now I've got away with it.

'Thanks.' I hang up, hoping she doesn't check on the shop too swiftly – I doubt Luc's going to be getting there promptly. I text him again to remind him to take his set of keys, and what

the new alarm code is. I lie back in bed, feeling lighter already —
until I remember my mission today. That makes it kind of hard
to relax, so I sit up again and open my laptop to check my email.
There's one from Marcy, as well as some new posts from her on
the various social media. I look through her smiling selfies, pictures of her snuggling up to a very hot dancer guy and pulling
a funny face, and her pithy side-of-stage commentary. I try not
to feel excited by her mentioning the dancer guy in her email
as well. I'm sure it's nothing, but maybe if her mind is wander-
ing too, it would make things easier. If she and Ryan both just
decided it wasn't working out, then maybe . . . ? No. For God's
sake, of course not.

I type a quick reply, glossing over her jokes about me looking
after Ryan and trying to ignore the uneasy feeling it brings to
my stomach. As if my mind is sending some kind of invisible
signal, he knocks gently on my door the minute I shut the laptop.

'Come in?'

Ryan pops his head round the door tentatively, as if he's worried I might not be decent. It feels uncomfortably intimate to
speak to him while I'm in bed. I sit up straighter and pull the
covers more tightly around my body.

'Hey. You all right? Just wanted to check you hadn't overslept.
Thought you were usually up and out by now?'

'Oh, thanks. Uh, yeah, I called in sick. But I'm fine.'

'Ahh,' he says, nodding. 'I get you. Fair enough.' He pushes
the door open a little more. 'Needed a break?'

'Could say that.'

He gives me a crooked smile that turns into a yawn and
stretch. I stare at the band of skin that peeks out from under his
T-shirt as he does, and the trail of hair that leads down his taut
stomach and into the loose tracksuit bottoms he's wearing.

'Got any specific plans?' he asks, looking at me a little

163

curiously as, for the umpteenth time, I find myself blushing at him. 'I only ask cos I'd said to this guy I'm sharing a couple of scenes with that we could run lines here this morning, but I can sort somewhere else—'

'No, no, that's fine, I don't want to disrupt your day or anything. I actually . . . I was going to go up to Kentish Town for a bit,' I say, reaching up to scratch my head and realising my hair is behaving like a follicle-based cloud around my head. I scramble unsuccessfully for a hairband on my bedside table.

'What's in Kentish Town?'

'Oh, um . . . I just want to visit someone.'

He nods, and his eyebrows draw together a little, but then he seems to recover his expression and raises them at me instead. 'Hmmm, mysterious.'

Shit, he probably thinks it's some sort of all-day booty call.

'It's not like—'

'Like what?' His expression is innocent, but his eyes are darker than usual.

'It's a woman.'

'Oh.' He grins, genuinely this time, teasing me. I fight the urge to throw a pillow at him, smiling a little. He leans his shoulder against the doorframe and sighs. 'Listen, Taylor, I just wanted to say sorry again about last night.' He glances at the floor, his voice lowering too. 'Apologising "about last night" – it's starting to become a bit of a habit.'

'Listen, like I told you, I was just being over-sensitive. It's, like, a sickness I have sometimes.'

'Well, it's a good thing you've taken some time off work then. You get too sensitive, and who knows what could happen?'

I gawp at him and he stares back. I don't think he'd intended it to come out the way it did, but now it's out there and all I can think about is things getting too sensitive. I take a deep breath and press my thighs together tightly. He shuffles his feet a little and swallows.

'I should say thank you, actually,' I say quickly. 'What you played last night was really . . . ' I trail off, my voice quiet. Things have taken a turn for the intense again.

'I'm glad you liked it.'

I fiddle with the duvet, and Ryan clears his throat.

'Do you want some granola?'

How does he make even that sound sexy? 'You mean that weird mixture you make in the plastic tub?' The stuff looks like what I used to feed my hamster as a kid.

'Don't knock it till you try it.'

'Hmm. Yeah, all right then. If it was good enough for Bubbles . . . '

'Eh?'

I begin to smile and explain, but I'm interrupted by a familiar ringtone coming through from the other bedroom. He's programmed one into his phone especially for Marcy. My smile falls a little.

'Sorry,' he says, glancing over his shoulder like it might stop.

'No, no, it's cool, I should jump in the shower anyway,' I say as brightly as I can. 'Say hi for me. I'll try her on Skype later.'

He nods and turns to head back to their room. I hear his voice rise, maybe sounding a little strained, like he's making an effort to sound happy and guilt-free. I sigh, getting up. I *have* to stop reading into things.

Their bedroom door is ajar as I make my way across the hall to the bathroom, and Ryan's eyes follow me. I bite hard on the inside of my cheek, hoping it will take away the bitter taste of jealousy; distract me from the pain of longing. I walk into the bathroom, shut the door and lean hard against it.

*

I'm kind of surprised at how busy the tube is in the middle of a Tuesday morning. I guess it's tourists and women on maternity leave, the unemployed, students, people bunking off . . .

I hate being underground. I'm too used to the bus now, and it feels a bit unnerving not to know I can just jump off and run if I have to, silly as that sounds.

I'm trying not to think about the fact that Ryan was still on the phone to Marcy when I left – it was nearly an hour; she must have bought a phone card or that will be quite a bill. But God, why *shouldn't* she want to speak to him for so long? It must be hard, being apart, her having experiences they can't share. I'm also trying to convince myself I only imagined his increasingly monosyllabic responses. Shame makes me quicken my steps as I head up the escalator at Kentish Town Station. Why am I trying to project some stupid negativity between them just to make myself feel better?

I swerve to avoid a woman absently pushing a buggy down the street while texting, and then shield my eyes as the sun breaks through the clouds. I'm not sure what side of the street Cynthia's café is on, but I check my phone's map and see I'm heading in the right direction. Finally I spot it across the road. It looks busy, but there are seats outside on the pavement.

I jog over the road and sit down at one of the small metal tables, and a waitress comes out almost straight away. I look up anxiously, but it's not Cynthia. She hands me a menu and says:

'Back in a minute to take your order, love. Drink in the meantime?'

'Uh, yeah, can I get a double espresso?'

'Course.'

As she heads inside, I wonder if that was a bad decision. I feel pretty wired as it is. I pull my coat sleeves down a little further on my hands. I'd forgotten just how chilly it was today, but I've sat here already, and I don't see anywhere to sit inside. I feel like now I'm here, I sort of want to hide out from Cynthia March too, which is pretty fucking stupid. At least the sun's out. I squint a little, wishing I'd brought my sunglasses for that full-on stalker look.

A well-heeled, portly old man in a light brown overcoat and what looks like a Panama hat makes his way slowly towards me, leaning on a walking stick, and lowers himself into a chair at the next table. He lights a cigar, and the waitress brings him a cappuccino straight away with a quick greeting, and with my espresso also balanced on her tray.

My eyes drift to the menu lying in front of me on the table as the waitress places my coffee in front of me and straightens up, looking at me expectantly.

'What can I get you?'

I stare at the menu again. The sandwiches, cakes and pastries listed are fairly standard, but one or two seem to have been named after people. Tina's Tuna Melt. Franklin's Cream Cheese and Chive Bagel.

David's Favourite Carrot Cake.

'I'll have the carrot cake,' I say, my voice sounding sandy. I cough a little.

'OK, lovely. That all?'

I nod and she smiles, heading back inside with that bustling efficiency decent waitresses have. My eyes follow her and I look through the window into the café. I notice her say something to a woman standing by the counter before she goes to cut my slice of cake, and then Cynthia turns round and looks right at me. I avert my gaze quickly, my heart pounding. Why am I so nervous? *Get it together; this is the whole reason you came here.* But now that it's really crunch time I'm having serious second thoughts.

What if she thinks I'm crazy? What if she really doesn't want to have to think about this at work, or talk about it with a stranger? The funeral was only a couple of days ago — if this wasn't her livelihood, maybe she wouldn't even have chosen to be back at work so soon.

I pull out a cigarette, lighting it and dragging on it hard as the waitress brings out my cake.

'Thanks,' I say as she hands me a fork wrapped in a napkin, then turns to head back inside. 'Um, excuse me, could I ask—'

'Oh, sorry, love, I should have checked — another coffee?'

'No ... I was wondering — is that Cynthia March?' I try to nod discreetly inside, and the waitress smiles.

'Yeah, she's the owner. Do you know her?'

'Um ... sort of,' I say, but then lose momentum. 'Actually, yeah, can I get another coffee? Single this time, I think,' I say with a half-smile, and she nods, looking at me a little curiously, then heads back inside. I sink my fork into the light cake and smooth icing. It's deliciously spiced, and I can understand why it was David's favourite. I find it weirdly comforting to discover something that might have made him happy, even for a moment, and I glance up and smile through the window at his mother, her back thankfully turned. Pushing my cigarette into the ashtray to stub it out, I savour the rest of the cake with my third coffee of the day. Then, heart pounding with caffeine and nerves, I make sure I don't have crumbs around my mouth or icing smeared between my teeth before I stand up. My waitress starts to come out when she sees me, but I head her off, walking quickly over to the counter. I stare at Cynthia's back for a moment.

'Could I ... sorry, is it OK if I pay? I was just outside at one of the tables.'

She turns and looks at me with an unreadable expression on

her face for a moment, before she forces a smile. 'No problem,' she says, going to the till. She rings up my bill and looks at me expectantly.

'Oh ... you're, uh ... you're David Barnett's mum. From the inquest, right?' I say, in the least convincing piece of acting ever.

She sighs but allows me a forgiving smile. 'Yes, that's right.'

'Yeah, I thought so.' I give her the money, my stomach crashing through my body to the floor.

'Taylor, isn't it?' she says quietly as she hands me my change. 'Johnny told me he'd bumped into you.'

'Johnny ... ?'

'Sorry, Jonathan. David's flatmate.'

Obviously. 'Oh, yeah.'

She lowers her voice a little more. 'He told me he'd mentioned the ... the note.'

'Yeah. I didn't ask him to, he sort of just—' I take a breath. 'I know it's private, all of this. I didn't mean to intrude or anything. I appreciate it's quite odd me turning up here like this.' At least I've admitted I looked her up.

'It's OK. No need to explain,' she says. She slips her hands into the pocket of her apron. It occurs to me that maybe she's embarrassed about the circumstances of David's death, and now I won't let her forget that I found her son the way I did. God, the thought of a stranger finding my mother like that ... That really is a private thing.

'I should probably ... ' I begin, but she shakes her head. A familiar sorrow begins to cloud her eyes, and I can't look away.

'No, really. It's quite all right.' She walks back around the counter to let one of the waitresses ring up another customer's bill. 'Do you want to come back in an hour? I'll be free to talk then. I'll meet you just outside.'

I can't conceal my surprise, but I nod quickly. 'I'd like that. Thanks.'

She smiles again. 'OK. See you then.'

I walk down the high street and kill fifty minutes in a bookshop before I head back up the hill. I hadn't meant to still be smoking when I got here, but Cynthia's waiting on the pavement outside the café.

'They're bad for you, you know,' she says with a wry smile as I walk up to her and stub out on a nearby bin. I pause for a moment, then pull out my pack and offer her one. She takes it, and I light it.

'Let's go up,' she says. I'm not sure what she means at first, but then I see that just next to the café is the door to a flat just above it. I notice Cynthia smokes like my mother used to sometimes, when she was tense – tight mouth, straight fingers, eyes darting like someone might snatch the cigarette away at any moment. She pushes open the door, and I follow her slowly up the stairs. I feel like I need to force and measure every movement I make, in case I do the wrong thing.

'Mind your step,' she says, edging around a mountain bike on the landing. I take a deep breath before heading inside after her. It's a bit dark, but warm, with wood floors and a bright orange runner down the middle of the hallway. I hear an insistent chirping, and as she leads me into the small living room, I see two parakeets in a cage in the corner, one blue and one yellow.

'Oh, they're pretty,' I say.

She squashes her cigarette into an ashtray on the coffee table and exhales the smoke quickly. 'Yes, sorry, they're a bit noisy. Come on, girls,' she says, and they quieten down a little. 'Can I get you a drink?'

'Uh . . . just water. Thanks.'

I glance along the mantelpiece I'm standing next to, noticing the smell of a row of small, unlit scented candles. But for some reason it brings to mind the faint smell that was beginning to come from David Barnett's body, and I wish the memory had never entered my mind. I hold my breath while I look at the photographs propped next to the candles. One of a little girl that looks recent – a niece maybe. A couple of Cynthia with an older man. And one that I know right away must be David – a school picture from when he was maybe thirteen or fourteen. He doesn't look too happy to be having his photograph taken. I think about his face, in the police photo, with the pebbles still pressed to his cheek—

'Here you go,' Cynthia says. She's holding out a glass of water. I hadn't even noticed her leave the room. 'Have a seat.'

Sinking further into the brown sofa than I'd anticipated, I take a sip of the water, and then settle it on a waiting coaster. Everywhere is very neat and dust-free. Maybe she stress-cleans. Better than drinking, I suppose. I realise I still have my coat on and I'm starting to get hot, but I'm not sure how long I'll be staying. I unbutton it but leave it on, following her gaze back up to the photos on the mantel.

'A year after that one was the first time,' she says quietly. I don't have to ask what she means. 'I keep it there because it's one of the last pictures I have before it all went . . . Before he began to *really* start to struggle.' She looks at me. 'Not that I'd try to *forget*, of course. No matter what, he was always my son.'

I notice she's holding something in her hand. A piece of folded paper. She sees me looking at it and unfolds it slowly.

'I think Johnny told you, David wrote something in here for . . . well, for you, I suppose.'

I look away quickly, shaking my head; it's not my place to read it.

'It's OK,' she says. My heart begins to race, but I glance back down at the scratchy scrawl on the lined notebook page, keeping my hands tightly clasped in my lap. Cynthia uses one long finger to point to some particular lines. There's not a lot written on the page, and the bottom of the paper feels too empty. The edge of the note is neat, torn carefully down the perforations. I look down to the dark ink where her finger indicates, careful not to read anything else.

> To whoever finds me, I'm very sorry. If I could just disappear, I would. Save all the trouble. What I've done isn't a judgement on life, it's just the way things have gone for me. But I'm very sorry you were the one to have to find me, after I've gone.

When I finish reading, I look up at her, my chest tight, and nod because I can't quite speak. She refolds the paper, then clenches her jaw to steady herself. 'Have you ... have you ever tried it?'

I frown. 'Tried what?'

'Suicide.'

For a brief, ridiculous moment, it sort of sounds like she's offering me a new drug – something illicit but potentially freeing.

'No, I haven't. I ... My mother.'

'Oh.'

'When I was sixteen.'

'I didn't mean to imply—'

'No. Please. It's OK.'

She's quiet for a moment, clasping her son's words between her palms, then sighs. 'I imagine all this has brought things up for you again, then.'

I glance at her. 'Yes.'

She thinks for a while, then turns a little on the sofa to look at me properly. 'I suppose we're a bit like the sides of a coin, the two of us. Me a childless mother, you a motherless child?'

I can't help but smile a little, and she does too.

'My mum used to sing that one. "Motherless Child"? She was a singer.' I start to tear up, and Cynthia looks at me, her brow knitted with concern. We sit for a while, letting the memories and the sadness settle back down around us.

'I can't believe he really did it,' she whispers at last, and I can't look at her. 'I can't believe I didn't stop him.'

I turn my gaze to her finally, and see a tear fall down her cheek that she wipes quickly away.

'I know,' I mumble finally.

'You were only a girl,' she says. 'But I ... I was supposed to be the one to look after him.'

'He was a grown man,' I counter. 'You couldn't be with him every waking moment. If he wanted to do it, then ...' I break off, shrugging. I feel angry and helpless and desperately sad.

I have to leave.

But we sit on in silence. Thinking, worrying, wishing.

Eventually I stand and start to button my coat, and she gets up too, and we both sigh hard again, helplessly beholden to the pain and the memories of the people who left us.

'Thanks, Cynthia.'

'Thank *you*, Taylor,' she says softly. 'For finding him. I'm glad it was you.'

She reaches over hesitantly, but then pulls me firmly into a hug. She squeezes, then lets go, tears threatening to fall. I bite my lip, then turn and head to the front door. I let myself out without looking back.

Chapter Sixteen

Cold envelops me greedily as I emerge from the Overground station and start walking home. It's been a pretty strange fake-sick day, and whilst seeing Cynthia has made me feel lighter in a lot of ways, her suggestion that things have been brought up again has stuck with me. Something unresolved, something caught on the bottom of a deep ocean, suddenly shaken loose and free to rise to the surface. Maybe it's a good thing, I don't know. She said she was glad I found her son, like it was meant to be, like I was the right person to have this experience. I sigh a little, thinking that's exactly the sort of thing Anita would say. The thing is, I hate even the idea of my mother as an 'issue' that I need to 'get over'. That's not what it is. I'll never get over her; I'll never stop wanting her back. But I carried on – moved on – rather than dwelling on it, because that's what I *had* to do. I didn't have a choice. I had to live my life, or else ... I'd end up like her.

I only realise I'm frowning so hard when I pass our downstairs neighbour walking out of the building. She holds the door open for me, her pale, wrinkled hand seeming to glow in the fading light.

'Oh, thanks, Mrs Buckley.'

'Hello, dear. Everything all right?'

I quickly rearrange my features into a smile. 'Yes. Fine, thanks.'

I climb the stairs two at a time, already mentally unscrewing the cork from the bottle of wine Marcy and I always keep at the back of the cupboard for emergencies. Rummaging for my keys, I pause, hearing Ryan on the other side of the door, trying to negotiate a few extra minutes from Charlie before he has to take him out. I take a deep breath and push my key into the lock. The minute I walk in, the dog bounds over to me, with an apologetic Ryan following close behind. Just seeing his tall, slim frame makes my heart stutter and still, all at once.

'Not yet, dammit,' he mutters, then glances up at me with a brief, tight smile. 'Hey.' He hooks his fingers into Charlie's collar and pulls him back so I can get inside properly.

'All right?'

Ryan rolls his eyes. 'Yeah, it's just been kind of a stressful day, that's all. And this bloody dog—'

I'd begun to take off my coat, but I shrug it back on to my shoulders. I can hardly believe I'm going to volunteer, but looking at Ryan's irritated expression – the tightness in the definition of his jaw, the dim in the glow of his honey-coloured eyes – I realise with a jolt that I'd do almost anything just to make him feel better.

'I'll take him out. It's cool.'

He straightens up and looks at me, finally breaking into a genuine smile. 'This is sort of becoming a thing, isn't it?'

He looks at me for a moment, and I struggle not to hear a double meaning in his words. I force out a chuckle. 'Seriously, it's cool.'

'To be honest, I could do with stretching my legs.' He

reaches for the lead by the door, and grabs his coat. Charlie trots between us, his tail whipping the air furiously.

'Well,' I say, before I can even think about it, 'why don't we go together?'

I push a cigarette between my lips out of habit. Charlie strains against the lead, but Ryan waits for me to finish lighting it before we set off at a steady pace. He quirks one side of his mouth up in a half-smile and I stare at his dimple, taking a hard pull on the fag. I blow the smoke away from him, then turn back.

'Want one? I won't tell.'

He laughs and shakes his head "no", and we walk on for a while in silence. The sky's turning an ominous dark purple as the sun sets, and the wind stings my face, flaring the cherry on my cigarette. I squint a little, smoking quickly so I can put my hands back in my pockets. Ryan edges closer to me as we walk, as though he might be able to keep me warm. I glance over at him, and he looks down at me, his gaze unwavering but backed with caution.

'Maybe the river?' he says, starting to turn down towards the side street that leads to the water.

'Uh, I don't know,' I say quickly and a little too loudly, panic starting to rise in my chest. 'Maybe just a circuit round here? It's sort of looking like it might start to rain soon.'

Ryan looks at me with a slightly quizzical expression, but he doesn't push. He nods and calls Charlie back the other way, and I glance down the street towards the river. Irrational, but it still feels too soon. It took months after Anita died before I could have a bath, and if I'm honest, I don't think forcing myself to confront that one small thing helped that much. Not that this is the same thing at all, but—

'Fucking freezing, isn't it? I shouldn't have let you come back out,' Ryan says, hunching his shoulders. He stops for a second to let Charlie off the leash, then falls back into step with me.

I blow the last of the smoke from my lungs and stub out my cigarette on a bin. "Yeah. Bastard.' I smile wryly, then remind myself not to flirt. Stuffing my hands in my coat pockets, I do an exaggerated whole-body shiver and Ryan grins at me, sparking something inside me alight. It burns steadily as a streetlamp clicks on above him, throwing the angles of his face into shadow, and I have to wrench my eyes away. We pace behind Charlie for a moment, and then I clear my throat. 'So, why was your day shit?'

Ryan keeps looking ahead, his sigh causing a cloud to form and disperse in front of him. 'Oh. Just my fucking agent – well, former agent. She reckons she's got too many on her books for now, and needed to drop a couple, including me. Survival of the fittest, I guess.'

In my head, like a cheesemonger, I think if it *was* survival of the fittest, he should have been top of the heap. Thankfully all I actually say is, 'Oh no. That *is* shit.'

'Yeah, well, I guess I'm just not getting booked enough for her liking at the moment.'

'But you got that BBC show the other day, right? And you were doing a play,' I say. 'That's not bad going, is it?'

He shrugs in answer, then flicks his gaze towards where Charlie's peeing up against a lamppost. 'Well it was that, and I had ...' He glances back at me, hesitating. 'I had a bit of a fight with Marcy today. Just stupid shit. I *hate* the phone, Skype, all this bollocks. It's just so hard to, I don't know ...' he laughs ironically, 'communicate?'

I feel my lips draw into a tight smile, my heart starting to pound at the thought of getting into a discussion about his relationship with Marcy.

'Yeah. It must be tough,' I say, concentrating on the grey of the pavement. 'I miss her too.' It's not a lie, but I feel guilty, and I hate admitting to myself why. I feel him looking at me, and turn my head back towards him.

'I think it's getting to me a bit, her being off doing her thing, you know?' he says.

OK. Jesus. We're taking it to this place. Why did I even suggest we come out together? His voice lowers, almost like he's talking to himself. 'And here I am, hanging around in your flat, getting in your way, and—'

'You're not getting in my way,' I interject quietly. I slow my pace and look over at him to make sure he knows what I mean. Takes two to feel painfully awkward tension.

'Well, that's good, I guess,' he murmurs, his own steps slowing too, his eyes holding mine. I look away, and hear him take a deep breath. 'I think it's just been a bad day for ... I don't know, my self-esteem. Makes you start questioning some of your choices.'

I glance at him, worried about what he means by that. Worried he's telling me that he wishes things were different. Again, hope flares dangerously inside me, and I swallow it down.

'Like ... with work,' he adds slowly. 'I just feel like, what the fuck am I doing sometimes, you know? This shit could all be a complete waste of time. Not everybody can make a living as an "*artist*".' He says the word sarcastically, and we both smile. 'I should probably jack it all in now, before it becomes a farce.' He quirks his mouth at the irony.

I nod, shoving my hands further into my pockets, remembering my mini-rant at Lucas about this very thing.

'You reckon I should, don't you?' he says, eyebrows raised.

I hesitate for a moment. If only he knew how jealous I am

178

that he's even trying. How much I admire it. Him. 'Well, are you any good?'

'What, as an actor?'

'Yeah.'

He laughs, but doesn't answer right away. Eventually, he looks up at the gathering clouds, then back at me.

'It depends. I mean, trying to make a living being somebody you're not, over and over again, seems like a pretty futile task, right?' His eyes shine with amusement.

I laugh, then notice that, across the street, Charlie's soiling the pavement with abandon. 'Ew. Have you got a bag?'

He nods and we cross over to where the dog is checking his handiwork. Ryan grimaces as he reaches down to scoop, then goes to drop it in a bin. When he comes back over, his expression is more thoughtful.

'I think I act because it's a challenge. And an escape, but also . . . a way to confront things, weirdly. I started doing it for that. I guess sort of like therapy? Seeing another person's troubles or emotions, *living* them . . . I think it helps you deal with your own.'

I stare at him for a moment, thinking of David Barnett, of Cynthia. Does Ryan know how much what he said could apply to my own life right now? I know he can't, but it still makes my heart pull towards him in a way I can't control. He frowns for a moment. We start walking again.

'Well, if it makes you happy, and if you can, you should keep at it,' I say. 'You're not delusional about it, so if acting ends up not working out, at least it won't be because you haven't tried.'

Ryan nods. 'True.'

I try not to think of the irony of my own words when it comes to myself. Why haven't I tried what I'd really like to do?

What risks have I ever taken? I'm so scared of *things going wrong,* sometimes I can barely move.

We bunch together a little as another couple comes towards us on the pavement, and Ryan calls Charlie to heel. We walk shoulder to shoulder a little longer than necessary, and I feel his warmth even through our coats.

'What about singing?' he says suddenly, like he can read my thoughts.

I move away a little. 'What about it?'

'You're good at that.'

'So?'

'So you agree that you are,' he says with a slow, gorgeous smile. I roll my eyes, struggling to stay nonchalant at the sight of it, at the way it makes the flame inside me burn harder.

'Yeah. I'm a secret egoist, didn't Marcy tell you?'

He laughs. 'Well, you should agree, because you are.' His face becomes serious. 'Maybe . . .'

I look at him expectantly.

'Maybe that's something that would make *you* happy? Even just doing it a bit more, like, in front of other people?'

How does he know? I feel my jaw clench. 'I don't seem happy to you?' I say, trying to make my voice sound jokey again.

He's quiet for a moment.

'Well, are you? Sometimes you seem like you're . . .' He stops walking, and I stop too, but when I turn to him, something about my expression – probably the angry, upset, tired, worried or hopelessly, desperately infatuated element – makes him trail off. 'It's none of my business,' he says, like he has before. Like I know deep down I want it to be. He starts to walk again, his brow creased. 'I'm sorry.'

'No, I seem like what?' Heat's rising on my neck, despite the cold. 'Go on.' I can hear the defensive tone in my voice.

He doesn't look at me. 'Like you're drowning,' he murmurs, then pauses. 'And I *wish* I could—' He stops talking suddenly. 'Dammit,' he whispers.

A wave of different emotions crashes over me, and I quicken my pace, swallowing hard to fight back the tears that I know will fall any minute, because they're always right on the edge. Because he seems so attuned to how I'm feeling. I get ahead of Ryan and pass Charlie who's trotting ahead of us. I light another cigarette, and just then, big fat cold raindrops begin to fall around me. I tilt my face up to mingle them with the couple of tears that have spilled from my eyes. I'm really embarrassed, and pissed off, and ... and ...

What does he wish he could do?

'Taylor.'

I can hear his footsteps catching up to me, but I don't turn round. I keep walking, fast. I need to get home, get to my room, alone. I feel his hand – he touches my shoulder, then runs it down to the crook of my arm, pulling me to a stop. I balance the cigarette between my lips and fold my arms against my chest, tucking my hands away. He moves to stand in front of me, and I look up at him.

'Hey,' he says, peering at my face. I pull out the cigarette, blow away smoke and take several deep breaths. I must seem like a freak show, but I can't help the irritation still knotted in my chest.

'Once. *One time*, I was very upset, and you were there,' I whisper. 'But I ... You don't know ... Just because I ...' I can't form a decent sentence about it all, and instantly wish I hadn't brought it up again, but when I glance up at him, he seems anguished. His eyes are stormy, and his breathing's fast, and he takes a step closer—

'I told you, that's not all I think about when I think about that. About you.'

181

His eyes are unrelenting, trained on mine. Panic and almost overwhelming desire replace the irritated knot in my centre, and I step away quickly.

'Taylor ...' he says again, and the way he does it makes my heart constrict.

I drop my cigarette to the ground. 'We'll all be drowning if we don't get inside soon,' I say, my voice shaky. It's really coming down now, and I'm shivering. I turn and start half walking, half jogging round the corner towards the flat. Ryan doesn't say anything else, but keeps pace, with Charlie trotting anxiously between us.

Our footsteps squeak damply through the silence as we walk up the stairs to the flat, Charlie's claws clacking rapidly alongside. I pull out my keys to unlock the door, but I drop them because my hands are so numb and I'm shivering. We both bend down to pick them up, and Ryan closes his hand around my fingers, squeezing them for a moment without quite meeting my eye. I don't get how his hand could still be warm, but it is. He lets go, then looks at me.

'It really *is* none of my business,' he says in a low voice. We're still crouched in front of the door, with Charlie huffing and wagging his tail expectantly. 'But I don't like it. You not ... not being happy. If you aren't.'

I don't know how to respond, and I'm still shaking, and I can still feel where his hand touched mine. I stand up straight, keys in hand, and open the door. Charlie trots inside happily, shaking rainwater everywhere, and we follow behind him. Ryan shuts the door.

'Shit,' I say under my breath. A fairly all-encompassing *shit*.

He shrugs out of his coat, and I step out of my wet trainers, wiggling my toes against the numbing cold. I can feel a pressure building in my chest, of everything rising up inside me.

Crushing sorrow for a stranger, and for my mother. The over-whelming feeling that there's someone who seems to understand without knowing, who is so near to me but so far away from something I can have. I clench my jaw hard, trying to take off my own coat. I can hear my breathing getting faster, and I know the tears are coming again. Once they start, it's hard to stop. Salt water blurs my eyes, but I concentrate on pulling my coat off. I finally get it off and walk over to hang it up, swallowing hard, but it's not working. The tears begin to fall, and a quiet sob rises out of my chest. Full-on cry mode, shit. With my back to him, I reach up to put my coat on the hook, feeling rainwater dripping from my hair on to my shoulders – but then something else is on them too, something warm. Ryan's hands.

He turns me around, and I lean in to him without even thinking about it.

His arms encircle me, one hand pressing my head gently to his chest. Another embarrassing sob is muffled in the soft grey fabric of his sweatshirt. His other hand moves in a slow circle on my back. I take a deep breath of him, and he tightens his grip. I can hear his heart beating, beating, beating ... He lowers his head a little, sinking it ever so slightly towards the crook of my neck. I feel surrounded by him, and my arms reach around his waist, gripping the back of his clothes tightly.

I don't ever want to leave this moment.

He doesn't say anything, just keeps rubbing my back, and when I can face it, I take a few more deep breaths and sniff hard, then pull myself away. I can't look at him.

'Shit,' I say, pulling my sleeves down over my hands to swipe at my cheeks. 'Sorry.' I point at the damp patch on his chest, and look up at him. His eyebrows are drawn together and his expression is so intense that my breath catches. 'Looks like a bloody Rorschach test,' I whisper, smiling shakily, and he laughs a little. He reaches up to my face and slowly brushes away a tear with his thumb.

'No worries.' He brushes my cheek again, trailing down towards the corner of my mouth.

I swallow. 'Uh, I should . . .' I point to the bathroom.

Ryan takes a deep breath. 'Yeah. OK.' He shoves his hand firmly down into his jeans pocket. 'I'm, um, gonna change then make some dinner. Do you . . . Do you want some dinner?'

I nod, and he turns and heads quickly into their room. I walk into the bathroom, slip inside and shut the door. I switch on the light and the extractor fan kicks in, drowning out my ragged breaths. I avoid looking at myself in the mirror until I've washed my face, letting the warm water wash away the last of my tears. For now anyway.

At last I meet my own gaze, with the water dripping off my chin. The tap is still running, and I cup my hands to take a drink, then blow out a hard sigh and reach for my towel to dry off. I can hear pots and pans clattering now, and wonder vaguely what we even have in the fridge. Maybe Ryan went shopping before I got home? Had he planned to cook for us both? Frowning at the mirror, I clench my jaw. Why would I even let myself think something like that? I massage some moisturiser slowly on to my face, stalling before I have to go back out.

Finally I duck back across the hall into my room to change out of my damp jeans. My eyes are drawn to the large David LaChapelle coffee table book I sabotaged, leaning against the side of my wardrobe. Another indiscretion. Pulling on some leggings, I check the time – it's only just after six, obviously too early to suggest I've changed my mind about dinner and I'm heading to bed, though I'd happily curl up under the covers and try to forget everything that has happened today. Well, maybe not everything . . . I close my eyes, recalling the way Ryan held me while I cried. It's as if everything with him is instinct. As though I know, deep down, that any self-consciousness I feel with him is really to do with the effort of fighting against myself.

Grabbing a sweatshirt off my bed, I nearly stop when I realise it's the one I'd thought was Marcy's, but turned out to be his. But I pull it over my head and put the hood up, pull the sleeves over my hands, maybe trying to recreate the feeling of being surrounded by him.

This is dangerous.

I don't know how strong I am.

'What are you going to do?' I whisper aloud to myself.

I don't know.

I open the door and step back out into the hallway.

Chapter Seventeen

The delicious scent of frying onions drifts towards me across the hallway, and I see Ryan's shadow stretching along the floor from the kitchen. Heading over, I lean against the kitchen doorframe and watch him for a moment.

'What are we having?' I say, and I see his broad shoulders jump, then relax slowly as he turns round.

'Jesus! Didn't know you were there.'

'Sorry.'

He looks me up and down, taking in his sweatshirt, and a flicker of a smile crosses his face, chased up by something harder to interpret. 'Oh, nothing fancy. Chilli. It's meant to cook longer, ideally, but an hour or so will do. That all right?'

'Sounds good. Do you need me to do anything?'

'Open that bottle of wine?'

I smile. 'Yep, I can definitely do that.' I grab the wine and undo the cork, then pull out a couple of glasses from the cupboard. I pour one, then raise my eyebrows enquiringly at Ryan. He nods and I pour the other, then pass the bottle to him to add a splash to the pot.

'Thanks,' he says.

I watch his forearms flex under his pushed-up sleeves as he stirs the chilli. Leaning back against the edge of the work surface, I take a long sip of my wine, closing my eyes briefly.

'So, what did you get up to on your sick-day in Kentish Town?'

I open my eyes, but he keeps adding ingredients to the pot, only looking over at me when I don't answer right away.

'Sorry, none of my—'

'You don't have to keep saying that,' I say quietly.

He turns back to the stove. 'OK.'

I take a breath. 'I went to a café there.' I scuff one toe along the vinyl on the kitchen floor. 'I went to see the woman who owns it, actually. It's ... it's a bit of a weird one,' I add, knowing I'm making absolutely no sense. Ryan keeps stirring.

'Were you seeing her about a job or something?'

I know I'm being way too cryptic, but I have no idea where to begin, or even if I should. Ryan puts the lid on the pot, turns and reaches behind me to pick up his glass of wine. Our eyes lock for a moment, and his gaze drifts down to my mouth, which is paused mid-sip. I pull my glass back down and swallow. Steam is clouding the air, fogging up the window over the sink.

'Not a job. OK.' He smiles a little. 'Are you going to make me guess, then? Or do I need to refer to my earlier, rebutted statement?' His arm is still half reaching around me, and I hear him pulling his wineglass around in circles on the laminate work surface.

'I don't think you'd be able to guess why I was seeing her,' I say, my voice coming out awkwardly breathless. I shift away a little, and he takes a step back, gulping some of his wine.

'Woman of mystery,' he murmurs. He has a slight red stain in the centre of his bottom lip, and I try not to think about my tongue tracing it.

'It's really nothing. Like I say, it's just a bit of a weird . . . It's—'
He holds up his hand and I stop.

'She's giving you tap-dancing lessons?'

I let out a short laugh. 'No.'

'You're helping her traffic a rare type of turtle?'

'Ohh, close. But no.'

'She's your contact in some low-level espionage?'

'Low-level? Harsh.'

'Fine.' He sighs. 'Well, I'm done with cooking for the time being. Just needs to simmer now.' He looks at me, his eyes glinting mischievously. 'And I've been thinking about that thing you said earlier.'

I frown. 'Which thing?'

'I think they were the words of an evil temptress.'

Jesus. I swallow more wine. 'Hmm?'

'Since you offered, I can't seem to stop thinking about it.'

He waits, and my muscles tense till the penny drops. 'Ah.'

I feel him watching as I pad out of the kitchen and go to my room to grab my pack and lighter. I find him in the living room, leaning out of the large window with his elbows resting on the frame, craning out into the dark to look down the side of our building. He moves aside a little so I can squeeze in beside him, trying to ignore the thrill of having a reason to be so close to him again. The cold air hits me like walking into a wall, and I pull the hood tighter around my head before popping a cigarette between my lips. He pulls the side of the hood back a little to see my face, his eyes like molten gold. I look away and hold the pack up to him, and he pulls out a cigarette wordlessly. Only one lamp is on in the room, so outside the sky is dark and vast above us. I flick my lighter, and exhale white smoke into the night. I turn to him, and he hesitates before leaning in to the flame I'm holding up.

'Don't let me corrupt you,' I say, taking another pull on my cigarette.

He laughs a little, and his arm rubs against mine. 'Too late,' he murmurs. We both stare out, listening to the crackling paper as we smoke. I flick ash and watch it float, shivering a little despite the warmth of Ryan next to me. I clear my throat, and realise.

I'm going to say it.

'The woman I went to see ... She's the mother of somebody,' I begin quietly. 'A man I found down by the river.'

He shifts a little beside me. 'Found?'

'Yeah. He'd ... washed up there, after he ...' I pause. 'He wore ankle weights. I don't know if I'd have thought of that.' I suck hard on the filter of my fag. I can feel Ryan's eyes on me, and I glance over at him. His cigarette is paused near his mouth, clenched between thumb and forefinger, his mouth open a little, awaiting the expression of his next question, but he's quiet for a painfully long time.

'When was this?'

'About a week and a half ago, maybe.' I flick more ash and take a breath, trying to sound more casual. 'So, yeah, I don't know. I found out his mother owned that café, and I just wanted to ... speak to her. It sounds bizarre, but—'

'Shit, Taylor, that's ... Jesus.'

I shrug, and feel ridiculous for doing it the minute my shoulders stop moving. 'Told you it was a weird one.'

He's silent for a while, smoking. I can see his frown even in the darkness.

'Have you told Marcy?' he asks finally.

'No.'

'Right.'

'It's ... I didn't want her to overreact. It wasn't a big deal. Well ... God, nobody expects to find a dead body, do they?' My heartbeat quickens, and I feel a sudden queasiness at the reality of what happened. 'I just didn't want a big fuss,' I mutter.

Ryan doesn't say anything, just stares at me, his jaw tight, his shoulders rising and falling as he breathes. Then, straightening up, he stubs his cigarette out on the bricks below the window outside and flicks his butt into the darkness. He pulls himself inside, and I stub my cigarette out in the same way. He waits until I've exhaled the last of the smoke and moved away from the window, and then he shuts it with a thud. I don't really know what to do or say. I run my hands up and down my arms and scrunch my toes up and down in their socks against the cool wooden floor. He looks down, watching them. I notice his hands move up slightly, and I get the sudden feeling that he's going to pull me into his embrace again. But then his fingers curl almost into fists, like he's fighting against it.

'I'd better go and check on the chilli,' he murmurs, and I nod, trying to catch his eye as he walks away.

Should I not have told him? Is he pissed off? But I really don't understand why he should be. Unless . . . It's possible he's annoyed because he feels like now he has to deal with this, with me, when I could have just talked about it with Marcy before she left. That doesn't sound like him, but who knows how men react to stuff like this? Lord knows I don't.

I sigh and turn on the TV, slumping into the sofa and pulling my hood down. I shouldn't have said anything. I've come this far without mentioning it. Why now? I drain the rest of my wine, but when I look up, Ryan's back, carrying the bottle. He sits down on the edge of the sofa next to me, fills my glass without asking, then his own. The light from the television flickers against his face, shadowing his eyes, bouncing off his lips, his cheekbones—

'You found a fucking dead body. A suicide,' he says quietly. It isn't a question. He seems to be sounding it out, trying to make sense of what I told him.

'Yeah.'

After a while, I reach out with the remote to change the channel, and we both stare at the screen. I'm barely taking anything in, and I'm fairly certain Ryan isn't either. He still hasn't leaned back in the seat.

'Did you have to ... Like, you spoke to the police about it and all that?'

'Yeah.'

'And you haven't spoken to anyone else about it.'

'No, not really. I guess that's part of why I went to see his mother. You know, to talk about it a bit, maybe.' I take a sip of wine.

Ryan turns to look back at me for a long time, with the little furrow still between his eyebrows. 'Taylor,' he whispers quietly, and shakes his head. His eyes remain in shadow, but I see his long lashes blink hard, and then finally he leans back on the sofa, slumping down low. The side of his body is almost touching mine, and he holds the bottom of the wineglass against his stomach, the red liquid at an angle. Even through his sweatshirt I can detect the taut muscles there.

'You're right,' he murmurs. 'I don't think I would have thought of that either. The weights.'

I look down at my lap. The smell of chilli is starting to fill the flat, and my stomach rumbles, once again at the most embarrassing moment possible. I clutch my palm over it and he looks at my hand, smiling a little. For a split second, I think he's going to cover it with his.

'It'll be ready soon,' he says.

My face is hot. 'Good.'

We fall quiet for another moment.

'I suppose that's the difference,' he says. 'You'd think of those things. If you're really serious about it, you'd think of all those sorts of things.'

I take another gulp of wine, and turn my head slightly to look at him. 'Do you know anyone who has?'

'Taken their own life? Nobody close. A friend of a friend at university.'

I nod, but then let out a short, mirthless laugh.

'What?'

'No, I just ... that expression. "Taken their own life".'

'Sorry—'

'No, no, it's just, taken it where? What the hell does that even mean? What, taken it away from us, from the people who—' I stop myself, and take another swig of wine. I should probably stop drinking. I sit forward and set my glass down on the coffee table. Ryan leans forward too, his leg right up against my own now, his arm pressed against mine as his hands fold loosely between his knees. I want to rest my head against his shoulder.

'Your mother did, right?' he says in a quiet voice. 'Marcy ... mentioned it once.'

'Of course.' I close my eyes. Pity party for one? I open them again, then turn and look at him; his face is so close to mine, I feel his breath on my cheek, like that night in the bathroom. His expression radiates concern. I turn away again. 'Yes. My mother killed herself.'

He's silent for a moment. 'How old were you?' he asks eventually.

'Sixteen.' I feel my jaw muscles clench. My eyes are cloudy with the threat of more tears. I swallow audibly. We turn to each other again, and I see a world of conflict in his huge, beautiful eyes against the flickering light of the TV screen.

'Taylor, I—'

'Listen, I'm sorry. I've been a bit of a basket case this evening. I'm sorry about all this. I don't want you to feel like you have to . . . I mean, you're making me chilli and—'

'Well' – the corner of his mouth quirks – 'I'm not making *you* chilli. I'm just making chilli.'

I can't help smiling back. 'Ah. OK. Cos I hate it when people make me chilli just because they feel sorry for me.' I bite my lip, remembering what he said to me when we were alone together for those brief moments at the restaurant before Marcy arrived. His eyes lock on to mine, seeing the memory in them.

When he speaks, he says each word slowly. 'I don't feel *sorry* for you, Taylor.'

He stares, like he's waiting for me to understand. I'm scared, because I do. I feel crazily aware of almost every cell in my body that is pressed against his.

'Good,' I whisper.

I can hear his breath getting louder – or is that mine? He moves a fraction closer, and I watch his tongue graze his lower lip. It's like I feel it. Somewhere I shouldn't . . .

Charlie's claws scrambling in from the doorway make us spring apart. I chuckle nervously as the dog nuzzles up to us both. He always was a mood-killer, but in this case I think it's for the best. I rub his head, and Ryan moves back, letting the dog jump up. I raise an eyebrow.

'You know Marce doesn't let him on the sofa,' I say, feeling awful just mentioning her name.

'Yeah. She doesn't care if he goes on the *bed*, though,' he says, grinning wryly. He pushes his face towards Charlie's and rubs his ears.

'Maybe she stops him for my benefit then?' I'd never considered that.

'Do you mind?'

Charlie turns to me, his doggy eyes seeming to plead for this to last. Once again, I know how he feels. Maybe we're actually kindred spirits.

'I suppose not.'

The dog settles between us, like Marcy's canine proxy. We watch the TV, Charlie's panting just audible under the canned laughter of the sitcom on the screen. After a while, Ryan gets up to make the rice, the dog rises with him, and I'm left alone on the sofa.

I turn on the table lamp next to the sofa, hoping the soft light it sheds will help break the spell.

Chapter Eighteen

'What the fuck? No, that's bollocks, he never said—'

'Drink! Charlie, she has to drink, right? Drink!'

My fingers close clumsily around the glass and I take another sip of rum. Any vague thoughts that I shouldn't be mixing drinks – on a school night, no less – went out of the window sometime after dinner, when we'd drained the wine and I'd somehow been talked into a drinking game like an impressionable sixth-former. I squeeze my eyes shut for a moment, worrying about what else Ryan could easily persuade me to do.

'Happy now?' I mutter.

Ryan nods, his eyes mischievous again, his movements languid from the alcohol floating through his veins. Charlie's been snuffling excitedly at our laughter, scampering between Ryan, sitting cross-legged on the floor between the coffee table and the sofa, leaning his head against one of its arms, and me, stretched out on the sofa with my head resting on the other. Teenagers warble dispassionately on the TV screen in the background, a late-night repeat of an earlier live show.

'You should go on this,' Ryan says, nodding at the TV and then sitting forward to pull off his sweatshirt. His T-shirt rides up his back and I stare at the muscles there, and the sinewy, defined ones that lead around his ribcage towards his abs . . .

I clear my throat. 'Are you serious? Why would I go on this shit?'

He chuckles, pulling his T-shirt down and leaning back against the sofa. My legs are behind his shoulders. He turns his head towards me. 'Yeah, you're right. You shouldn't . . . ' He seems to lose his train of thought, his eyelids blinking slowly as he stares at me.

I look up at the ceiling, and breathe out slowly. When I look back at him he's taking another sip of rum, not even noticing if the correct phrase has been said on the screen. I gradually sit up, swing my legs round and plant my feet on the floor beside him. The movement sets my head swimming, and I wait for it to stop.

'Bollocks,' I mutter. 'I'm going to be a mess for work tomorrow. I can't believe you let me do this.' I nudge him with my leg, and he lifts his arm, resting it over my thigh, his hand on my knee. I try to keep air moving in and out of my lungs.

He looks up at me with his big, dark-amber eyes. 'Sorry. You can slap me if you like.'

Those words set off all sorts of incredibly dirty thoughts in my head. I could just lean over and . . . *Marcy, Marcy, Marcy.*

'Coffee. Water,' I force myself to say. 'Going to make water and have some coffee.' Just as soon as I can stand up.

'You won't be able to sleep if you have coffee,' Ryan murmurs.

'I will, it's fine.'

'What time is it anyway?' he asks, attempting to squint at his watch on the arm that's leaning on my knee. I reach down and take hold of his wrist, leaning forward to read the dial, feeling his forearm muscles tense as I close my fingers around them.

'Two. Fuck, two.'

My curls have fallen in my face from leaning forward, and

Ryan's hand is suddenly in my hair, pushing it back again so he can see my face, like he did with the hood, and my hand is still clutching his arm, which is so warm and strong, and he's leaning his weight in to me ...

We both sigh hard at the same time, and I finally manage to stand up.

'Yeah, coffee will be good,' I say hoarsely. 'I'll make us coffee.'

I head to the kitchen and manage, with an epic effort of concentration, to scoop coffee into the cafetière, boil the kettle, pour on the hot water, stir. While it brews, I gulp down two glasses of water, fighting the queasiness it brings, and feel marginally better. Charlie lumbers in and settles into his basket for the night with a smug look on his face.

'Yeah, all right, Captain Sensible,' I murmur.

Pulling out two mugs, I put a teaspoon of sugar in each, then carry everything gingerly through to the living room and set it down on the table. Ryan's moved back up on to the sofa, one leg crossed over the other. He's muted the TV and is softly picking at his guitar with his eyes closed. He doesn't open them until I sink into the sofa beside him, but he keeps playing. I close my own eyes and listen, leaning my head back, knowing he's watching me. My head stops swimming and I feel still. I start to hum along with the melody, then sing wordless notes, and together we become music for a while. So easily, so unselfconsciously. It feels beautiful.

'Mmm. That's nice,' he whispers. And it is.

Eventually I remember the coffee, and lean forward to plunge it, pouring us both a cup. Ryan balances his guitar flat on his legs and takes the mug grudgingly. It's quiet now, but that crackle of awkwardness, that need to fill space with words, doesn't descend. I sort of wish it would. I breathe out, feeling the steam from my mug mist against my face.

'Yeah, actually,' Ryan says after a while, holding up his mug like a toast. His voice has become gravelly with liquor and the late night.

'Told you,' I murmur.

He cocks his head to one side as he looks at me.

'Taylor . . .'

'Mm-hm?'

'Why Taylor?'

'What do you mean?'

'I've just realised what a strange name that is for a woman.'

'Ah. Cheers.'

'No, I mean, unusual.'

I shrug, then reach forward and put down my mug, slumping back on the sofa, a little closer to him. Maybe I could just sleep here . . .

'Why do you think they called you that?' he says. He sets his mug down on the table too. The neck of the guitar juts out over my lap, and I try not to think about it as any kind of metaphor, though I can't help reaching up and running my fingertips along the tiny ridges of the metal strings. Ryan's eyes follow them.

'There was no "they", really,' I reply, my own voice husky too. 'It was my mum. She called me Taylor because it was my father's name. She told me she didn't know anything but his first name – not that she was generally *that* kind of girl, mind you,' I add.

'Of course not.' He pushes his head back against the sofa, turned towards me.

'He was a session musician, from somewhere in the States apparently. I don't even know where. A trumpeter. She only met him once or twice, they did their thing, and hey presto, here I am.'

'Wow.' He taps his fingers on the wooden body of the guitar. 'And you've never found out any more about him?'

'Nope. Mr Taylor *Blank*. American. African-American, apparently.' I gesture to myself with a small smile. 'That's about it.'

'And you've never wanted to find out more?'

I think back to what Ryan told me about his birth mother, and feel a little guilty. 'Uh . . . no, not really. The odd curious moment, but I guess since he was never in the picture – it was always just me and Anita, you know? – I just . . . She was really all the parent I needed. Most of the time, anyway. All the parental drama I could handle, that's for sure.'

Ryan nods, quiet for a moment, then my favourite slow smile spreads across his lips. 'What if he was, like, Miles Davis or something?'

I nudge him in the ribs. 'Just putting it out there, but I *think* my mum might have noticed if she was shagging Miles Davis, cleverly slipping under the radar by telling everyone he was a session musician called Taylor.'

'True.' He takes a sip of coffee then sets the mug down again. 'Quite the back-story you've got.'

'What, are you doing a study of me, like somebody in one of your scripts?'

'Hmm.' He lets out a small chuckle. 'No. Just . . . noticing. It's hard not to.' I stare down at the neck of the guitar. 'You know, this whole air-of-mystery thing you have going on—'

'I'm not mysterious,' I interrupt.

'I beg to differ.'

'Well, I've never heard that one. I've heard "quiet", "uptight", I've heard "stuck-up", I've heard . . . I don't know . . . '

'You shouldn't be so hard on yourself,' he says softly, picking up his guitar, setting it gently on the floor so he can stretch his long legs out on to the coffee table.

'I – I'm not.' My voice is a bit shaky.

He's quiet for a moment. 'OK.'

One of my hands is resting on the sofa between us. Slowly he reaches over and brushes his little finger against mine, the way he did that day at the cinema. I hold my breath. We look at each other, and he moves his hand more, entwining our pinkies for a moment. Then he pulls back, reaches underneath and clasps my whole hand in his, interlacing all of our fingers. We both stare down at our hands pressed together, like we're surprised they're there, that they belong to us. He starts to run his thumb up and down the back of my hand, up and down, the lightest stroke. My heartbeat doubles.

After a while he blows out a long, quavering breath and slowly, painfully slowly, unfurls his hand from mine, squeezing his eyes shut. I rise tentatively to my feet, but he doesn't move.

My voice comes out hoarse. 'Well ... thanks for letting me have some of the chilli you made.'

He smiles, but doesn't say anything, his eyes still closed, head against the back of the sofa. I glance at the mugs and cafetière on the coffee table, and decide I'll deal with them in the morning.

I want to reach down, touch his face, trace my fingertips across his eyelids, kiss them ...

Instead I turn and walk to my room, feeling both heavy and light.

Chapter Nineteen

I've only just begun to feel vaguely human as five-thirty rolls around and I can finally think about locking up the shop. When Luc saw how green around the gills I was, he stayed to man the till an extra hour so I could sit in the darkened back room for a while. I'm not sure if it made me feel any better, though; I sat with my head resting on my arms at the staff table, replaying last night, sometimes augmenting the later moments in my mind. *Ryan gets up off the sofa and follows me, comes into my room, into my bed . . .*

Even through the thick fuzz of my hangover, I knew thinking that kind of thing, especially now that he and I were maybe, possibly, dancing on the edge of something, was a very bad idea. I tried to focus on Marcy, on the sense of betrayal she'd feel if any of this shit really went anywhere. I tried to think about the word 'loyalty', but that just made me feel queasier.

I still can't believe I told Ryan about finding David Barnett. I don't regret it, but I worry what he really makes of it, and of me not telling anyone. Does he think it's some sort of perverse, masochistic thing? Maybe that's true. I worry too about the fact he knows he's the only person I've told – what kind of significance might he attach to that? I suppose he wouldn't be wrong in any assumptions he made. Maybe 'dark confession' is a very twisted way I have of trying to get an unavailable guy to find me attractive? Jesus.

I wrap my scarf tighter around my neck as I trudge to the bus stop, and just as a bus pulls up, I hear my phone beep. I pull it out as I get on and sit down, cringing at the fact that I hope it's Ryan, even though I'm not even sure he has my number. My heart sinks when I read the text.

Hey hon, class starts at 8.30 pm, meet u there 8.15 yeah? xx

Beverly. I totally forgot I'd agreed to try a new yoga class with her. Even though there's ten months before the wedding, she's become obsessed with getting into shape. Much as I'm dying to sack it off, I think it might be a good idea to be out of the flat for a bit. I don't want to let her down, and some exercise and meditation might help me work on my self-control.

Cool. In a bit xx

My stomach clenches with hunger as I get through the door of the flat, despite having had a mountain of chips at lunch in an attempt to soak up the last of the rum and wine. Thankfully, it seems Charlie's been fed and walked already – he raises his head as I come in but then goes back to snoozing contentedly in his basket. The flat is quiet. Ryan's out – but on the stove is the pot of chilli, with a sticky note attached to its lid. A thrill of happiness goes through me before I've even read it, chased by discomfort at feeling so gleeful that he left me a bloody Post-It.

Back later. There just happens to be some left-over chilli, if you just happen to be hungry. Not you specifically, just anyone generally. Hope work was OK. I'm only just feeling less like a ball of C's matted fur. Hope you are too. R

I grin like an idiot, and look into the pot. I'm not sure if it's a good idea to eat a bowl of chilli before doing yoga, but I can't resist. I click on the burner to heat it up, and then check through the post on the counter. Bills, junk – and a letter from the police, addressed to me. I grab the letter and head to my room, like I need to hide away to read it. Not that it really matters now Ryan knows – and he's not even here. He might have seen it when he brought the letters up from downstairs, but ... I know I'm stalling, and I rip it open, only to find that it's a generic 'victim and witness support' letter with a number and email address to contact if needed.

'Bit late for that,' I mutter, and scrunch it up, then get changed for yoga and go to check on the chilli.

'And whenever you're ready, stretch out in your final resting pose ...'

I have to suppress a smirk at the woman's breathy voice, but it really does feel good to sink down on to the mat – I was wrong in thinking this might be a gentle workout. I'm covered in sweat, but at least I feel like some of my kinks have been forced out, which is definitely good. Except now I'm thinking about kinkiness, and being worked out by—

'God, I feel like I could fall asleep,' Bev murmurs from her mat next to me.

'Mmm, yeah, I reckon I'll come back. It's a good class.'

'We could make it a regular thing, you and me,' Bev says, sitting up slowly. 'I don't get to see you enough.'

I hoist myself up too, and we start to roll up our mats with the rest of the class. 'Definitely. Sounds good. Us mortals have to stick together – I can't keep up with Marcy's exercise regime.'

Bev laughs. 'Maybe I should get her to drill-sergeant me when it gets closer to D-Day.'

'Babe, you don't need to lose any weight, seriously.'

She raises an eyebrow at me, but she honestly can't be more than a 12, and even if she was, I don't really see what's wrong with that. I'll have to try and bite my tongue on the wedding-prep stuff, but other than that it would be nice to see Bev more.

We head to the changing rooms to shower, and I watch Beverly retwist her new braids artfully into a bun after she's rinsed off, and smooth lotion into her already velvety skin. I wonder if I should make more of an effort with myself sometimes. Maybe if I gave more thought to looking after the outside, the inside would start to feel better too? Although, since last night, I've hardly thought about everything that finding David's brought up.

'So what's the low-down on Marcy's bloke?' Bev says, and my eyes flick up guiltily as I finish getting dressed. 'I never got to meet him at that party last month.'

'Ryan?' I clear my throat, feeling like she knows something, even though there's nothing really to know. 'Yeah, he's cool. He's . . . yeah. He's quite different to her usual. I mean, remember Saul?'

Bev scoffs. 'Yeah, he was a prick.' She stuffs her toiletries back into her bag, then pulls it on to her shoulder along with her yoga mat.

'I'll need to get one of those,' I say, pointing to it. 'The ones you borrow in class smell like feet.'

She chuckles and wrinkles her nose, but she's clearly not done with the topic of Ryan. I wish she would be. I know it makes me a terrible, awful person and an even worse friend, but it twists my gut talking about him being with Marcy.

'They've been a thing for, what, six months?' she asks.

'Four, I think.'

'Blimey. Still, that's practically a lifetime for Marcy, right?'

Bloody hell. If my stomach sinks any lower it'll be in my shoe. 'Yeah, it's a pretty long time for her. Would be for me, too, to be honest.'

Beverly nudges me with her shoulder as we head outside. 'Aw, come on, hon, you're just biding your time.'

I smile. 'Oh yeah,' I say wryly. '*Or,* actively repelling men. Potato, potahto.' She laughs, but I have to force myself to join in. *Or,* I think, *I've already found the person I want, but too late – or it was too soon to know, and* now *it's too late.*

Yup, there goes my heart, sinking down into the other shoe.

'Look at you. Even in sweats and a smile any man would be lucky to have you,' she says, giving me a quick hug as we get to the tube station.

'Are you flirting with me, Bev?' I say with a chuckle.

'I would, but I'm taken, hon,' she says, flashing her rock again. 'See you next week!'

I wave as she descends the steps, and turn to start the walk home. It's a good twenty-five minutes, and I could get the bus, but now that I've started on some exercise, I suppose I might as well carry on. It's not raining for once, and milder than it has been for a while. I stroll along, looking in at the windows of bars and at the couples sitting in restaurants, feeling an odd yearning – so much so that when I spot a familiar figure through the window of a pub, I think I'm imagining him.

But no – Ryan really is in there, on a small stage, sitting on a stool with his guitar. I stand at the window like a pauper in a

Christmas advert, looking in. The room's quite dark except for lights at the bar, and one warm spotlight is trained on him as he plays. Blood surges into my veins, as if it had forgotten how to move through them before my eyes fell on him again. The light hits the contours of his face, and his dark hair, which is starting to grow out, reflects it. His brow furrows earnestly, his lips part as he breathes in between phrases. He's singing. I've never heard him sing, and I can only hear the faintest strains out here, but I'm scared to go inside because I've never felt so painfully drawn to someone in my whole life. It's as though I could be pulled in without even trying, cracking the glass of the window until it shatters.

So I just stare, from outside. There's a handful of people sitting at tables near the little stage, some chatting, some watching him. Further back, people are standing, drinking, carrying on as though nothing's happening. I start to edge closer to the door, but then back away. Ryan wouldn't want me to just turn up like this, would he? He would have mentioned it otherwise – he's never suggested he wanted me to come and see him perform. A couple push their way outside for a smoke, and the man holds the door open for me as I hover. Then I walk slowly inside.

Ryan picks the guitar strings intricately in a sort of acoustic solo, then, eyes closed, launches into the final lines of his song. His voice is deep and rumbling, both surprising and also exactly how I would have expected him to sound. I edge towards a pillar near the middle of the room and lean against it, hoping the crowd will hide me a little. His music fills the air, and I know he's written the lyrics himself – they're so *him*, somehow. He holds one last, long note, strums a final chord, and comes to a stop. I feel myself panting, as if I have been holding a note too. The handful of people around the stage begin to clap, one or two whoop, and then the rest of the crowd in the room politely joins in the applause.

'Thanks,' Ryan says, his mouth a little too close to the microphone as he stands up. Just as he does, our eyes meet. A look of surprise crosses his face, and I swallow hard, holding up my hand in an apologetic wave. I'm about to turn and leave, but he gestures for me to wait.

Will he be angry? I'm worried he'll think I've followed him, like some kind of lovesick stalker. I watch him put his guitar away carefully in its case, leaning it against a table near the stage before making his way over to me.

'Hey,' he says, a hint of a query in his voice, looking behind me, like he's expecting somebody to be with me.

'Hi. Sorry, I . . . I was just at a yoga class over in Old Street – Beverly dragged me, our mate from uni? – and I was just walking past and saw you. I didn't mean to—'

'No, no, I'm glad you're here.' He parts his lips to say something else, then stops.

'That sounded great. I wish I'd heard more,' I say quietly.

'Oh. Thanks, I don't really . . . This is a bit of a new thing for me, just trying out my own stuff, you know?'

No, I know nothing about trying something new.

He glances back over to the table where his guitar is resting. 'Um, my mate Mark's over there; I think he's the only one who's heard anything much of my warbling before now.'

'Lucky Mark,' I say, looking down at my trainers.

'Well, he's mainly here to make sure at least *one* person clapped,' Ryan says with a grin. We both look over at the table and Mark waves, gesturing to the full pint glasses he's just set down on their table.

'Right, well, I should let you get on with—' I stop as Ryan shakes his head.

'Stay for one. Hair of the dog, so to speak?'

He raises his eyebrows and I find myself flushing, like we have a shared secret. Maybe we do.

'OK, one. You guys are all right for drinks . . . ?'

'Oh, no, I'll get it.' He starts towards the bar and I follow behind him. When he leans against it to order, I want to press myself into his strong back and put my arms around his waist and close my eyes and breathe in—

'Taylor?'

'Sorry?'

'What would you like?'

'Oh, uh, glass of red?' I chuckle, embarrassed. His eyes glint as he looks at me for a moment before turning back. He orders and hands my drink to me, his fingers brushing mine slowly, deliberately. I take a sip and just about manage to murmur my thanks before following him over to the table, taking a deep breath. I set down my wine and smile at his friend as I pull off my coat and scarf, feeling a bit self-conscious in my zip-up Adidas top and wishing I'd at least put on some eyeliner when I left the yoga studio.

'Taylor, this is Mark. Mark, this is Marcy's best mate, Taylor,' Ryan says, looking down at his beer. I feel a pinprick of awkwardness at the way he put me in context. But then I remember that I *am*, of course, Marcy's best mate and also a terrible, disloyal, jealous human being.

'Nice to meet you,' I say, and Mark reaches out to shake my hand over the table, smiling warmly, an assessing look in his eye. Maybe Bev's right – some guys clearly do like sporty.

'Likewise,' he says, still holding on to my hand. I smile with more enthusiasm than I'd initially mustered and pull it away. I can't pretend it's not an ego boost: he's good-looking, in a dishevelled sort of way. Ryan takes a large gulp of his beer.

'So Ry's been freeloading at yours while Marcy's off around the world, eh?' Mark says, looking teasingly over at Ryan, who rolls his eyes at me, clearly starting to regret inviting me to the table. Or maybe he wishes we were alone.

'He pulls his weight,' I counter. 'His chilli's pretty damn good.'

Mark glances between us and takes a sip of his pint. 'Fair enough,' he says with a hint of a raised eyebrow. Ryan grins into his drink.

I realise Mark might start to get the sort-of-right wrong impression, so I make an effort to turn my attention fully on to him.

'So, how do you know Ryan?' I say, looking Mark in the eye and running a finger absently around the rim of my wine-glass. A little flirting will hopefully distract him from thinking about Ryan and me like that. Though I should probably worry less about how things sound, and more about how they really feel . . .

'Oh, we were at uni together. English and Drama. But I gave up the artistic dream and went into the glamorous world of recruitment consultancy. Been nearly a year now,' he says with a self-deprecating laugh. He has very straight teeth, and his smile does make him seem more handsome.

'Well, a job's a job I suppose,' I say, taking a sip of wine. I can feel Ryan looking at me, and I resist the pull of his gaze.

'What do you do?'

'Hah, speaking of "a job's a job". I work in an art bookshop. You know, fancy over-priced coffee-table stuff.' I shrug. 'Pays the rent, just.'

'Do you want to be an artist?' he asks, leaning his elbows on the table.

'No . . . I . . . Not like . . . ' I stop myself, and sigh. 'To be honest, I don't really know what I want to do.' A lie, but I don't want to get into it. I smile quickly, and Mark smiles back. From the corner of my eye I see Ryan already draining the last of his beer, and I finally let myself turn to him again.

'What are you guys up to tonight then?'

'Not sure . . .' Mark begins hopefully. 'Fancy staying for another?' He sort of says it to both of us but I know he means me. But I don't want another drink. I want to go home and be alone with Ryan, dancing on the edge.

'I'm pretty knackered,' Ryan says, and my heart lifts and sinks, over and over. 'I might head home.'

Does he think I want to stay? 'Well, I'm not exactly dressed for a night on the tiles,' I say quickly. 'I think I might head back too.'

'You look pretty good to me,' Mark says boldly, and I smile.

'Oh yeah, this make-upless post-workout look is all the rage now.'

He laughs, but I take one last sip of my wine and start to stand up. Ryan stands too, slightly holding on to the back of my chair to help me. It's the subtlest cock fight, but I kind of like it. I smile a little to myself and reach down to pull on my coat.

'It was really nice to meet you, Mark,' I say. 'Hopefully see you again sometime.'

'Yeah,' he says, standing up too. We all start to make our way to the door, and he edges a little closer to me, lowering his voice, though of course Ryan can still easily hear. 'Listen, I hope you don't mind me asking, but I'd love to get your number? If that's cool, I mean . . .'

'Oh. Yeah, sure.' I swallow a little as Ryan holds open the pub door for me, and we all walk outside. Mark pulls out his phone and I give him my number, having a sudden flashback of giving my details to the policeman beside the river. My stomach lurches and I force a smile on to my face, feeling a churning mixture of anxiety, sadness, guilt, and pleasure at the flattery.

'I'll give you a call,' Mark says, and I nod, keen to get away.

'See you later, mate,' Ryan says, giving him a brief half-hug. He shifts his guitar on his shoulder impatiently as Mark says goodbye to me with a kiss on the cheek, and I flush and pull away.

Mark heads off in the opposite direction, and Ryan and I begin walking back to the flat in silence.

Chapter Twenty

'Sorry about that,' Ryan says at last.

Our pace is quick, our gazes mostly on the pavement in front of us. I glance over at him. His knuckles are pale as he clutches the strap of his guitar case, tense.

'Sorry for what?' I say cheaply. I'm baiting him, and it's childish, but I'm only doing it because I can't just reach out my hand and—

'Mark. He cracks on to practically everyone he comes into contact with. It's painful really.'

'Oh, right.' Jesus, my voice comes out too high; I genuinely sound like a four-year-old about to have a sulky fit. 'Cheers for the vote of confidence.' I try to sound light-hearted, and fail miserably.

'Taylor, I didn't mean that you're not ... Of *course* he ...' He sighs hard. 'You know that's not what I meant.'

The way he says "you know" makes my heart stutter. I stop walking, pretending I need to retie my shoelace, so Ryan can't see my face. He waits for me, and I draw in a few breaths, staring at his boots, before I stand, ending up unintentionally close to him – which negates the attempts at calming myself down. *Walk. Start walking again* ...

I pace off, and he turns to catch up with me.

'Is he a serial killer?' I ask before he can say anything.

'No, obviously n—'

'Does he cheat on his girlfriends? Does he *have* a girlfriend?' I wince at that one.

'No, look—'

'Well then, what's the big deal?'

'It's just *embarrassing*. He's my mate, and I didn't want you to feel uncomfortable, that's all.'

'Well, I didn't. Feel uncomfortable.' I avoid his eyes, sure this is *totally* convincing.

'OK. Well, good, I suppose,' Ryan mumbles as we turn the corner towards the flat. He sighs. 'I mean, he's a good guy. Obviously, he's my mate. I just, I don't know ... I'm probably just jealous.'

My eyes dart up to him.

'I mean, he was always more confident than me,' he adds, jaw muscle clenching.

We fall quiet while I attempt to process what he's said – whether he means what I want him to mean, or if I'm just allowing my feelings of desperation and hopefulness to cloud things.

We finally get to the door of the flats and Ryan gets his keys out. We walk up the stairs to our front door and I hover behind him as he unlocks it. He steps aside for me to go through, openly gazing down at me as I pass by him, and takes a deep breath. I'm conscious of every beat of my heart, feeling my pulse travelling around my body, everywhere, especially right *there*.

I move slowly, and he follows me inside, so close behind me I can feel him, but we don't say anything, and he doesn't quite touch me ... And I step away.

And the moment's gone.

I head to my room, close the door, lean against it, like I can barricade myself in. After a while, I take off my coat and dump my stuff on the bed, letting out a little groan of frustration and worry and pent-up desire. I'm not leaving this room until it's safe.

I could be here some time.

I hear a knock, light and tentative, but I try to ignore it. I've spent forty-five minutes trying to read my book, an hour internet-surfing crappy sites, and I'm about to launch into my second downloaded episode of a trashy American soap, but I still can't feel a veil of tiredness descending. I'm worried if I switch off my laptop and try to sleep, I'll end up thinking too much about the ache running through the centre of my body, and doing what I'd usually do to relieve it – while thinking about him. But now I can't, because it just feels too close to possibility. I think. I wish?

The knock again.

'Taylor? Are you awake?'

Shit. It's like he can hear me thinking. I glance at the clock – it's edging towards one in the morning.

'Uh ... yeah. Come in.'

Ryan opens the door and peers into the darkness. I realise my laptop is the only light in the room and maybe it looks a little dodgy. I swing the computer around to show him the ladies paused mid-bitch-fight on the screen, and he laughs.

'It wasn't too loud, was it? I should have put my headphones in—'

'No,' he says quickly. 'No, I just wanted to see if ... I mean, I wanted to check if you were ... ' He sighs and starts again. 'I was a dickhead earlier, and I was worried you were pissed off with me,' he mumbles.

I reach over and switch on my bedside light, squinting a little at the change in brightness. It looks like he's been to bed then got up again. He's leaning against the wall next to the door, his hands in the pockets of his jogging bottoms, wearing an old T-shirt of soft, worn cotton that makes me want to reach underneath it and touch his warm skin; the way his jogging bottoms hang off his hips makes me want to reach over and—

'I'm not pissed off with you,' I say with a sigh, shutting my laptop and setting it next to me on the bedclothes. 'I thought maybe it was a good idea if we got a bit of space.'

He looks down at the floor. His feet are bare. 'OK. Yeah. You're probably right.' He pushes off from the wall like he's going to leave.

'But ... I don't know,' I murmur. 'I tend to overreact to things sometimes.'

The side of his mouth turns up a bit. 'Oh. OK. Me too.'

He doesn't move, and we stare at each other, indecision crackling across the distance between us. I clench my hand into a fist under the bedclothes, between my crossed legs.

'You know what?' I whisper.

'What?' His voice is a low rumble.

'I might get up and have a smoke.'

He clears his throat. 'OK. Yeah ... I might join you.'

I nod, and swing my legs out from under the covers to stand up. Then I remember I'm only wearing a T-shirt and pants as sleepwear. No bra. Ryan's lips part as I turn to face him, reach down for some discarded drawstring bottoms and slip them on. I can't help smiling a little as I pull the strings and tie them, and he lets out a disappointed sigh. I grab a cardigan and my cigarettes.

'Come on, then,' I say, striding past him into the dark corridor.

In the living room, I feel my way over to the table next to the sofa and switch on the light. My feet are already chilly against

215

the floor, and I reluctantly crack the window open a bit, then change my mind. 'It's too fucking cold for the window. Couple of cigarettes won't exactly turn the place into a smoking den.' Ryan raises an eyebrow.

'Such a rebel,' he says with a smirk, and I roll my eyes.

'Why don't you make yourself useful and get an ashtray? There's one hiding on top of the fridge.'

His grin widens at my bossiness, and I can't help finding it impossibly sexy. 'Yes, ma'am,' he says.

I look at the sofa, think better of it, and head for the armchair. I cross my legs, tucking my feet in to warm up and pulling my cardi closer around me. Then I light up, watching the smoke float around the room, feeling naughty. Ryan comes back with the ashtray and puts it down on the table, then he slumps on to the side of the sofa nearest to me and reaches over for the cigarettes. We're quiet for a while.

'My dad used to smoke. My biological dad,' Ryan says eventually, then shakes his head. 'That sounds so ... clinical.' He flicks his cigarette into the ashtray, and I lean in and do the same. 'But the smell of it, that's one of my earliest memories.'

'Like what age?'

'Must have been maybe four? He didn't ... He was older, and he didn't live with my mum. I don't really remember any of that very well, but I found out later. Anyway, yeah, he'd come round and give me a toy or whatever, and smoke the whole time. I suppose that's why smoking makes me feel ... like I'm being rewarded, or like a bribe maybe? Sense memory.'

'Sense memory,' I repeat with a small smile, nodding. I think I understand that. 'So if that was with your bio – I mean, if that was with your birth parents, how old were you when you were adopted?'

'Six, going on seven. I wasn't adopted straight away. I was

216

in foster care for nearly two years before Mum and Dad came along.'

'Oh, right.' I clear my throat, suddenly picturing Ryan as a little boy. Vulnerable. He still seems that way sometimes. I feel a swell of emotion towards him, and try not to let it show in my voice. 'And why *were* you . . . ?'

'Put in care?'

He says 'care' like it should have quotation marks around it. I nod, and he shifts a little in his seat, taking a long drag on his cigarette.

'Well, like I say, my father wasn't really in the picture, and he died around the time I turned five. And my mum, she was . . . She found it hard to cope. She was an addict.' He coughs, his translucent brown eyes looking distant. I desperately want to reach out for his hand, touch his face, but somehow I stay put. 'It wasn't a good time. I suppose people at my school were concerned, and eventually they decided it was best if I didn't stay with her. Obviously I didn't really understand – I just wanted to stay with my mum.' He stops for a while, and I stay quiet, not wanting to interrupt. 'Even that young, I felt like . . . A wall went up against her inside me, after it happened. After it seemed like she didn't fight to keep me. But I get it now. Well, more or less.' He flicks more ash. 'I reckon . . . God, it sounds shit to say, but it was the best thing that happened to me.' He looks over at me, and I realise I've left my cigarette to burn down. I stub it out, and try to find my voice.

'Is she clean now?'

He shrugs. 'She's still struggling, I think. But she's better than she was. And I know she wishes things could have been different.' He looks down, then takes one last puff of his cigarette before putting it out too.

'Ryan.' He closes his eyes briefly when I say his name, when he hears the emotion in my voice. I have to fight with myself not to move next to him, to wrap my arms around his neck. 'I don't think it sounded like a shit thing to say, by the way,' I say quietly. He looks up, and I try and hold his gaze, try to reassure him with my eyes the way he does with me.

'Thanks,' he whispers.

'I mean it,' I reply. I blow out a long, slow sigh. 'I think you're ... God, especially with all that, I actually don't get how you're so ...'

'So ...?' he leads, and I get a flashback to our fight when we were walking Charlie.

'So considerate.' I blush. 'And ... I don't know. Calm. It just doesn't seem like you're carrying it on your back. It doesn't seem to weigh you down.'

He looks at me, his eyes roaming all over my face before meeting my gaze again. 'I have my moments,' he murmurs.

I arch an eyebrow.

'I do.' His eyes hold mine. 'Sometimes I feel like there's knives in my chest, like there's somebody inside me, punching, kicking, screaming, angry, *trapped*. Sometimes I have to fight with myself not to do something crazy, something stupid, to let the frustration out. I have to channel it. I have to try not to let what happened, or what still happens ... Things that are outside of my control ...' He blinks at me. 'I try not to let them overwhelm me. You know?'

I don't say anything, because I don't know what to say. I want to *do*. I want to touch. I want to fold myself around him. His eyes are shining with emotion.

'Elaine, my, um, my birth mum. She had this thing printed out on her wall in a frame, when I went to visit her that first time. Well, I'm sure she still does. It was the Serenity Prayer. You know, the thing they say in twelve-step programmes?'

218

I nod. I've heard it on TV or in films, I think.

"'God grant me the serenity to accept the things I cannot change; the courage to change the things I can; and the wisdom to know the difference.'" His eyes return to mine. 'I don't know about the God bit. I don't know if anyone or anything can *grant* you the serenity. I think it has to come from inside you.' He touches his chest, and my eyes drop to his hand. *I want I want I want* . . . 'But I love that word. "Serenity". If you can be serene, serene enough to know what you can control and what you can't? I reckon that's the key. That's what I try to do.'

I nod, blinking away tears that I hadn't realised were starting to form. 'That is a beautiful word,' I whisper. I want him to say it again. *Serenity.*

He draws in a breath and then leans closer to me. 'Taylor, I—'

I shake my head, stopping him, because I'm scared of what he wants to say. 'You do hide it well, though,' I say quickly. 'The turmoil, I mean.' I chuckle, but it comes out mirthless. 'I mean, look at me: you've said it yourself, I'm a fucking mess—'

'I don't recall ever saying that,' he says firmly, his expression chastising. 'Anyway, it's not a competition. If it was, I'd fucking win.' He's grinning slowly now, and I bite back a genuine smile.

'I don't know about that.'

'No, actually, me neither.' His face grows serious again.

I look at my hands, my fingers playing with the edge of a thumbnail. 'I have moments too. But in the other direction,' I say, my voice quiet. 'It's like, most of the time I'm fairly low, frustrated. Sad.' I glance at him. 'But there are moments where I feel . . . unburdened, happier, lighter. Maybe even serene.' Ryan smiles. 'And then when something happens – like . . . finding David Barnett?' I pause, biting my lip. 'I know that's not an everyday thing, finding a dead man. Obviously. But I feel so *heavy.* It's weighing me all the way back down.'

'But that's not strange, Taylor. That's—'

My eyes flick up to his. 'I know that. But it's like it's pulling at me when I'm already sinking. And . . . And . . . ' My breath is speeding up, I feel panicky. 'And the thing is, it's not quite bad enough to say, "Oh, there's something wrong, a doctor could help," or . . . or, you know, it's not like I'm at *their* level. David Barnett, or my mother. Not *depressed*. I'm just *low*. But sometimes I worry I'll *always* be like this, Ryan.' I hear my voice getting more strained, and I blink away tears quickly. 'It's like she conditioned me. Even when she was alive, I was always waiting, waiting for something awful to happen, worrying, getting angry with her, with myself, and – and . . . It's not something she could help. It wasn't her fault. I mean, if *I* feel low? God, it was so much worse for her. Otherwise she never would have done what she did. I have to believe that. She wouldn't have left me if it wasn't. A-and I *hate* what she did, and I'm scared of ending up like her, but then sometimes I think, at least it would be a *decision*, d'you know what I mean?' I look at him again, hearing myself rambling, saying stupid stuff. He's frowning, and I exhale a trembling sigh. 'I just don't *want* to always feel like . . . like I can only remember the bad things, feel the bad feelings. I don't *want* to feel abandoned, I want to feel—'

'Hey, hey.'

I'm breathing hard now, and I feel anxiety rising in my chest. A tear brims over and spills down my cheek. 'Sorry.'

'Come here.'

I shake my head, but find myself standing up, and Ryan sits forward, holding his hand out towards me. I'm trembling a little. I put my hand in his, and he guides me over next to him. I slump down on to the sofa and pull my hand away, make fists in my lap, but he reaches over and unfurls my fingers. He runs his fingertips over the palm of my hand.

'Breathe,' he whispers.

I look at him and take a deep breath, which he mirrors, like he did that first day. I feel another tear spill on to my cheek, but somehow I feel steadier already.

'It's OK,' he whispers. 'I understand.'

He's telling the truth.

Ryan pulls my hand up towards his mouth and presses my knuckles to his lips. I sigh, my muscles relax a little, and I give in and rest my head on his shoulder. He blows out a long breath, ruffling my hair, and I feel his cheek lean against the top of my head. After a moment he lifts his arm so I can settle under it, reaching around me and pulling me close. I turn towards him, press my face into the warm skin of his neck. His grip tightens, and his breathing gets faster for a moment, then calms again. One of my hands rests on his stomach, then twists into the fabric of his T-shirt so I can hold him tighter. I feel his lips press against my hair, and he sighs again, but says nothing. My eyelids sink shut.

He doesn't let me go.

Chapter Twenty-one

I open my eyes. It's still dark outside. I realise I must have fallen asleep, still entwined with Ryan on the sofa. His chest rises and falls steadily as I lean against him, my hand still on his stomach, one of his resting gently on top of it. Eventually I pull away a little to sit up, and he moans groggily. I twist, stretching my arms up, trying to reanimate my muscles, and feel his hand slide around my waist, gripping me and pulling me back towards him.

'Mmm.'

'Ryan . . .'

I reach down, not wanting to prise his arms away but doing it anyway, because I know I should.

'Stay,' he whispers.

I inhale deeply, fighting with myself, trying to resist. 'I should go to bed.'

He sighs, and we both sit up straighter. He leans forward, elbows on his knees, face in his hands as he rubs his eyes. I squeeze at the muscles around my neck, blinking hard, and then get up, looking down at him. He holds a hand out sleepily for me to help him stand, and I pull him up. He rises to his full height, and his position blocks my path to the door. He looks down at me, his body close, heat in his eyes.

'Ryan ...' I say again, a note of warning in my voice. I reach up a hand to push past him, but it lands on his chest, and I feel the muscle there tense under his thin T-shirt. I should move my hand away, but somehow I don't.

'Hmm?'

'I'm gonna go to bed.'

'OK ...'

He reaches his hands up to the sides of my face, brushing my loose curls back, sinking his fingers into them, tilting my head towards his. I find my arms slipping around him, my hands sliding up the muscles of his back. He leans his face down towards mine, and I rise up on to my tiptoes. He presses his forehead to mine, his breath brushing over my face in rapid pants. I feel him stir against my hip as I press my body in towards him, and I let out a quiet, faintly embarrassing whimper. I move my lips closer to his, barely brushing them, and his breath comes out more ragged now. We could stop. We should stop ... I pull back a fraction, and he licks his lower lip, slipping his hands around to the back of my neck, his fingertips brushing lightly against the nape. And then slowly, ever so slowly, he leans down, and finally presses his mouth against mine. Firmly, resolutely, warmly, softly ... A low sound emits from deep in his throat, and he begins to move his lips, tilting my head in his hands, and I moan, and my own lips part, and his tongue presses inside, the tip of it lightly teasing mine, then moving deeper, and I press my whole body against his, my hands slipping under his T-shirt, against his burning skin. He groans again, his hands tousling my hair, one breaking away to run down the length of my spine, then up, under my T-shirt, around to the front, slowly up my ribcage, under my naked breast. He exhales against my lips and I drink it in with my own gasp. The very tip of his thumb grazes up against my nipple, and I think I'm going to burst. He's hard and long against me through our clothes, and the pulse of needing him throbbing right through the very centre of me, and just as we stumble towards the sofa, just as he bumps against it with the back of his legs, just as we're about to sink down on to it, just then.

He stops.

He pulls his lips away from mine. We look at each other, breathing hard. Our hands slip slowly away from one another's bodies, fall to our sides. I feel the blood drain from my face, watch his stricken expression as my face falls.

'Taylor, I—'

'No.'

'Please, I just—'

'No. This was a mistake.'

'*Please* . . .' He reaches for my hand, but I snap it away. 'Wait. Taylor—'

'No. No.' My voice is a whisper, tears pooling like acid in my eyes, but I don't let them fall. I push past him, like I should have done before.

I can't get into my room quickly enough. I slam the door, pressing my eyes shut and letting the burning liquid spill down both my cheeks. I feel sick. How could I have let that happen? How could I have let it go this far? Marcy's name pulses through my mind over and over. How could we do this to her? I clutch my stomach, waiting. Hoping he'll leave me alone.

Hoping he won't.

I hear Charlie scrabbling against the door, woken by the slamming, I guess. I tense as I hear Ryan shoo him off, and back away, sitting down hard on the bed, facing the door, as the light goes on in the kitchen. Biscuits hit the dog bowl, then the light goes off again.

Then I can ... feel him, on the other side of the door.

He doesn't say anything. He doesn't knock.

After what feels like for ever, I hear his bare feet slap against the floor as he walks back to his room. *Their* room. The door closes.

I shuffle back on the bed, switch off the bedside light and slip my legs under the duvet, pulling it up around me, trying to pad myself against the feelings that threaten to crush me, and stare out into the darkness of my bedroom, stunned.

How could I have been so utterly, utterly stupid?

I've barely closed my eyes again before my alarm clock goes off. I slam the button too forcefully and the whole thing slides off my bedside table and clatters to the floor.

'Fuck!'

I can already feel the heavy bags under my eyes. This feels worse than the hangover yesterday. Much worse. I squeeze my eyelids shut and cover my face with my hands, remembering afresh what happened last night. Remembering what Ryan told me. *Be serene* ... Remembering the warmth of his body next to me, holding me. Remembering his hands in my hair, his lips, his tongue, his fingertips against my skin ...

Thank God he stopped us before we— But why did he? For the same reason I should have, the same reason I'm so glad he did. Because of Marcy. Every time I think about it, I get a stabbing pain right in my centre: guilt, frustration, relief, guilt, rejection. Rejection. Rejection. Guilt. Guilt. Guilt. Even though I know it's better than whatever I'd be feeling now if we'd gone further. If we'd slept together – well, we did sleep together. But if we'd had sex? Made love ...?

'Dammit,' I whisper.

I jump as the front door closes. Ryan, taking Charlie out.

Avoiding me. I exhale, push the duvet away and go to shower quickly. If I scrub hard enough, maybe I can get rid of some of the mortification that's still clinging to me. The hot water runs down my face as I wash quickly, trying not to let more tears come.

It was a mistake. People make them all the time. Humiliated and guilt-ridden as I am, it's better that it happened, and now there's no way it's going to go any further, no way we're going to let it, I can just get the fuck over it all. Over him.

But I know this feeling in the pit of my stomach isn't just guilt because of Marcy. It's also emptiness – loss. Something's ruined, something I hadn't realised I needed quite as much as I did. As I do.

Tears spill. Water washes them away.

For once, I'm actually pleased to get to work, away from the mess at home. I wonder if I could sleep here, make a little cocoon of books and live among them? I spend the morning rearranging the shelves, updating the software on the till, taking an inordinate amount of time to discuss time-lapse photography with a weird old man who wanders in looking for an atlas, and even start researching books for a new display table. I've never cared about work quite so much, as long as it means not thinking about Ryan's fingers brushing against the nape of my neck ...

Thankfully Lucas's arrival snaps me out of an errant daydream replay before I get to the heart-stabbingly painful part. I swing by the deli round the corner to get lunch, and when I come back, Luc's striding down the centre aisle, exaggeratedly running his finger along a shelf to check for dust.

'Very impressive, Ms Jenkins, very impressive indeed.' He arches an eyebrow. 'What's with the sudden assiduousness?'

'Word-of-the-day loo roll again, eh?'

He chuckles.

'Nothing really,' I say, hoping to distract him by handing him his baguette. 'I suppose if I'm going to be in this shithole, I might as well make it the best shithole it can be.'

'Nothing like chat of shitholes before lunch,' he says, taking a big bite of his sandwich anyway, and striding back behind the till. I head into the back to dump my stuff, then join him on the other stool. It's quiet today, but my new-leaf work ethic should be preventing me from letting us eat front-of-store. Oh well.

'So, what's new?' he asks through a giant mouthful.

'Urgh, Luc!'

He swallows, unapologetic. 'Come on. I haven't really seen you properly since we went to the pub. I'm going to start thinking you don't love me any more.'

I pop my Coke can open with a half-smile. 'Nothing's ever new with me.' I know my new-found interest in shelf alignment betrays that statement, and he studies me for a moment before nodding. As ever, he doesn't press me.

'Well, I've taken my affections elsewhere anyway.'

'Really? A girlfriend, seriously?'

'Try not to sound quite so fucking surprised,' he says, and I laugh, genuinely intrigued. He's getting all dewy-eyed just talking about it.

'Is it that zebra-crossing lady you were all excited about the other night?'

'*Xiomara*,' he says scoldingly, then looks slightly embarrassed. 'Uh ... yeah, no. She was an amazing shag though ...' A wistful look clouds his eyes.

'Focus, Luc. Who is it then?'

'I met her in the laundry place round the corner from my house. I was doing my wash and taking a few pictures in there while I was waiting—'

'You do laundry?' I interrupt, and he throws a piece of cucumber at me.

'And anyway, this beautiful girl looms into my viewfinder, and I snap, and she smiles and . . . the rest is very recent history. Her name's Heather. She's a trainee horticulturalist.'

'That's not just a fancy way of saying she grows her own weed or something?'

Luc purses his lips. 'Mrs Cynicism today, aren't we? No. She's, like, a gardener.'

'Sorry, I didn't sleep very well. I'm happy for you, Lucas. That's really cool. Quite the meet cute.'

He grins. 'I know you're jealous really.'

'Definitely.' It's true, though not in the way he's joking about. He gets off his stool and holds out his hand to take my rubbish, throwing our sandwich wrappers in the bin. He pats my shoulder in a gesture of understanding as he edges back past me to straighten the postcards next to the till. I take a breath, and he looks over at me.

'Have you ever regretted . . . ?' I begin, then stop myself.

'Oh, I've definitely regretted.' He smiles a little, then waits.

I shake my head. 'Forget it. Ignore me.'

'Well that would just be rude.' He looks at me patiently.

'I'm . . . ' I take a sip of my Coke. 'I'm thinking if I can impress Rosalind a bit more, maybe I could get a pay rise. And if I get a raise, maybe I could try and find my own place. It's just feeling a bit . . . crowded at mine.'

He nods carefully. 'Isn't Marcy on tour?'

'Yeah, she is. But her boyfriend's there and—'

'Right.' He looks at me, comprehension all over his features now. 'I'll keep an ear out. In fact, Xiomara has a one-bed in Bethnal Green, and she's leaving for New York in a few weeks, she's got a new contract out there. I'm sure she said something about sub-letting. I can attest to its cleanliness and convenience for swift exits.'

I smile, feeling intense gratitude loom up in me for his general Lucasness. I shuffle over and touch his arm. 'Thanks.'

'No probs.' He winks and pats my hand. 'You'll sort it all out, T.'

Before I can respond, he heads into the back room to grab his stuff.

'Right, I'm off.' He hoists his bag on to his shoulder. 'Take it easy. See you on Monday, yeah?'

'Yeah. See you then,' I say, watching him go.

Oh, yeah. The weekend.

I stare out of the bus window, swiping at it as it begins to fog over. There are some really weird things on the top of bus stops. A shoe, a potato with coloured sticks coming out of it, an over-sized bracelet, a pint glass. I try to focus on these sorts of things, and not the rising panic about seeing Ryan again. If he's home. Maybe he's still avoiding me, but part of me just wants to rip this plaster off, start at the business of behaving like nothing ever happened. I'm deliberately heading straight home, and I've got no real plans for the weekend other than cotching in bed and searching the internet for vaguely affordable new accommodation. And trying not to think about Ryan's tongue slipping gently between my lips . . .

My phone vibrates suddenly, and I nearly puke on the screen when I see who the message is from.

Guess what?!? ;)

I stare at Marcy's text, puzzled and afraid – until I realise that, unless she's more ruthless than I've ever given her credit for, she

229

wouldn't put a winky face after a message meaning she's made the discovery that her best friend and her boyfriend have been— Fuck, I need to stop this. We've 'been' nothing. Nothing really happened. And Ryan surely wouldn't be so stupid as to tell her anyway. Would he?

I realise I'm approaching my stop and press the bell, looking at the text again as I get off the bus and start walking home. I think back to Marcy's last email, trying to remember if she'd been waiting for some kind of news. Maybe the tour's been extended? Jesus, I'm not sure if I could handle that – what's left of her being away already feels like a lifetime stretching ahead of me. But no, I'm pretty sure she'd just been bitching a little about their tour manager, joking warmly about the other dancers, and missing a decent cup of tea. And me. And, of course, Ryan.

When I get to the flat I'm too busy trying to open my email inbox on my phone to think about prepping myself for seeing him, but when I let myself in, I hear voices in the living room. Does he have friends round? That's one way to avoid having to confront each other. Good plan. Although it might get weird if it's Mark ... I shut the door loudly to announce my presence, and nearly jump clean out of my skin when I hear a wail from the end of the corridor.

'Teeeeeeeee!'

I'm almost bowled over as Marcy comes steaming out of the living room towards me, wrapping her arms tightly around my neck and giggling hysterically. I can't help joining in, she's just so damn enthusiastic and great and ... here. But my heart feels like it's ricocheting around the walls of my chest with shock and happiness and guilt and worry.

'Fucking hell, Marce. What are you doing here?'

'The boss lady has the flu, so they've rescheduled the

continental Europe dates, so we're picking back up for the London shows early next week, so BLOODY HELL!' She squeezes me again. 'It's so good to be home, I can't even tell you. I've missed you guys so much!'

As she pulls me into another hug, I finally notice Ryan standing in the living-room doorway. He bites his lip as my eyes catch his, but I quickly look away. Obviously he hasn't mentioned anything about last night, and when she pulls back and grins between us, we both manage fairly genuine smiles back at her.

In spite of everything, I feel a huge flood of relief. Maybe it will all be all right; maybe I just imagined everything I was feeling towards Ryan. Yeah, OK, bullshit.

I have to get away for a moment. As I go and dump my stuff in my room, I hear Marcy chattering and giggling. The ache turns into a stabbing pain. I count down from ten, trying to hypnotise myself into a convincing show of nonchalance and mellow happiness, especially given that Marcy already knew I was on a bit of a downer before she left, and I don't want her asking questions. I suddenly wonder: even if Ryan wouldn't be so crazy as to tell her about the kiss, he may well have mentioned me finding David Barnett. I worry Marcy would be pissed off that I told him and not her. Would he do that, share something I told him privately? Another item on the list of secrets between us. Although – awful as it is – I still like the idea of having things that are just between him and me, and I hate the possibility of those bonds being broken.

'Come on, babe!' Marcy shouts, and I walk out of my room, pushing the corners of my mouth into a smile, hoping it reaches my eyes. 'We're going out!' she announces, then holds up a hand immediately as I open my mouth to protest. 'Uh-uh. No way. Don't want to hear it. I've got one night off before we start rehearsals again, and I want to spend it with my two favourite people.'

I grin, but along with my warmth for her, I feel like if I really was a friend I'd tell her that what they say is true – it's the ones you love that can hurt you the most.

I should know.

Chapter Twenty-two

Balloons of relief lift my mood when Marcy tells me that she's booked dinner and the cinema for our little triple date, saying she's sick of loud music, and dancing feels too much like work at the moment. The tour must *really* be bloody hard work, because she never passes up the opportunity to shake her ass.

Marcy's reserved us a table at the bizarre cabaret-meets-fine-dining place where she used to perform sometimes, about a fifteen-minute walk from the flat. She links arms with Ryan and me as we stride down the street, making other pedestrians pass around us. I mention that one of our favourite DJs is in town – I figure now I'm out, I might as well go for it – but she shakes her head.

'Nah, honestly, this is better – we can hear each other talk, catch up. I'm really up for just doing something mellow, getting an early night ...' Marcy looks up at Ryan, and I watch him too, gauging his reaction. He smiles quickly and somewhat awkwardly at her, and I fail to dodge his eyes when Marcy looks away. They hold the same look they did last night, when he stopped the kiss and I stormed away. Like there was something unfinished, that he wanted to explain. I jump guiltily as Marcy releases my arm, but it's because we've arrived at the restaurant.

She breezes inside and her mate Stefan is there to greet us at the door, taking our coats in a flurry of laughter and air kissing. The music's actually pretty loud in here, and there's a weird acrobatic show going on in the centre of the room, so it's maybe not as conducive to chat as Marcy was suggesting. But the vibe boosts my energy a bit.

After we order champagne and Stefan persuades us to let him surprise us with a tasting menu, Marcy sighs and reaches over to squeeze my hand.

'So, how the fuck are you? How's work?'

I grin as she tries to keep a composed facial expression while a lady in a white unitard does the splits next to our table. 'Um, it's good, the same, you know,' I say with a laugh. 'Oh, Luc's found himself a girlfriend apparently.'

'Seriously? Bloody hell, there's hope for us all,' she replies. I pull a wry expression, but she ignores it. 'Speaking of which,' she continues, 'anything more with that guy you met the other night? I can't believe I didn't get to scope him out—'

'From the club? No,' I say quickly, glancing at Ryan, then down at the table. 'God, no, that was just . . . That wasn't anything.'

Stefan comes over, pausing the conversation, and pours out our champagne. The three of us clink glasses, and Ryan's eyes lock on to mine for a moment. He nods towards me. 'Actually, Mark asked Taylor out,' he says, then looks over at Marcy, taking another sip of his drink.

'Oh *really*?' Marcy purrs, a grin spreading across her face. Why the hell is he bringing that up? I sigh and force a smile, gritting my teeth and firing invisible darts at Ryan with my eyes. *Thanks a lot.* Maybe I wasn't misinterpreting his comment about being jealous. Well, I guess obviously not, in fact. *Him asking me to stay . . . his lips on mine . . .*

I feel a twinge in my heart at the lack of possibility between us, and hate myself for having these thoughts with Marcy right next to me.

'He didn't ask me *out*,' I retort stiffly. 'He just asked for my number. It was no big deal.'

'When was this?'

'Uh, the other day at the pub,' I say, deliberately vague. It's actually hard to believe it was only yesterday evening, given what happened afterwards. I take another sip of my champagne. 'Ryan was performing.' *If he's going to play throw-you-under-the-bus, I will too.*

Marcy's loose body language becomes ever so slightly less fluid. 'What, playing guitar?' She can't hide the surprise in her voice, though she tries to stay casual.

'Yeah, and singing one of his songs,' I say, and her expression tightens a tiny bit more. Jesus, I'm a bitch. But it's not *her* I mean to make feel bad, I tell myself.

I need to stop. This is a very stupid road to go down.

Marcy turns to Ryan, nudging him with one bare, silky-skinned shoulder. 'Finally putting it out there, eh? So to speak,' she says with a wink. 'That's great.' Her smile is still a bit forced, and Ryan shrugs.

'I've just been trying a few things out, yeah. I'll play them for you.' He leans over and kisses her cheek, a gesture of appeasement. I stare down at my plate. 'Taylor just happened to pass the pub when I was playing.' I look up again, and his eyes are hard to read. I nod at Marcy, confirming what he said. 'That was when Mark made his move,' he adds, with a tight smile. 'He was there for moral support, since I didn't have you here, and he's heard stuff from back at uni, so ...' He tails off as our first course arrives, and we all eat quietly for a bit. It's delicious, but over in about two bites. I think I'm going to be hungry later.

'Mmm,' Marcy says, clattering her knife and fork down dramatically and leaning back in her chair. 'That was fucking good. Anyway, so back to Mark ...'

'So glad this came up,' I say sarcastically.

'But babe, it would be perfect. You with Ry's mate?'

'Marcy, I only gave him my number. We're not exactly headed down the aisle.'

'All right, all right. I'm just saying.' She chuckles, and I stab a stray pea with my fork.

'Anyway, forget the boring shit that's been happening here,' I say, raising the excitement levels in my voice with some effort. 'What about the tour? Tell us all about it!'

'Yeah, can't wait to see the show,' Ryan adds, though his tone lacks conviction. I sigh with relief that he's finally helping me change the subject. Did he bring up Mark because he's trying to put some distance between us? I feel confused, jealous, anxious, the emotions all piling up alongside my guilt. I'm very glad when a waiter causes more distraction by clearing our plates.

'Actually, that reminds me,' Marcy says. 'I need to sort your comp tickets.' She starts mumbling distractedly to herself. 'I'd better do it now while I remember, cos everyone in the show will be trying to ... Oh, maybe Stefan has Rick's number from when he was in that other production. One sec, guys.' She gets up absently from the table, mobile in hand, and goes to find Stefan.

Ryan and I watch her retreating back as she wends her way between the tables. I concentrate hard on wiping all the condensation from my freshly poured glass of champagne with one finger.

'Taylor.'

I don't look up.

'Are you OK?' he asks quietly, leaning towards me, his voice low.

'You need to stop asking me that,' I say, while loving that he did. I risk a glance. His eyebrows knit together and he sits back in his chair, rubbing his forehead. It makes me want to touch his face, and I hate myself all over again.

'I'm glad she's back.' He pauses, and I wonder if he's telling the truth. 'But I wish she hadn't come back tonight. Taylor, I need to talk to you about—'

'Ryan, let's just not. Just forget about it. She's my fucking best mate.' My chest feels like it's being crushed.

'I know. God, I know that. That's why—' He stops, exhales hard, and I swallow. He leans forward again, closer. 'I'm sorry,' he whispers, fiddling with the edge of the tablecloth. 'Listen, I don't want you to think that last night I didn't *want* to . . . I mean I really, really, *really* wanted to . . . ' He hesitates, and I press my thighs together and stare down at the table as the sound of his really, really, really wanting to moves through me. 'Taylor, please look at me.'

I do, my breath catching at the intense, conflicted expression on his face.

'The problem is, I don't want to forget it,' he whispers urgently. 'I *can't*. Taylor, I can still feel you.' He looks down at his hands like he can't quite believe it, and my pulse begins to pound faster. 'And not just like that. I'm . . . I can't think about anything else *but* you.' He blinks at me. 'I have to tell her.'

My eyes widen, and I stare at him, my heart floating traitorously even as the words escape my lips: 'No. Ryan, no, absolutely not. Please, I . . . ' My voice is shaking; I feel like my whole body is. This is what I want, so badly I can taste it, but panic hits me square in the gut. I can't do this to her. Not to Marcy. 'I . . . ' His eyes bore into mine. My voice is barely audible now. 'I just

237

want to pretend none of this ever happened.' I don't want that. I'm sure he can see it all over my face. 'Please don't tell her anything. Please.'

His expression falls, and I think I see devastation in his eyes. He's silent for what feels like for ever. 'You want to pretend,' he says finally. Not a question.

'Ryan . . .' I try to swallow the quiver in my voice.

'OK.' His eyes say otherwise. His eyes say nothing's OK. 'If that's what—'

He breaks off abruptly. My pulse is still pounding, but I quickly follow to where his gaze has suddenly snapped away from mine, and I try to relax my face. Marcy's grinning, striding triumphantly back towards us with a glint in her eye.

'Wicked,' she says. 'All sorted. I got you a plus-one, T. I think Mark should come to the show too. In fact . . .' she bites her lip faux-guiltily, 'I might have just messaged him and he might have just said he's well up for it!'

'What?' I'm dazed, still trying to recover from what Ryan said.

'Yes, babe! Date night. Well, sort of, I mean Ry will be there, but that could be good, keep it casual at first . . . But baby, you'll keep your distance if things get interesting for T, won't you?' She chuckles and rubs her fingers over Ryan's outstretched hand, then sits back as our next course arrives. 'And then you guys can all come backstage after. It'll be great.' She picks up her fork with a satisfied smile.

'Christ on a bike, Marce,' I mutter, and she snorts.

'Just call me Cupid.'

Ryan studies his napkin closely, and I can see his jaw muscles working. We're both shrouded in a haze of guilt and emotional conflict so thick it might almost be visible. Oh God, what if it is?

He doesn't want to forget. Those words fill me with awful hope.

But I'm afraid, too. I'm so afraid of what all this could mean.

I shift uncomfortably as Marcy, sitting between us, leans over and rests her head on Ryan's shoulder, lifting up his arm so she can nestle under it. I want him to show more willing, but I'm also, in some nasty place in my mind, glad that he's not. Being here is probably stirring memories in him too, though the relentless explosions on the big screen are a bit different from the film we sat in front of That Day. And what he said? That he wants to tell her? I pray silently that he'll respect my asking him not to. I think he will. I try to push down the ache of knowing he'd choose me, if I could let him.

But I can't.

I try to take my mind off it all, staring at the elaborately choreographed car crash unfolding by the side of the Thames on-screen. Next to me, out of the corner of my eye, I can see Marcy's own eyes shining with excitement – she loves action movies, and usually so do I. But seeing the river unexpectedly draws me back to the sight of David Barnett's body lying on the pebbles, stiff and bloated, and Charlie's anxious barks ... I breathe deeply, overwhelmed by the memory that had been pushed to the back of my mind by the boulder of guilt.

'I'm going to the loo,' I whisper quickly, and Marcy nods, distracted. I feel Ryan's eyes on me as I shuffle my way down the row, away from them so I don't have to squeeze past and risk brushing against him. I don't think I could take him touching me in any way right now. I might just break into pieces.

Stepping gratefully into the quiet of the lobby, I take a few deep breaths and rub my fingers lightly across my palms like Ryan did before we fell asleep.

Sense memory . . .

I head to the toilet, but an attendant is cleaning the ladies' when I try to get in. I'm happy to wait. I actually debate leaving altogether, texting Marcy to say I'm feeling ill, but I know I shouldn't just run away. When the attendant finishes, I head into the loos, shutting the cubicle door and closing the toilet lid, sitting down heavily, sinking my head into my hands and resting my eyes for a moment. I feel like I might keep on sinking for ever.

God. I need to snap out of this. Move on, from all of it. From things I can't help, things I can't change. Things that can't be, things I can't have; Ryan, Anita. *Grant me the serenity* . . . I suppress the first prickling of tears, and think about my mum reading all those ridiculous self-help books, though ironically that would usually be when she was in one of her good spells. They'd always say stuff about 'triggers', things that could easily lead you down a negative path. Like falling for your best friend's boyfriend, or finding suicides lying on riverbanks, I'm guessing.

Something led me to David Barnett, though. He was hard to avoid, in all senses. I thought I'd handled the whole situation OK, got past it, but obviously not. Look at this mess. Never mind triggers, I'm looking down the barrel of the gun. I've been reckless, letting myself lose control. Letting Ryan realise the effect he has on me, even if it's not one-sided . . . Perhaps that's why it aches so badly. I shudder, thinking of how easily I told him all those things I could talk to nobody else about. How *natural* it felt.

How much I trust him.

I head out of the ladies' without even using the loo, and get back to my seat just as the credits start to roll.

'Oh my God, T, I can't believe you missed the ending. It was *sick*!' Marcy says as the lights come on.

240

'I know, I just think that weird foam thing from earlier disagreed with me,' I say with a grimace. She gives me a sympathetic glance, and I shake my head. 'It's cool, I'm fine now. I'll catch it on DVD, eh?'

We head outside, and Marcy entwines her hand with Ryan's. 'Right. Time we got home.'

I follow a few paces behind, but Marcy turns and waits for me to catch up.

The pillow's cool against my cheek as I adjust the headphones over my ears and turn the volume on my phone up. I made my excuses as quickly as I could, and there were certainly no complaints from Marcy. As the next track shuffles, I hold my breath against the silence, genuinely afraid of hearing anything that might be coming from the next room. Sometimes, hearing a couple is kind of sexy, but the very thought of what might be happening in there right now makes my stomach turn over anxiously. I don't know if Ryan would, after what he told me at the restaurant ... But it would be worse still if he felt that urge to be honest with her again? Shit. I'd rather they were having sex. Well, maybe not. God. I pull the covers tighter around me, squeezing my eyes shut, but they fly open as I hear my one of my mother's favourite songs begin to play in my ears. Lena Horne, her voice rich and heartbreaking, singing about having it bad.

My thumb hovers, ready to skip, but I relent and let her continue. 'Listen ... listen,' Anita used to whisper over and over again as this song played, her eyes closed, her fingers flitting through the air, tracing the notes. 'So beautiful ...' she'd murmur. My mother was beautiful, too, especially when she was like that. Lost in beauty rather than darkness. I swallow back tears as I listen. Sometimes I hate missing her. It goes against everything I taught myself after it happened, against my means of survival. Anita wanted it like this. She left me alone, in an attempt to make me strong perhaps, able to handle things by myself. Her lesson of life for me, and probably the only one I've ever really learned. But if that's true, I should be better at this all by now.

I imagine Ryan here now, comforting me like he did last night. But it just makes me feel worse, because I have no right to feel this way. He's not mine, not as far as Marcy is concerned, and that's what matters. I feel tears run down the side of my face into the hair above my ears as the song finishes. It's not like he can make it go away anyhow. He can't stop me feeling these things.

But when I'm with him, I don't feel like I'm wrong for feeling them.

Eventually I risk it – pulling off my headphones, I wait and listen. I peer at my bedside clock: it's been at least two hours since they went to bed. I strain my ears, but there's only silence. I exhale with relief and sit up in bed, wipe my face with a tissue, take a sip of water. I read for a while, until finally my eyelids begin to droop. I switch off the light, but then swing my legs out of the bed, deciding I might need to go to the loo first.

I freeze as I hear their bedroom door open.

Quiet footsteps pad in front of my door. They pause, then move away, perhaps towards the kitchen. Maybe getting something to drink? I hold my breath, straining to listen, then after a while the footsteps return. I jump – suddenly, something slips under the crack below my door. Large, square, flat. I look down in the gloom from the moonlight outside the window, and somehow I know immediately what it is, though I'm completely confused as to why.

Marcy would have knocked, so it must be from him.

It's a record. Vinyl. I can just about make out a Post-it stuck to it, but I can't make out the album cover or anything. It's hard to tell if Ryan's still outside my door. I walk over and rest my fingertips on the handle. If I open it, will he be standing there? Then what? I pull my hand away and reach down to pick up the LP, taking it back to the bed and switching on my lamp again. I look up and see a shadow disappear from under the door, hear the other bedroom door close quietly.

I peel off the note but delay reading the dense writing, like a kid saving the best present until last. It's an old jazz record, by a singer I don't recognise, though perhaps my mother would have – she was like an encyclopedia, and even though she managed to impart a lot of her knowledge to me, gaps remain. The woman on the cover is beautiful, with coffee-coloured skin, wild curls and dark red lips. Her eyes are closed and her hands outstretched mid-song. I think again about how my mother looked when she listened. When she sang.

Finally I look at the note, written in Ryan's tiny scrawl on a Post-it he's obviously taken from the pad in the kitchen. The writing spills on to the other side of the sticky square of paper, and I have to squint to read it all.

You don't have a record player, so I know it's stupid. Her expression just reminded me of you, how beautiful you looked that night in the kitchen. Well, you're always beautiful. But I bought this just after that night, when I barged in on you singing, and then I didn't know if it was weird to give it to you. I noticed later, the trumpet-player credit is a Taylor. Fate? Anyway, she sounds kind of like you too, actually – I listened in the shop. I know you don't want me to say anything, so I won't. But Taylor, I wish—

He's crossed something out.

I can hardly—

More scratching out.

The look on your face when we—

Hard scribbling.

I want to live that moment again. And our first moment. I wish I could start again.

I swallow hard, reading it twice more, going over his words again and again. I stick the note to my bedside table, with hope and fear rising in my chest once more, along with that feeling I'm scared to confront.

Because I think that it really might be love.

I stare at the record, run my fingers around the edges of it. It feels so familiar, reminds me so much of my mother. I wonder if he knew it would. He can't have done – but I think somehow he understood deep down.

That's just how it is with him.

I reach out for my glass of water, my mouth dry. Forgetting about going to the toilet, I get back under the covers and switch off the light, settling the album on the pillow next to me before I fall asleep.

Chapter Twenty-three

'Taylor!'

Marcy's shout echoes across the narrow street as she jogs down the steps and out of the building towards me, waving.

'Hey!' I say with a smile. Other dancers begin ambling out behind Marcy on to the cobbled side street, looking lissom and loose. She reaches the patch of sunlight where I've been waiting, trying to keep warm, and tugs at my scarf. I reach over to give her a quick hug. 'How was rehearsal?'

'Yeah, good. Mate, I'm so gassed for tonight, I can't wait for you guys to see it. I mean, I know she's not so much your bag, but the pyro alone is unbelievable. You'll blatantly get swept along with it all.' She grins. 'Anyway, if not, you can always watch me.' She writhes against my side suggestively.

'Save it for the stage, babe.' I chuckle, and we link arms.

'So, I'm thinking since you've got the afternoon off, we should go shopping,' she says, already pausing in front of a store window and leaning in.

'Mmm, I don't know. I'm trying to save up—' I stop myself. I haven't mentioned the idea of my moving out yet.

'Save up? For what? Come on, don't you want to look fit for tonight?'

'What are you on about?'

'Mark! You know, the big date?'

'Oh, God ...'

'Well even if it ends up just being a bit of fun, might as well use the occasion to dress up, eh? How often do we get to do that?'

I pull a face, but Marcy's locked into relentless mode, there's no stopping her now. Seconds later, I'm in front of a mirror next to racks of clothes, with Marcy holding things up to me, tilting her head and frowning.

'I can chose my own clothes, Marce,' I say, swiping away a frighteningly short sequinned dress.

'OK, OK, but come on. These.' She holds up a pair of black leather jeans. I roll my eyes, but she folds them over my arm, no arguments. Eventually I pick up a few more things and we head to the changing rooms.

As I slip the jeans on, I have to admit, the fit is pretty sexy. Marcy really does understand how a surface thing can make a difference to how you feel inside. And it's a fact that my arse has never looked quite so slappable. I sigh and blush simultaneously, thinking about who I'll be on the date with, and who I'd prefer to be slapping my arse. *Stop it.*

'OK,' Marcy announces, and we emerge from our respective cubicles to inspect one another. She's wearing a gloriously impractical rubberised body-con dress, in which her figure looks eye-poppingly good. She looks me up and down appreciatively. 'You're getting those. Yes?'

A smile twitches at the corner of my lips. 'Yes,' I admit grudgingly.

'Hm ...' she says, inspecting herself from all angles in the mirrors, as if there were something to criticise. 'Nah.'

We go back into the cubicles, and Marcy's muffled voice floats through the divide. 'How have things been with Ry? I know I kind of threw you in at the deep end there, babe, and I've been meaning to say thanks for putting up with it. I suppose it must've been a bit weird at first. I hope he's been a good boy.'

I hear the curtain of her cubicle slide back, and she waits for me outside mine. I clear my throat. 'Uh, yeah, it's been ... Yeah, fine.' In the mirror, my face has gone pale as I pull on my coat and scarf. I gingerly pull back the curtain, and Marcy looks up from checking her phone. 'It's been no trouble at all, really,' I add, hoping to draw a line under the topic. 'Toilet seat down, walking the dog, you name it. He's been well trained.'

She laughs. 'Good! Glad to hear it.' We head over to pay, and she dumps a pile of tops and a skirt on to the counter with a sigh. 'Being away, it was starting to feel sort of like ... God, I hate to say it, but hard work. It's easier face to face, but it's still a bit ...' She shakes her head. 'Forget it. Anyway, I'm glad it's been all right.' I nod mutely, and Marcy hands her credit card to the cashier with a flourish. 'Fuck it, eh? You only live once.'

She finishes paying, then looks at me hesitating. 'Get them. Honestly, you won't regret it.' She grabs the jeans out of my hands and hands them to the cashier. I pull a face but pay for them anyway, and can't help smiling when the cashier says they're actually half-price.

'Fate!' shouts Marcy, grinning. 'There you go, shouldn't cut into your "saving up" too much.' Her smile remains, but her eyes betray a slight curiosity.

I am assailed with yet more guilt about everything I'm not telling her. I read Ryan's note over and over again when I woke up this morning, before tucking it into my barely touched journal for safe keeping and risk-reduction purposes. I feel my whole body go hot at the idea of Marcy scrabbling around on my bedside table for some change or something, only to find—

'Cool, let's go,' she says, passing me my shopping bag. 'This was good. You deserve something nice – treat yourself, you know?'

'I don't know about deserve,' I murmur. 'Anyway, I think we *both* deserve two dozen of those sugar-pastry-ball thingies and a caramel latte.'

'Hell, yes.'

We head to the café nearby, but as Marcy strides towards the door and smiles at the guy who holds it open for her to pass through, my breath catches in my throat. And when I see the older lady waiting behind him, I have to blink several times to make sure I've not manifested some strange vision.

'Taylor,' the woman says. 'Oh. How are you?'

'Cynthia, hi. I'm . . . yeah, I'm fine. How are you?'

'Yes, fine. You remember Jonathan, don't you?' She gestures to him as he holds the door. David Barnett's flatmate. What are they even doing here, together? Well, they're obviously fairly close with each other, I could see that at the hearing. Or at least, brought close by circumstance. And there's no reason why they shouldn't venture outside their local areas, for crying out loud.

I can hear my pulse in my ears, and I can definitely feel Marcy's eyes flitting between us all with mounting curiosity. I'm increasingly aware that we're blocking the doorway. Cynthia smiles weakly, seeming a little dazed as well.

'Oh, um, this is my friend Marcy,' I say. They all nod hello briefly, and I can feel the hanging expectation from her that there will be some kind of explanation of how I know these two strangers. 'Well, I'll let you guys get on,' I say quickly. 'Nice to see you again.'

Jonathan smiles benignly. 'Yeah, good to see you too, Taylor. You look well.'

I highly doubt that I do, given how discombobulated I feel

as Marcy and I make our way over to the counter to order. She peers over her shoulder to where Cynthia and Jonathan had been, her face crumpled into a baffled frown.

'OK, who were they?'

I hesitate, and her eyes widen.

'Wait, that's not Mr One Night Only, is it? Cos actually, he's pretty fit—'

'No, no. That's ... No.' I take a breath, staring intently at the muffin display.

The frown returns. 'Right ... Well, good. It would have seemed a bit weird that you knew his mum too – that would have been some fairly kinky shit!'

I chuckle hopefully, thinking her joke might distract her, but she's not smiling.

'So who are they? Spill, come on.'

'They're just ... people, who I met. That's not his mum, she's actually ... She's the mum of a friend of his.'

Marcy folds her arms, exasperated. 'What the fuck, T? Are you going to tell me what's going on?'

There's no escaping it now. My stomach flips. I'm kind of wishing there was something stronger on offer than coffee.

'Let's order and sit down, and I'll explain.'

'I just ... I can't fucking believe you didn't tell me.'

'It really wasn't that—'

'Taylor, I'm not joking, if you say it's not that big a deal one more time ...'

'It wasn't, honestly. I mean, it wasn't great, but I got through it, and I just didn't want it to be ... I didn't want to dwell on it, that's all.' I sigh and play with the crumbs from my cake, draining the last of my coffee. It's gone cold, and I grimace at the grounds that end up on my tongue. The conversation went

249

pretty much as I imagined it would. Her hurt, concerned stare as I explained, almost overpowering my ability to speak. Her restless anger at not having been able to do something about it. I almost feel like I took something away from her. I know it's wrong, but part of me is starting to feel irritated by her reaction to the whole thing.

'And you went to the hearing on your own?'

'Yes. I told you.'

'But Taylor, I just can't imagine ... I know you're saying it wasn't a big deal, but I just don't get how it couldn't have been. I mean, with Anita ... ?'

I won't meet her eyes, and she reaches out a hand to still mine as I fiddle with my fork. I immediately think of Ryan doing the same thing, and my hand twitches. I pull it into my lap. How had it been so easy for me to talk to him about this? Marcy's my best friend, I've known her for years. She knows me better than anyone. Maybe that's why it was easier with Ryan – because he doesn't know me. Not really.

Or maybe it's because he sort of does, deeper down. On a level that has nothing to do with time spent.

I finally look up into Marcy's concerned brown eyes, and I know she only wants to look out for me, but I'm still feeling that unshakeable irritation. Is that how Marcy sees me? As the suicide-bereaved orphan (or near enough), all alone except for her, the one shining friend who will see me through? I swallow. Jesus, why am I so cruel? She's been with me through thick and thin. But the look of pity on her face makes my heart sink. I suppose I want to pretend I'm strong, undeserving of that pity, a fearless survivor. I probably *don't* deserve her pity. I don't really deserve anything from her.

'No wonder you started smoking again, eh?' she says eventually, with a mirthless laugh.

'Right?' I try for a smile. 'And to be fair, M, it was your bloody mutt that found the body, so you should really be berating him.'

Marcy smiles too, but it doesn't last long. 'I'm not trying to tell you off, T. I'm just amazed you've been going through all this without telling anyone.'

I stare at the dried coffee in the bottom of my cup. Shit. 'Mm. Well, I guess I'm made of sterner stuff than we thought,' I murmur.

'What, fucking Kevlar?' she retorts wryly. 'Listen, I *know* you're tough. Obviously. I'm worried, though, that ... I mean, I thought we told each other everything?' she says, her voice quieter now. 'You felt like you couldn't tell me about this?'

I lock eyes with her, wishing I could get her to understand. Wishing I understood it myself. 'Marcy, no. Your friendship means the world to me. It was stupid of me not to say something. I just thought I could deal with it on my own. I'm really glad you know now, though.' I reach over and we squeeze each other's hands again. 'Thank you, honestly.'

I do mean it sincerely, but I'm relieved when she seems appeased.

'Fucking hell. Heavy coffee break,' she says with a sigh, smiling over at me. 'Listen, we better head back. I've got to get to the venue for six, and I need to dump this stuff.'

'Yeah, cool. Listen, I'm sorry, M.'

She smiles briefly and we pull on our coats and head out. The light mood we had before we go to the coffee shop is gone, and I'm scared it will never come back. She knows now that we can have secrets between us.

Chapter Twenty-four

I lean closer to the mirror, finishing off my mascara. The black leather jeans squeak a little, but as I step back and look at myself and adjust my knitted silk top, I do feel pretty good. Confident. Comfortable. I'm fairly sure that won't last, but for now at least. I slick on a final touch of red lipstick, smiling at Anita's picture, missing her. I wonder what she would have been like, watching me head out on a date, if she'd lived to see me go on my first proper one. Hopeful? Worried? Knowing? I'm fairly certain she wouldn't have been the 'When are you going to settle down, get married?' type of mother – she was never one to call the kettle black.

I'm sort of dreading this whole evening, but also perversely looking forward to it. It's not like Mark is a bad guy, and the idea of having his attention is nice. But also, much as I'm ashamed to admit it, the idea of Ryan perhaps feeling jealous about it is a turn-on too. I glance at the record he gave me, propped next to the bed semi-out-of-sight, and then look at myself in the mirror again. Like a massive loser, I try the pose the singer is doing on the cover, and I kind of see what he means about us being similar. I enjoy the idea of seeing myself the way he sees me.

OK, take a breath. I need to remind myself that I'm about to go and watch *Ryan's girlfriend – my best mate –* do her thing on stage for two hours. While I'm on a date with his friend. And after Ryan wanted to tell Marcy that . . .

Why did I agree to this again?

I chuck my lipstick, mobile, keys and purse into a smaller bag and check the time – it's heading towards eight. I'm meant to be meeting Mark at the tube in North Greenwich at half-past. I'm not sure where Ryan is, whether he's meeting us there or what, but I know I'll probably be late if I don't get going soon. And I know Marcy will be pissed off if we miss anything – I'm sure we'll be quizzed afterwards. I smile, sort of excited to see her up on such a massive stage, even if still a bit irritated that she's responsible for this journey into awkward upon which I'm about to embark.

Just as I hoist my bag on to my shoulder ready to leave, I hear the front door open and close, and footsteps quickly hustle into Marcy's room. Taking a deep breath, I leave my room, and I'm outside their open door just in time to see Ryan pull his T-shirt over his head. He turns round at the sound of my footsteps and our eyes lock – then almost simultaneously sweep down each other's bodies and back again. The overhead light in the bedroom casts shadows that emphasise every nook and cranny of the muscle definition in his chest and abdomen. I swallow audibly.

'Wow,' he says. 'You look incredible.' He clenches his jaw a little, like he hadn't meant the words to come out.

'I was just about to head out to meet Mark,' I say quickly, feeling my face heat up.

'Wait for me?' he says hopefully, grabbing a shirt off a hanger on the wardrobe door. 'Please?'

He starts to head towards the bathroom, and as he squeezes past me, still without a top on, I lose all sense of where I'm going

253

or what I'm doing, because I can literally feel the heat coming off his body, see the small dusting of hairs on his chest so close I could just—

'Um, I'll . . . ' I watch his chest rise and fall. 'I'll just be two minutes,' he murmurs. He moves away, the bathroom door shuts, and I hear him sigh loudly on the other side of it.

Trying to be normal and do normal stuff, I check my bag for my Oyster card and pull on my long winter coat, which looks a bit better with this outfit than my usual hooded number.

Ryan emerges from the bathroom, shirt on now, and word-lessly holds up a finger to say he'll be ready in a minute.

I pull out my phone and text Marcy a good-luck message. There – normal.

A moment later, Ryan's ready.

'OK,' he says. 'Shall we?'

Shall we . . . ?

I know we're going to be late. We should be walking faster, but as I look over at Ryan, hands in his pockets next to me strolling towards the station, I know he's in no hurry either. He smiles, but says nothing, like he's waiting for me to start. I can almost feel sentences hovering in front of me, shuffling in order of importance. I want to thank him for the record. I want to tell him we can't think about each other the way we have been. I want to tell him how much I want to kiss him again. I want to tell him how much I want to—

OK, stick to the thank-you.

'Ryan, I—'

'How was—?'

We both laugh as our words clash. He gestures for me to speak, and I take a deep breath of cool evening air.

'No, I just . . . I wanted to say thank you. For the LP. It's really

254

great.' I roll my eyes at myself. 'I mean, you're right, obviously I don't have a record player, but I looked up her stuff online and it's really ... Really beautiful. I think it's a bit of a reach to say I sound anything like her though.' I smile, and he shrugs.

'Well, it's more just a feeling, sort of,' he says, looking at the ground almost bashfully. 'The, um, the feeling I got when I saw the cover, and then listened to her voice.' He looks over at me, and there it is again. A pulse right through me. Head, heart, and further down.

'Oh,' I say feebly.

We fall silent the rest of the way to the Overground, but when we finally arrive and reach the barriers, he moves aside so I can swipe my Oyster card first, and then I feel his hand, very lightly, on the small of my back as we move towards the stairs. It's like he's holding a flaming torch to my body, and he walks close behind me as we descend to the platform, so close I can smell his smell, feel his warmth ... I almost stumble, and reach out to grip the railing.

We hear a train coming and jog down the last few steps to catch it. It's not too busy, and we find two seats next to each other pretty easily. The train moves away, and we sit quietly, rocking gently with its movements for a while. I make to speak but then hesitate, and Ryan turns to look at me. Without taking his eyes from mine, he reaches up and brushes his fingertips along the back of my hand as it rests over the end of the armrest. I look down and slowly pull my hand away.

'Sorry,' he whispers. 'I just ... wanted to touch you.' His face reddens a little, and I lose the ability to form a sentence. 'You were going to say something.'

'Um ... yeah,' I finally manage. 'I was thinking about the vinyl. You know what you said before, about sense memory?'

He nods.

'Well, I haven't really even held a record for years, since my mum died. But the minute I held it in my hands ... I don't know, it just immediately took me back.' I see his face begin to look concerned, and shake my head. 'In a good way, I mean.' I can't help smiling at his slight panic, and my heart blooms at the idea that he cares about upsetting me. 'She had loads of vinyl,' I continue. 'I kind of wish I'd kept some of it, and her record player.'

'You don't have any of them?' he says, surprised.

I shake my head. 'It's stupid. I do kind of regret not keeping more of her things. But back when it happened – and now too, I suppose – I just thought, her things aren't *her*. They were just her belongings. I didn't want to trick myself into thinking they held some special essence of her, or ... '

'Yeah. Sometimes *things*, objects, can become a burden. I think memories are probably better keepsakes, good or bad.'

I look at him and nod. *Exactly.*

My eyes hold his, because I can't hold him. My stomach is shaky with how much feeling I've built up for him – it's an ache, deep inside me, that just won't go away.

'I think we need to change here, right?'

We step out of the train, and as we head down the escalator to change on to the tube, we're jostled apart slightly. I feel the loss of him being close, but it's probably best. As we jump on the next train, we stay quiet. He stands, I take the free seat nearby. When we finally reach our stop, things are pushed to the background, swallowed down, hidden again.

'Mark's meeting you here, yeah?' Ryan says finally as we reach the top of the escalator. I turn back to him, a couple of steps behind me now, and nod, then check my watch.

'Yeah, he should be here already.' I am thirteen minutes late, after all.

256

Sure enough, when we pass through the barriers, I see Mark just outside the exit, smoking a cigarette. I wave, and he exhales and squashes his butt underfoot to come and meet us.

'Really sorry I'm late,' I bluster.

'No worries. You look great,' he says smoothly, kissing me on both cheeks then nodding at Ryan with a grin. 'All right, mate?'

'Yeah, mate, you good?' I can hear in his voice that he's making as much of an effort as I am. 'Listen, we'd better go and collect the tickets from the window thing, it'll be starting soon.'

'Cool, yeah,' I say, and then smile gratefully when Mark offers me one of his Silk Cuts. He holds my hand a little longer than necessary as he helps me shield and light my cigarette. Ryan strides on ahead of us, and I feel a stab of guilt – I suppose because slowly developing lung disease was *our* thing.

As we collect our tickets and head into the arena, I stare around, always amazed at how huge these places are, and that one person can hold the adoration of ten thousand in one space, and give them the experience they long for. It suddenly makes my heart hurt for Anita and her dreams. Perhaps for my own as well.

We make our way to our seats, and I'm glad that Marcy did choose seating, rather than leaving us to be jostled and bumped by the masses in the standing area. Ryan moves aside, and Mark obligingly settles between the two of us. I know it makes sense, but I'm irritated that I don't at least get to be in the middle. If it's going to be messy, I might as well get the most out of it. I make an effort to smile as Mark hands me a plastic cup of red wine. Voices swell around us, the pre-show DJ's music pounds, and I focus on making small-talk as Ryan stares silently down towards the stage. Eventually Mark tries to fold him into the conversation, and he joins in stiffly.

Finally the lights dip into darkness, and the electric anticipation that has been building in the expanse of the arena bursts into life. Familiar music starts to blast out, and a spotlight illuminates the stage. It's hard not to get swept up in it all, and I stand up with the rest of the crowd. Straining to look, I whoop loudly as I spot Marcy strut across to the centre of the stage and join in with the elaborate dance routine that's unfolding. I lean over Mark to point her out to Ryan, and his eyes finally spark into life. We all begin to cheer loudly, clap, sing along even. I feel a welcome lift in my spirits, and at last I don't have to force the smile that's on my face. For a moment, I forget everything but the music.

Marcy hadn't been wrong about the sheer spectacle of the show, and the crowd cheers rowdily for a second encore as it all draws to a close. I feel pretty exhausted by the end of it, and the three of us slump back into the hard plastic chairs as the rest of the audience finally accepts that the show is over and begins to stream for the exits.

'I've got to admit,' Mark says loudly – our ears all still ringing – 'that was better than I expected it to be!'

I nod, then tense slightly as I feel his arm begin to snake around the back of my chair. He leans towards me so he can lower his voice, and I turn to look at him. His face is close, his large blue eyes looking down at me. He *is* handsome. Why do I sound like I'm trying to convince myself? Oh, because I am. 'Really glad Marcy sorted this out,' he says. 'I guess I was a bit too chicken to call you.'

'Chicken?'

'Well, yeah, I mean it's not every day I meet someone as stunning as you, who hears the words "recruitment consultancy" and still agrees to give me her number.' I chuckle, and he smiles. 'So you're not regretting saying yes, then?'

I don't want to tell him that I didn't have much of a choice, and I'm feeling very conscious of Ryan in the next seat, fiddling with his phone so he can ignore us.

'No, no. It's been fun,' I say, trying not to pitch my voice too high. Mark's hand slips on to my shoulder.

'Good,' he murmurs. Before, this *would* have been good. Before, I wouldn't have tensed as he leaned towards me and brushed his lips to mine; a good-looking, fun, polite, *available* guy. I wouldn't have had to concentrate in order to make my lips pucker and return his kiss. I keep my eyes open a little, wincing at Ryan's stiff body language as he looks up from his phone and glares deliberately out at the rapidly emptying arena. I pull back and give Mark a tentative smile, hoping he can't see the awkwardness behind it. I clear my throat and move to stand up.

'We should go and find Marcy,' I say briskly.

Chapter Twenty-five

The arena is virtually empty now, the tremendous energy having drained from the vast space like water from a bathtub, taking my high spirits with it. I shudder involuntarily at the thought of the word 'bathtub', and my mood is well and truly sunk. Mark reaches an arm around me, pressing me to him a little.

'Cold?'

'A bit,' I reply, but I keep my arms folded tightly in front of me, and he loosens his grip until his arm hangs by his side again. I glance up at him, but he doesn't seem too perturbed. The man has perseverance, I'll give him that.

'Come on, Marce,' Ryan mutters, hitting the dial button again on his phone, frowning. A nearby security guy eyes us, his walkie-talkie crackling like the police officers' radios that morning by the river. Finally I can hear Marcy's muffled voice from Ryan's phone.

'Hey! Babe, we're at the stage door, where are you?' Ryan says, irritation barely masked in his voice. I try to give him a supportive shrug, but he looks away, then shakes his head at what Marcy's saying. 'No, on the left-hand side as you look at the stage ... Yeah. OK.'

He ends the call and turns to us. I make sure I'm not standing too close to Mark. I want him to know I'm not . . . that I couldn't even think about—

'She says she's on her way,' Ryan sighs, exhaling his frustration.

'Keeping her adoring public waiting,' Mark jokes, and Ryan smiles half-heartedly. A moment later the door we're waiting next to swings open and Marcy poses in the doorway for a moment before giggling and apologising. She's still in her revealing stage outfit, all legs and boobs, and even my eyes are on stalks. I pull her into a hug, and Mark gives her a quick peck on the cheek. She hands us all passes for the backstage area.

'You were incredible, Marce,' I say, feeling a genuine swell of pride.

'Thanks, love. That really means a lot.'

Then Mark and I stand awkwardly off to one side as Ryan leans in to give her a quick kiss, but Marcy leaps into his arms and kisses him emphatically. Heat begins to prickle at my neck and I give Mark a half-smile, which he returns. Shoe-on-the-other-foot time, I suppose. But it sets off an awkward, jealous churning in my gut that I find hard to shake, even as they finally break apart and Marcy grabs my hand. 'Come on,' she says, leading us into a warren of corridors backstage. Through various doors I can see half-dressed dancers laughing and singing, technicians rolling up cable, huge containers of equipment being taken out to loading bays. Marcy points down one corridor.

'Main dressing rooms,' she says, then mimes smoking a joint. 'We'll stick to bubbly though, eh?' She introduces us to some of the dancers she's sharing a dressing room with, and then pours out several plastic cups of sparkling wine from their rider. We toast enthusiastically, then Marcy demands a full breakdown of each of our thoughts on the show. The buzz of being behind the scenes brings me warmer memories of my mother, and I let the alcohol relax me a little. Cracks of sunshine really *did* lurk in the darkness back then – I just need to remember that. I need to let more of it break through when I can.

After a while, reviews well and truly given, Marcy sidles over to where I'm leaning on a dresser. She nudges me and smiles, her features exaggerated by the stage make-up. 'So ... how's it going?' She flicks her eyes towards the guys, who are chatting more easily now they've had a couple of drinks

I swallow more bubbles. 'Er, good, yeah. All right.' I don't want to get her hopes up, but I do smile over at Mark almost as a reflex when a tall, slender dancer goes over and starts to chat to him. He returns it, making sure it's clear he's not returning her flirtations. Marcy eyes me closely – she can tell my heart's not in it.

'Well, you had fun anyway, yeah?'

'Mate, definitely,' I say sincerely. 'It was great, and you were phenomenal. I'm so proud of you.'

She squeezes my hand, and we tap our plastic cups together again. I drain mine down.

'*Sure* you don't want to come back for a drink?' Marcy says, looking between Mark and me with a mischievous expression. I think her reasoning is that I may as well get a shag out of this. I shake my head at her imperceptibly, but I can practically feel the waves of gentlemanly politeness coming off Mark as he half smiles at us both.

'Honestly, I'd love to, but I genuinely do have to get up early tomorrow,' he says, looking down at me apologetically. 'I'd love to take you out again soon, though. Maybe without the thousands of people and stuff?' he says hopefully. I chuckle non-committally, but I realise he's too good a guy for me to let this go on. I clear my throat and turn to Marcy and Ryan. He's holding her hand but watching me closely.

'I'll be up in a sec, guys, OK?'

Marcy raises her eyebrows a little at me, and Ryan shakes his mate's hand. Mark thanks Marcy for the tickets, and then we watch as they walk round the corner to the flat's entrance.

I turn to face Mark, half expecting him to throw caution to the wind and say he's changed his mind about coming up, but he remains polite.

'This was really nice,' I begin, cringing at the word. I can see a flicker in his eyes that suggests he knows what's coming.

'It was,' he says diplomatically. 'But . . . ?'

'I'm sorry, Mark.'

He shakes his head, shrugs. 'It's cool.'

'It's just bad timing. I'm being one hundred per cent honest,' I say, looking up at him. 'You're a great guy, seriously. It's just not a good moment in my life, which always seems to be the case when it comes to these things.'

'You don't have to explain—'

'I just wouldn't want to string you along and then—'

He puts a hand on my shoulder. 'Taylor, honestly. I get it. I'm sorry too, though,' he says with a wry smile on his chiselled face. *Shit, shit, shit, what is wrong with me?* 'Listen, let me walk you to your door.'

'No, I'll be—'

'I insist.'

We walk along for the minute it takes in silence, and then turn to each other outside the downstairs doors. He leans down and kisses my cheek. It's probably turning red.

'Thanks,' I murmur.

'No problem.' He starts to leave, then stops and turns back to me for a moment. 'I hope . . . I hope it all works out for you.'

He glances up towards the flat, and I wonder if he understands what's on my mind. 'Bye, Taylor.'

I stand outside for a moment longer, worried and regretful. Then I let myself in and climb the stairs, concerned about what might greet me on the other side of our door.

Marcy and Ryan seem to be in the living room, and I walk slowly down the hall, hoping not to find them *in flagrante* while Jonathan Ross mumbles on in the background or something. But they're just on the sofa, with only a marginally discomfiting amount of body contact going on. A bottle of red is open on the coffee table, and Marcy has her legs stretched over Ryan's lap as he rubs her feet gently. Charlie sits on the ground next to the sofa, curled up happily. Domestic bliss.

A jealous gremlin inside me growls.

'Hey.'

'Hey! Grab a glass,' Marcy says, her words sluggish with exhaustion and alcohol.

'Mm, yeah, in a sec. I'm just going to get changed.'

Before I turn, she adds, 'Was that all right?' She bites her lip sympathetically. I glance at Ryan, who looks away quickly. He's said nothing by way of greeting, but when I reply 'Yeah' to Marcy's question in a half-hearted, mumbly way that clearly conveys what happened in my chat with Mark, I feel his eyes return to me.

'OK, hon,' Marcy says, settling back on the sofa arm. 'Well anyway, yeah, go and get changed.'

I go and put on a T-shirt and loose jogging bottoms, feeling oddly clammy and hot, then return to the living room and slump into the armchair. I don't bother bringing a glass for the wine – I'm feeling light-headed enough from the backstage drinks earlier. Instead I glug from a can of ginger beer I found in the back of the fridge, but Marcy doesn't seem to notice. She stares blankly at the TV, and I can sense the weariness in her bones. But after a while she smiles languidly over at me.

'He can do you next,' she says, nodding at Ryan still kneading her feet. I nearly choke on my drink, but manage to just shake my head and smile a bit. The corner of his mouth twitches a little, but then sinks down into a frown. Marcy pulls her feet back and swings her legs to the floor gracefully.

'Loo,' she mumbles, and heads out of the room.

Ryan and I are quiet for a moment. I stare at the TV, then realise the reality show that's just started makes me want to stab myself in the eye. I begin to look around for the remote, but there's no sign of it.

'Is the zapper over there?' I mutter, but Ryan shakes his head. I sigh and get up, going over to the sofa to check where Marcy usually tucks it down between the cushions, and he looks up at me as I move closer to him.

'Taylor,' he says quietly. His voice sounds hoarse, probably from cheering earlier at the show. 'I know I'm being . . .'

'No, you're not.'

'I am. I don't know how to . . .' He tapers off again, his eyes searching my face.

'Then don't do anything.' I stare into amber.

'Taylor.'

'What?' My eyes are starting to mist.

He looks at my hand as I lean down on the sofa cushion, and then reaches over, trailing his fingertips across the delicate skin on the back of it again, and then a little way up my wrist—

'What's up?' Marcy's voice, in the doorway. I look up, and feel Ryan's fingers move away.

'Just trying to find the remote,' I say, keeping my voice smooth, controlled. I do it immediately, like a trained liar. I hate myself. But it's too late – I see it. The flicker of doubt in her eyes.

Maybe it's been there all this time, and I just haven't noticed. My fingers finally close around the remote control in the space between the cushions, and I try not to sigh audibly with relief. 'Hidden as usual,' I say, retreating to the armchair and flicking channels quickly.

Marcy settles back beside Ryan, leaning against his shoulder and stifling a yawn. 'Actually, I think I'm going to need to hit the sack in a minute,' she says. I think she really is tired, rather than asking for sex. Ryan plants a kiss on her forehead, then stands up straight away, and helps her up.

'OK then,' I say. 'Well done again for tonight. It meant a lot to me, seeing you up there.'

She reaches down and squeezes my shoulder as she passes, holding Ryan's hand as they head to their room. 'Thank you, hon.'

Their door closes, and I pull my legs up to my chest, hugging them close.

I try to press away the suspicion that things won't be the same in the morning.

Chapter Twenty-six

I rub at my wrist as I lie in bed, like I can erase the feeling of Ryan's fingertips tracing up it. Erase the moment, the flash of hurt and confusion and suspicion I think I saw in Marcy's eyes.

I think about him. Him on the train, saying, 'I just wanted to touch you.'

I know I can't carry on like this – I can't risk it. And what if this is nothing really? What if I've read too much into it? Sure, maybe Ryan understands some of my issues better than most. And maybe there is a physical attraction … I close my eyes and think of his lips moving over mine, the heat of him against me. But maybe it was just that he was lonely, she was away and I was there. And maybe he's confused right now, but he'll realise soon that it's a mistake. Just like he did when he stopped us, before we went too far. Then, for a moment's misplaced feeling, what would I have risked? Something way too important to lose.

I look down into the darkness between my bed and the night-stand, where I've propped the gift Ryan gave me. I should throw the record out of the window, and I should get my lighter and burn the note he wrote. None of this should ever have happened. But somehow, if nothing else remains, I need to keep those. The note especially. We'd talked about how *things* could weigh you down, but somehow words – especially words written down on a page, directly from someone's mind, considered, deliberate – words like that are hard to take back, and hard to forget.

My gut twists all over again at the choice I'm making – to give up the first person who's ever really helped me confront what happened with my mother, to start sifting through those issues without feeling like a crazy person or a failure. Who's made me feel safe to express whatever I need to. The first person who I've ever felt such a pull towards that a look from him makes everything else fall away, makes all my senses focus only on him.

I look at the clock. It's only just past midnight but it feels later. Right now I can't imagine ever getting to sleep. But I'm so tired . . . and thirsty. I forgot to get water before I went to bed.

I get up and pad out of the darkness of my room to the kitchen. Charlie stirs in his basket, snuffles lightly, then drifts back to sleep. I stare at him in the moonlight enviously for a moment, and then get a glass out of the cupboard. I try to do it quietly, but manage to clink into the others as I do, and then when I run the tap it gushes out loudly as I nudge it open too far. Slick. Must remember never to try and be a cat burglar.

I freeze as I hear the other bedroom door open – exactly what I didn't want.

The light footsteps and Charlie's more eager response tell me straight away that it's Marcy. A moment later I see her dark outline in the kitchen doorway.

'Hey,' I whisper tentatively. 'Sorry, I was trying to be quiet.'

She shakes her head. 'Couldn't sleep.' She flicks on the overhead light pointedly, and we squint at each other. She walks over to the sink to get herself a glass of water too, and then turns and leans against the sideboard, sipping while we eye one another silently.

'Shame about Mark,' she says after a while. Her jaw is tight.

'I know.' I swallow more water. 'I just couldn't ... I didn't want to lead him on. It just wasn't there for me, I don't know why.' I know why. I'm scared she does too, from the way she's looking at me.

'I really thought that could work out, you know? Like, if I had to choose a bloke, rack my brains for someone, I would have thought he'd have been a good pick.' Her voice is tight, sarcastic.

We look at each other.

'You can't force these things, though, M. They just happen, or they don't.'

'Yeah.' She falls quiet, thinking. 'These days I suppose it would be harder for me to guess where your head is.'

I roll my eyes. 'You're still pissed off, aren't you? That I didn't tell you about finding David Barnett.'

She smacks a hand down on her leg in frustration, then gestures it at me. 'You say the man's name just like that – like you didn't find him *dead* at your feet and neglect to mention it to me at all.' Her voice is louder now. Charlie stands up and trots over to her, curious, anxious.

'Why does it bother you so much?' I put down my glass, angry though I know I shouldn't be.

'I've told you. I thought you trusted me, I thought we were ... God, since when do we have secrets?'

'You don't live inside my mind, Marcy. I don't live inside yours. You don't – you *can't* – know every single thing about me. You don't know how it feels. You think you do, but you don't. To have your mum, the only person ... to have her fucking top herself and leave you—'

'No. That has nothing to do with you keeping secrets.' She folds her arms, not letting me play the 'Mum abandoned me' card. Her voice grows softer. 'That has nothing to do with you not talking to me about how you're feeling. If you just told me . . . '

'I'm sorry! Jesus. Maybe I don't want to always be that person with a problem, something that can be solved by you. So I can be *fixed* by you. Cos you don't have problems, right? *I'm* the fuck-up.'

She stares at me, incredulous, and I regret saying that immediately.

'When have I ever—?'

'Sorry, I didn't mean it like that. Shit.'

She looks away from me, and I sigh, feeling tears beginning to sting the back of my eyes. I take another sip of water, my hand shaking. 'Marcy . . . '

'You know what? I just don't get why you told him, but you couldn't tell me,' she says, nodding towards their bedroom door. I feel a jolt as my heartbeat speeds up. '*That* really hurts,' she continues. 'Because of what we've been through. Together.' She gestures rapidly in the air between us. 'I mean, I know I'm not in your bloody head, but Taylor, come on. I was *there*. I was the best friend I could be. And now all of a sudden—' She breaks off, blows out air hard.

Ryan told her that he already knew? I feel like I can't breathe. My stomach twists with anguish at the look on her face, and tears spill free from my eyes and begin to stream down my face.

'Marcy, I'm so sorry . . . '

'I mean, he only let it slip about you finding the body.' She closes her eyes for a moment, then opens them. 'I told him I'd just found out about it.' She blinks again, and now her cheeks are wet too. She looks at the ground, a mirthless smile on her lips, then her eyes whip back up towards me, narrow and accusatory. 'But still, I thought, you know, *Why is he looking at her like that?* There have been times before, other times where I thought

270

something might be going on, but I pushed it out of my head, because, well, that wouldn't even be possible, right? But then tonight I suddenly understood. I'm a fucking *mug*.'

'Marcy, please.' My words are caught in a sob. Somewhere vaguely in the back of my mind, I think Ryan must be awake by now, if he was ever even asleep. He must be listening. Is he going to come out here? Is this all going to play out between the three of us, right here, right now? 'It wasn't like ... I think I just wanted to confide in someone,' I say, panic and desperation quaking in my voice. 'Somebody who didn't know me, not like you do. Someone objective. Does that make sense?'

She doesn't say anything.

'I wasn't going to tell *anyone* about finding the body, Marcy. But it just ... Ryan was there, that was all. But there's nothing else going—' I stop short. I don't want to lie to her, not now. I take a breath. 'Well, I mean, if – if I had any feelings, they were mispl—'

She scoffs, stopping me in my tracks again. '"You can't force these things though," right? "They just happen, or they don't,"' she shoots back at me.

I deserved that. I deserve all of it.

'He's yours, Marcy. I get that. I would *never*—'

'Is he? Is he fucking mine, Taylor?'

I swallow. 'Yes. Of course.'

She blows out a shaky sigh, and rubs her cheeks free of tears with angry swipes. 'I can't do this right now. I'm going back to bed.'

'Marcy, please, I'm sorry,' I say weakly.

She puffs out a laugh laden with disbelief. 'Me too, Taylor.' She stares at me for a moment longer, her eyes dark and glistening, then slowly walks back to her room, carrying her glass of water.

'Marcy ...' My voice is thin, trembling. She ignores me. Their door slams.

What will she say to him? What will he say to her?

I can hear myself sobbing, like it's someone else. I take deep breaths until the tears subside to a steady trickle. I'm barely able to hold myself up to walk back to my room. I stumble to my bed, get in and press my face into the pillow until it's soaked through.

The numbers – 04.03 – are fuzzy, my eyes blurring. About an hour after Marcy and I spoke in the kitchen, I heard the front door open and close. It must have been Ryan, leaving. Maybe she asked him to go, maybe he offered. How much has he told her? I feel sick at the thought of her knowing more about our betrayal. Emotional. Physical ...

But I'm also scared – terrified – that I might not get to see him again.

My head's already pounding from crying, and it's a familiar feeling. How many nights after Anita died – sometimes before – had I ended up with a headache and a tear-stained pillow?

The look on Marcy's face, the hurt and anger in her voice. Why was I so selfish, so fucking *foolish*, as to think that the one person who had always been there for me, who'd never let me wallow for long, who'd supported and encouraged me – that I should keep all of this from her? Instead, I've plunged a knife in her back, and stabbed myself in the heart in the process.

I sigh as the arguments go round and round in my head again. Would it really have made a difference? *If you just told me ...* But how? When? OK, obviously I could have told her about finding David Barnett any time before she left for the tour. But that would have meant facing up to whatever finding him had dislodged inside me, and I was too weak to do that. Maybe I still

272

am. Maybe she could have helped me, like she always did. That's why I'm a fool, of course. But *Ryan*? Did she mean I should have told her about all that too? What could I have said? What difference would it have made, other than to humiliate me, and make things horribly awkward? Before she left, I had no reason to think he felt anything back. Then Marcy returned so suddenly, and there was no chance for me to just pull her aside and say, 'Oh, by the way, I think I'm having some intense feelings for your boyfriend.'

Fine, maybe that's not true either. I could have told her. But then what?

I shift under the bedclothes, like I'm trying to crawl out of my skin. I wish I could. Basically, I've taken Marcy's friendship for granted, and now I don't know what's going to happen. Waves of tears push up from my chest again, and I swipe at my face with the corner of the duvet. How am I ever going to look her in the eye tomorrow? The night's edging away from me too fast – soon the world will have to be faced. Perhaps I could stay in bed all day, like my mother used to: *I can't get up. Do you think I want to be this way? Don't you think I'd get up if I could? I just CAN'T.*

But this is not the fucking same. What's wrong with me, almost wishing it was? I have to face the fact that Anita had a reason, a real, medical reason, and I don't. But I think I understand some of the helplessness of feeling this low.

God, thinking about it now, I can hardly forgive myself for those times when I'd lose it, shout at her to just get over it, just get up. Letting exasperation get the better of me. Or, even worse, thinking sometimes that it was better she stayed in bed – that there, away from me, she was more manageable. That I could almost pretend she wasn't there.

And then she wasn't.

Fresh tears choke me. I feel like they'll never stop.

When that had been my life, my every day – there, all of a sudden, was Marcy. A friend, a real friend, despite all my faults and all of hers. How could I have done this to her?

A small voice inside me answers.

Because I fell in love with him.

Because it started the minute I first saw him.

Because I couldn't control it.

Is it always going to be like this? Love wrapping itself up with misery, the two twinned and inseparable? I wonder if I'll ever be able to explain myself. I wonder how anyone ever even tries. I think about what Anita wrote in her last note. *She* didn't try. 'Don't Explain', another of her favourite songs, especially in Billie Holliday's resigned, beautiful tone. 'Don't explain . . .'

I throw off the covers and stand up, pacing and taking deep breaths, trying to stop the tears. Without thinking, I start to sing softly to myself. When I was a child and a nightmare woke me, Anita wouldn't get into bed with me, or embrace me, or indulge my urge to get up and have a hot chocolate like I'd seen on TV. She would turn on the cheap Woolworths desk lamp by my bedside, and point it up towards herself in the darkness. A spotlight. She would clear her throat and look at me expectantly, until I nodded. Then she would begin. With a smile glinting in her eyes, she would launch into some beautiful melody, starting strong and getting softer and softer, until I drifted into a calm sleep.

I finish singing, and I do feel calmer. Like she was just here. I switch on my bedside light, half expecting my mother to be standing beside me, arms outstretched.

She's not. But I still feel her.

I still love her.

I lean down to the drawer and open it, pulling it out as far as it will go, and rummage until my hands close around her note. Slowly, carefully, I unfold its worn creases and stare at the neat lines of writing. I take a breath, and read out loud in a quiet voice.

'Taylor, my darling—' My voice shakes. I take another breath, staying steady.

> I'll miss you. I can't even begin to tell you how much. I look at you and I wonder how I ever managed to raise such a beautiful, clever, strong girl. You're a wonderful young woman now. I'm sorry I've been such a mess. But now you can move on, and have a fresh start. I know you'll do a much better job of all this than I ever did. Just know that I love you. I stayed here because I didn't want to go off and you not know where I was. Your Aunty Sylvia will make sure everything's OK. Be good for her. I'll miss you, my sweet girl. I love you so much.
> xxx

The usual emotions swamp me as I finish. Anger, grief. The impotence of not being able to argue back. What would my mother think of me now? Haven't I fucked things up just as badly as she did? I've been miserable, self-indulgent, inert. I've hidden my feelings. I glance again at her note, and then at Ryan's – I got it out of my journal to read again after my confrontation with Marcy.

Confrontation. That's what I need, what I have to do – confront it all. Marcy was right to force me.

I refold Anita's note, feeling exhaustion sink over me, and finally allow myself to fall asleep.

Chapter Twenty-seven

It's after midday when I wake up, still feeling exhausted. Part of me wishes I hadn't taken the day off work today; at least it would be an excuse to distract myself for a while. But then I remember: I'm done with excuses.

I listen for a while at my door, but the flat is quiet. I come out of my room, noticing that Marcy's room is empty, but the door to the bathroom is open, and I hear movement before she appears in the doorway. She glances at me disdainfully, and then stuffs her hairbrush in her handbag. She's dressed to go out, and Charlie snuffles around her legs, eager for his walk.

'Marcy, can we talk?' My voice drags along sandpaper.

'I'm going out,' she replies, stalking towards the door.

'Well, I can come with you if you're walking Ch—'

She turns around towards me. 'I don't want you to. Anyway, I'm meeting Ryan at the caff. He needs some of the stuff he left last night. Though I'm sure he could have got it off you.' Her mouth curls tightly as she speaks, and I don't think I've ever seen her this angry with me.

But anger begins to build in me, too.

'So you'll see *him*, but you won't talk to *me*, is that it?' I say, regretting the tone of my voice but wanting to know all the same.

She's nodding her head, and Charlie is looking between us, anxious. 'You know what, yes. Jesus, Taylor. I've known him all of six months. I've known you for half of my *life*.' She strides over to me, her slight physique suddenly seeming to tower over me. 'Do you have any idea how fucking hurtful it is to tell me that I'm smothering you? That my friendship is not of a . . . a satisfactory quality for you? What, you want me to be fucking closed off and secretive like you – that's how we're doing this now, is it? After all these years?' Her voice grows louder with every question, and tears spring into my eyes again.

'No, Marcy, I . . . No! But you have to understand my side of this. I wasn't looking to hurt you, I really wasn't. Sometimes you have to just let me go through stuff on my own.'

'Or with him,' she says, quieter now, turning away from me. There's a hint of sarcasm, but somehow less accusation in her voice when she says that. It gives me a faint glimmer of hope.

I try and think of how to respond, but Marcy clips Charlie's lead to his collar and opens the front door.

'I have pre-show rehearsal in a couple of hours cos they're changing some of the songs for tonight,' she tells me stiffly, then swallows hard. 'And tomorrow we're heading to Paris early. So I'll be away for a few days.'

Shit – I forgot about the European dates. 'Oh. OK. So . . .'

She looks at me; her hurt, disappointment and sense of betrayal all shoot daggers into my heart. 'It's probably for the best that we won't be seeing each other. For a while, anyway.'

I bite my lip. 'Yeah. OK.'

She closes the front door without saying goodbye. I try not to panic. I have to believe we can survive this. We *have* to. I can't allow myself to think otherwise, because even thinking it makes me want to sink into a pile on the floor and not move. And I have to move, because inertia is what got me into this mess in the first place. The next few days are going to be torture, but I hope Marcy is right. I hope it's for the best.

I wash my face with cold water, take a few long, deep breaths and then go back to my room, suddenly purposeful. I open my laptop, find a property website and start to search. She's right: distance, perspective. Starting again.

I scan the page, chewing the inside of my cheek. I won't be able to do a flat-share with strangers. I know Marcy's habits like the back of my hand; I couldn't imagine living with anybody else.

Well, almost anybody.

I take another shaky breath, and start to look at studios and one-beds around this area. Even with all this 'fresh start' bollocks, I can't stand the idea of living too far from Marcy, if she stays in our flat – I think she could afford it on her own now. Or . . . or with Ryan. I don't know if they're definitely over, after all. The thought makes my stomach clench, but I have no right to assume anything any more.

I sigh hard, but I'm relieved to find there are a couple of little places I could just about make the rent on by myself. I bookmark a few other potentials on my computer, and call up to view one of them this afternoon. It suddenly starts to feel real. I'll be out there on my own. It makes me nervous, I admit – but not afraid, like I thought it would.

Seeing as I have a few hours before the viewing, I decide to go and catch the movie that I failed to watch properly the other day: distract myself. It's been quite a while since I went to the cinema by myself – not since That Day. But I think now's as good a time as any.

I shower and dress, grab my bag and head out, but as I cross the street, I stop short. I actually rub my eyes, like I might have conjured up him with my mind, but it's really not *so* strange that he's here, I guess.

With Charlie trotting by his side, Ryan is coming straight towards me, his head down, lost in thought, his free hand in the pocket of his pea-coat, his hair lifting in the wind. He looks beautiful. I almost want to run away.

'Hey,' I say.

Ryan looks up, surprised. 'Taylor.' His eyes roam over my face, like he's drinking me in. 'Sorry, I was in my own world.' He pulls Charlie's lead so he comes to a stop. 'Marcy ended up running late, so she asked if I could bring him back to the flat. I think she'd been trying to avoid me coming back here. Understandable, I guess.' I get a sour taste in my mouth, and he's quiet for a moment. 'Are you . . . all right?' he asks eventually.

I look down at the pavement. 'I've been better.'

'Yeah. Me too.'

I meet his eyes again, and he regards me searchingly. I have to squint against the wintry sun.

'What are you up to?' he asks tentatively. 'Do you want to . . . I don't know, go for a walk?'

I glance down at the dog. 'I don't know if that's a good idea, Ryan,' I say quietly. 'Anyway, aren't you kind of all walked out by now?'

Charlie starts wagging his tail enthusiastically, and Ryan pulls a wry expression. 'I don't think he'll mind.' The imploring look in Ryan's eyes melts away any little resolve I had. 'Please?' he adds.

'Yeah,' I whisper. 'All right.'

I pull out my cigarettes and offer him one, but he doesn't accept. I look at him questioningly, though I understand. We've done enough betrayal of Marcy. I put them away without taking one out for myself.

'How was she?' I say quietly as we start to walk.

He shrugs. 'OK, I suppose. I don't know.' His face looks drawn, tired suddenly. 'The idea that I might have ... If the way I've acted means the two of you might—'

'Did she say something? About her and me?' Panic edges my voice.

'No.' He rubs his forehead with his free hand. 'Not really. But she's angry, Taylor.'

I nod. 'I know she is. I'm angry with myself.'

'I'm angry with myself too,' he says quietly. I look up at him, and he shakes his head. 'Not because of anything to do with you. Definitely not.' The way he says that makes my heart begin to race. 'But for ... for not just being honest from the start.'

Remorse floats into the silence that settles between us. We reach the path that leads down to the river, and Ryan starts to pull Charlie away.

'No. It's OK,' I say. 'Let's go this way.' I start walking faster, and Ryan catches up to me, glancing at my face, but he doesn't comment. I tuck my hands into my armpits against the wind. We walk in silence until we see the river ahead of us. I stop, and Ryan stops with me. Charlie gets to the end of his lead, then returns, panting. We stare out ahead of us for what feels like an hour.

'Where was he?' Ryan asks finally.

I point. 'Bit further down there. Next to the water.' I shield my eyes, taking a deep breath. Ryan moves a fraction closer to me, his shoulder just brushing mine. I close my eyes, and when I open them he's looking at me.

'You're OK.'

I nod. I actually am. 'I know.'

He reaches down and lets Charlie off his lead. There's a couple of other dog walkers around, and an older man jogging past. Charlie barks loudly and joins his fellow canines. Now that I'm here it feels ... normal. Not ominous or special. I look over at Ryan and smile a little half-heartedly, but I see the muscles in his jaw clench.

'I don't know how I thought this would all end up,' he murmurs, staring out to the river. 'I mean, I wasn't prepared. It's not like I *meant* to ... Marcy, she's ... But with you ...' He turns back towards me, pausing like he needs to gather his words.

'Ryan ...'

'With you it just hit me. Just like that. I mean, I didn't think that was a real thing. But now that I think back, I'm pretty sure it happened the minute I first saw you. If I'd known then ... If I'd had any way to find you, or—'

'Please, don't.' I walk away a few paces, but he follows, and I whirl around. 'Honestly, Ryan, haven't we fucked things up enough already? She doesn't deserve any of this shit.'

He shakes his head, helpless, exasperated. 'We *have* to talk about this, Taylor. If ... If I could stop feeling this way, or thinking about this – about you – every single second, I would. If I could stop wanting to touch you, to hold you, to talk to you, to *be* with you—' He stops, swallowing hard. 'Do you think I want to hurt her? Or you?'

I open and close my mouth a few times, like a demented goldfish. 'Listen to me,' I finally say quietly. 'It's there, fine. But we don't have to do anything more about it. If we just—'

'What, ignore it? Yeah, great idea. That's worked brilliantly so far.'

My mouth stays open this time, and I feel hot inside my coat. 'Nice.'

'Taylor ...' He tries to take my hand, but I pull it away and turn to start walking. 'Taylor, wait!'

I do, and I feel him behind me. He turns me around, and keeps his hands on my shoulders for a moment, staring into my eyes, his brow furrowed, his lips parted, his shoulders heaving up and down. I want to kiss him. I want him to kiss me. But eventually he lets his hands drop to his sides.

'Look,' he says softly. 'I'm staying somewhere else. And ... I mean, Marcy's obviously going to be away for another week, and then ...' He tails off, shaking his head. 'I don't know.'

I swallow. 'Yeah.' I can barely fight the pull I feel towards him. When I look back up, his eyes bore into mine, pain and uncertainty pouring out of them. 'I don't know either.'

'Taylor, I really hope we can talk. When you're ready. OK?' His voice is strained, desperate, and I want more than anything to reassure him, but I don't know if I can.

'Maybe.'

We're both silent.

'Well, I should take Charlie back to the flat,' he says eventually.

'I'm going to stay out for a bit.' My voice is hoarse. I shuffle my feet on the tiny rocks.

'All right.'

He sighs, and I look up and study his face. I'm not sure when I'll see him again, and the thought makes me want to scream. His cheeks are stubbled with dark hair, his nose red from the wind. His amber eyes glow in the sunlight. He looks exhausted and gorgeous. I see his Adam's apple bob as he swallows again nervously, like he doesn't know what this means either. He reaches for my hand, and I don't pull it away this time. He squeezes my fingers, interlacing them with his, his eyes never leaving mine.

Until they do.

He calls Charlie and hooks on the lead, then turns and walks away.

Chapter Twenty-eight

'Taylor?'

I drop the bunch of keys I've been using to lock the shop's shutters, and try to catch my breath from the surprise of hearing my name called. As I turn around, I squash down the rising disappointment – it's not Ryan. I've spent all of the last few days at work dreaming that he'd come to the shop. I'd lock the door. We wouldn't need to speak. I'd lead him past the shelves to the back room, and—

'Hey! I thought that was you.'

'Mark! Um, hi.'

'Hi. Yeah, I remembered you saying you worked at a book-shop round here. Not that I'm stalking you, I just was seeing a client round the corner, and . . . Anyway. I'll stop rambling.' He smiles at me.

'Good to see you,' I say, not insincerely. He's wearing a suit with no coat, just a scarf. He fills it out pretty well.

'Closing up for the day?' he says, then presses his lips together, knowing it's obvious. I can't help feeling flattered that he's still a bit flustered around me.

'Yup.' I finish with the shutter and turn fully towards him. 'What are you up to now?'

'Nothing much. I was just about to head home.'

I nod towards the end of the road. 'There's a little pub on the corner, if you fancied a drink?' I don't really know why I'm offering, given my vow not to lead him on. I think it's just the fact that I'm not keen to go back to the empty flat. Well, empty apart from Charlie. Ah, Charlie. 'I can only stay for one though. I've got to take Marcy's dog for a walk, or who knows what damage could ensue?'

Mark smiles. 'No problem. Lead the way.'

He insists on buying the drinks, and I sigh at the first sip of the gin and tonic he sets down in front of me.

'Needed that, eh?'

'Yeah. Been a stressful few days.' I put my glass down on a beermat. 'It's nice to have some company actually.' Wait, did that sound like I'm coming on to him? My paranoia levels have been pretty high since all this happened; I feel like I have to be careful of everything I say and do. 'I mean, we don't really get many people coming into at the shop. You can go a bit stir-crazy by the end of the day.'

He nods. 'Do you think you'd ever quit, try something new?'

I take a sip of my drink, considering it. 'I'm trying to decide. I need the money, but I think I've let myself get a bit stagnant. Maybe I need to take a risk or two.'

We both let the awkwardness of that statement settle between us.

'So Marcy's off again on the tour, right?' he says finally.

'Yeah, the last few dates in Europe. She's back after the weekend, for good. Well, till the next one, I suppose. It just feels a bit quiet in the flat at the moment.' I pick up my drink again, thinking of Ryan's key still on the table where he left it days ago. 'Uh, I mean, not that it's not nice to have a bit of space to myself,' I add, worried I sound too morose, or like I'm coming on to him. Why am I acting like such an idiot? *Stop thinking he's going to suggest coming back home with you and banging your brains out.* Though if I wasn't worried about hurting yet another person, I might suggest it myself – one more stupid attempt to take my mind off everything. The flat sometimes feels like it's swimming with my thoughts – Marcy, Ryan, David Barnett, my mum. I wade through them all every night, sifting, trying to resolve them in my mind.

'Mmm,' Mark says. 'I suppose now that Ryan's not there, you've got a bit of space to ... consider things.' He looks down into his beer. Right. I guess a shagfest wasn't on the cards anyway then.

'You've spoken to him?' I begin tentatively.

'He's staying on my sofa, actually.'

Shit. Couldn't he have found someone else to crash with?

'Oh. I didn't realise.'

'Yeah, well, I'm the only single one out of our mates, so it's cool. Nobody to piss off at mine, and the sofa's pretty comfortable, so ...'

We sip our drinks.

'Right. I mean, I wasn't pissed off with having him at ours ...'

'No, I know.' He looks at me pointedly. 'He's a good housemate.' He swallows more beer, then sighs. 'He's a good mate, too.'

Fuck. I wonder how much Ryan's told him about what happened. Obviously enough to make this conversation increasingly uncomfortable. I'm starting to wonder if it was really a coincidence that Mark bumped into me tonight, but maybe that's just the paranoia again.

'I probably need to start getting used to living by myself anyway,' I say at last, transitioning horribly, but I need to make things clear if I can. 'I've been flat-hunting. Think it's time to get my own place.' I crush the lime wedge into the bottom of my glass with my cocktail straw. 'Ryan and Marcy could ... I don't know, I think they could use a chance to spend more time on their own. I don't want to get in their way.'

'Oh. OK.'

I frown, look at him quizzically – doesn't he believe me? Maybe he shouldn't. 'What?'

'Well ...' he begins slowly, 'it's just that from the way he talks about you ... and I sort of felt a bit of a vibe between you two when we went to the concert ...'

'Oh. No.' Wow, was it really so obvious? I feel myself blush. 'Uh, I mean ... no. Marcy's my best friend,' I say, and hope he gets that that's the end of it. I drain my drink. 'I should think about getting home.'

He looks worried. 'Taylor, I wasn't trying to imply anything ...'

'Yeah, I know. Honestly. It's fine.' I get up and start to put on my coat, and he rises too, coming round the small table to help me as I struggle to put my arms in the sleeves in my haste. I feel idiotic and embarrassed, and sad in both senses. As he settles my coat on my shoulders and I start doing up the buttons, he wraps his scarf around his neck and puts his hands in his pockets, watching me.

'I shouldn't have said anything. It's just, like I say, Ryan's a good mate. A good person. He's a fucking mess at the moment, if I'm honest.'

I look up, my heart doing a strange constriction thing.

Mark shakes his head. 'I mean, I know him pretty well. He doesn't do things lightly. He's not one of those arsehole guys who don't give a shit who they hurt. He really does give a shit.' He smiles a little. 'That sounds kind of rank, but you know what I mean.'

I nod, and think for a minute. 'Do you know what? You're *both* not arsehole guys.'

'Well, thanks,' he says with a chuckle. We head towards the door.

'Cheers for the drink,' I say, as we step out into the cold.

'Yeah ... Listen, sorry if I overstepped the mark.'

I hold up a hand. 'No, honestly, you didn't.'

He turns up the collar on his suit jacket against the wind. 'OK. Just ... think about things carefully. If we're both nice guys, I reckon at least one of us shouldn't finish last.' He smiles again. 'If that's not too contrived.'

'Maybe just a touch,' I say with a small smile, knotting my scarf. 'Well, I guess I'll see you around, Mark. Thanks again.' I decide a hug may not be the best idea, and we both give an awkward wave, and then begin to head off in different directions. But I quickly come to a halt and turn round.

'Mark?'

He stops and comes back to me a few steps. 'Yeah?'

'Can you tell him ... um ... Just, can you say hi for me?'

He pushes the side of his mouth out in a half-hearted smile. 'Sure.'

I walk to the bus stop and sit on the cold hard seat to wait.

Charlie settles on to the sofa next to me and rests his head on my lap. He really never gives up. A bit like his owner – or at least I hope so. I've heard nothing from Marcy for days, other than a brief request to look after the dog while she's gone. I guess she really meant it about us all having a bit of space. I wonder if she and Ryan are in touch. I wonder what he's doing. I stare at my phone, then turn it face-down on the arm of the sofa. I'm about to reach over for the remote to switch on the TV, but I wait for a moment, finally almost enjoying the quiet, and the sound of the dog's gentle breathing. Suddenly the phone vibrates and slides to the floor with a clatter.

My heart racing, I scramble down to pick it up and turn it over, but when I see who's calling, another flavour from the variety-pack of guilt I'm carrying around in the pit of my stomach makes itself known.

'Aunty Sylvia?'

'Hello? Hello, dear,' she says. 'Is now a bad time? I can call back—'

'No, no, now's fine. Now's good. I ... I'm sorry, I've been really busy the last week or so, I've been meaning to give you a call. Did, uh, did the rest of the party go well the other day?'

'Well, Linda and her mates got a bit too involved with the champagne ... But yes, it was fine. She had fun.'

'Good.'

'Listen, sweetheart, I'm in town a week on Monday. I just thought maybe ... I know it will be just after Anita's, um. The anniversary. But I can't make it up on the day, so I thought we could go and have a coffee, or ...'

I swallow. I've been trying to avoid thinking about it. 'Yeah. That would be nice. I'd like that.'

'Like I say, I'm really sorry I can't come on the day.'

'No, no, that's no problem. I think, uh, afterwards is better anyway. That day's always a bit hard.'

'I know, darling.'

I clear my throat. 'But yeah, why don't you text me when you know what time you'll be around on the Monday, and we'll go for that coffee.'

'Oh, text you, yes. I'll get Linda to show me,' she says, then chuckles, and I smile. Mum was always useless at that too. My face falls, and I sigh as quietly as I can.

'OK,' I say.

'You're all right, aren't you, dear?'

'Yes. I am. Really.'

I hear her assessing my voice. 'All right. Well, take care. I'll be in touch soon.'

'Bye. And thank you, Aunty Sylvia.'

Thank you, thank you, thank you for always making sure everything's OK, just like Anita said you would.

I'm only now beginning to realise how lucky I've been – to have the people I've had around me, even when I thought I was alone.

What Mum said in her note was true of Sylvia; I want it to be true of me too.

I want to do better.

Chapter Twenty-nine

I'm dreaming. I know I am, but I can't wake up.

Anita's calling out my name, and it echoes around me, her voice like a chorus, repeating it over and over again. I'm shouting, but I can't make her stop, and soon the syllables of my name become meaningless, like a song without words. But it's not a helpless call, it's like a chant. And now we're underwater, and the noise is silenced as we sink. I see my mother, floating down below me in a red dress; her skin is deathly pale and her lips are shocking red. Her hair streams upwards slowly as she descends in the green water surrounding us, and she reaches her hands towards me, smiling, her features blurring in the aquamarine. She's not afraid, but I'm so scared, and I want to cry, but the water is stealing my tears. Now there's more red – thin ribbons of it, streaming up past me to the surface, and I look down, and I see it's coming from my mother's outstretched hands, from her wrists. I panic, I can't breathe, but Anita still smiles. Someone else is with us. His skin is dark, then paler. He has my face, then no face, and his skin is white now. His body expands, his features familiar once more, he's David Barnett, lifeless and bloated, and he floats away into the darkness beyond. Mum and I are still sinking, sinking, faster, and there's no air in my lungs. Anita drifts down, serene, but I know I can't go with her. I mustn't touch the bottom. Bubbles burst in front of my face, and finally I tell myself: *Kick. Kick. Kick.* But there's no air, and I don't know if I—

I wake with a start, gasping, tears running down my face. I sit up and reach over to switch on my light. The flat is so quiet, and I feel so lonely. I look at my mobile and check the time: 1.07. Late. But I pick it up, scroll through the numbers and hover over the one I've stared at a hundred times in the last few days. Finally, I hit dial.

It rings three times.

'Taylor?' His voice is even deeper than usual, and croaky. He must have been asleep. Obviously.

'Hi.' I realise I'm still breathing hard, and it could sound extremely dodgy. I try to slow down. 'Sorry, I ... Shit. I shouldn't have rung.'

'No, I'm—'

'I had a dream. It was kind of fucked up, and I just ... I wanted to hear your voice. I thought maybe I'd just get your voicemail, that you'd have your phone off, and I could just, um, listen to it. I used to do that with my mum's, but they cut it off eventually.' I take a deep breath. 'Sorry, that sounds really morbid.'

'It's all right.'

'No. It's stupid. I shouldn't have woken you up.'

'I'm awake.' There's shuffling, like he's sitting up.

'Well, you are now.'

Ryan laughs softly. 'I'm glad you called me.'

'OK.'

'And I'm glad you didn't get my voicemail. I never set it up properly – I've just got that robot voice thing.'

'That would have been disappointing.'

'Yeah, probably.'

We're quiet for a while.

'Well. I should probably say stuff. I mean, if you wanted to hear my voice.'

He sounds so beautiful. I feel my muscles begin to relax. I swipe some tears from my face. 'Mm-hm.'

'What shall I say?' His voice is almost a whisper now.

'I don't know.'

'I miss you.'

My heart stutters. 'Ryan ...'

He's quiet for a moment. 'What was your dream about?'

I sigh. 'Drowning.'

'Oh.'

'I've had it before. My mum, she's sinking down ... I'm not usually in it though. Tonight I was in it. And I was floating down with her.'

'Shit.'

'Yeah. Don't need a psychiatrist to interpret that one.'

'Hmm. So what happened?'

'Huh?'

'In the dream.'

I think for a moment. 'I couldn't breathe ... then I remembered that I should kick, so I did. But I woke up before I reached the surface.'

I can hear him breathing, and I try to match my breaths to his.

'I think you made it to the surface,' he says.

I let out a small laugh. 'Oh, you're in my head, are you?'

'I hope so. On your mind, at least.'

I bite my lip to stop myself saying a million different things.

'Sure you're all right?' he asks when I don't say anything. 'Do you want me to come over?'

I swallow hard, then chuckle.

'Taylor?'

'Sorry, it's just ... Why even ask?'

He's quiet for a while, understanding what I mean.

'But you shouldn't,' I add quickly, hating my stupid rational self.

He gives an odd little growl of frustration. 'OK,' he says eventually. 'Yeah. I know.'

We both sigh at the same time, and I can tell he's smiling just a bit, like I am.

'I should go,' I say.

'I can stay on for a bit ... '

I consider it. But the phone isn't enough. I want him here, in my bed. 'No. It's OK. I'm – I'll be fine.'

'Yeah,' he says.

'Ryan?'

'Mmm?'

'Thank you.'

'Any time, Taylor.'

I hang up. The sleek surface of my mobile screen is fogged, and I run it along the duvet cover until it clears. I feel calm as I settle back on to the pillow.

I switch on the table lamp in the living room against the gathering night, drain the last of my wine, then take my plate through to the kitchen with Charlie trotting hopefully at my heels. I scrape the leftovers from my takeaway into his bowl, and he tucks in happily.

I'm almost used to it now – being alone. Not alone, in fact, that's not really right. I realise that that now. Being *by myself*. I know I can do it, and I know I don't have to do it. That feels pretty important, and I feel like an idiot for not having realised it before. I feel like an idiot about a lot of things, of course.

I really wish my mother had realised it too. That she wasn't alone, that she had something – lots of things – to live for. I wish I'd been equipped with the tools to show her.

Heading back into the living room, I put in another of the pile of trashy DVDs I've collected for my Saturday-night entertainment. I feel like I need some mindless rom-com action after a day of looking at flats and filtering estate-agent jargon. I think I've found one or two that I can definitely picture myself in, and I've nearly got everything together for the deposit, thanks to dipping into some of the small savings I'd been surprised to find Anita left me when she died. I'd been trying not to use any of it until I had to, but now seems like a good time. I just need to talk to Marcy about it properly, of course. We've emailed a bit. I've never been so relieved to see a name – and a subject heading that wasn't 'Fuck off out of my life'. I've tried to explain to her what's been going on with me, but I know writing stuff down isn't her thing. She wants to see me, to talk face to face, and I wouldn't want it any other way. Only a couple of days to go.

But I have to get through tomorrow first.

Don't worry about it right now. The jauntily scored opening credits of the film start to roll, and Charlie trots back to join me on the sofa. My phone beeps, and I smile.

He's sent the same text, three nights in a row, since I rang. Nothing more, without any expectations.

Call me if you need me. R

I need him. Jesus. Tonight is the hardest not to reply, but I don't. I put my phone down, and focus on the painfully unlikely scenario unfolding on the screen. When I open my eyes a while later and realise I've missed at least ten minutes of a romantic montage, I decide I'm tired enough to fall straight to sleep.

Still, when I wake up the next morning, I see Charlie still asleep curled up at the bottom of my bed, and the sun barely risen in the sky. I know immediately. I don't have that fug of trying to understand why I can feel this pronounced gap in my heart, today especially.

Six years ago today, I woke up not knowing it would be the last time I'd see my mother. But every year since, she's been gone.

I get up, make some coffee and go and watch television for a while in my pyjamas, trying to neutralise my thoughts. Two hours later, I've barely comprehended anything in front of my eyes. It's not working, and I know it. I've decided.

This year, I'm going to go.

It feels right.

I step into the shower and scrub until my skin tingles. I go and get dressed. Red sweater, red lips; an homage. A reflection of her, of what she left behind. Her legacy.

I head out of my room, pulling on my coat, and Charlie trots out into the hallway.

'Not just yet. I'll be back in a bit,' I say, and he sits obediently. 'Good boy.'

I jog down the steps and out on to the street, my footsteps resounding determinedly along the pavement towards the station. There's hardly anyone around, and those that are seem to have the same sense of purpose. Clearly this time on a Sunday morning isn't for the aimless. I touch in with my card and head down to the platform, remembering the journey with Ryan to Marcy's show. Having him on my mind right now comforts me. But I know that I can do this for myself.

The stop comes up more quickly than I expect, and I head out, moving up the escalators and on to the street. It's only a ten-minute walk from here. I still remember the way, even after all the time since I last came.

It's so familiar – the long brick wall, the black iron gates, the gravel, the overgrown grass, the dying bunches of flowers. It hasn't changed. And why would it? Nobody here ever will, after all.

I find her section. Fifteen over, three up.

I stand and stare down at the gravestone for a moment, then crouch and run my fingers over my mum's name and dates. There are no flowers here yet, but I know Sylvia will bring some tomorrow. I didn't think to bring any, but Mum had enough flowers in her lifetime. I'm going to leave something more permanent behind for her, or at least try to. I promise, in this moment, that I'll spend my life trying. I won't waste it.

I remember Sylvia talking to her at the grave, like Mum could hear her. It always came across to me like they'd had a fight and Anita was just refusing to answer her sister through her bedroom door or something. I smile, and a tear bubbles on the edge of my eyesight.

'Hi, Mum,' I whisper. 'Yeah, I know, sorry ... I haven't got a good excuse. Yeah. I am actually. I'm really good.' I clear my throat. 'I miss you too.'

'Taylor.'

I straighten up and turn, surprised but half expecting my aunt. Instead, the figure standing a little way down the path makes the tears fall straight down my cheeks.

'Marcy? Wh-what the fuck are you doing here?'

Her hand rests on the handle of her wheelie case, and she adjusts her huge handbag on her shoulder as she shrugs. 'Changed my train to this morning. I was at St Pancras anyway so I thought I'd just jump on the tube over.' She rummages in her bag and pulls out a half-bottle of Bollinger. 'Got this for your mum, wanted to drop it off.'

She comes over to me, swearing under her breath as little

pebbles get stuck in the wheels of her suitcase. We look at each other, my tears leaving cold trails down my face, but I smile. Marcy blinks, rubbing her eyes, and then sighs.

'Hi, Anita,' she says, looking down at the gravestone, then back up at me. 'All right? I wasn't sure if you'd be here.'

'Yeah.' I wonder suddenly if Marcy comes *every* year. For me. I try not to let the realisation overwhelm me.

'You remembered,' I murmur.

'Course, babe.'

I shake my head at her, tears streaming. 'Course.'

We hug tightly, then Marcy pops open the champagne. We both take large swigs, then pour the rest on the ground.

'Cheers,' Marcy says, then props the bottle next to my mother's gravestone.

We stay there for a while. Then I offer her my arm, she takes it, and together we make our way back towards the gates.

Chapter Thirty

'Oh, mate. It's gonna be weird though, isn't it? Us both on our own.'

'I know. Really weird.' I sit up straighter on the sofa and cross my legs to mirror Marcy as we face each other.

Charlie trots over to Marcy and paws her. She pats his head and makes a baby voice. 'I know, sweetie, I'll have you.' I can't quite believe it, but I feel jealous. I think I might actually miss that mutt.

'I . . . I spoke to Ryan,' she says, turning back to me. 'I think we've sorted things out.'

I look at her nervously. 'Oh.'

'I mean, we're not together any more, obviously. Just so you know.' She looks away for a moment, and I unfold my legs and turn to stare around the room, not sure where to begin. I look at her half-unpacked suitcase on the living-room floor, and notice the little stuffed bear I gave her when we were fourteen, that she said was her good-luck charm, peeking out of one corner.

'Marcy, I'm so sorry. I don't know what to say.'

'Say . . . Say you'll take care of him.'

My eyes widen. 'What? No. I mean, I'm not going to—'

'Well then what was all this for?' she says quietly but firmly. Her eyes meet mine, jostling emotions in her gaze. Anger, irritation, sadness. She looks away again and shakes her head. 'Sorry, T. I didn't really want to get into it all, not today.'

We sit in silence for a while.

'It wasn't what I wanted it to be,' she says at last. 'Him and me. I thought it could be, but I'd known for a while that it wasn't, if I'm honest. I did – I do – feel something for him, but—'

'Marcy, I don't deserve this. I don't deserve *you*. I honestly don't even understand how you're still my mate.'

'Jesus, T! Fucking listen to me, OK? It's not about what you deserve. Don't you get it?' She levels me with a stare. 'You'd do the same thing for me. Wouldn't you? Honestly. I *know* you.'

I hope she's right. I look down at my lap. I can't believe I have any more tears, but apparently I do.

'It's not like it's a choice,' she continues, standing up and starting to pace, almost shouting at me. 'I know they say you choose your friends and not your family, but bloody hell – I don't agree. OK?' She's breathing hard now. 'Deserve? You deserve *to be happy*.' She arches her eyebrows at me pointedly. 'And by the way, so do I. Ryan and me weren't really right together. I sort of knew it before, and I definitely know it now. The way he talks about you? Jesus, do you think I'd be happy carrying on with a man who loves my best mate, not me?'

I'm stunned. 'Marcy, I—'

'It's not like I don't understand. I get it. I wouldn't be saying any of this stuff if I didn't. You're my best mate. I *love* you. And he's . . . If he wants to make you happy, then he's pretty fucking special in my book.'

I stare up at her. I think my heart might shatter. Much as I want him, I know now that I would force myself to ignore it, to never let it go any further, if she wasn't certain.

'But Marcy, I *couldn't* be happy if it meant you weren't. I love you, too.'

Marcy frowns and strides back over to stand in front of me. 'No, you don't get it. I will be happy. I plan to be. You're going to *help* me be the fucking happiest woman on this planet, like a fucking best mate should. This is important to me, OK?'

'I can see that.'

'Exactly! Look at me!' she shouts, raising her arms and laughing. I can't help smiling back. 'Listen, I'm not going to let you get away with not at least trying this, out of loyalty to me,' she says. 'Jesus Christ, T, I can't believe we're here fighting over a man. One of us has to have him, all right?' she says with another laugh that brings tears behind it, matching my own. I need lessons in loyalty from this woman, says the guilt still lurking in the back of my mind. But I know she wouldn't have said all of that if she didn't mean it. If she still wanted him. Marcy falls back on to the sofa next to me and I wrap my arms around her familiar frame.

'OK. I hear you. Bloody hell.'

'Good.'

We both pull back and smile, wiping away each other's tears with our sleeves.

'I'm going to try not to fuck this up,' I murmur.

'Well, whatever happens, I think it's fair to say you're stuck with me.'

I grin. 'Same.'

You never realise quite how much stuff you have until you try to pack it all up and move it. My whole body aches. But as Marcy and I open the first bottle of wine in my new flat and I pull out two glasses from the pack of six I've bought to kit out my kitchen, it hits me. This is it.

We toast, then we slump on the sofa in my tiny living room, and then eventually she says she'd better go before she starts to beg me to put it all back in the hire van and come home with her. As the door closes behind her and Charlie, I turn and look around at all the boxes and bags I need to unpack. A new chapter.

There's something I still haven't done. I'm not quite the 'life warrior' I'm aiming to be yet, but hey, everyone's got to start somewhere. I pick up my phone, thinking this time I'm finally going to return Ryan's calls. That familiar excitement bubbles up, followed by several minutes of self-chastisement as I chicken out. Thing is, I know as soon as I dial, it will be fine. Maybe it's some kind of delayed-gratification thing. I've waited this long and now that I finally have permission . . .

A worry hits me – maybe that was the appeal? That it was forbidden? Now that I can, I won't want to?

Nah.

No.

Absolutely not.

I notice there's a text on my phone from Beverly about yoga, which I've managed to skip a couple of weeks in a row. I text her and tell her I'm going to miss one more, then I'm all hers for exercise and general hang time; boot camp and all, even if she's going to make Marcy train us within an inch of our lives. But tomorrow's Thursday, and I remember. Thursday nights.

A mic and a spotlight.

My hand is actually, visibly trembling. This is my third brandy. I'm pretty sure Anita used to say one was best, for the throat, but I needed the first two just to get me over to the guy with the clipboard to sign up. When I did, I scanned the list, but I already knew Ryan's name wouldn't be on there – there's no sign of him in here. It's not a big pub; I'd have seen him. But now

I've committed, and I'm next, and it would look pretty fucking weird to get up and run out. Though maybe I don't care how weird it would look.

Come on. I start my pep talk again, nerves churning my stomach like a washing machine. Why didn't I ring Marcy? Like Ryan said about Mark, I should have a mate in the crowd so at least one person claps. Maybe Bev's finished her yoga class? I glance at my phone, but just then the MC steps on to the stage and looks down at his notes.

'OK, next up we have ... Taylor Jenkins. Let's have a big round of applause for him. Taylor?'

I stand up, swallow the last of my drink and force one foot in front of the other towards the little stage.

'Oh, sorry!' the MC says, then moves off.

I fumble with the mic, eventually lowering it. I can hear myself panting loudly through the speakers, into the silence of the room.

Shit shit shit shit— 'Uh. Hi. I'm ... Sorry ... it's ... it's my first time doing this.' My amplified voice is high and awkward-sounding. I squint out at the crowd, but can't really see much. Thank God. I take a deep breath. 'This is for my mum.'

I don't have any music, and I almost don't know what I'll sing until I take my first breath, but I can suddenly hear the opening piano notes in my mind. Of course.

'The Nearness of You'.

My heartbeat slows. I close my eyes, fill my lungs, open my mouth and let it all go – until the music overtakes me, until I forget where I am, until the notes bend and my voice soars. Until I have only one wish.

OK, maybe two.

When I finish and open my eyes, I see a silhouette making its way to the front, near the stage.

302

He sets his guitar case down, straightens up, and I hear him start to clap. He steps closer until I can see him, his eyes – beautiful glowing amber, locked straight onto mine.

'Ryan!' I breathe, my voice still amplified by the microphone, reverberating around the small space. My heart takes a running leap, trying to breach the confines of my chest.

I'm vaguely aware of the sound of more applause joining him.

Wishing works. Who knew?

Well, one wish came true. As for the other – I'll just have to hope she would have been proud.

I jiggle the key in the lock.

'Still getting used to it,' I say over my shoulder. I hear a click. 'Ah.' I push open the door, and kick an empty box to the side. 'It's still a bit messy.'

I hesitate for a moment, feeling Ryan close behind me. 'It's nice.' His breath is next to my ear.

I step away, switch on the hallway light. 'You haven't even seen it yet.'

He's smiling. I shut the door behind him. We stare at each other. I undo my coat, let it drop to the floor. He's still staring. I walk over and start to unbutton his, concentrating because my hands are shaking. He reaches down to steady them, and then finishes taking it off by himself, looking down at me while he does. I actually, genuinely feel light-headed just being this close to him, being *allowed* to be.

'You sounded beautiful, by the way. I forgot to tell you,' he murmurs.

'No, you didn't forget.'

'Oh. I was just thinking about it again.'

'Do you want a drink?'

'No.'

He leans down, his face so close his features blur into one gorgeous mess. He presses his lips to mine, taking in air through his nose as we kiss, as though he's trying to breathe me in too.

'Mmm,' I say, through my mouth and into his.

His hands tighten on my waist and he pulls me closer. I can feel his heartbeat as he backs me against a wall, pressing his body into mine. He moves his lips down, along my chin, and the tip of his tongue traces into the crook of my neck. 'You taste beautiful too,' he murmurs.

I can hardly breathe. Goosebumps break out all over my skin. 'Is this real?' I can barely hear my own voice it's so faint. Ryan pulls away and looks at me.

'It's real,' he says. He moves his hands up to the sides of my face, holding it gently.

I nod, my head still in his hands, and smile, looking into his eyes. 'I think I'm ready.'

He grins too. 'God, I've been ready since the day I first saw you, Taylor.' His hands wander away from my face, slowly on to my shoulders, down the sides of my body, feeling every curve, and his lips return to my neck and begin to suck.

I stifle a moan. 'No,' I say. 'Well, yes. Definitely, yes.' He nips gently at my skin, and I can't stop the noise in my throat this time. 'But I mean . . . I think I'm ready to be happy.'

Ryan's lips stop their movements, and he pulls away to look at me again.

'So, thank you,' I whisper.

His eyebrows draw together a little. 'Don't thank me, Taylor. I'm an idiot. I just felt . . . *stuck*. And every time I'd hear you laugh, or see that look in your eyes, where you looked adrift at sea, that look I understood so well, I just . . . I felt like I couldn't do anything, couldn't say anything about it without somehow . . . I don't know. I think I was scared.' He takes a breath. 'I'm always scared.'

I reach up and smooth my fingers along his brow. 'Well, you're here now,' I say quietly. 'We can be scared together.' I press my lips to his. We get lost for a moment.

'Mmmm. Scared and happy,' Ryan murmurs. He pulls me close to him once more, his hands under my clothes, his lips crushed against mine, our tongues moving desperately against one another. I feel like I'll melt or explode or just disappear altogether if we don't—

'Come here,' I manage to say. I take his hand and lead him to the bedroom.

I walk over and switch on the bedside light, then turn to him and slowly pull my jumper over my head to reveal the tight vest top underneath. Ryan hasn't moved from just inside the doorway. He pushes his hands into the pockets of his jeans and sighs, his eyes roaming my bare arms, my cleavage, before locking back on to my gaze. I kick off my shoes, then undo my jeans, taking my time with each button. I push them down my legs and step out, then peel off the vest slowly. I stand before him in just my pants and bra, and I can see his chest rising and falling faster now. His eyes still make little journeys away, around my naked skin, but always return to mine.

I take a step towards him, and another, my need for him pulsing between my legs. He pulls his hands from his pockets and I curl my fingers under the bottom of his jumper and T-shirt together. He looks down at me – his eyes deep, wide, dark – and puts his arms in the air. I trail my fingertips against his stomach and chest as I pull his clothes up over his head and throw them on the floor. He makes a noise deep in his throat, and I move my hands back to his belt and fly as quickly as I can. He beats me to it, unbuckling and unzipping, his hands urgent as he pushes his jeans down off his legs.

Then he reaches around me, pressing warm kisses against my shoulder as he undoes my bra and watches it fall down my arms to the floor between us. My nipples harden as his breath brushes against them, as he bends down and runs his tongue ever-so-lightly against each one. I moan, savouring it for a moment before my fingers find the elastic waistband of his boxers, reaching inside to ease the material over his erection. Ryan's breath hitches. He pulls me into a tight embrace, wrapping his arms around me, just to feel us, finally, skin to skin, burning hot—

'Taylor,' he whispers, his voice trembling with emotion.

'I know.'

I lead him back towards the bed, slipping off my pants.

Hands, lips, tongues . . .

He moves over me, pressing against my opening, his Adam's apple bobbing as he swallows. 'Can I . . . Are you on . . . ?' He can barely finish his sentence, and I know we should have talked about it earlier.

I nod rapidly, truthfully and thankfully, and he exhales and sinks into me. He draws in a ragged breath, and then we both sigh again together, long and low. He doesn't move for a moment, and I just feel him. Inside me, everywhere, all around me.

'I love you,' he whispers. Maybe he doesn't even say it, maybe I just feel it. I wrap myself around him.

'I love you too.'

Then he moves. He moves and moves and moves, into me and into me, over and again, harder, faster, deeper, deeper, deeper, again and again and again, until we can't any more. Until we reach that sweet release. Together.

Together.

When there's no space left between us, I realise.

I feel no weight, no pressure, no heaviness.

Just light. Strength. Beauty.

I am serene.

I am free.

That's what I wanted. What I needed. It's all any of us want, isn't it?

Perhaps we just take different paths to get there.

THE END

If you enjoyed this book, please review it
and help us to spread the word!

We are also delighted to offer an
exclusive bonus scene from Ryan's POV!

Go to www.sareetadomingo.com/
exclusive-extract.html

If you are affected by any of the issues in this book,
please consider contacting the Samaritans:
08457 90 90 90 or www.samaritans.org

Acknowledgements

This novel would not exist without the support and encouragement of a number of wonderful people. My husband Will, my parents Larry and Valda, and my brother Lawrence – thank you so much for your love and belief, and, in the case of Lawrence and Valda in particular, your very helpful notes on the manuscript. I must also thank my friends Lauren Baker and Anne Marie Ryan for their extensive and invaluable notes, and Noam Hollander and Deirdre Domingo their kind words on the early draft.

Thank you to Brett Goldstein and Mel Freilicher, both of whom took the time to encourage my writing at a very early stage, when they really didn't have to, and for which I am incredibly grateful.

I would also like to thank all my other family and friends, especially Micallar Walker-Smith and Cicelia Deane, for being so supportive and excited for me. And I will never forget the encouragement of the wonderful Michelle Richards – your belief and positivity are still with me.

I am incredibly grateful to my agent, Sara Keane of Keane Kataria, for her tireless work, and to Anna Boatman and the whole team at Piatkus, for believing in this book and for all their insight and support.

Most of all, I'm grateful to you for reading this story. Thank you.

Newport Community
Learning & Libraries

The item should be returned or renewed by the last date stamped below.

Dylid dychwelyd neu adnewyddu'r eitem erbyn y dyddiad olaf sydd wedi'i stampio isod

St. Julians

To renew visit / Adnewyddwch ar
www.newport.gov.uk/libraries

Sareeta Domingo is the author of *The Three of Us* (previously *The Nearness of You*), and creator, editor and contributing writer of romantic fiction anthology *Who's Loving You*. Her novel *If I Don't Have You* is longlisted for the Diverse Book Awards 2021. She has also written numerous erotic short stories and an erotic novella with Pavilion Books, and her books for Young Adults are published under S.A. Domingo, including *Love on the Main Stage*, recently shortlisted for the Lancashire Book of the Year 2021. She has contributed to publications including, *Nous*, *gal-dem*, *Black Ballad*, *Stylist* and *Token Magazine*, and has taken part in events for Hachette Books, Primadonna Festival, Winchester Writers' Festival, Black Girls Book Club and the Royal Society of Literature among others. She lives in South East London.

sareetadomingo.com // @SareetaDomingo